PRAISE FOR *RASPUTIN'S BASTARDS*

"Bram Stoker Award winner Nickle's (*Eutopia*) latest novel tells a complex story of supernatural horror and psychological suspense crafted with the somber foreboding of a Russian novel and the genre-breaking freedom of magical realism. VERDICT: This novel is supernatural eeriness at its best, with intriguing characters, no clear heroes, and a dark passion at its heart. Horror aficionados and fans of Stephen King's larger novels should appreciate this macabre look at the aftermath of the Cold War."

—*Library Journal*

"As always, Nickle is right on point. The prose here is thoughtful, energetic and sharp. Most importantly of all, the plot of *Rasputin's Bastards* is complicated and it's told in a complex way. Despite this, it's stiffly compelling. Once you're done, there's no question: the hours spent enfolded in Nickle's imagination are well spent. You won't ever feel the desire to ask for them back."

—**David Middleton,** *January Magazine*

"I'm almost certain the book *isn't* an attempt on the part of ChiZine Publications and author David Nickle to subconsciously program an army of sleeper agents. That said, there are times when *Rasputin's Bastards* feels like a twenty-first century answer to *Catch-22*. Both books are complex, revel in asynchronous storytelling, and left this reader eager to reread if only to mine for details, subtexts, and plot threads missed on a first read through."

—**Adam Shaftoe,** *Page of Reviews*

"While recognizably 'genre,' whatever that may mean to the reader (and their prejudices about the same), *Rasputin's Bastards* is not of a genre. Instead it's an ambitious melange of them all. Nickle's horror is the theft of body and will; the revelation that one's father is 'A cold, soul-dead killer.' His science fiction feels like '50s pulps, his fantasy a dark-lensed fairy tale with literary heft. Rasputin's Bastards is a testament to the fact Nickle can write *anything*."

—**Chadwick Ginther,** *The Winnipeg Review*

"*Rasputin's Bastards* is a fever dream of a novel. It's something you must jump into and allow to take along through the tides and currents. And sense? Don't depend too much on that. Rather depend on your senses, and on Mr. Nickle's ability to take you along on a journey you won't soon forget. Highly recommended."

"[Nickle's] novel *Eutopia* is a gloriously original American historical horror, and his follow-up *Rasputin's Bastards* is a bold and disturbing Russian epic spy thriller that takes drastically disparate elements (there are echoes of James Bond, John le Carré, China Miéville, and Simmons' *Carrion Comfort*) and mashes them together in a fantastical narrative that crosses POVs and dimensions with an assurance that is staggering. Have I got your attention yet? Good. Because David Nickle is *that* good."

—Corey Redekop, author of *Husk*

"*Rasputin's Bastards* is an utterly unique novel; I've never read anything quite like it before. It's a mind-blowing blend of science fiction, political thriller, and understated horror."

—Paul Goat Allen, *Barnes & Noble Books Blog*

"Part *Bioshock*, part *X-Files*, part *Sopranos*—and 100%, uncut Nickle—*Rasputin's Bastards* is a glorious, chaotic delight. I wish I'd written it; in fact, I may yet steal the domesticated giant squid."

—Peter Watts, author of *Blindsight*

"A journey from the depths of the sea, the heart of Mother Russia, to the darkest corners of the soul, this book appeals to the reader's intellectual curiosity, and engages the heart with surprising moments of emotionality."

—K.E. Bergdoll, *The Crow's Caw*

"[David Nickle] has a talent for spinning a phrase to make it much more than the sum of its parts, and surprisingly, there's quite a lot of humor as well: clever and dry, popping up just when things start to get really serious, but never disrupting the flow. The author dives deep into his main characters and paints very complete pictures, weaving the stories together amidst a surrealistic landscape of dream walkers and mind control. This reminded me very much of Dan Simmons' *Carrion Comfort* (one of my all time favorites), and it's been quite a while since I've read a book with this much teeth. Lovely, rich writing only serves to make the creepy bits (of which there are plenty), well, even more creepy, and fans of subtle horror will find much to like in *Rasputin's Bastards*."

—My Bookish Ways

PRAISE FOR *EUTOPIA*

"Nickle (*Monstrous Affections*) blends *Little House on the Prairie* with distillates of *Rosemary's Baby* and *The X-Files* to create a chilling survival-of-the-fittest story. . . . [His] bleak debut novel mixes utopian vision, rustic Americana, and pure creepiness."

—***Publishers Weekly***

"Toronto author David Nickle's debut novel, the follow-up to his brilliantly wicked collection of horror stories *Monstrous Affections*, establishes him as a worthy heir to the mantle of Stephen King. And I don't mean the King of *Under the Dome* or other recent flops, but the master of psychological suspense who ruled the '80s with classics like *Pet Sematary*."

—Alex Good, *The National Post*

"Try to imagine a collaboration by Mark Twain and H.P. Lovecraft, with Joe R. Lansdale supplying final editorial polish. Or if that's too difficult to imagine, read the book and see for yourself."

—Joe Sanders, *The New York Review of Science Fiction*

"[*Eutopia*] is immensely readable: a quick-paced mountain stream of a novel, cool and sharp and intense, and terrifically adept at drawing a reader in. . . . *Eutopia* accomplishes what the best horror fiction strives for: gives us characters we can care about and hope for, and then inflicts on them the kind of realistic, inescapable, logical sufferings that make us close our eyes a little at the unfairness of not the author, but the world—and all the while with something more to say for itself than *the world is a very bad place*."

—Leah Bobet, *Ideomancer*

"*Eutopia* crosses genres in a world where folks from a rustic Faulkner novel might clash with H.P. Lovecraft's monstrosities. Add a dash of Cronenbergian body horror to atmosphere worthy of Poe, and you get one of the most original horror stories in years."

—Chris Hallock, *All Things Horror*

"This novel is seriously creepy. Do not read it on your own, at night, with the bedroom window open. I ended up jumpy and paranoid and then had to sleep with the window closed even though it was muggy and uncomfortable."

—Ellie Warren, *Curiosity Killed the Bookworm*

E FOR *MONSTROUS AFFECTIONS*

ites 'em damned weird and damned good and damned dark. He is poetic and vivid. Don't miss this one."

—Cory Doctorow, author of *Pirate Cinema*

"Bleak, stark and creepy, Stoker-winner Nickle's first collection will delight the literary horror reader. . . . This ambitious collection firmly establishes Nickle as a writer to watch."

—*Publishers Weekly* (STARRED REVIEW)

"These stories work so well in part because of Nickle's facility with the language of the place he's created. He is comfortable writing in different voices . . . and he knows the idiom of his semi-rural environment. . . ."

—*Quill & Quire*

"The cover is creepy. . . . The stories themselves are also very creepy, drawing you into believable, domestic worlds, then showing you the blue pulsing intestines of those worlds."

—Kaaron Warren, author of *Slights*

"[L]ike the cover, the stories inside are not what they seem. But also, like the cover, the stories inside are brilliant. . . . You'd think that you were reading a book full of what you had always expected a horror story to be, but Nickle takes a left turn and blindsides you with tales that are not of the norm, but are all the more horrific because of surprise twists, darkness and raw emotion."

—January Magazine's Best Books of 2009

THE 'GEISTERS

DAVID NICKLE

ChiZine Publications

FIRST EDITION

This book is a work of fiction. Names, characters, places, and incidents are either a product of the author's imagination or are used fictitiously. Any resemblance to actual events, locales, or persons, living or dead, is entirely coincidental.

Distributed in Canada by
HarperCollins Canada Ltd.
1995 Markham Road
Scarborough, ON M1B 5M8
Toll Free: 1-800-387-0117
e-mail: hcorder@harpercollins.com

Distributed in the U.S. by
Diamond Book Distributors
1966 Greenspring Drive
Timonium, MD 21093
Phone: 1-410-560-7100 x826
e-mail: books@diamondbookdistributors.com

Library and Archives Canada Cataloguing in Publication

Nickle, David, 1964-
The 'Geisters / David Nickle.

Issued also in electronic format.
ISBN 978-1-77148-143-4

I. Title.

PS8577.I33G43 2013 C813'.54 C2013-900795-4

CHIZINE PUBLICATIONS
Toronto, Canada
www.chizinepub.com
info@chizinepub.com

Edited and copyedited by Sandra Kasturi
Proofread by Kelsi Morris

Canada Council for the Arts Conseil des arts du Canada

We acknowledge the support of the Canada Council for the Arts which last year invested $20.1 million in writing and publishing throughout Canada.

Published with the generous assistance of the Ontario Arts Council.

Printed in Canada

for Madeline Ashby
who shows me the way

ALSO BY DAVID NICKLE

Monstrous Affections
Eutopia: A Novel of Terrible Optimism
Rasputin's Bastards
Knife Fight and Other Struggles (2014)
Volk (2015)

WITH KARL SCHROEDER:
The Claus Effect (Tesseract Books)

CONTENTS

THE 'GEISTERS

A Glass of Gewürztraminer

i

Was it terror, or was it love? It would be a long time before Ann LeSage could decide. For most of her life, the two feelings were so similar as to be indistinguishable.

It was easy to mix them up.

ii

"Family, now . . . family is far away," said Michael Voors, and as he said it—perhaps because of the way he said it—Ann felt a pang, a prescience, that something was not right with him. That perhaps she should leave now. Until that moment, she'd thought the lawyer with the little-boy eyes was the perfect date: perfect, at least, by her particular and admittedly peculiar standards.

To look at, Michael was a just-so fellow: athletic, though not ostentatiously so; taller than she, but only by a few inches; dirty blond hair, not exactly a mop of it, but thick enough in his early thirties that it would probably stay put until his forties at least. He'd listened, asked questions—the whole time regarding Ann steadily, and with confidence.

Steadiness and confidence were first among the things Ann found attractive in Michael, from the night of the book launch. He'd approached her, holding her boss's anthology of architectural essays, *Suburban Flights*, and asked her: "Is it any good?" and she'd said: "It's any good," and turned away.

He hadn't been thrown off his game.

She had been enchanted by this easy confidence. After everything that had happened in her life—everything that had *formed* her—it was a quality that she discovered she craved.

But now, that confidence crumbled, leaving a man that seemed . . . older. And somehow . . . not right.

It hadn't taken much. Just the simple act of asking: "What about you? Where's your family from?"

He tapped his fingers and looked away. His suddenly fidgeting hands cast about and found the saltshaker, a little crystal globe the size of a ping-pong ball. His eyes were momentarily lost too, blinking away from Ann and looking out the window of the 54th-floor view of Toronto's financial district, a high hall of mirrors up the canyon of Bay Street. They were in Canoe, a popular spot for lunch and cocktails among the better-paid canyon dwellers. It should have been home turf for him.

"Just my father now. In Pretoria. But—" and he twirled the near-spherical glass saltshaker, so it spun like a fat little dancer "—I don't hear from him. We have had—you might say a falling out."

"A falling out?"

"We are very different men."

Their waiter slowed as he passed the table, took in Michael's low-grade agitation and met Ann's eye just an instant before granting the tiniest, most commiserative of nods: *Poor you.*

He picked up his pace toward the party of traders clustered at the next table, and Ann suppressed a smile. She was sorely tempted to stop him and order a big, boozy cocktail. But it was early—in the day, and in the relationship—for that kind of thing. Particularly because the way things were going, she didn't think she'd stop at one.

"He is an Afrikaner," continued Michael. "You understand? Not just by birth. By allegiance. When the ANC won the elections in 1994 . . . He wasn't a bigot—isn't a bigot, I mean. But he'd seen the things that the African National Congress could do—the business with the tires . . ."

"The tires?" Ann said, after a heartbeat.

Now Michael made a half-wise smile, set the saltshaker aside. His hand must have been trembling: the shaker kept rocking.

"My God," he said, "you'd think I'd been into the wine already. I'm sorry. They would put tires around fellows they thought were traitors, and light them on fire, and watch them burn to death in the streets of Soweto. And then they became the government. You can imagine how he felt."

"I remember that," said Ann. She nodded in sympathy. *That* was real terror, now. In the face of it, her own inexplicable instant of fear vanished. "I was small. But didn't Nelson Mandela have something to do with that?"

"His wife. Winnie. Maybe. Probably. Who knows?"

Ann smiled reassuringly and they sat quiet a moment; just the chatter in the restaurant, a burst of boozy mirth from the day traders; the pool-hall swirling of the saltshaker on the glass tabletop.

The waiter scudded near and inquired: "Need a minute?"

"Just a minute," she said, looking at her menu.

Michael studied his too, and without looking up, said: "Share an appetizer?"

"Is there real truffle in the wild mushroom soup?"

"You want to share soup?"

"Is there a law says I can't?"

That, thought Ann as she regarded Michael, was how you kept it going on a second date: make a little joke about the appetizer. Don't talk international politics. For that matter, don't start asking a lot of questions about how international politics and tires kept father and son apart for so long.

In fact, don't start talking about family at all. Because as grim as the tale of Michael Voors' own family turmoils might be— if Michael then started asking after the LeSages, and she was compelled to tell *that* horrific story . . .

Well. He was already thrown enough to fidget—she could hear the rolling sound of the saltshaker again.

"What about the salmon tartar?" she asked before he could answer. She allowed herself a smirk: why, Mr. Voors was actually blushing! "We don't have to share soup."

"No, I—" he was frowning now, and looking down at the table. "My goodness," he said softly.

"What is it?"

Ann lowered the menu, and looked down at the table. And froze.

The saltshaker was dancing.

It twirled in a slow loop across Michael's place setting, rolling along the edge where the curve met its base. Then it rocked, clicking as the base touched the tabletop, and rocked the other side, turning back. Michael held his menu in his left hand—his right was splayed on the tabletop near the fork. His pale cheeks were bright red as he stared. First at the saltshaker, then up at Ann.

"Isn't that incredible?"

Michael set the menu down, well away from the perambulating saltshaker.

"Incredible," said Ann quietly, not taking her eyes off the shaker as it continued to rock.

The Insect, she thought, horrified.

It was back.

No, not *back*.

Really, it had never left.

Ann wanted to reach out—grab the shaker in her fist, stop it physically. But she knew better. Already, she could hear the rattling of glasses at the long bar. Two tables down, one of the traders commented that the air-conditioning must have kicked in. One of his lunch-mates asked him if he were a woman and everyone laughed. Michael's eyes were wide as he watched the saltshaker.

Ann reached under her chair and lifted her handbag. "Don't touch it," she said.

He looked at her and asked, "Why not?"

"I'm going to the ladies room," she said and stood. "Now please—don't touch it."

Ann drew a long breath, and pushed her chair back to the table. Michael didn't stop her, and he didn't try to touch the spinning saltshaker either.

Their waiter, carrying a tray of two martinis and a fluted glass of lager, stepped past her—and without her having to ask, directed her with a free hand to the restrooms. "You have to go outside," he said. "By the elevators. Just past them."

Ann smiled politely and, shoulders only slightly hunched, head bowed only the tiniest, hurried between the tables, out the doorway and past the elevators—and there to the women's washroom where she finally skulked inside. It was as safe there as anywhere, now.

One blessing: the washroom was empty but for her. She made her way to a sink, spared herself a glance in the tall, gilt-framed mirror. Her makeup was holding. That was something.

Ann fumbled with her phone.

It was a new one, and she hadn't had time to program her numbers into it. Not a catastrophe—she knew the number she had to call now like she knew her own name—but speed dial would have helped.

Finally, a signal. *One ring.*

Would the glasses still be on the rack now, or sliding, one by one, along the rails, crashing into the plate glass windows overlooking Bay Street?

Two rings.

Would frost be forming around the edges of those windows, irising a circle of white, evil crystals to block out the sun?

Three.

Would one of the traders hold up his hand, wonderingly, examining the steak knife that had penetrated the back of it as he sat, turning it this way and that while his mind processed the impossibility of it, and itself began to unravel?

Four.

The first might be dead—the only question would be who . . . who it would choose. Not the waiter! Not Michael Voors—

Oh God . . .

"Come on, Eva," Ann said to the empty washroom. "I need you."

And click: and *five*. And . . .

"Hello?"

"Eva!"

"Ann?" Eva Fenshaw was on her own cell phone—she'd obviously figured out the intricacies of call-forwarding since last they spoke—and her voice crackled. She sounded as though she might be in some large space—maybe the Wal-Mart where she liked to spend hot afternoons before her consultations started in the early evening. Ann should have remembered, and called the cell phone first. "Ann, how nice to hear from you!"

"Not so nice, Eva," said Ann.

"Are you all right?" Pause. "Ann, dear?"

"It's coming," said Ann.

"Oh oh. The Insect."

"The Insect."

"Oh."

The acoustics shifted—maybe as Eva moved down an aisle, someplace more private. "All right, Ann. It's all right."

"It's not all right. It's back, it's coming out, I can feel it."

"Where are you? At work?"

"At lunch. With a date."

"With that Michael?"

"Michael Voors."

"Dear Creator," Eva whispered. She had, of course, warned Ann about Michael; Eva Fenshaw had a lifelong distrust of lawyers, born of the needless troubles in her divorce thirty years ago. When Ann told her about Michael's interest in her, Eva had had some unkind things to say.

She didn't repeat them in the Wal-Mart. "All right, Ann. Were you drinking?"

"God no."

"Good. Now. How did it manifest?"

"The saltshaker," said Ann. "Moved on its own. That's for sure."

"In the restaurant."

"In the restaurant!"

"Telekinetically."

"Yes!"

"Don't shout," said Eva. "Stay calm. We're going to visualize the safe place."

Eva gave a yogic huff, and Ann drew a deep breath.

"It hates him," she said. "It's the same as before."

"Ann!" Her voice was sharp this time. "Visualize the safe place, Ann. It can't harm you there. And if it can't harm you . . ."

"I can control it. All right." She shut her eyes.

"Good, dear," said Eva, in a voice that seemed to recede down the long corridor that was the first part—the gateway to Ann's safe place. Eva had helped her construct it—*how long ago*? Not important. *Ten years ago. At the hospital. You remember the hospital, don't you, little Annie? I know I do—*

Ann concentrated on opening herself up, seeing the hallway, walls made of cut stone with bright, leaded glass windows along both sides. There was a sunrise—Ann was always happier with the onset of light than she was the spread of darkness—and it manifested in pinkish rectangles along the flagstone floor.

The safe room was at the far end of the corridor. It would take a moment to walk, but by the time she had made the journey, she would have shed the tension that had brought her here. That was how Eva had explained it, all those years ago as they sat together in the lounge in Fenlan, waiting for word of her brother, of Philip after the crash.

"You're going to walk as slowly as you need to, and at each window, you can pause and throw any worry you have out there into the light."

"Light of the rising sun?" young Ann had asked, and Eva had replied: "Just the light." And she had held Ann as Ann described how that hallway would be: like the hallway between high towers in a wizard's castle.

The wizard wasn't there, because she was the wizard.

This was Ann's castle.

She stopped at the first window. Ann always had a leather satchel with her when she walked the Hall of Light, and she reached into it this time. She found a small parcel, wrapped in a dark, oily cloth. It was warm to the touch.

It wasn't important—it might even be counterproductive—to try and determine what worry, exactly, was contained in this package. Whatever it was, it was heavy, and warm, and alive. She pushed open the first window, and threw the package out. It fell into the hot sunlight, down the mountainside, and disappeared.

She was inclined to hurry, to the thick oak door at the far end of the hallway. She certainly could do so; the castle existed only in her imagination, as guided by Eva's own counsel. She could simply imagine herself all the way down, in the tower room, her fears cast from windows in retrospect. She could simply say to herself that she had unlocked the twelve sturdy locks, and removed the bar, and raised the miniature portcullis that led to the tower chamber, where it—the Insect—was contained.

And I could, she told herself, *watch as the whole, fragile construct collapses to dust. While God—excuse me, Creator knows—what havoc the Insect is wreaking in the restaurant.*

So, meticulously, Ann went window to window, tossing cloth packages and poisonous apples and broken daggers and twisted candles from her bag, until it was empty, and then removed the key ring, and set to work on the door. And then, free of all burdens, she stepped inside—to the tower room.

"Do you see it there?"

"I don't." The chamber was a circular tower room, with a single window overlooking a bright kingdom, far, far below. There was a chair. A table. A little flask of iced mint tea (in the past, matters had gotten uncontrollable when there was wine in the room). It was otherwise a bit of a cliché: but what was to be done about it? They'd devised it during the depths of Ann's teenaged Dungeons & Dragons obsession. And circular tower rooms in wizards' castles, as Ann had explained seriously at the time, were both pretty comfortable safe places, and made awfully good prisons.

Good, but obviously not perfect.

"It's gone. It's escaped."

"Look up, dear."

"Of course." She looked up, into the rafters of this room—where just a few years ago, during the big blackout, when she was sure the thing had gotten out again, running amok in the dark corridors of her residence, flinging knives, she'd found it hanging like a great chrysalis, grinning down at her, long hair dangling like the tentacles of a man-o-war.

Not this time, though.

"Not this time," said Ann.

"Keep at peace," said Eva. "All right dear, let me tune in."

Ann couldn't help imagining Eva in the Wal-Mart, moving her hands so they hovered inches apart from one another, eyelids fluttering . . . the little rituals that she invoked, to tune in to Ann, and her safe place, and the prisoner that she kept there.

Imagining Eva in Wal-Mart, or indeed anywhere but in the circular tower room, was of course exactly the wrong thing to do. The safe place *was* an unreliable construct . . . a lie, really, although best not to think of it in those terms. Hurrying would knock it over, and so would distraction. Start thinking of some other place, particularly a real place (like the Wal-Mart) and that place intrudes.

"Stupid," she hissed, as the door to the stall farthest from the door slammed shut and her eyes opened. "Sorry," she said to the closed stall door. The woman who'd presumably gone inside didn't answer, and suddenly Ann felt nothing but foolish—imagining how she must have appeared to the woman now sequestered in the stall, a moment earlier quietly passing the sinks, and wondering: what a strange young woman, leaning over the sink with her eyes shut tight. *Some of us can't hold our liquor.* That's what she would think.

"Ann?" said Eva, and Ann said, again: "Sorry." She shut her eyes, and reassembled the tower room, re-inhabited it. "Got distracted."

"All right," said Eva, "now hush. I'm sending you energy."

Indeed, as Eva said this, the tower room flooded with light—appearing through the mortar between the stones, and the narrow slit-like windows that gave a tantalizing view of the realm. Ann thought she'd have a look at that realm—cement some details in her mind—the bucolic roll of hills, a silver river that wended between them . . . that mysterious, snow-capped mountain range in the distance—and take in the energy that Eva insisted she was sending her.

Was she really? Sending energy? From Wal-Mart?

Questions such as those, Ann had long ago learned to suppress. And she did so now. After all, they did nothing to help her take control, to give her the strength she would need to wrestle the Insect.

A clank, as the door to the stall rattled. And a voice—echoing off the tile of the washroom. *"Are you all right out there?"*

"Fine," said Ann, keeping her eyes shut this time, "thank you. I just need a moment."

"Don't we all."

The hollow rumble of toilet paper unwinding now.

"You know what you really need?"

Still unwinding.

"I'm fine," said Ann, while on the phone, from Wal-Mart, Eva said: "Shh."

"That fine-looking young man out there. He's a crackerjack!"

The door to the stall rattled fiercely. It slammed open, and closed again, and somehow Ann was turned around, the cell phone on the floor. Watching as the door to the stall slowly rebounded open. Showing nothing but an empty stall, with a long line of toilet paper, draped over the toilet bowl in a mandala form.

From the floor, Eva's voice buzzed. Like a bug, Ann thought crazily (*like an insect*) and she watched, transfixed, as the silver button on the side of the tank depressed, and the toilet began to flush.

"*I am satisfied*," said the Insect, as it settled back into its chair in the shadowy part of the tower room, crossing its hands on its lap, slender fingers twitching and intertwining. "*I approve*."

"Thank you," said Ann when she'd collected her phone from the floor.

"Did that do the trick dear?" asked Eva, from Wal-Mart.

"That seemed to do it," said Ann.

"You sure now?"

"Sure," she said—not sure at all.

Eva sighed. "I'm glad, dear. Be at peace. Now you call, if—"

"I will."

From one tower to another, Ann LeSage made her way back. She could find no evidence of mayhem en route. The glasses hanging over the bar gleamed in the afternoon sun, which shone through windows clean and clear. The traders gesticulated at their tables, hands unblemished, while their cutlery stayed safe in front of them. The waiter was cheerful and intact behind the bar, tapping lunch orders on a computer screen. And Michael sat back in his chair, ankles crossed, hands palm-down on the table, while the saltshaker sat unmoving between them. His face was strangely, beatifically calm.

When Ann recalled that July day—months later, outside Ian Rickhardt's Niagara vineyard, while she cradled an unreleased Gewürztraminer on the south-facing veranda and looked down upon the rows of grapevines, with just a moment to herself before their other guests arrived . . . this moment, not any prior or subsequent, was the moment that defined it. She, folding her skirt beneath her as she resumed her seat; Michael, looking steadily at her, unblinking, as he lifted one hand, and lowered it on top of the saltshaker like a cage of fingers.

"Gotcha," Michael said as he lifted the shaker off the table and studied it with real glee.

Was it terror she felt looking at him then?

Was it love?

Love, she guessed.

Yes. Love.

iii

To say that Ian Rickhardt played a large role in the planning of their wedding was like saying the sun was a bit of a player in the solar system. The old man *threw* the wedding—planned it and drew up the guest list and staged it, taking things over and riding them all like a bride's nightmare mother.

When Michael had told her about him, Ann thought Rickhardt might have been a father figure, standing in for the angry Afrikaner Voors. Michael had met Rickhardt in South Africa, over a rather complicated real estate deal. Rickhardt, who'd made his fortune in deals like this, saw something in Michael—clearly—and over the course of the years took an interest in the young South African. "He encouraged me to be my own man . . . eventually, to come here, and make my own life."

Ann nodded to herself. *Like a father, like a father should be.*

When she eventually met Ian, for dinner one August Sunday at Michael's condo, she scratched that idea too. He was more of an uncle.

He was near to sixty, but in fine shape for it. Had all his hair, which had gone white long ago and hung in neat bangs an inch above his eyebrows. He was lean without being gaunt, with a thin brush-cut of beard over a regular jawline. His eyes were pale blue and his skin a healthy pink.

Ian came to dinner in a pair of faded old Levis, and a motorcycle jacket over a black T-shirt. A wedding band, of plain gold, bound a thick-knuckled finger. His socks had holes in them, and he displayed them like hunting scars.

"The house at the winery is ancient," he said. "Century house and then some. Very romantic, oh yes. Floors are the original oak, and they're fucking stunning. But they spit up nails like land mines. The socks put up with a lot."

Michael laughed at his joke and so did Ann—not because it was funny, but because it cut the tension that ran just beneath the surface of this casual little dinner party.

Because of course, it was barely a party, and anything but casual. Ann figured it out even as it began.

She was being interviewed.

So they sat down to a meal of lamb and collard that Ann and Michael had prepared together, with a bottle of Rickhardt's cab franc, and as the sunlight climbed the bricks of Michael's east wall, Ian genially put Ann through her paces.

"You are an orphan?" he asked as he poured wine into their glasses.

Deep breath: "My parents died when I was fourteen."

"Car accident, I understand."

"Yes. I was very lucky. But my mother and father didn't survive."

Rickhardt made a sympathetic noise as he sat back down. He gave her a look that said, *Go on. . . .*

"My brother—"

"—Philip."

"—it was Christmas."

"Michael was telling me. You two were very close, I understand?"

"I don't think of him in the past tense. Philip survived."

Ian nodded. "But not whole." He took a sip of his wine. "That's very hard, Ann. I'm sorry. And you've really been on your own since then."

She sipped at her own wine. It *was* really very good.

"No one's really on their own," she said.

"That's not always true," he said. "But it's lucky you haven't been. And now you've met Michael, and that's fine. You two are getting married."

Needless to say, when Rickhardt arrived, he'd demanded to see the ring Michael had bought her and Ann obliged: a two carat emerald-cut diamond, set in a smooth band of platinum. Yes, they were getting married.

"I think marriage is good," he went on. "Good for Michael, good for you. I wish my wife could be here. She'd like you."

Michael nodded.

"What's her name?"

"Susan," he said.

"Sorry she couldn't come," said Ann. "I'd love to meet her."

Rickhardt made a small smile and sipped his wine. "You're young," he said. "How young?"

Another sip of wine, all around.

"Twenty-six," she said.

He nodded. "Michael's ten years older. Practically an old man. That doesn't bother you?"

Michael met her eye and smiled a little, shook his head, and Ann said: "Horrifies me, actually," and Rickhardt laughed.

"She's not in it for the money," said Michael, and stage-whispered: "Don't worry. *She's loaded.*"

They didn't really talk about money after that, although Rickhardt did ask her about her job at Krenk & Partners. He knew more than a little about them; Alex Krenk himself had joined forces with him in the 1990s, on an office development in Vancouver that had gotten some attention. Rickhardt had hired Krenk on various projects off and on since. They'd been asked to bid on designs for the restaurant and retail structures at his vineyard but had fallen short.

He told this story with clear expectation that Ann might jump in, but it was difficult. She was junior enough at the firm that she had no real knowledge about the Vancouver development; she'd helped out on some of the design for the vineyard, though, and she mentioned that. Rickhardt managed to say something nice about the bid, but facts were facts: the bid had fallen short. Ann attributed his words to a belated attempt at basic good manners.

There had been no mistaking when he'd finished his interview with Ann. He asked her a question about the type of care Philip was getting, but he clearly wasn't interested. Halfway through her answer, he was refilling his glass.

She was in the middle of a sentence when he looked up, right past her, and asked Michael, "Hey, do you remember Villier?"

Michael frowned, snapped his fingers, and said, "John Villier? From Montreal? Of course! What's he up to?" And so they launched into a long, context-free reminiscence about a trip the three of them had taken somewhere, some time ago, involving a seaplane and a great deal of liquor.

After Rickhardt left, they fought.

"He's a jerk," Ann said. They were standing on the narrow balcony where it overlooked the reclaimed industrial lands of the city's east end. Across the street, patrons from a café built from an old auto body shop sat under glowing orange lanterns and wide umbrellas outside the open garage door, getting happily buzzed before another work week.

"That's not fair," said Michael, his voice taking a plaintive edge. "Ian's just of a different generation."

"Fair enough," she said. "What's your excuse?"

They'd both had some wine by then, and Ann's tone was sharper than she'd intended. Two glasses ago, she might have stopped herself from pressing the matter.

"You left me out to dry," she said. "Ian Rickhardt treated me like a piece of property, a new car you brought home. He came over to check it out. Check me out."

Michael tucked his chin down, put both hands on the balcony rail, and pretended to study the seventh-day revellers in the café. "That's not what was happening," he said.

"Wasn't it?"

"I told you he could be a little off-putting."

"Yes. You did. And it was off-putting. So off-putting you abandoned me."

Michael stepped back from the railing and held his hands in the air, a gesture of retreat. He stepped back through the doors and retreated further, to the kitchen. Ann looked away from him, down at the café. As she watched, one string of lanterns flickered, and went dark.

Good, she thought, and was immediately ashamed.

Now, at the vineyard, staring out at the stand of fiery golden maple trees, watching the van make its way up the drive, and wondering if there might be some more of that delicious Gewürzt inside, Ann winced at the memory. She swilled down the last dregs of the wine from her glass, and drew a deep breath of the smell of this place—woodsmoke and loam—and turned to go back inside Rickhardt's winery. This was the place that Krenk & Partners didn't design, and from the look of it, wouldn't have if they'd been asked: all glass and oak around the tasting bar, faux-Bavarian beams demarking a first-storey ceiling below a dark loft above, railing hung with even-more-faux grapevine. Home Depot had won that bid, no question.

Rickhardt is a jerk. Also no question.

Ann swung around the tasting bar and pulled the half-empty bottle of Gewürzt out of the cooler. She poured herself half a glass.

He was a jerk. But so was she. She realized it when later that August Sunday, she'd come inside and started drying the dishes Michael was washing, and Michael had told her: "He wants to pay for the wedding. That's why he wanted to meet you. He thinks of me as a son. I'm sorry you didn't hit it off."

Ann took a sip, and then another. She started to take a third, but stopped herself as the wine touched her lip and set the glass down on the bar. The place would fill up in just a few hours with the guests at her Ian-Rickhardt-Productions wedding. From the sound of things, it was already starting.

Outside, she could hear the van pulling up. For a moment, she considered finishing the wine. But she resisted.

There would be plenty of time for wine later.

iv

Ian Rickhardt's list of guests was longest, at seventy-seven; Michael Voors' list less so but still respectable at twenty-six. Ann LeSage invited just five people to her wedding and Ian and Michael both looked worried. But she insisted it wasn't so sad as that. She loved four of them, and she was sure they loved her too, and that counted for a great deal.

Jeanie Yang had been Ann's roommate for two years at the University of Toronto, and together they had explored the delicate art of old-school pencil-and-paper role-playing games, the subtle art of Anime, and the numbing craft of single malt scotch. She was working across the border in a lab outside Chicago, but caught up with Ann in G-chat as soon as she got the invite and said she'd drive out.

ANN: It's a long drive.

JEANIE: OMFG its not. im a midwestrn grl now. everywhere goods 5 hours drive.

will lesley be there?

ANN: ummmm

JEANIE: :p

It was not awkward in the least, Jeanie insisted, that also attending would be Lesley Chalmers—another member of their little circle, with whom Jeanie had shared a bed for a semester. Lesley was in the architecture program with Ann, which was how she had met Jeanie, and it had been a terrible drama that year, Ann mediating their courtship, affair, and breakup.

Lesley was in Toronto, still; in school, still. She and her partner,

Bec, would rent a car and make a weekend of it. Lesley was old-fashioned. She confirmed by telephone.

"Who's going to be your maid of honour?" she asked.

"It's awful, but I haven't really picked one."

"Wow. And the wedding's—when?"

"October."

"This October."

"That's right."

"You know it's already September, right?"

"I suppose I should pick one."

"I suppose you should," said Lesley. "It's awfully last minute. It would have to be a very good friend."

Ann stifled a laugh. Sometimes, the time since graduation seemed like a lifetime. Sometimes, like no time at all.

"Lesley," she said, "would you do me the honour?"

"Given it a lot of thought, have you?"

"A *lot*."

"Do I have to buy a lime green dress with shoulder ruffles and a big fucking pink bow on my ass?"

"Yes."

"Does Jeanie have to wear one?"

"No."

Quiet on the line, then: "She's invited, right?"

Sometimes, it was like no time at all had passed. Ann reassured her friend that all was well with Jeanie, and fielded a few questions about how she was doing, and explained that yes, Lesley was maid of honour because Ann liked Lesley better and had secretly taken her side in every dispute—and agreed with her that Jeanie would not look as good in lime green and pink as Lesley, and would be madly jealous when she saw her, teetering on those stripper heels through the Chicken Dance.

Ann did not ask Lesley if she had asked about Jeanie because she was still hung up on her . . . if it would have really been better if one or the other of them hadn't been invited. In return, Lesley did not ask Ann about the quickness of the marriage, and if she mightn't have jumped into it less from the dictates of desperate soul-searing love, and more as a consequence of her general isolation from the world; if her minuscule guest list might not indicate a more dangerous isolation, for a young woman set to marry a wealthy lawyer she'd only known for a few months.

Questions like those were best left to Eva Fenshaw.

Eva booked into a bed and breakfast in the little village of Vanderville on the Bench almost a week before the wedding.

What the hell? Ann wondered.

But Eva said she could afford it, and she loved the fall colours, and she wanted to be well-rested for the celebrations. And she didn't want to be any trouble for the Rickhardts at their fancy winemakers' house, which was where Ann and Michael were staying.

"I know I'm welcome," said Eva before Ann could say it herself. "But I'm more comfortable here."

When she drove out to see her, Ann admitted she could see how. The bed and breakfast was a two-storey, red brick, pink-gabled Victorian, just off Vanderville's miniscule downtown. A chestnut tree shaded a big garden, still lush in the early autumn with nasturtiums overflowing clay pots and poking between field stone and little concrete gargoyles, still-flowering stalks of zabrina mallow growing everywhere. Its owner was a woman who might have been Eva's baby sister: a menopausal earth-mom in peasant skirt and T-shirt decorated with the Mayan alphabet.

The ground floor was filled with crafty knickknacks that somewhat-less-than-casually suggested Christmas. Yes, Eva said when they settled down for lunch at Stacey's, a diner on the town's main strip—not five minutes from the B & B—her bedroom followed the festive theme.

"It's like sleeping in a Christmas window display," she said. "Quite some fun, actually, if you're open to it."

"If you say so."

"I say so." Eva smiled, and Ann smiled back. Although they spoke very regularly, they didn't see each other in person much anymore, and that fact hit home with Ann as they sat there. Eva had aged visibly since they'd last had a meal together, a year or so ago; gained some weight, bent a bit here and there . . . her light brown bob was more grey. When Ann looked at her, she remembered her from a decade ago, taller, more tanned, not more than a wisp of grey in hair that went to her shoulders, telling Ann and her Nan about Tibet. The intervening years hung from her like debris.

"Thank you for coming," Ann said. "It means a lot to us."

"Oh, don't say that." Eva shook her head. "'It means a lot.' What's 'a lot'? A lot of what? A lot of hooey."

"It's something people say," said Ann, knowing even as she spoke the direction the discussion would take, and so was utterly unsurprised when Eva said, "People hide behind words like that. They don't say what they mean and then it's all lies. Not that I'm calling you a liar."

"Of course not."

"And yet . . ." Eva lifted up the menu and read from it: "Chinese and Canadian Food. Do you suppose they have poutine?" She scanned down with a fingertip. "Oh they do!"

"That takes care of the Canadian part," said Ann.

"I think I'll have poutine. Imagine, living here all my life—and I've never had it before."

"You're on your own," said Ann.

Eva clucked her tongue. "I wonder if they have herbal tea here? All it says is tea."

"Should I ask?"

"I can ask." Eva shut her menu, and signalled the waitress she was ready.

"Now tell me about this ceremony we're having on Saturday," said Eva after confirming that there was indeed herbal tea available, and that yes, the poutine was "any good." "You've got your wedding dress. I bet you look lovely in it."

"I do," said Ann. She took her phone out of her purse and showed Eva pictures on the tiny screen.

"Wow," said Eva as she flicked through the images. "You're a beautiful girl. Your Nan would be so—"

Ann put her hand on Eva's and gave it a squeeze and Eva squeezed back. Eva and her Nan had come to be good friends before she died. Almost as good friends as Eva'd become with Ann in that time.

"So proud," said Eva. "You're getting married."

"So I am."

"Are you sure?" Eva looked at Ann levelly. She had been smiling the whole time, but now it faded. "It's very soon."

"Sometimes you know," said Ann.

"That's true," said Eva. And as the steaming plate of fries, cheese curds and gravy arrived: "Michael is a nice fellow."

"I'm glad you like him."

Eva stabbed a french fry with her fork. She sniffed it. "You think I don't like him," she said, watching with fascination as a string of melted cheese curd snapped off the bottom of the fry.

"I—" began Ann, but Eva kept going.

"You think I'm coming here to bust this up, don't you?"

Ann opened her mouth and closed it again. Yes, she had to admit, deep down she did think that. Eva didn't like to travel. She didn't like to sleep away from home. Ann had idly wondered if Eva wasn't coming to town early to set up her B & B room as a kind of base camp for a more intensive campaign.

Eva squinted, popped the fry in her mouth and nodded as she chewed it.

"You know, we used to talk. A lot more. You'd tell me everything. And I'd tell you everything too. And when I said I thought somebody was a nice fellow, it was because I meant it. And I mean it now. Michael Voors is a nice man."

"For a lawyer?" asked Ann.

Eva shrugged. "Can't say I've known very many," she said, and her smile broke out again, and they both laughed.

"You're taking a step in your life," continued Eva. "You're taking it more quickly than we would have, when I was your age. . . . My God—Creator—that's an awful thing to hear yourself say. . . . But it's a good step all the same. I'd be more worried if we were sitting here five years from now, and you hadn't taken any kind of step—that's an awful thing to say too, because there's nothing wrong with being independent either." She put her fork through a clot of gravy and starch and twisted it like it was spaghetti. "But you know what I mean."

"I don't really have any idea," said Ann.

"Only this," said Eva. "You've got my blessing. Michael . . . He is a nice man. I can tell, you know. And you . . . If you've got any doubts or second thoughts . . . Well, like you said, sometimes you know. I don't think you really have doubts, now do you?"

She raised her eyebrow, and Ann said, "I don't. No."

Eva nodded, and leaned in forward, a little confidentially. "And he is a handsome young man. I assume he's good . . . you know."

"Eva!"

"Oh, I'm not a prude," said Eva, laughing. "Don't you be. Sex is important. It's part of a marriage."

Ann didn't know what to say. Sex was important. And it was . . . fine with Michael, she guessed. Not great . . . not as frequent as she'd have thought. Something, she'd supposed, they could work on, on the honeymoon.

"Don't worry, Eva," she said. "Michael keeps me more than satisfied." She made a show of winking. "If you know what I mean."

Eva nodded again, and this time had the good grace to blush—at least a little. "Well good," she said, and they sat quietly.

Ann had ordered a grilled chicken sandwich. The waitress came with it, finally.

"I had a dream about you last night," said Eva when the waitress had gone. "Very vivid. I think it might have been the new place I was sleeping; all that Christmas stuff. It was a good dream."

"Oh?"

"It was at the house by the lake," she said. "Before . . . well, before it sold. We were all younger—your Nan was there. It was Easter I think, because I remember a basket of eggs on the dining room table. You weren't actually in the room. . . ."

"That's not surprising," said Ann. "I didn't go back there once during the time you knew me."

"Oh, I know, believe me. That was the last place you should have been, then," said Eva. "Your Nan and I sometimes went back there. Particularly as it was getting ready to go on the market."

"You didn't tell me."

"She didn't want to be there alone. I didn't want her to, either." Eva paused for another bite of poutine. "We had good talks there."

"So it wasn't really about me."

"We were talking about you. You were going off to a new school in the fall—a private school. Your Nan thought it would be good for you."

"I probably hadn't studied for the exam," said Ann. "That's how my dreams about going off to school usually end up."

"This wasn't going to be like that."

"You could tell that?"

"She knew you could do it."

"Of course she—" Ann stopped and swallowed. Eva sat quiet, waiting. But Ann didn't cry. Outside the window, a truck pulled by, gears grumbling as it crawled down the street.

"The marriage is a good thing," said Eva. "Michael—he's lost his family too, really. They've driven him off, it's the same thing. So it's no surprise that you want to make a new one quickly, now that you've found each other. And you must be feeling pretty secure in each other. In everything." She punctuated with a raised eyebrow.

Ann raised both, to say: *Go on, Eva.*

And Eva went on: "I mean to say, if you weren't secure—if you didn't feel really safe . . . you never would have invited *him*."

The van had pasted on its side a photograph of trees, blue sky—across its tail, hands joined together, pale as clouds. MARGARET HOLLINGSWORTH RESIDENTIAL CARE, written in fine script. If you passed it on the highway, you might mistake it for a minibus—something that would carry residents well enough for day outings to the nearby mall. Stuck in traffic, you might notice some other things about it—the reflective shades drawn down over the windows; the eighteen-inch caduceus stencilled above the license plates . . . the small blue light on the roof.

While it was true that the Hollingsworth Centre had those other kinds of buses, the ones for the mobile residents—this one wasn't one of those.

Ann knew about this kind of bus. Point of fact, she knew *this* one. Ann recognized the attendants, although she couldn't remember their names: the woman had short brown hair and a deep tan, she liked to snowboard; the man was black-haired and balding. He waved at Ann where she stood hesitating on the ramp to the winery, and jogged across the drive while the woman *(Ellen? Alana?)* opened the tailgate of the van and manoeuvred the hydraulic lift into place.

"Hey there!" said Ann, and squinted at the name tag, and (when he was near enough) finished: "Paul."

"Hi, Ann." He stopped and put a hand on the railing, looked around and nodded—taking in the grounds. "This is a beautiful spot. This where it's going to be?"

"This is it." Ann spread her arms as if to indicate the world. "Ceremony and reception."

"Very nice." He regarded the ramp and nodded again. "Elaine—" *(Aha! Elaine!)* "—is getting him ready."

"Was the trip okay for him?"

"Very comfortable. Traffic was smooth, so we made good time; he didn't need anything until the last leg. So he'll be a little sluggish now. But trust me—he's in great spirits."

Ann sighed. "That's good," she said, in a way that was apparently unconvincing.

Paul suddenly became very earnest. "Ann—it *is* good. He's very excited to be here for you today. He called this his 'road trip.' He's been cracking wise about dancing at your wedding all week."

Ann laughed—more convincingly this time. That being the kind of gag she'd have expected, from him.

Paul stepped back from the railing and beckoned her back to the van.

"Let's go say hello," he said. "I've got to help with this next part."

"Let's," said Ann. And she smoothed her skirt, and crossed the drive to the van.

"Hi Ann!" said Elaine, poking her head out of the back of the van. "Do you want to come up inside before we send him on his way?"

Ann peered inside. The interior of the Hollingsworth minibuses were well enough lit for their purposes; but in the afternoon light, the compartment looked like a black pit. She swallowed, and drew a breath, and said: "I don't want to get in your way."

"Okay," said Elaine. "Paul, give me a hand?"

And when Paul turned away, and it was clear no one was looking, Ann shut her eyes.

She was in the corridor. Sunlight streamed in through the tall windows facing the east. At the end of it, in a deep shadow, the ironclad door stood still. Ann walked carefully down the hallway, not tossing anything out this time, until she could lay a hand on the door, run her fingers over the cool iron locks and bolts there. She pressed her ear against the wood, and listened.

Inside, it was silent.

Good, she thought. *Stay that way.*

She opened her eyes at the touch of a hand. "Hey," said Elaine, "say hello."

"Hi big brother," said Ann, as the wheels of Philip LeSage's chair rolled off the lift platform. She stepped closer, Elaine still holding her arm. Philip wore a green Roots sweatshirt that she remembered hugging his shoulders like a skin. Now, he was lost in it. His head lolled in its brace, and his lips pulled back over his teeth in the thing that he did these days to smile. His eyes blinked over hollow cheeks, under brown hair sheared competently, by the hand of a Hollingsworth nurse.

Hello little sister, came the whisper.

THE VOYAGE OF THE *BOUNTY II*

i

Philip was tall for his age then, and strong.

To Ann he'd been a giant. They lived in a giant house by a giant lake, with their mom and their dad and their dog, all giants too. There was a town nearby but it was small, or that was what Philip kept calling it. Littleton, he called it, even though it was really called Fenlan.

Viewed from a certain angle, however, it too was giant-sized.

Ann had turned ten only a month before they came there. She wouldn't remember much about that house for long because it was very boring. There was a little yard with a plastic slide in it. She had a little room in the back with a window too high up for her to see out of without climbing on the top bunk. Her dad hated the kitchen. Her mom hated the basement. She hated that window.

As far as Ann knew, Philip didn't hate anything. Not there, anyway.

Ann would remember the house at the lake for a long time—first, because she watched it being made. Her dad was a structural engineer and when she was little he started his own company. He was good at it and soon he was making buckets of money. The first bucket went to buying the old lot on the lake. The second bucket, to buying a beautiful sailboat to tie up there. The third, to figuring out the best house for them. The money they got from selling that other house went to building it.

It was built of cedar logs, mostly, with some concrete and stone around the foundation and slate for the roof. That summer, the summer they went there, it wasn't finished yet. The foundation was in and the walls were up, but it was a hollow box: a maze of two-by-fours and plastic sheets, conduits and copper pipes all exposed—open holes where windows would go. So they couldn't live in it. But the last place there had had a nice dock and a boathouse next to it, and that was where they stayed, while the crew their dad had hired finished the job.

Philip thought the boathouse was worse than the old house. It was small, shaped like a shoebox, and it was damp, and in the night the water from the lake lapped under the floorboards.

"I think it's nice," said Ann as they lay on the air mattresses at the far end of the little boathouse from their parents, and Philip said, "It makes me want to pee."

"So pee," she said.

"You first." Philip knew the one thing that Ann didn't like about this place was the facilities, as her dad called them: an orange outdoor toilet that got emptied weekly and smelled . . . well, of pee, of course.

"You don't need to go there," she said. "You can just go outside."

"I can go right here," he said, and Ann rolled over and gave him a kick.

"I would," he said. "I'd pee all over you."

"Gross."

"Yeah. It would be gross," he said, slowly so as to emphasize each word.

"Quiet time," said her mom from behind the sheets they'd hung at the far end of the boathouse, for privacy. She was there alone with them that night; their dad, down in the city taking care of a contract with some condo dwellers. Philip pulled his headphones over his ears and changed CDs in the blue Discman he'd brought with him. He rolled over and opened the book he was reading. It was an old spy book by Len Deighton. *Yesterday's Spy*. There was a picture of a rusted automatic pistol on it. Ann wanted to read it next.

When he turned the page, Ann got up and tiptoed over to the window. It was an old-fashioned wood-frame with nine panes. The glass rippled like tree gum. Outside, night settled over the lake, but she couldn't see it, for the reflection of Philip's reading light.

She squinted, and put her thumb on the lower left pane, and traced the crack there. When they'd arrived, it had only been as long as her middle finger. Now, it was long as her hand, heel to fingertip.

She didn't care what Philip said: even though it was small, and temporary—and it smelled like lake, and she didn't yet have her own space—she liked this little boathouse better than the old house. The window was just her size. And as far as the lapping water went: it was nice.

It sounded like home.

They had a beautiful boat.

She was a sailboat, made of rich brown wood—oak, and mahogany—and although even Ann could tell she wasn't very big, she was big enough, with a long cabin where you could cook a meal and sleep overnight and use the bathroom if you needed to. That was half the reason they were here in the summer before the house was finished—their dad was in love with the boat, which he'd named the *Bounty II*. The first *Bounty* being the boat he'd owned for a while when he worked in the Caribbean, back in the day. He was in love with that one, he was in love with this one too—or so Ann's mom said.

"That's your true love, Bill, right there in the water. Children, say hello to your new mom." And everybody laughed.

But even young as she was, Ann thought her father's feeling toward the boat was more complicated than love, and maybe not as nice either. Her father bought the boat in February from a dealer he'd met when they all went to the Boat Show the month before. Their parents had agreed a small power boat made the most sense. They might use it for errands to the marina across the way, or visiting other cottagers, or fishing, or water-skiing.

When they got there, it was a different story. Ann didn't notice anything strange about her parents at first—she fell under the spell of the fancy booths and the music, the smell of beer nuts and the pretty women who stood at all those booths, and all those boats. There was a stage show with dancers in the middle. They had scuba divers too, in a big glass tank. You could knock on the glass and the diver would knock back.

But once that magic wore off, Ann started to pick up on things. Her mom was talking constantly—more than usual, in fact. Philip hurried ahead of them, almost too far to shout. Her dad, meanwhile, became very quiet. He stopped for a moment, in the space underneath a parasail that dangled from the ceiling and stared into the fabric until Ann nudged him. When they paused at a dealer's show space, it was usually at their mom's suggestion. He jammed his fists into the pockets of his coat and nodded while she asked him what she thought about this, or that, and he hurried them along.

Ann was starting to wonder whether her dad really wanted to buy a boat. He looked like he just wanted to leave.

But after lunch, they stopped at a booth from a North Bay company called Clinker. There weren't any boats here—just photographs that were wrapped in plastic, of sailboats for the most part, and a stack of three thick binders. The booth was being run by an old woman who wore a white Clinker sweatshirt and a sun visor. Her skin was wrinkled and brown as leather.

Their dad stopped, and looked at the photographs, and said to their mother: "Go look at the jet skis. I'll catch up." And as they went off, mom shaking her head, Ann watched as their dad stepped uncertainly up to the booth and introduced himself to the woman there.

The next month, as they sat in the tidied-up kitchen of the old house waiting for an appointment with their realtor, it emerged that he had bought them a boat. The *Bounty II*. Not, he admitted, exactly what they'd discussed. It had a motor on it, true, but that wasn't the point of it. The boat was made for sailing. It was made, really, for sailing on bigger water than the lake. Twice, he said, the previous owner had sailed it down the St. Lawrence River and out into the Atlantic Ocean, south as far as the Caribbean Sea. That was where the photograph had been taken—on a bright day in the Caribbean, no land in sight. The water was a deep green, the sky uninterrupted blue. The boat was still, its sails down, mast stretching above the top of the frame. Someone—an old man, with a baseball cap and a white beard—sat in the cockpit, right hand frozen in a cheery wave.

Yes, their father said, in fact it had cost more than they'd planned to spend. "But she's a beautiful boat," he said, and their mother looked at the photograph, and then at him, and said nothing.

Were it not for the boat, they would not likely have moved to the new property so quickly. Their dad wanted to sail—wanted to make up for lost time, he said. And he wanted his children to sail also, and he was very keen not to waste the summer. So when school finished in June, they moved most of their possessions into storage, the family into the boathouse, and the *Bounty II* alongside the dock beside the boathouse.

They didn't take the *Bounty II* out every day. But it quickly began to feel as if that were the schedule. Their dad was an enthusiastic sailor, and was also pretty good at it, or so it seemed to Ann. He could find wind on a still July morning and he knew about sailors' knots and he could read a nautical chart.

They crossed the lake and back again, explored what little there was to see, waved at cottagers, and spent two nights on board, crammed into a space even smaller than the boathouse. Their mom knew how to play guitar, and the second night out their dad persuaded her to bring it along. They all sang old songs: "Puff the Magic Dragon," and "Let It Be," and most of "The Wreck of the Edmund Fitzgerald" (until they cracked up laughing and had to stop).

They didn't go out every day. But they got in quite a lot with the boat in the time they had with her.

ii

It was July 19th, and a Tuesday. The sky that morning was a clear blue bowl, and even on the lake, it was hot. Ashore, the contractors were putting up drywall between the master bedroom and the second-floor hall. The LeSages were out, on the *Bounty II*.

Philip and their parents were up top in the cockpit, and that was fine with Ann. Their dad was intent on teaching him how to run the boat, so Philip was stuck behind the wheel while his dad swung the boom around and hollered for anyone topside to duck.

Ann wasn't topside. She was below, just out of sight of the companionway, making her own fun. She didn't have a lot to work with—most of her toys were shut up in storage. But her mom had bought her a Barbie doll in town. And she'd finally had a look at that Len Deighton novel.

So she did what she could.

At 11:22 a.m. (by the clock over the stove), Barbie awoke: trapped in the hold of a big steamer bound to Egypt with a shipment of bomb parts that the master-spy Mr. Champion was sending to terrorists. Barbie was wearing her tennis outfit, because the last thing she was doing before the bad men had stuck her with a needle was getting ready to meet her spy handler Ken for a double set of tennis and a briefing. She wobbled back and forth unsteadily, coming to herself by degrees.

"Don't panic, girl, just figure this out—before they come."

"Panic and you're through," said Ann aloud.

Outside, the weather was getting choppy, but Ann was okay with that. The steamer was going through a storm, crawling up huge waves and crashing down . . . lightning flashed between clouds blacker than . . . than, um, night. The darkest night! The men who'd captured Barbie were distracted, trying to keep the ship on course.

It all gave Barbie precious seconds, as she worked out where she was—explored the space around the spare gas tank, clambered over the wooden keel and looked for ways out.

"You'll never escape, foolish girl."

Ann tried not to giggle. Philip was doing voices, she figured; she could feel the coolness as his shadow blocked the sun on her.

And it was a great voice. She played along: "You can't keep me here. My family will come get me!"

"Your family? What makes you think your family is in any position to get you?"

"My family has a helicopter," said Ann (as Barbie). "It's got a big machine gun on the bottom of it. And when it flies? It goes so fast!"

"Never faster," said the voice, *"than when it's falling."*

"They have parachutes! Let me go or they'll machine-gun you!" Ann made machine gun noises with her mouth: "CH-CH-CH-CH-CH-CH-CH-CH!"

"They can't machine-gun me."

"They can!"

"No."

"Let me go!" shouted Ann, delighted.

"You don't want to go."

A blast of water hit Ann in the back of the head, and at that, she turned around, to give Philip hell. But he wasn't there. The companionway was empty but for a dark, rolling sky.

Ann put Barbie down and climbed the steps.

Her dad, at the wheel, told her to stay down and make sure her life jacket was tight. The boat was rocking and rain was coming down hard, flying in all directions. They'd taken the sails down. The motor was on, chugging desperately. Philip and their mom were at the back of the boat, bailing, and looking away—

—to a huge spinning ribbon of water, climbing higher than the trees.

It was moving from side to side, twisting prettily under the fat, black clouds, like a towel spun tight between hands. It made a sound like a big waterfall, like Niagara Falls.

Her dad shouted something at her, and he met her eyes, and Ann froze. She had seen many things in her dad before, some of which she couldn't put a name to. This was the first time she'd seen such naked fear. She had no trouble naming it.

The boat wheeled around and another big wave rocked them as she ducked back into the cabin. Water rushed in after her.

Ann grabbed onto the side of the steps as the water ran down the deck toward the bow and then came back again, a tea-coloured mix of lake water and the sand she'd trekked in with her flip-flops. It dragged Barbie along with it. She was facedown in the water. The storm had not been a lucky break for her after all.

The boat pitched and the water deposited Barbie at Ann's feet. Still holding onto the ladder with one hand, Ann reached down with the other and grabbed Barbie by the hair. She pushed the doll into the crook of her arm and held it there as another sluice of water came through. It was freezing cold down her back, and she squealed.

"Hang on, honey." Mom was on her knees. Hands gripping the hatch. Everyone was on their knees, because the boom was swinging wildly as the boat turned in the water.

"Close the hatch!" Ann shouted. Her mom shook her head: "No honey! I don't want you trapped. Just stay there," and Ann screamed, so that her breath steamed in the cooling air:

"Close it!"

And at that, the boat pitched, and her mother slipped back, and then Ann couldn't tell anything, because the hatch was shut, and she was back in the hold of the steamer.

"Where is the girl?"

"She was knocked right out when we left."

"Well she isn't now, dumkopf. *She has escaped. We must search the ship."*

"Who's there?" The cabin—the hold—was dark as night. Ann held Barbie tight, and felt the deck pitch underneath her. A lash of rain and water hit one of the portholes and drew back. A latch clicked, and she heard one of the drawers sliding open. Then came a clattering—a sound of cutlery dumping onto the deck.

"Not here."

"Philip?" The voice didn't sound like Philip—it seemed deeper than he could manage, and . . . somehow foreign, and . . . it seemed to be everywhere.

Maybe at her shoulder.

"The little bitch is crafty," it said.

"Only so many places to be crafty," it said, *"on this ship."*

Something covered the porthole then, for just an instant—and Ann felt a plastic bowl bounce off her ankle. When the porthole reappeared, Ann could see a rime of frost forming around its edges.

"Not there."

Ann felt her stomach turn then, and the light shifted and shifted; the wooden hull moaned and the water that had gotten in sloshed frantically. Ann swallowed—tears of panic crawled from her eyelids. She held the Barbie tighter, and thought: *We're in the waterspout!*

"Here?" Something snapped, and dishes clattered and Ann felt herself being pressed against the ladder now as the spinning grew quicker.

"Where is that little bitch?"

The boat was going to break apart!

"Give yourself up!"

"No please no!"

Ann squealed, as she felt something squirm under her arm. She reached in and pulled out Barbie, still soaking wet in her tennis outfit. She looked the doll in the face—and then turned her away, to face the dark—and (hating herself), she shouted to the dark hold: "Here she is!"

The boat pitched again, and Ann slipped in the water puddling in the bottom of the boat, and when she righted herself, she was empty-handed.

Something whistled—maybe the kettle they had for making tea. . . .

Maybe Barbie, in the clutches of the bad men . . .

Screaming.

Whichever it was, whistle or scream—the noise cut short with a great *crack!* sound, and a sudden listing, as the *Bounty II* struck rock, and the spinning stopped for good.

Philip had scraped his hand raw on a rope. The *Bounty II* would need a new mast, a new propeller, and all or part of a rudder, and someone would have to come by to look at the hull just to be sure. But with those exceptions, no one was hurt, and dad's precious boat had survived.

Later, that night, their mom would call it that: *your precious boat*, as a way to contrast the preciousness of his daughter, his son, his wife . . . himself.

When Ann opened up the hatch and climbed onto the deck, there were no harsh words. The boat had tangled in some water-rounded rocks that peeked out of the lake near a stand of pine trees on the shore. It was listing heavily to port, so the whole family was as much leaning against the deck as they were sitting on it. The whole deck was in shadow. The sky was brilliant blue directly overhead; to the east, towering thunder-headed clouds sped away. Her mom was there by the hatch, prying it up.

"My God, baby, you're cold as ice!" she said as she drew Ann into her arms. "It's like a freezer in there!"

Ann held on to her mom tightly as she pulled her into the sunlight. Their dad scrambled around them, and reached into the hatch. He unstrapped the first aid kit and hauled it to the wheel, where Philip hunched over his injured hand.

Her mom chided her for shutting the hatch, but gently. "It might seem safe to lock yourself in there, but it just traps you, honey. If the boat had turned over . . ."

"I didn't shut myself in there."

"It's okay if you did this time. It was pretty scary up here."

"But I didn't."

"Just remember not to do it again."

"It wasn't me," she said.

iii

There was pizza back at the boathouse. Dad bought enough for the family and the contractors too, and some beer besides—"to drink to our good fortune," he said, which sounded like a funny thing to say, at first. But Ann didn't have to think long to realize that it had been a lucky day all around, and as the sun set on it, they all sat around a fire pit on the beach, going over just how lucky.

Cal, one of the drywallers, had been taking a smoke break on the lawn when the storm came in and he'd seen the twister come.

"Never seen anything like it," he said as he reached for another bottle. "I go out, and it's clear and hot. Couple clouds in the west, but nothing to write home about. Not even a breeze when I'm lighting up. You were out pretty far by then, but I could still see you fine. I remember thinking you were going pretty good for how calm it was on shore."

"Calm, and fuckin'—sorry—and hot," said Luc, a carpenter in from Montreal.

"Yeah, until then. I'm not even half finished my smoke, and suddenly it gets dark, and cold. The wind's picked up, and there's a cloud—a black cloud—right overhead. Blacking out everything. Thing snuck right up."

"Forecast didn't say anything about it," said Dad, nodding.

"Forecasters don't know their ass," said Luc.

"Not today," said Cal, and clinked the bottom of his beer bottle with Dad's.

"Did you spot the funnel cloud?" asked Dad, and Cal nodded.

"Didn't know what it was at first. Never seen one of those before. But yeah. It was sort of dipping down toward the lake . . . and screw it, I thought. I pinched off my smoke and headed back inside. Figured we'd get hit. It was that close."

"Fuck."

"Luc!"

"Ah. Sorry. Hey kid! Sorry!"

Ann looked where Luc was waving. Philip had gotten up and was heading toward the boathouse.

"It's okay," Philip called back. "I'm just taking a walk."

Ann had another slice of pizza and chewed on it as the workmen continued their tale: how they'd shut off the generator and headed to the basement, occasionally glimpsing the rising swirl of water from the lake. Cal insisted he'd said a prayer for the LeSages, and another workman who Ann didn't know said he tried to get to his truck to radio for help. But the wind was too strong.

They started to talk about how best to fix the boat, then. It was still tangled in the rocks—tomorrow, their dad would hire another boat from the marina across the lake, to come out and haul it back—so the conversation was pretty theoretical. As it dragged on, Ann asked if she might be excused and her mother sent her on. "Go find your brother," she called after her and Ann said she would.

It was, after all, what she'd been intending all along.

Philip was inside the boathouse.

Not the second floor, where they were living, but the bottom—a garage, basically, where you might actually house a boat or two, if you bought the right size of boat. He wasn't hard to spot; he'd turned the light on, and was sitting inside, along the dock and in a torn old canvas chair that had been left by the last owners. The light reflected up off the lake and made everything seem underwater.

"I peed in the lake," he said when she came in. "So don't go swimming."

"Ew." Ann sat down on the edge of the dock beside him and peered into the water. It was black. It wasn't quite still enough to see her reflection. Philip tapped his heel on the dock. "How's your hand?" she asked.

"Good. Better."

Tap-tap-tap, went his foot. Ann looked out the front of the boathouse, which was open. The sun was pretty much down, but she could see the distant line of trees at the lake's far side against the slightly lighter horizon. Soon there would be all kinds of stars out; since the storm, the clouds were all gone.

"Were you talking to me?" she asked. "Right before the storm hit?"

He was silent.

"And after? When the hatch closed? Were you talking to me then?"

"No," he said.

Tap-tap-tap-tap.

"Because I thought you were," she said. "I heard you talking. While I was playing. With my Barbie."

"I was kind of distracted," he said. "Big storm. Remember?"

Tap-tap.

She nodded. "I remember," said Ann. "And . . ."

Tap.

"What?"

She leaned back and put her hand on his foot.

"I'm sorry," she said. "I think it was my fault."

Philip pulled his foot back and kicked a little. She let go.

"Fuck off."

It was the worst thing you could say to someone, but Philip said it in a way just then that made her want to hug him.

He drew his feet underneath the chair and he looked at her.

"It's not your fault," he said. "It's Dad's."

"What?"

"This never would've happened if we'd just stayed at home. If he didn't buy that boat. And make us go out in it."

Ann turned around so her back was to the water, and she could face him directly.

"Tell me the truth," she said. "Swear. You didn't say anything to me when I was down below? You weren't, like, fooling around?"

"*Fuck.*" He held up his bandaged hand like he was taking an oath. "*Piss. Shit. Goddammit.* That good enough swearing?"

Ann rolled her eyes, and swung back around to look at the water. She pulled off her shoes, and dipped her feet in. It was freezing, but it felt good. It was numbing in its way.

Feet still in water, she lay back on the dock and looked up at her brother. This was how Barbie would see things, she thought.

"Good enough," she said.

"Someone was talking to you?" he said after a while. "During the storm?"

She nodded.

"Think it was a ghost?"

Ann shrugged. "I thought it was you."

"Did it sound like me?" He tapped the side of her head with his toe, but gently.

"At first. But then—"

He nodded. "A ghost."

"On a boat?"

Philip leaned forward so his face loomed over hers, upside down. "It's an old boat," he said. "Remember that picture of it? With the old guy, sitting at the wheel, waving?"

"Yeah."

"Maybe he's dead. And maybe he doesn't like being dead. And maybe he came all the way up here, to get—"

His toe tapped again, against her ear.

"—his—"

"Ow!" It was harder this time, and Ann sat up fast.

"—boat back!" he shouted, and leaned forward, started tickling under her arms, yelling "Bwa-ha-ha!"

Ann's feet came out of the water in a spray, and she kicked so more water came up, soaking them both. She squealed. He rolled out of the chair and onto his knees and dug in, tickling her waist. "Bwa-ha-ha-ha-ha-ha," he said.

Ann brought her knees up from the water and gasped, "No no no!" And at that, he relented, fell back on his haunches, looked down at her with a grin.

"I hate you," she said, grinning back.

"I hate you more," he said, and slapped her on the shoulder.

"No I hate you more." Ann rolled over and got up. Her ribs hurt from laughing, and she was wet, and freezing cold.

"I'm going to get changed," she said, and stuck her tongue out. Philip gave her a pro-forma middle finger, then nodded. Made a show of shivering.

"We're both soaked," he said. He got up too, and together they went outside and climbed the stairs to their temporary home in the boathouse. They paused at the door. On the beach, one of the workmen had just tossed another log on the fire, and the sparks climbed high over the roof—nearly as high as the roof of the main house, which towered tall and black behind them. The storm, the tower of water *it* made, hadn't touched the house. It hadn't touched *anything* here.

But for the evidence of the boat on the rocks tonight, and Philip's rope-burned hand, it might never have come at all.

Ann heard a sob, clawing its way from her belly. She shut her eyes.

Philip put his arms around Ann then, and hugged her close. She hugged her big brother back. She didn't know if he was crying, then, but she sure was. He let her finish before he opened the door and took them both inside.

"I don't think it was a ghost," said Philip as he turned the light on, "for what it's worth."

The Joining of Two

i

The production company Ian Rickhardt had hired was to be editing the wedding video while Michael and Ann were off in Tobago; Ian Rickhardt had led Ann to expect that she wouldn't see it until the honeymoon was over.

"These guys are good," he said. "Normally, they'd take a month on this thing. For me—for you, they'll cut it in two weeks. One way or another—they'll get it perfect. And when you're back, we'll sit down with bowls of popcorn and check it out."

As far as anyone knew, that was Rickhardt's plan all along.

And it was—until he drove into town, met with the editor, had a talk about just how much he'd been able to achieve, and sat down with a rough cut.

That changed everything.

Ann and Michael were on the Buccoo Reef, snorkelling under a clear Caribbean sky with a glass-bottom-boatload of Venezuelans. It was very non-exclusive. The whole honeymoon had been managed by a business contact of Michael's—Steve Clifford, a Trinidadian banker who either owed Michael a favour or was building up some credit.

He'd found them a beach house—a two-floor cinderblock affair not technically on the beach but within sight of the sea. It was near the airport at the capital town of Scarborough, but not too near. Coconut trees surrounded it, and it was far enough from the road that it might be considered remote. Michael liked it because it was "off the grid," the grid being the line of resort complexes that had breakfast buffets and swim-up bars and a list of activities.

"Sounds like my kind of grid," said Ann when they discussed it. But she was persuaded by photographs of those palm trees, and the promise of a housekeeper and driver.

Steve Clifford would, in that spirit, have organized an exclusive just-the-two-of-them trip out to the reef and had in fact made the offer. But Michael and Ann had agreed: Steve had done enough already, setting them up in that beach house with their own housekeeper and cook, arranging a car and driver to be on call for them.

By the time they decided to check out the local sea life, stepping back on the grid, getting to see some people, didn't seem like such a bad idea.

So Ann arranged for two spots on the *Calypso Empress*, a big outboard shaped like a shoebox, and they settled around the glass floor to watch the bottom of the sea scoot by.

The Venezuelans were in a group, and they were tied up in wedding business too. They were all guests, though; the bride and groom were holed up at a resort by the airport, getting ready for the big day. These ones were friends of the groom; they worked with him at a newspaper in Caracas. It was one of the newspapers that didn't much care for Chavez—or so Ann surmised from the conversation.

When she pointed this out, several of the Venezuelans laughed. "We all hate Chavez," said one. "Even in death. That is what they pay us for!"

The ride to the reef was just under a half hour. It went quickly. The Venezuelans were delighted to hear that they were on a boat with honeymooners, and peppered them with questions. When were they married? Where were they staying? Were there going to be lots of kids? Did they have an opinion regarding President Obama?

They played a guessing game about their nationalities. The newspapermen pegged Ann as a Canadian right away, but guessed wrong twice about Michael. German? Swedish? Or (the closest one) Dutch?

He seemed pleased when he finally had to tell them: "South African. We should have put money on it."

Soon enough, the glass-bottomed boat rendered up its rewards: a sand shark, schools of yellow sunfish, great crabs. A manta ray paced them for a while.

The boat paused at a nondescript shallow that had been named the Nylon Pool by visiting royalty. It was rumoured to have rejuvenating powers, and everybody climbed into the water with that in mind. Rejuvenated (and a little bored), they climbed back out, and moved on to the reef, while the guides admonished them about the penalties to befall any visitor tempted to break off coral or do anything else to upset the ecology.

The guides passed out masks and snorkels, black rubber shoes. No need for fins: the reef was shallow enough here that a tall person would have to crouch a bit to get the mask underwater. They all climbed down a little steel ladder that extended from the boat's stern.

Ann didn't have to bend very far to get a look at the reef. It was a revelation! A school of tiny silver fish swirled around her ankle, and not far from her toe, a barnacled crustacean of peculiar origin moved aside. Her first impulse—to jump back, away from the world that she was invading—passed in an instant. The guides were right: this was an ecology, a whole world unto itself.

She made her way across the coral—itself a huge living entity, maybe seven kilometres across, if you stretched the definition of living and entity.

The water deepened and she was able to stand straighter, and she went deeper into that strange, drifting land, and thought: *I could get used to this place.*

That was when the fish struck.

Later, the guide would proclaim it a parrot fish, so named because of the hard, beaklike jaws it had, perfect for biting off pieces of coral. It was not a fish known for its aggressive tendencies. It was not a very big fish.

But it could bite.

Ann actually watched it approach. It came close, circled her waist, spiralled down her legs. It slowed as it reached her knee. It was then that it made up what passed for its mind.

Ann screamed more in surprise than pain—although the bite certainly hurt. The fish took a small piece of her left knee with it as it spun into the deeper parts of the reef. Michael splashed over to her side, accompanied by two of the Venezuelans and a guide.

"Fuck!" she shouted as she hurried back to the boat. The mask dangled from her neck. Her knee hurt fiercely. She explained, at some volume, what had happened and that she was probably bleeding. The guides shouted to the others to come in.

"Sorry," she said aloud.

It wasn't as bad as she thought, but it was bad enough. The *Calypso Empress* had a first aid kit on board and the guides were trained. To take her attention away from the pain, the guide handed her a cold bottle of Red Stripe, and asked her to describe the fish. When she was finished, he nodded. "Parrot fish. Eats the coral, not the tourists. You didn't make much of a meal for it if that makes you feel any better."

"She is a pale girl," said one of the Venezuelans, and his friend punched him, and added, "skin like alabaster, he means," and the first said, "like fine coral."

Michael held Ann's shoulders and gave a squeeze.

"Maybe we should get a bit of sun tomorrow," she said to him, "just as a precaution." And she reached around and stroked his chin, and he laughed.

"Maybe," he said.

Ann got the injury looked at properly at a clinic in Scarborough that Steve recommended, and after that they had a meal of fresh-caught sea bass and plantain, grilled for them by Thea, their housekeeper.

That night, they had another go at it in the bedroom.

It would be wrong to call it a failure, at least from Ann's point of view.

Michael Voors was an attentive lover. He had a box of scented oils, which he would apply with great assurance, using hands here, a feather there, the tip of a tongue in the tricky spots. He would kiss her, and do this and then that—and then, with a piratical leer, he would vanish beneath the sheets for quite some time to "bring the boat home." Ann wondered how he managed to get any air during these dives, but she didn't want to discourage him, so kept the question to herself.

As far as it went, that was fine—wonderful, really. She only wished she could return the favour so adeptly.

In a series of failed attempts, she had developed a solid repertoire of tricks, and she drew on them that night, mixing up the order of things.

First—rather than waiting for him to roll off her, disentangle him from the sheets, she slid her right leg underneath him, brushing against him lightly with her calf, sliding up to tweak him with her toe. In the past, she'd lingered there to diminishing effect. This time, she pulled away, and rolled out of bed. She walked naked to the French doors, taking time to stretch with calculated languor. She glanced back at him, noted his eyes on her, and flicked the latch. She complained that she was freezing. But the moon was very nice. Michael obligingly got out of bed and joined her. He put his arms around her, rubbed warmth back into her arms.

Got him! she thought.

This was a new trick, and she held out great hope for it. With a nudge and a bit of pull, she manoeuvred his hands from her arms to her breasts. Hands free, she reached down behind her, and took hold of him. "Nowhere to go but up," she whispered, too quietly (and just as well), because he only said "Hmmm?" as she pressed him against her hip.

Ann smiled to herself. This seemed to be working; Michael was stiffening appropriately, his breathing was quickening as it should. But she didn't declare victory yet: they'd been here before.

So she proceeded with care. She turned. She pressed. She stopped pressing. Turned. Led. Sat. Stroked. Kissed. Stopped kissing, then started again, now with the tip of her tongue—in a different spot than the night before. Made sure to keep eye contact, as she drew him into her mouth.

"How is your knee?" he asked.

"What do you like?" she asked some time later.

"What do you mean?"

"You know what I mean. What's your fantasy?"

"My fantasy?"

"Deepest and darkest."

"Hum. I must think about this. My deepest, darkest fantasy . . ."

"Give it up."

"I'm thinking. Why don't you tell me yours?"

"I just wish I knew what you liked."

"Don't be worried," he said, and stroked her hair.

And she said, "I'm not worried."

What she was, was more than a little pissed.

ii

While Ann was busy being pissed, Ian Rickhardt was on his way from Toronto. It was not until he touched down in Grenada for fuel, at about four in the morning, that anyone knew he was coming.

He contacted Steve with instructions: get a car to the airport at Piarco, and work out a route to meet the fast ferry: Rickhardt didn't want to get on another plane after all this flying. It gave Steve just enough time to arrange a car at the airport. They drove through the morning to make it to the docks on time.

"Shall we call ahead?" Steve asked. "I have the numbers for Michael's Blackberry."

No.

"Do they have any idea you're coming?"

"None."

"Do you think they'll be pleased to see you?"

"Don't call."

Ann and Michael weren't expecting him, and they were out for the day. When they came back, they ran into Steve at the roadside by the drive to the beach house, sipping shandy and munching a double.

"He is inside," said Steve, after filling them in on the back story. "Try to act surprised. I think he wants you to act surprised."

The beach house smelled of the sweet curry that had been simmering stovetop for the afternoon. Thea was sitting in the dining nook with Ian. They could hear her laughter from the steps from outside.

"Surprise," said Ian when they came in. He was wearing a white cotton shirt and nylon walking shorts. He had trimmed his beard down to white nubs. His bare feet were propped up on a chair. Thea, dressed as usual in a long red skirt, her hair tied under a yellow kerchief, covered her mouth and looked at them apologetically.

"Dinner's comin' up," she said.

Ian nodded. "It's fantastic. Coconut prawn curry on rice and peas. Side of okra. And there's a fresh case of Caribe in the fridge. I brought it myself. Surprise," he said again, and grinned.

Ann waved her hands at shoulder height, and said, "Surprise." Michael took the hint, and went to fetch the beer.

"Sit down," said Ian, moving his feet, and before Ann could say anything else, "Thea tells me you were bitten by a parrot."

"A parrot fish, Mr. Rickhardt," Thea said.

"Of course. It all gets mixed up in my mind. While I was at the airport, in Piarco—I picked up one of the local newspapers. There was a story about a widow who was convinced that her dead husband had been reincarnated in the body of her pet parrot."

Thea nodded. "They write the story once a year."

"Hush my darling," said Ian. "She knows he has returned, she said, because the parrot walks on her just the way he used to. Did you hear that, Michael?"

In the kitchen, Michael shut the refrigerator door with his heel. He had four beer bottles, two in each hand. "A parrot who walked on her? Did the husband walk on her in life?"

Rickhardt appeared to consider this. "The article didn't say. It also didn't explain how it was that her husband was reincarnated in the body of a parrot that was hatched before he died."

"This woman, she believe the spirit of her husband entered right into the parrot," explained Thea, and tapped the side of her head. "She ain't right here."

"That's not reincarnation," said Rickhardt. "That's possession."

"Oh, best I not," said Thea as Michael put an open beer bottle in front of her. He shrugged, slid the beer over to Rickhardt, who slid it back to her and she laughed and shook her head and sipped the beer. "Thank you Mr. Voors . . . Mr. Rickhardt."

"You were bit by a parrot fish?" said Rickhardt. It took Ann a moment to realize he was asking her the question. She nodded. Bent her leg up so she could display the knee, a thick square of gauze conveying the enormity of the wound.

"The fish mistook me for coral," she said.

Rickhardt squinted at the knee and shook his head. "That sounds farfetched. My money's on possession."

Tobago delivered up sunsets out of postcards every night. They used that one to set the mood for dinner: still waters, swaying palms, a flamethrower igniting the sky. As they tucked in, Ian laid bare the dual purpose of his visit. He wanted to show them the wedding video, and talk a bit of business with Michael. Either one by itself, he said, could have waited. Put together . . .

Michael didn't object.

Ann found herself in the kitchen as Thea was cleaning up for the night.

"Quite a fellow," said Thea, lifting a thumb to the saloon door leading to the dining table, "that Mr. Rickhardt. He doh eat nice."

"I'm sorry?"

Thea smiled. "He say all sorts of things, don't he?"

"Did he say something to offend you?"

"To offend me?" Thea laughed. "Oh no. Nothing to offend me."

Ann opened the fridge, took out another beer and a fresh lime. "Thanks, I'll cut it myself," she said when Thea offered.

"He pay for your wedding, that one. Must have a lot of money."

"He does."

"And you don't like him."

Ann carved out a wedge of lime and stuffed it down the neck of the bottle. It fizzed and twisted in the amber liquid.

"You *should* not like him," said Thea. "Here he is, uninvited, on your honeymoon. He pay for your wedding, think he can do that? Come here and vex you so."

Ann took a swig of beer. It was tart and hoppy and just what she needed. "I don't like him," she said. "But I suspect we won't see that much of him once we're settled."

You suspect that, do you?" Thea smiled, shook her head. "He flew in a plane to show you a movie of that wedding he bought you. On your honeymoon. Ah," she said, and turned back to the dishes, "I'm overstepping. None of my business. But I will tell you something, Mrs. Voors. He's very charming that fellow, yet he not going to leave you be. That monkey know what tree to climb." She smiled and shook her head when Ann tried to hand her a bottle. "No thank you. Better I loll off no more."

Ann put the second beer back in the fridge.

"You're not overstepping," she said to Thea, "and I won't tell."

"Tell if you like," said Thea. "It don't really matter to me."

"You were gone awhile," said Michael when she came back and fell into her chair. Ann smiled at Michael, then at Ian.

"Just thought I'd give you two a chance to catch up." She raised her bottle, now half-empty, and made as if to toast.

Ian and Michael had been hunched together, talking in low tones, as Ann was talking to Thea; Ann had noted it over the saloon doors from the corner of her eye. Now Ian was leaning back, hands behind his head—Michael, arms crossed.

They both looked, she thought as she sipped the dregs of her beer, vaguely guilty.

"You didn't have to do that," said Ian.

Ann smiled and said, "Liar."

She'd meant to say it sweetly—but she'd had . . . three bottles of Ian's beer now? That sounded right . . . and her ire must have leaked out. Ian and Michael shared a glance.

She tried to recover. "Nice liar, I meant. You two have business to talk about. I can leave you to it. . . ."

Ian smiled and shook his head. "Taken care of," he said. "And really, I wanted to show you this." He lifted a DVD in a plain white case from the table. "What can I say? I'm an old woman. They really did a fantastic job of it. I couldn't wait."

Ann shook her head. "I can't believe you flew all the way down. Couldn't you just upload it onto YouTube? Send it by courier?"

Ian's eyes widened and he clutched at his chest theatrically. "YouTube? A courier? Heathen! This is special stuff! You don't just fling it on the internet, give it to some lackey. It's a treasure!"

Ann and Michael shared a glance themselves at that.

"Why don't we watch it," said Michael, "right now."

"Excellent idea," said Ian. He looked out the open French doors. "It's about dark enough."

It certainly was getting dark; the sun had pretty much set—there was just a tiny line of purple at the horizon. Stars were emerging overhead. But Ann didn't see what that had to do with watching a video and said so. Rickhardt laughed.

"You didn't think I was going to show it to you on the TV set they've got here." The TV set being an old 27-inch Toshiba that occupied a corner in the living room. "I've set up something special," he said, and got up.

"What—" Ann began, but Michael put a hand on her arm.

"It's all right," he said, "Ian told me about it while you were in the kitchen. Speaking of which—Thea?"

"Yes?" she called from the kitchen.

"You can finish up," he said and they stepped around the kitchen to the living room. Ian was already there, unzipping a black nylon case and pulling a laptop computer out. As he plugged it in, and pulled out what Ann recognized as a projector, Michael lifted down a framed lithograph of a tall sailing ship and set it aside. The frame left a faint outline on the white wall.

"You're projecting it," said Ann, "like a presentation video."

She'd done this more times than she cared to admit in the service of Krenk & Associates.

Ian nodded. "Full cinema experience," he said. "Nothing but the best."

Thea popped in to say goodnight as she left, and patted Ann on the shoulder where she sat.

"Funny ideas," she said, so only Ann could hear. "Don't let 'im spoil things."

And then she was gone, and Ian slid the DVD into the side of his laptop and said, "Enjoy."

Michael set an open beer down in front of her and flicked off the lights.

And their wedding began, anew.

iii

A black screen.

A cool, descending bass line for a few bars, and then a trumpet joined in, blowing all over the place. The screen shifted to blue—the sky, over the Rickhardt Estates winery, two weeks ago—while on the soundtrack, Louis Armstrong put the trumpet down and wondered what good melody and music was without swing.

"Did you pick the song, Ian?" asked Ann.

"Hey, be thankful," said Ian. "Michael wanted Sinatra. 'Love and Marriage.' Or was it 'The Tender Trap?'"

Michael barked a laugh as Ann punched him in the shoulder.

The camera came down on the treeline, then the rooftop, and then the milling guests outside Rickhardt's winery. The image faded to sepia and froze, and the title faded in.

THE JOINING OF TWO

And there was a date, and a location, and their names, and then the whole picture swam out of focus.

Literally.

As the trumpet faded out, it seemed as though the picture spun—as though Ann were spinning herself, dizzily reeling in a dance across the floor of Rickhardt's winery. She couldn't say how he did it—the screen simply shifted from a sepia exterior to an interior pan across a row of inverted wine glasses, a fiery stand of maples seen through a window.

And yet . . .

"Wow," she said, and looked down and took a sip from her beer.

"Wow," echoed Rickhardt, softly.

The camera was moving along the floor now, or near to it, past rows of guests seated in front of the dais where she and Michael would say their vows. Michael was at the front, hands crossed in front of him, smiling in genial terror. She would have been in the limousine still, sipping a small flute of champagne with Lesley at her side.

This was the part of things she hadn't seen.

Faces, now—most of them strangers, some of whom she might know the name of—some of whom she knew more intimately. The lens drew across each of them, fading between so that sometimes one might seem to morph into another. Drew Sloan, one of the partners at Michael's firm, laughed as he blended into the hollowed cheek of an older woman, who brushed a lock of her blonde hair from her eye and looked past the camera with wry approval, as she melted into the face of a young African boy, who looked bored and sullen, sitting in his chair beside his mother and transforming—into Jeanie Yang.

"Shh," said Ann, as Ian kicked off a sandal, and it thumped on the floor. She leaned forward.

Jeanie was wearing a dark blue satiny dress, her black hair braided tight at the back of her neck. She was standing and talking and laughing, her purse under one arm, her other reaching out as if to touch the shoulder of her companion. But the camera pulled out to show her standing, alone. Who was she talking to? Someone on her Bluetooth maybe? Hard to say, because she quickly slid away. In her place sat Susan Rickhardt, Ian's wife.

She had not been having a good day that day (Ann had never seen Susan having a good day), but this shot made the most of her. She was seated by a tall window that overlooked the vineyard. The sun came in at a high angle. It caught the fringe of her pageboy haircut, illuminated the ridge of her wide nose and perhaps, the hint of a smile—and bathed it all in a warm, golden glow. She might have been in Tuscany that afternoon. She saw the camera, turned, broadened her smile to just shy of Mona Lisa amperage, and with two fingers made a tiny wave.

And the screen went black.

It couldn't have stayed black for as long as it seemed to; the single breath that Ann drew as Susan Rickhardt ended her wave couldn't have sustained her.

The editor was working his art again, and the act of transition was somehow transformed into something more. But this time, Ann didn't feel as though she were spinning; she felt herself a fixed point in space and time. All of it slowed to an instant, and that instant stretched.

At first, Ann thought she couldn't look away, that something was holding her gaze on the screen. As the breath rasped through her throat, she began to think that she *could* look away, could look anywhere she wanted in fact—but the blackness had replaced everything else, so it didn't matter. Ann began to panic. It manifested in attempts—at screaming, at getting up, at just asking Ian Rickhardt: *Please could you turn it off a moment?* Nothing would come of it, though. She wondered if she might be dead.

And here was the fulcrum of it, as Eva might say. The point where we can make a choice: dead or alive.

Ann wasn't going to be dead.

And thinking of Eva, Ann began to imagine—to construct—to inhabit—the safe place.

It was a struggle; she recalled that first time, sitting with Eva at the hospital, building the castle stone by stone in her mind, clearing the woods around it . . . fashioning, or at least conceiving, the architectural details. It was a true act of creation.

Here, creation was barred from her. She saw the place she and Eva had made as through a dense fog. Standing in the high corridor, the fog's tendrils clutched and flowed through the tall windows. Ahead, a blackened branch poked through. She could barely see anything; when she willed a candle, it snuffed out.

She shuffled down the corridor, which was, she discovered, covered in mud. Sensation returned to her as she did. She felt the cool mud between her toes, rotten leaves sliding beneath her bare heel. She ducked beneath the branch, felt its bare twigs catching in her hair.

She stood in front of the door to the tower room, the rot of swamp, of cesspool, filling her nostrils.

And there, she stood and listened.

Wood scraped against stone—as though a great trunk were being dragged across the floor of the tower room, one end to the other. The dragging stopped. There came a creaking sound then. And a great exhalation of air, as though an old man, an old woman for that matter, had just finished a big job.

Then came a humming, and a scratching—with an occasional rending sound, as though a claw had found purchase in the wood.

The humming sounded like a man. The tune was hard to place. It might have been random. It sounded like insanity.

Quiet down, Ann wanted to say. *Behave.*

But she still couldn't summon the voice to say that. She was still drawing that single breath, and she could only watch—as her lungs filled—as the door buckled—

—and cracked.

"Hey li' si'."

She was looking at Philip. He was wearing his jacket-and-tie wedding uniform, although she could only see the collar, the knot of tie, because the camera was in close. His mouth was twisting like it was its own creature; his eyes, though, were steady, gazing straight into the camera as he tried to say, *Hey little sister.*

"Con'a—hin," he said. *Congratulations.*

Ann coughed, and gasped, and sucked in lungfuls of fresh air.

"Oo boofoo." *You're beautiful.*

She looked around, sat up on the sofa, and took stock of her situation.

The living room was darker than it had been when the video began. Michael and Ian were gone.

"Uv oo," said Philip from the wall.

I love you.

Another wicked bass line came up—"Bang a Gong" by T-Rex; actually one of Ann's choices—and the scene cross-faded to a shot of Ann and Michael and Lesley dancing, very badly, while Mr. T-Rex went on about how dirty, sweet, skinny and black-clad his girl was.

Ann got to her feet. She was unsteady. Her mouth tasted sour—of too much beer. Had she had too much beer? That might explain things. She rubbed a chill out of her arms.

T-Rex's girl was weak, and also had hydra teeth. This was Jeanie, bopping side to side as she breached the fringe of the dance, showing every one of those teeth in a broad grin. She and Bridal-Ann faced off on the screen and yelled at each other to bang gongs, get things on.

Where were the men? Ann did a check of the main floor. The kitchen was empty, pristine. The entry hall. A little coat closet. She called out: "Michael? Ian?" as she climbed the stairs to the second floor, the bedrooms.

T-Rex went away and laughter and squealing replaced it. "Congratulations Mikey!" shouted a woman on the TV. People clapped.

Partway up the stairs, Ann steadied herself and flicked on the hall light and climbed the rest of the way. The doors to the two bedrooms were open, their interiors dark. The bathroom door was closed. So was the door to the linen closet.

"Guys?" she called as she stuck her head in one bedroom, then the other. "Guys?"

Nothing. The beds were made.

"Insect?" she whispered as she touched the freezing cold doorknob to the bathroom, and as she thought of that other door, she pulled this one open.

The bathroom in the beach house was nice but nothing fancy. There was a biggish bathtub with jets, next to a fibreglass-formed shower stall opposite the toilet, whose tank was high on the wall. You flushed it by pulling on a chain at the bottom.

Ann flicked on the light. Everything was as it should be at first glance. Towels were hung neatly by the sink. The mirror was clean, and uncracked—and while it was true, her arms and legs were gooseflesh, there was no frost or even mist on the mirror. The water in the toilet bowl was clean and blue. There was nothing amiss.

Other than the fact my husband is missing.

Ann shut the bathroom light off and crossed the hall to their bedroom.

The French doors there opened onto a miniscule balcony; they were cracked open. Had Ann left them that way this morning? Had Michael? Wouldn't Thea have shut them while they were out?

Yes. She would have. She most certainly would have.

Ann closed her eyes—tried to visualize the safe place. That, she knew, was the one sure way to deal with the thing that was happening. But she couldn't get far—the memory of the shambles that she'd found there, just moments earlier, was too strong. She might be able to reconstruct it, but it would be well-nigh impossible to do it herself. And she couldn't face that door—not without Eva. And Eva was far away.

"Fuck," she whispered, and opened her eyes. "Fuck."

It was darker now; the door to the hall was shut. The French doors were wide open. Her mouth tasted copper-salty; she had bitten her lip hard enough to draw some blood.

Outside, the palm trees swayed; the leaves sounded like knives on a sharpening stone as they rubbed against one another. And underneath that—

A humming sound.

It sounded like a man—humming a tune to himself while he worked. What tune, Ann couldn't say. It was coming from outside the room though. She made her way around the bed, and peered out the window.

The bedroom was badly placed for any view; it looked out on the small cleared garden behind the beach house, which ended not twenty-five feet off, in thick foliage. There was a moon tonight, but also some cloud. So while Ann could hear that the humming was coming from the edge of that foliage—she couldn't see much, at first. Just something moving, swaying back and forth. She went to the edge of the railing, and leaned over to look.

It was a man. Who, she couldn't say. But she could see arms outstretched on either side—a head that seemed to loll back, far enough that the neck might have snapped. He was turning like a dancer. She wanted to call out—but her throat felt full of sand. She couldn't even open her mouth.

She also couldn't look away.

Because she began to realize that he wasn't turning like a dancer at all—he was spinning, as though he were dangling on the end of a string, or a wound up elastic band; there was no contact with the ground. And as he turned, he seemed to rise up: a half-dozen revolutions, and the tips of his toes soon hovered at Ann's eye-level—not more than a few metres out.

His rotation had slowed—he might have been making one revolution every two seconds. His close-cropped beard caught the faint moonlight in a stippling of silver, as he spun to face her for an instant. Then the moon struck silver hair—bare, suntanned shoulders—the flank of pale naked buttock.

He corkscrewed higher still, and when he turned, Ann found herself face to face with Ian Rickhardt. His eyes were shut—his jaw clenched.

Ann stumbled back into the room. She fell against the bed and righted herself with her hands. When she turned back to look, the French doors were shut again. The room was like ice now.

Ann pushed herself up and tried to open the doors. They were stuck—of course. She drew the curtain aside and peered out through the glass. There was nothing there but the trees. She put her hand on her racing heart and drew a deep breath, and shivered. When she exhaled, her breath condensed on the glass, and made a lattice.

"Get back in your room," she said. "Back into the tower."

But she didn't have the stamina to do what she had to do—go back to her safe place, visualize the necessary repairs . . . toss those things out the windows on her way to the door, which she might then secure with . . . something . . . something that would keep the Insect in its place.

"Get back!" She hoped to sound strong. But she was all too aware how her voice broke over the words—how the terror manifested, in her quaver.

The room hummed back at her—mocking.

Ann stepped away from the window as a crack started to grow along the frozen pane.

"Get back!" She tried to turn on the lamp, bring real light to drive away the dark, but it was dead.

She rounded the foot of the bed and found the door to the hallway. She twisted the doorknob and pulled hard, and the door opened. She stepped out of the bedroom, and into the tropical warmth of the beach house again.

The hall light was out too—but it wasn't dark.

A warm yellow glow was coming from one of the closed doors—not the bedroom or the bathroom. But the utility closet.

Was there a light fixture in there? Ann didn't think there was; when Thea had given them the grand tour, she'd shown it to them: the place to get towels and clean sheets, and light bulbs in case one blew.

"Shit." Ann swallowed. The light bulbs.

She had to be careful if that's what it was.

The light bulbs had sent her mother to the emergency ward one time; she'd have lost an eye if the glass had flown just an inch higher. Ann approached the closet carefully, one hand shielding her eyes. She pulled open the door, standing behind it as light spilled out, accompanied by the crackling whiff of ozone.

Ann stepped around the door, and looked in. That's what it was, all right.

The dozen sixty-watt bulbs were yin-yanged in their little corrugated cardboard sleeves, next to the stack of towels. They were all glowing bright and hot.

The packaging was starting to smoulder.

She could see how this would end—how it had almost ended, the last time.

Ann opened the washroom door and turned on the tap in the sink. The pipes moaned, but no water came out.

Fuck you, she thought, and found a small bucket by the toilet. She dipped it into the toilet bowl and pulled out a half-bucket of water. The first bulb popped, then, and as Ann turned she saw the fire had started, flames licking around the edge of the cardboard.

Ann flung the water into the closet. But she was too far away, and the water that got there just hissed, just threw up steam. Another bulb exploded, and then two more, in fast succession. The fire grew, as though someone were standing close fanning it. Ann dipped the bucket back into the toilet and stepped closer this time.

"Fuck you!" she shouted, tossing the bucket directly into the flames, which had now spread to the doorframe, making of it a gateway of fire. Steam and smoke billowed from the middle, forcing Ann back.

She dropped the bucket and coughed. There was a sparking and a hiss over her head, as the ceiling light fixture shorted beneath the inverted dome of the cover, sending a scar of black across the frosted glass. Fine white smoke poured out around the edge and cascaded down like the foam from an overflowing draught.

Ann bent low and her hand flailed behind her and caught hold of the bannister. She pulled herself to the stairs and, on hands and knees, backed down them to the dark main floor as her injured knee protested. The smoke followed her in grasping tendrils but she was faster, and soon she was on the main floor. Only then did she let herself draw air. She struggled not to let it turn into a sob.

The Insect was out. And tears? Tears only fed it.

The door to the front steps was jammed, as was the sliding door to the balcony; a part of Ann knew this would be so even before she checked. She tried various things to smash the glass—a chair, a frying pan, and finally Ian Rickhardt's laptop, still playing their wedding on its draining battery. Any one of them would have done the job. But Ann wasn't surprised, when at the end of it the only thing shattered was the laptop. Ann wasn't that strong to begin with, and the Insect had a way of pulling her punches for her, at times such as these.

Smoke rolled down the stairwell, crawling across the ceiling of the living room, lit as if from within by the flames from the second floor. Ann bent low and drew in what air there was.

She wouldn't be breathing long and she knew it. The smoke, the heat of the flames . . . she would suffocate, immolate, one or the other or both, very soon now.

The Insect had her, and it knew it too. It pounded triumphantly on the walls, shook the windows in their runners. Outside, it would be stirring up a storm. Nearer: flames roared and the room lit orange, as something caught. The smoke pressed her down further, and she rolled off her knees, so her face touched the floor.

It would not be long. And there was no way out.

Ann shut her eyes, and went the only other way she could.

In.

"Why?"

She stood in mud, among the shattered foundations of the castle tower that she and Eva had built together. The sky overhead was a rolling storm. The stones of the tower stretched like the spine of a huge beast, over a dark hill and into twisted branches of a ravine.

It was no place Ann had dreamed. Yet when her eyes closed, when she sought the safe place—this was where she landed. The field of her defeat.

She wished Eva were here now, or available somehow, to help her—to reconstruct, to find the Insect . . . rope it back inside. What might she say? First, she would tell Ann to banish this ruin from her mind; to think of bright banners and trumpets sounding, of victory marches. Set her subjects to work, reconstructing the tower, while riders spread out across the land, accompanied by hounds who had gathered the scent of the Insect.

Above all, she would tell Ann: *Step out of the mud.*

But Ann could not; it was thick and deep, and her ankles were mired in it. And as she looked down, Ann realized there was no need to send trackers after the Insect. For in that mud, it crawled and clicked in a multitude of itself, centipedes and blue-backed beetles the size of her fist churned through the mud, spun about her ankles, crawled up as if to consume her.

"*Why?*" they clicked and whirred, mocking with their tea-coloured wings and mandibles—with their pounding, growing louder, on the walls of the beach house, "*Why does it ever go so?*"

"Why are you trying to kill me?"

"*The heart wants what the heart wants*," sang the Insect through the buzzing of its flies, the chirps of crickets . . . the sharp crack, of a wooden doorframe.

Ann felt arms underneath her own, and then the floorboards dragging against her legs. She tried to open her eyes but couldn't—the smoke stung too badly. Then she was off the ground entirely, draped over shoulders. Someone was shouting, and coughing—and she was moving. At once, there was a sharp pain as her shoulder hit against something hard. And then a wash of cool air—a stomach-lurching shift—and gravel biting into her back, her thigh.

"Ann!"

She opened her eyes, and looked up into Michael's. He knelt over her. He was shirtless, the thin blond hairs on his arms, crawling up his shoulders, turned into a halo of orange sparks by the light of the burning building behind them.

He slapped her lightly on one cheek. She stopped him from doing the same on the other with her hand. She coughed, and coughed, and eventually managed to sit up, and tell him she was all right.

"Thank God," he said. "Oh thank God."

He took her in his arms, and she held him too—and they sat like that, as the flames climbed into the night sky, until the sirens announced the arrival of the firefighters and the ambulance.

iv

Ian Rickhardt was apologetic, but not to Ann. Michael kept him away from her after the fire. The two men had their conversation in a courtyard of Tobago County Hospital, while Ann drew oxygen and waited for the results of a chest X-ray and a blood test in the emergency department. Ian wheedled and bargained, but Michael held to his guns.

When he returned to Ann's bedside, he was alone.

"He's going back," said Michael. "What an awful idea he had, coming here. I won't let him do that to you again."

Ann shook her head and pulled the oxygen mask aside. "I'm fine," she whispered.

And she was fine. Ann hadn't taken in very much smoke at all before Michael got to her, and she'd kept clear of the flames, so there were no burns to treat. She'd re-opened the fish-bite on her knee, but that was a simple matter of cleaning and re-dressing. Her throat still felt raw and her voice deepened half an octave. But Michael thought it sounded sexy and so did she.

Given all that, Ann agreed when Michael suggested they could book a suite at the Coco Reef resort and ride out the rest of their honeymoon in style. That made sense in more ways than one. It would be nice to restart the whole honeymoon, and draw some good from it; and really, Ann wasn't sure she wanted to get on a plane just now.

Given all that.

As for Ian Rickhardt: he sent a card and a basket of fruit and rum to their suite, but otherwise had the good sense to make himself scarce.

He wasn't the only one. Ann tried calling Eva Fenshaw five times. She left four messages. But Eva didn't seem to be answering. Eva didn't seem to be around.

Ann hoped she was all right.

"It's the fish woman!" said the man at the beach.

Ann opened her eyes and squinted out from under the beach umbrella.

The man was tall and thin, with a long face and a thick beard, olive skin and light brown hair. He wore a pale blue tank top shirt and swimming trunks that went down to his knees, and carried two bottles of Corona: one with the lime stuffed inside, the other with fruit still peeking out the neck. She recognized him from the expedition to the reef. But she had no idea what his name was, so she smiled and waved and said hello. He solved the mystery instantly.

"I am Paolo. We met on the *Calypso* boat."

"I'm Ann. We did."

"I remember your name," he said. "You were devoured by a fish. You don't forget something like that. How is your knee?"

She was wearing a flesh-hugging patch of a bandage now, and underneath, it was feeling a good deal better. She said so.

"I see you're without a drink," he said, and offered the fresher of the two Coronas. She smiled and fended it off with a hand.

"Thanks but no. I hope you didn't get that for me," said Ann. "I'm giving my liver a break."

He shrugged and grinned. "No loss in trying," he said, eyeing one beer, then the other. "But my work is cut out for me. May I join you?"

Ann was sitting in a wooden chair joined to another by a small table, and the other chair was empty. She motioned to it.

"Where is your dashing husband?" he asked as he took the seat and set the beer bottles between them.

"Inside. He's sleeping off a sunburn." It was true; Michael had pulled her from the burning beach house unscathed. Their first afternoon here, he'd fallen asleep on his stomach by the pool, stayed there for an hour, and that was all it took. Funny old world, he'd said.

"He won't mind me sitting here?"

"I don't think so. He's sleeping."

"Okay," said Paolo. "I don't want to make trouble on anyone's honeymoon."

Ann laughed, and it must have been a bit too hard because Paolo frowned. She waved a hand and shook her head, and asked him, "On that subject . . . how was the wedding?"

"Oh, it was very beautiful. We all took off our shoes. Danced in the sea as the setting sun turned the bride and groom to gold." He took a deep pull from the Corona. "Now they are gone, to a house down the coast. And the rest of us will be back to Caracas in a day or so."

"That sounds lovely."

Paolo smiled and squinted out at the sea.

"Weddings are often lovely," he said. "Now tell me, Ann. What are you doing here? Sitting by yourself on the beach. Not even a drink beside you. Not an iPad or an iPod or even a book. No husband. And you are here! Weren't you staying at a beach house?"

"Burned to the ground," she said, and he laughed.

"The heat of passion," he said, and when she didn't laugh, he apologized.

"It's all right," she said. "No offence taken."

Paolo finished his beer. "You probably think I'm hitting on you," he said. "And probably, I am a bit. I shouldn't be. You're on your honeymoon after all. And your husband is much handsomer than I. Even all burned up."

He stood up, and made a small bow of his head.

"Excuse me, please, Ann. I hope your husband's sunburn recovers as well as your lovely knee."

Ann smiled and thanked him, and Paulo made his retreat. He was out of sight, when she noticed that he'd left the untouched bottle of Corona on the table, within easy arm's reach.

She contemplated it a moment. From the sweat on the bottle, the beer was still cold; bubbles of carbonation traced up its side and gathered around the triangle of lime stuffed in its neck.

Ann shut her eyes. Another bottle of beer was not what she needed right now. Because there was work to do. She took a deep breath, and imagined a spectrum of colour, in sequence, and dreamed a verdant land at the foot of a range of mountains. It was a place near, but out of sight of the tower where she had imprisoned the Insect long ago. But it was a good site; the mountains would yield stone to build a new tower; the land would yield crops to feed the men and women who would raise the walls that would soon make a home for the Insect once more.

The last time she'd done this, it had been hard work. But she thought that this time it might go quicker; after all, when the closet had lit bright at the Lake House that winter, the first time, Eva had not told her about the safe place. No one had known what to do.

They had all done the best they could, with what tools presented themselves.

The Lodge

i

The offices that Charlie Sunderland used in those days were situated in a strip mall at the south end of Etobicoke, smack between a medical centre and a pharmacy. But he made it clear to all of his clients who made the observation, that the proximity was entirely coincidental.

"I'm not going to write you a prescription. I promise you that. Because you know by now, drugs aren't going to resolve anything. And as for the clinic? If you needed a physician, you wouldn't be here."

Ann's mother lifted her bandaged right hand. Two days ago, those bandages had been applied in the emergency room at Perth County General, on top of deep, stitched-up cuts from which the doctors there had extracted three thin shards of glass. They had pulled six more from her shoulders and chest, but the bandages from those wounds were hidden under a thick sweater.

"I wouldn't say we don't need a physician," she said.

Sunderland smiled a little sheepishly and looked down at his own hands. He was a tall man with very dark hair and a prominent chin, a deep tan for this time of year. He didn't look like a physician to Ann; he wore an open-necked sweater and pale blue jeans, and he smiled too much.

But maybe that was fine. Maybe he was right.

A physician wouldn't be able to do much for the problem at the Lake House.

"What happened to your hand?" he asked.

Ann's mother looked down now, and Ann's father put his hand on her shoulder, and she looked up at him, and said: "The ghost did it." And then she looked back at her hand, and her lips pressed tight together.

The ghost did it.

This was a hard thing for her to say. Of the four of them, she had held onto her skepticism the longest, edging out Philip by about a week. Until then, Ann's mother had answered Ann's complaints with a hug, and a trip to the closet or the basement or the bathroom with a flashlight to say: *There's nothing here.*

Not now there's not. But before—

Not ever, Ann. Imagination's a powerful thing. But it's not real. It's all in our heads.

It's all in the closet.

You just think so. But really, baby—it's you.

Saying that was like a challenge—and after the thing had happened in Ann's brother's room, the thing he wouldn't talk about, not yet, Philip tried to tell their mother so. But she wouldn't listen. She just kept on opening doors and moving curtains aside, shining her flashlight into the dark corners of the bright new house—until she opened the hall closet, and looked into the light.

"Why do you say it was a ghost?" asked Sunderland. Outside, it had begun to snow, and as he spoke, the heating system kicked into higher gear.

"There was . . . a stack of light bulbs. They weren't connected to anything—just in the closet. They were . . . on."

"On?" Sunderland's smile faltered.

She looked down at her bandaged hand, and said again: "They weren't connected to anything. They weren't just on—they seemed to be pulsing, showing me a pattern. When I got close enough . . ." She made an exploding sound with the roof of her mouth—the kind of sound some of the boys that Ann knew would make if they were pretending to blow things up. Dr. Sunderland nodded. He had a computer on his desk, and he glanced at the screen, tapped some keys, and pushed a disk in the three-and-a-half-inch drive.

"We both saw it," said Ann's father.

"But you had the presence of mind to get a fire extinguisher," she said to him.

"You were bleeding."

"You were right there," she said. "Thank God."

Sunderland left them to it, and turned his attention to the computer. He typed something. Ann met Philip's eye, who was sitting in an old plastic-covered chair by the window. He pursed his lips and nodded with resignation, jammed his fists farther into the pockets of his fleece vest.

"Please excuse me," said Sunderland. "I'm opening a file for you. That way, we'll have everything in one place."

"I thought you had a file already," said their father.

On the desk beside Sunderland was an old school notebook that Ann had half-filled with what she could remember about the incidents. She had also made some drawings and they were in there too. Philip had used his own computer, and his homework was in a stack of printouts underneath the notebook. Underneath that, a yellow questionnaire that Ann's mother and father had filled out, and signed.

Sunderland pressed a key and the drive started to write. It made a squonking noise, Ann thought.

Squonk squonk.

He turned his attention to the notes, picking them up and holding them, like a restaurant menu.

"These are great," he said. "Ann, Philip—you've done a great job setting things down. I'm really impressed with you."

Ann nodded *you're welcome*. Philip regarded Dr. Sunderland, but didn't say anything.

"What's your prognosis, then?" asked their father.

He shook his head. "Prognosis. That's a doctor's word. We're not dealing with a medical situation, Mr. LeSage. Aside, I mean, from the injuries you sustained from the electro-kinetic event last week, Mrs. LeSage. We're dealing with something more . . . complex."

"So you can't fix this?" said Ann's mother.

Dr. Sunderland bent his head and regarded her, as though over the top of invisible glasses.

"We can learn," he said, "about the phenomenon." He gestured to the bandaged hands. "Make you safer."

Ann's mother was about to say something, but stopped at the touch on her hand. "That's what we want," said her father. If it weren't for him, Ann thought they all would have walked out right then and there.

If it had been up to their mother, they wouldn't have come in the first place.

Their mother had been the last of them to shed her skepticism, but that only became clear after the incident with the lights. Until then, it seemed as though both parents were on the same page when it came to understanding the presence that their children described. When Ann's mother took the flashlight into the laundry room, Ann's father would hang back, nodding in tacit agreement that yes, *the only thing to fear is fear.* He was the one who ordered the parental control box for the cable TV service, after they agreed that Ann was just scaring herself. Their father gave no sign that he understood the things that were happening in the Lake House to be anything other than a child's overactive imagination.

It was, as it turned out, cover. After he had emptied the kitchen fire extinguisher into the closet—after he had gotten their mom home, stitched up and swaddled in bandages—he'd sat them down in a family meeting to explain some things. It was a fiercely cold night, and on other nights like this they might have lit a fire; sitting around the fireplace in the high-ceilinged living room was almost to the point of a religious ceremony with the LeSages. But their dad said no.

"We'll turn up the furnace if you're cold. I don't want to start anything. Now sit down," he said. "I have a confession to make."

Their father, as it turned out, had not been nearly as skeptical as he'd made himself out to be. Which, he admitted, was another way of saying that he had lied to them—kept things from them. He hoped that they would forgive him.

"I've seen this thing too," he said. "Bottom line. Three months ago."

What had he seen? Ann wanted to know, and demanded details. Their dad seemed flustered at the request, and tried to avoid answering. But their mom said: "No, I want to hear this too. What did you see?"

He clamped his hands together and sat very still. He laughed a bit, and said he felt like he was telling a ghost story but that he didn't want to frighten anybody more than they already were.

"Don't worry about that, dad," said Philip. "That ship's sailed."

And their dad laughed, and unfurled his hands, and started into it.

"It was down by the water's edge," he said. "Near the boathouse. Very early in the morning.. We'd had a movie night the night before."

"So, Sunday," said Ann.

"I got up before everybody and took my coffee out to the lake." In fact, he had taken his coffee and a pack of cigarettes outside. But that was one of the things that he left out of the story, then.

"I remember that it was very still out. The mist was on the water. The first thing I heard was some splashing."

"Under the dock?" Ann had been caught by that one more than once—what seemed like a fish caught under the floating part of the dock, splashing and twisting and pushing the whole structure out of the water and dropping it again. But her father shook his head.

"No, it was pretty clear that the splash came from the lake. First a big one, like a fish jumping out. Then they became rhythmic. I could see where it was coming from—the lake mist was swirling and spreading about a hundred feet off the dock, maybe further. It looked like someone swimming, but not well—it was like they were maybe in trouble. I called out and asked, and I heard something—it was like a cry for help—it sounded like a woman.

"I kind of panicked. If it were earlier in the year, the boat would have been in the water and I'd have been able to make it out there to pull her out. But we'd put the boat away. And it was pretty far out. So I put down my coffee cup—" and he stubbed out his cigarette under his boot "—and I pulled off my shirt and boots and jeans."

"So you were going to swim out to her? In October?" asked their mother.

"Did you at least take the life ring off the dock?" asked Philip.

"I did that, yes. And yes, I was going to try and swim out there and help her. What else was I going to do?"

"The lake's freezing this time of year. You'd give yourself a heart attack."

"Yeah." He went quiet for a moment. "I didn't end up going in the water. Before I got my pants off my ankles, the swimmer had come closer. I thought maybe I could just throw that ring. But by the time she got close enough . . . well."

The newest log burning in the fire place cracked and popped twice before he continued.

"There was no she. No swimmer. It was just the water. Splashing and swirling by itself."

"Why didn't you tell us?" asked Philip.

Their father shut up again. There was no good answer for the question.

Finally he said: "I've got in touch with somebody. I'm told he can help."

They wound up staying at Dr. Sunderland's offices until late that night. Most of the time Ann spent waiting around.

Dr. Sunderland explained it: "We're going to do individual interviews and tests. So we've got a room for you kids to hang out in while you're waiting."

The room was off a long hallway in back of the main office. There were no windows, but it was nice enough. There was a couch and a chair and a TV, a little table with a pitcher of ice water and cups to one side—a coffee table in the middle. There was nothing to read, Philip noted.

"You won't be here that long," said Dr. Sunderland as he shut the door.

"This is bullshit," said Philip.

"Bullshit," agreed Ann, and giggled.

Philip got up and opened the door, looked up and down the hall.

"Is the coast clear?"

"The coast is clear."

"Are we going to escape?"

"We'll make a break for it at shift change. Hotwire the minivan. Hit the border by sundown."

Ann giggled, and Philip let the door close, fell back on the couch beside her. They looked at the blank TV screen, and Ann found the remote control on the arm of the couch. When she turned on the set, the screen went snowy.

"No cable," she said, and Philip nodded.

"Ghost-busting doesn't pay like it used to."

Ann punched him in the arm and clicked up three channels before shutting the set off. Philip looked at his watch. Outside the room, they heard footsteps, but they didn't stop and no one opened the door. The light from the fluorescent fixture overhead flickered, made everything seem a little dead.

"I'm scared," said Philip.

It was the first time he had admitted that, and looking at him, eyes straight ahead, Ann thought he was joking. But he wasn't, and told her not to laugh.

"I don't like this place," he said. "I don't think Sunderland's a good person."

"What do you mean?"

Philip sat up. He frowned, opened his mouth like he was going to say, then stopped. "I think he's going to try to talk to us by ourselves."

"That's what he said he was going to do."

"He's not a real doctor. He said so himself."

Ann nodded. "So?"

Philip looked right at her. "When he talks to you," he said, "promise me something."

"Okay."

"Don't let him make you take your clothes off."

"Are you blushing?"

Philip *was* blushing. He looked away. "Just promise me. He might say it's part of the tests he's got to do. He might say something else. But he's got no business taking your clothes off. So don't do it."

"Okay," she said. "I promise."

"Thanks."

"Is that what you're scared of?"

"Maybe." He bit his thumbnail. "I don't know, exactly."

"Well I'm scared too," said Ann, and took her brother's hand. The thumb tip was still damp with spit. "But not of that."

"I just don't like him. That's all."

They sat waiting for a half an hour by Philip's watch, before the door cracked open and Dr. Sunderland peeked in. Ann got up, but he shook his head. "You stay here," he said. "Philip, it's your turn."

"How long will it be?" she asked.

"Not long. Why don't you watch television?"

"It doesn't work," said Philip. "No cable."

Dr. Sunderland frowned. "What? Sure we do. Hold on a second." He went over to the TV, reached around behind, jiggled something, and turned it on. A music video came up. "Hm. Sir Mix-a-Lot." He looked at Ann. "Your kind of thing?"

She wrinkled her nose and shook her head.

"Well," he said, pointing to the remote, "there are plenty of channels to choose from. Take your pick."

And with that, he and Philip left Ann alone in the room. She started to flip channels.

ii

"Mr. Spock had to have his brain put back in," she said. "Dr. McCoy didn't know what he was doing, but Mr. Spock talked him through it."

Dr. Sunderland grinned and nodded. They had talked about the music videos and the cooking show and now they were on to the *Star Trek* show.

"That was quite an episode," he said.

"It was pretty stupid."

"It wasn't one of their finest," he said. "I haven't seen the old series in years. When I think about it, I prefer Mr. Data to Mr. Spock."

"They're both the same. Basically."

"Basically. That's true. Each is very alone, even in a crowd. Do you watch a lot of *Star Trek*?"

"My brother does. So sometimes I do too. Where's my brother?"

The two of them were alone in the little waiting room. Dr. Sunderland had returned with a clipboard. He was wearing a deep blue fleece jacket, and he'd brought a blanket for Ann, along with her coat.

"He's with your parents," he said. His breath made frosty clouds over his chin. "We'll go see them in a minute."

Ann pulled her coat tight around her. "Soon," she said.

"I promise." Dr. Sunderland made a note on his clip board. "Did you enjoy the news any better?"

"It was all about the war," said Ann. "What does SCUD stand for?"

"I don't really know. We can check later. But you didn't answer my question. You were watching the news for a long time. Did you enjoy it?"

"No."

"Well I guess nobody really enjoys the news. Was there something about it that interested you?"

"How do you know I was watching the news so much?" Ann looked around. "Is there a camera in here?"

"Yes."

Ann shivered and drew her knees up to her chest. "And you've been watching us the whole time?"

He didn't answer.

"Is Philip in trouble?"

He shook his head. "Philip is a good boy," he said. "A good brother. He gave you excellent advice. Do you worry about him?"

"I worry about everybody."

"Because of the poltergeist?"

"Is that what it is?"

"It's what your brother called it. In his notes he used the word, and when we spoke just now, he said that's what he thought was going on. Is it okay for me to call it a poltergeist?"

"If it's a poltergeist," said Ann, "that makes it my fault. Philip says poltergeists are made by little girls."

"No one's saying anything is your fault. Should I call it something else?"

"Poltergeist is fine, I guess."

"Okay. Tell me, Ann. What does the poltergeist look like?"

"It doesn't look like anything."

"That's what you wrote in your journal. but everything looks like something." He put the clipboard down on the coffee table. There was a yellow tablet of paper on it, Ann saw, filled with messy writing. "If you could imagine what it looked like, how would you describe it?"

"A bug."

"You said that very quickly. Are you sure?"

She closed her eyes and made a show of thinking about it.

"A big bug."

"So like a spider?"

"Spiders aren't bugs. They're—" she shut her eyes tighter and it came to her "—arachnids. Like scorpions."

"You're right." He patted her shoulder. "So it's an insect?"

"Sure."

"Would you rather we called it that?"

"The Insect," she said, and nodded. "Can I go see my family now?"

"Soon," said Dr. Sunderland. "But first—" he reached over and picked up the water jug "—can you remember what the Insect was doing when this happened?"

The jug had been full, but nothing came out when he tilted it. The water inside was frozen solid.

The video cameras told it better than Ann could—and later, in her new bedroom at the lodge, she'd wonder if things might have turned out differently if she'd been more forthcoming.

There were two cameras. One up near the ceiling behind the TV; the other, over the door with a view of the TV. They watched the tapes back in Dr. Sunderland's office, on a big TV. First one, then the other.

They showed enough, by themselves, to make the decision easy.

"Three definite manifestations," said Dr. Sunderland. "At the fifty-seven minute mark, the subject—that's you Ann—huddled down in the corner. The temperature dropped six degrees according to the thermostat. At fifty-seven fourteen, the channel changed on the TV. Ann, you didn't move."

Ann shrugged. What could she say? She was sitting still.

"Did you even notice the temperature change?" asked her father. "It getting colder, I mean?"

"Sure," said Ann, but she knew that was a lie. "That's why I scrunched up."

He nodded, and she could tell by the sad expression on his face he knew it was a lie too.

"And finally at sixty-two oh three," said Dr. Sunderland.

They'd watched that part twice on each tape to make sure. The event wasn't very much, Ann thought. But it was enough.

There was Ann, curled up on the couch, watching the NewsWorld channel. They were talking about the war, and showing pictures of what missiles looked like when they shot up into the night sky in that part of the world. Ann rubbed her nose with the palm of her hand then jammed the hand back into her armpit for warmth.

The room darkened for an instant, as though the light had shorted out. Or something had moved in front of it. When the light came back, the coffee table was half a metre closer to the couch than it had been.

"It's not so dark you can't see," said Ann's father. "But I can't make out what happened there. Can we see it move?"

Using a wheel on the remote control, Dr. Sunderland tracked back and forth on the ceiling camera, and the table jumped back and forth as he did so.

"It did move," said Ann's mother. She looked at her bandages almost wonderingly—as though seeing them there for the first time.

"Yeah," said her father. "It did. I didn't think these things would be so easy to call up. Right there."

Dr. Sunderland froze the frame. "You thought you'd have to convince me," he said with a sympathetic smile. "Because you were sure this . . . phenomenon . . . would only manifest at home, that it would have the good sense to keep hidden here."

Her father gave a small laugh. "That's about right. Sorry."

"Why apologize?" said Dr. Sunderland. "Most of the time, when people worry about that, they're right to. Because most of the time, they're not dealing with anything real. Just their own overheated imaginations."

"But this isn't imagination." Their mother folded her bandaged hands in her lap and looked up. Her eyes were wide, and frightened. Later, she would identify this moment as the point where the solidity of what was happening to the family sunk in. Broken glass was nothing, she'd say, compared to the proof of videotape.

"No," said Dr. Sunderland. "This is real. And as you've already learned—" he indicated the bandages with the remote control "—it can be extremely dangerous."

"So what's next?"

Dr. Sunderland didn't speak. He reached over to a book case behind his desk, and pulled out a videotape. It was homemade, but it had one word on its label.

The Lodge.

He swapped tapes in the VCR, and hit Play on the remote.

iii

"This isn't like the tape said," said Ann.

"Well it's winter," said Philip.

"And how."

They were standing at the top of a long dock, on a lake much smaller than the Lake House's. And it was winter all right. They were far north and the lake was solid. Ice fishing huts huddled on it in a lonely village.

There was more snow than Ann had seen before. It smothered the branches of the trees. Deep paths the width of a shovel snaked through it like trenches. The cloud was thick and the hour late, and what sun was left made the snow the colour of a wound.

"I know what you mean," said Philip, and took Ann's mittened hand in his own, gave it a squeeze. "It's not just winter. The video totally oversold this place."

"I don't like my room. There's nothing in it."

"I think that's the idea. So you don't . . . you know, start throwing shit around."

"Don't *swear.*" She looked at Philip with wide eyes, and waggled her other mitten at him, then said in a spooky sing-song: "The Insect doesn't *like* swearing!"

Philip smiled and made a little puff of breath out of his nose and looked at her sidelong as she cracked up at her own joke. But she knew he didn't think it was funny because he let go of her hand.

"Look," he said, pointing back up the hill to the Lodge. "The innkeeper's waving at us to come up."

Ann waved back. "We better go," she said.

Standing on the long porch in his heavy blue parka, lobster-handed mittens, Dr. Sunderland—the *innkeepah* as Philip had taken to calling him—grinned and waved again, and headed back inside.

"It's going to be okay," said Philip. "It's two weeks. We'll all be here. And then—"

Then the Insect will be gone. Ann nodded. That was what Dr. Sunderland had said back at his clinic.

"Ann will undergo a form of behavioural conditioning. Nothing unpleasant. It will be really easy; most of it, she won't even be aware of—because it's not conditioning for her. It's for the Insect. You can all stay and watch over her—in fact, that's an important part of the process. It will last about two weeks."

"And then?" asked her mother and Dr. Sunderland leaned back in his chair, folded his hands on his belly, as though he had already finished the job.

"Then the Insect will be gone."

The Iron Butterfly

i

Eva's phone went to voicemail for four days after the fire in Tobago. When Ann made the connection, it was not with her, but with a man who said he was Eva's nephew—not Ann's old childhood friend Ryan, which was a relief. Another one. David. He didn't let her speak with Eva at first. Ann begged, and he still wouldn't put her on, but explained to her what had happened.

"Eva's suffered a small stroke," he said. "She's all right—recovering nicely here at home. But she's resting."

"Can she talk?"

"She can talk. But it's a bit of work." It was clear that David was not relishing this conversation.

"Could you tell her it's Ann?"

"Ann? Sure. I'll tell her you called. But don't expect a call back soon. Do you have any other message for her?"

"Sure." Ann's mind raced—she needed to tell Eva what had happened—the fire, the manifestations . . . the thing she'd seen happening to Ian Rickhardt. She couldn't pass that on in a message though. Certainly not through David.

"Tell her to pray for me," she said, and feeling immediately awful, added: "Tell her I'm praying for her."

"Sure thing," said David, and disconnected. Ann switched

off her phone and turned back to the bar, where the server had thoughtfully deposited another Caribe for her. She took a deep pull from it, and doing so calculated just how much of a self-centred bitch David must think she was.

"That's how drowning people must seem when they're on their own." she said to no one as she set the half-empty bottle down.

So all on her own, on the beach and in the bar and in their suite, Ann went to work, using all the things that Eva had taught her.

She built a great fortress in her mind; felled forests for thick timbers, quarried a whole range of mountains for the hard stone walls, mined them for the rare ores that made the unbendable steel bars. She made guards this time, from a tribe of hard and watchful men cursed with sleeplessness by the waterfall beneath which they lived. The fortress climbed into the clouds, where winged lynxes circled its highest chambers, watchful lest anyone attempt escape.

Far below, there was a moat filled with smoke and mud and bones. Ann figured she had the place locked down. It would be an escape-proof prison for the Insect . . . if she could ever get the Insect inside it.

If she could find the Insect at all.

Ann made them miss their flight back, by a simple expedient—she refused to wake up. She was in fact so determined about it that Michael later said he had considered calling the hospital.

She would not explain herself, so Michael surmised a theory, that she had been more affected by the fire than anyone had thought, and was having a post-traumatic stress episode. Ann did not disagree, at least not out loud. It wasn't so far from the truth. She wasn't asleep when he'd shaken her. What she was, was uncertain.

No, she was worse than uncertain.

She was terrified.

"It's all right," Michael said as she curled up tight on the bed. "We'll miss the flight. You don't want to fly in this state."

She didn't want to fly in this state; not with the Insect at large somewhere around her, somewhere inside her. What if what happened at the beach house happened in the air?

She couldn't fly.

They couldn't stay at the resort any longer either. The place was booked solid, and another couple were checking in later in the day.

So Michael made a call to Steve on Trinidad and explained their situation. Steve, he said, was very understanding, and had offered a very generous favour. He had a house in Port-of-Spain in Trinidad, one that he rarely used. If they would like to, they could stay there until Ann felt better. Until Ann felt safe.

They stayed a week.

Ann didn't call Eva again before they left—it was clear from her one conversation with David that more calls weren't welcome. But she was not entirely neglectful. She did send her friend emails to her Hotmail address. Two of them.

The first one was perfunctory:

"Dear Eva,

I spoke with your nephew earlier and he told me about your stroke. He said you were doing well but in no shape to talk, so I didn't push him. Hopefully you can read this? Hopefully you're feeling better? I'll see you when I get back, but I don't know when that will be. I've had Insect trouble here. There was a fire. No one got hurt. Well, not badly. But it was very strange. And I am having trouble getting the Insect back into its cage. Don't worry though. I will keep at it and get it right before I come back.

Can't wait to see you,

Ann

She wrote her again from Steve's house in Port-of-Spain, on Sunday. It was more perfunctory.

Dear Eva

Pray for me please. Do your thing. I can't find it—it could be anywhere.

Ann

And a third one, on Tuesday, the night before they left, before they went out for one final adventure in the city.

Dear Eva

I'm feeling much better. There's nothing like letting your hair down to get a bit of perspective. I think everything's all right. I think. Leaving tomorrow.

So you look after you. I'm fine. I'll see you when we get back.

xox, Ann

ii

The air was still over Piarco as the taxi pulled up to the main terminal building in the pre-dawn. It felt like a blanket; a little suffocating, Ann thought. She didn't want to think about what it would be like when the sun rose. She was not necessarily feeling better, she decided as Michael hopped out of his side of the taxicab and helped the driver pull their bags from the trunk.

Michael rolled the baggage to one side and paid the driver in U.S. dollars—something that went over well here—and Ann got to her feet. She smiled as Michael met her eye.

"Well, this time at least you're awake!" he said. "Might be better asleep once we got on the plane, though. Take a nap once we've cleared security, maybe?"

Ann pulled a bottle of water from her purse and took a swig. "You should have stopped me last night," she said, and Michael laughed.

"Nah," he said. "You needed to unwind. Therapeutic."

She swirled another mouthful of water and swallowed. "A lot of unwinding." They had been out every night in Port-of-Spain. Last night was a club calling itself Zen that was anything but. It was dark, and purple, and throbbing, and Ann felt that way too. She had had rather a lot of rum. Michael had apparently had not so much rum as she had. He'd been up before her, had finished packing, and now he was loading the larger of their bags onto a luggage cart with what looked far too much like enthusiasm.

They were early for the flight; the Air Canada counter was just opening up when they arrived, and they were second in the queue. Security was nearly as quick; this wasn't an American airport and neither Michael nor Ann set off a single alarm.

They didn't, after all, have a scan for the thing that Ann might be carrying.

"Do you want coffee?" asked Michael as they found their way to their departure gate and settled down to wait.

Ann shook her head. "Another bottle of water would be fine," she said.

"I'll bring it with mine," he said, and hurried off to a coffee shop—it was called Rituals, Ann noted.

Ha.

While he was gone, she sat down and closed her eyes, took a breath. Oh yes, she was hungover; maybe even still a little drunk. She listened for her mantra; she descended the spectrum of colour, from red down to violet.

A row ahead of her, a baby began to fuss. She cracked her eye open, looked over the mother lifting her child above her knee, at the gathering dawn over the tarmac. Their plane was stopped at the gate. A baggage truck approached out of the rising sun.

Damn.

She shut her eyes again and ran the sequence of the colours. Red and Orange and Yellow . . .

No good. It had been no good trying to do this for the past . . . how long? Three days? Four? Longer?

She recalled the architecture of the fortress, its sheer walls, latticed with capillaries of ivy crawling up from the base. Which of course made no sense; she'd just constructed it a week ago. Ivy grew quickly, but not that fast. She tried to imagine how that might happen; maybe with some amped-up engineered fertilizer from Home Depot. . . .

Ann smiled and shook her head. *Home Depot.* There was the problem. She was imagining her fortress, the prison—trying to rationalize it—not seeing it. The baby, who had moved from fussing to a full-on wail, was easier to visualize; she didn't have to open her eyes to know what was happening two rows over, the mother putting her child close up to her shoulder and patting its back as its little legs gyrated and pushed.

Or Ian Rickhardt, stretching naked, suspended in the air beyond flames, his face pulled taut in an expression of . . . what?

Ecstasy?

"Here. Drink up."

Ann opened her eyes. Michael sat down beside her, and handed her a bottle of water, slippery with condensation. The terminal air-conditioning wasn't keeping up; Michael's linen shirt was spotting with sweat.

His sunburn had cleared up a week ago, and he was left with the kind of deep tan that only the fair-haired could really pull off. He smiled, and his teeth flashed.

This—not the fortress, nor the beach house on fire—was the world she inhabited. In this world, she had a home.

"You're a good-looking man," said Ann.

"What?"

"I thought you should know." She cracked the bottle open and took a swig. The water was icy on her throat.

"You had more to drink than I thought last night."

"I had a lot to drink last night, but that's neither here nor there," said Ann. "I just wanted to make a note of it. I've been spending a lot of time in my own head these past few days. All stuck in myself."

"It's understandable."

"Maybe. But it's not good for us. You hauled me out of the fire. Got burned."

"By the sun."

"Details."

He laughed. "Well thank you then."

The boarding call came just a few minutes later, and when the attendant called their row, they queued up for the last time in Trinidad while outside, the morning sun burned off the last of the mist and the North mountain range resolved itself, a high wall of green between them, and home. Ann took another swig from her water bottle and slipped it into her purse as she handed over her boarding pass.

iii

The in-flight movie was on a little LCD screen on the back of the seat in front of her, and there was a touch-screen choice. She scrolled around through the first run movies, Canadian cinema, "silver screen" classics and television, eventually settling on a John le Carré adaptation. Michael smirked a bit.

"You watch movies like an old man," he said, and Ann mouthed "fuck off" at him and put in her earbuds.

She had the window seat, and after a few minutes pulled down the shade—the sun was too bright. The movie started up in a café in Eastern Europe somewhere, a couple of old men meeting over demitasses of coffee. Soon there would be a shooting.

Michael had put on a science fiction film. It might have been a Terminator movie; might have been a zombie movie. There were a lot of guns going off and some blurry CGI. The seatbelt light switched off. Michael touched her arm. He leaned over and said something in her ear, but she couldn't quite make it out. She leaned back a little bit, watching through drooped eyelids as the action shifted to London, and a pair of British actors she vaguely recognized had another conversation as they stood in an elevator. And easily, happily, she felt herself doze off.

She started awake some time later with a lurch—as though she'd lost her breath. The seatbelt light was back on, and the movie had stopped. The time, according to the screen, was shortly after 11 a.m.—they'd been in the air two hours.

Michael wasn't beside her.

The plane lurched again. A baby—maybe the same one that she'd heard in the departure lounge—started to wail. Ann lifted her window shade and looked out. Water was accumulating on the plexiglass, as the plane flew among thunderhead clouds that climbed like gigantic trees around them.

A bell sounded.

"Good morning, everyone." It was the Captain's voice. "Just letting you know what you've probably already figured out. We're hitting a little turbulence right now. Nothing to worry about; whatever it is, it's very localized. I'm going to take us higher, to ride over it. Until we get there, please stay in your seats, and please keep your seatbelts fastened."

Where the hell was Michael? Ann rubbed her arms; they were suddenly chilled. She looked to the back. The stewards had already strapped themselves in, along with everyone else in the passenger compartment. Michael should be too. Had he gone to the washroom?

The next lurch was particularly violent; it felt as though the plane had actually struck something mid-air. Lightning flashed outside the window.

It's all right. You heard the Captain. We'll get through this—and in a matter of hours, we'll land at Pearson Airport and get on with life.

It's all right, Ann.

Ann looked across the aisle to the centre row of seats. A lean young South Asian man was sitting there, arms crossed over his chest, fingers digging into the sleeves of his long black T-shirt. His jaw was set as he looked ahead, wide-eyed, the muscles in his jaw working up the side of his close-shorn scalp. Ann leaned over, couldn't quite reach to tap his arm, but she got his attention.

"Have you seen my husband?" she asked, and pointed to the empty seat. "I fell asleep."

He shrugged. "Don't know—maybe in the latrine? You should just stay put."

"I know," she said. "I'm just worried—"

As she spoke, the cabin lurched again, and she felt a sickening rush as she lifted out of her seat for an instant. Somewhere to the front of the plane, something crashed. The bell chimed again, but this time no one came on the intercom. The crying baby made a noise that sounded like a shriek, and Ann felt her ears pop. The rest of the plane was dead quiet. She and the man in the centre aisle didn't take their eyes off one another.

"*Your husband is in the latrine*," he said.

"What?"

"*He's not alone.*"

Ann leaned forward, hand on the aisle-side armrest. "What do you mean, not alone?"

The man shook his head and reached across the aisle, put his hand on hers. "Easy miss," he said. "It's going to be okay. Now sit back, miss. We all got to stay calm."

Ann slowly pulled her hand away and did as she was told. The man gave her an uneasy smile and settled back into his own seat, hands gripping the armrests tightly as the cabin pitched again. The baby was gasping with terror; the only other human sound in the aircraft was its mother, singing something gentle to her child.

It's going to be okay. What a kindly lie, thought Ann. She shut her eyes tight.

It wasn't going to be okay. This wasn't just a storm that you could fly over, or through.

The Insect was out. Michael was gone. *And it's my fault.*

There was a loud crash to the fore of the aircraft—and a thump, a sound like metal buckling. A man shouted something, and other voices rose up around him. Ann felt a sluice of the old terror. She was in her father's boat, watching the sky draw the lake to its bosom; she was in the women's room at Canoe, hiding from the spinning saltshaker; she was in the minivan, and the wind rose up . . .

The Insect was out.

Ann kept her eyes shut, and drew the spectrum to her mind. Red and Orange and Yellow . . . She swore and opened her eyes.

She couldn't even imagine the colours; she was just reciting the words in her mind. She was cut off from the fortress, and everything that Eva had taught her.

The plane lurched again—this time, seeming to twist, hard, and Ann felt her hips press hard against the buckled seatbelt. Her purse slid up from underneath the seat where she'd stowed it, and emptied on the empty seat beside her as the plane righted. The water bottle rolled out and settled—bisected up the middle by a line of solid ice.

"Insect," said Ann, and then louder: "Insect!"

No one paid her any heed. Another chime sounded, and Ann flinched as an oxygen mask fell in front of her, and rocked back and forth on its tubing like the watch of a hypnotist. She took hold of it and drew it to her mouth, pulled the straps over her head like they'd explained.

"Where is my husband?" she said into the mask.

The man across the aisle caught her eye. He pointed to the front of the plane.

"He is in the latrine," he said, quietly but clearly—in a way that left no doubt to Ann.

"Is he safe?" she asked.

"He is raping me," replied the man. *"Help."*

The cabin went dark and the plane seemed to spin. Ann was dangling from her seatbelt for a moment, then pushed hard back into her seat. Lightning skittered across the windows behind her, then across the far side as the plane turned hard. The man across from her shouted now, along with a dozen others, as several of the overhead storage compartments popped open and luggage spilled out. He blocked a hard-case carry-on bag with his forearm, and it crashed into the aisle—where Ann saw running lights had turned on. If she were to follow them—if the plane would steady enough that she could follow them—she'd find an emergency exit.

They would also take her to the latrine—where Michael was holed up. Doing what exactly?

Raping the Insect?

A laptop backpack struck the floor and bounced up again as the plane lurched and spun. It felt like a barrel roll.

Jesus, she thought. *We're going to fucking crash.* She looked out—and was relieved at least to see that the wing was intact. There was nothing to see beyond that but soot-coloured cloud. She wondered how near they were to the ocean now. The plane steadied, and the engines whined.

Ann waited a moment. The aircraft seemed to have steadied. Was it safe now? She would take the chance.

Ann unbuckled her seatbelt. She took off the oxygen mask, drew a breath and confirmed that the cabin pressure hadn't dropped that badly. She pushed herself out of her seat, and stumbled into the aisle. Someone shouted at her to get back in her seat. She shook her head.

"It's fine," she shouted, but it wasn't. The cabin lurched again, and Ann's feet came off the deck. If she hadn't been holding onto the side of a seat, she would have fallen.

Lucky me, she thought, and it seemed to be true.

The cabin had become a cylinder of flying debris, but none of it came near Ann. It was as though a path was being cleared for her as she forced her way forward. At one point, she floated down the middle, the plane dipping into free fall. Near the first emergency exit, she fell to the ceiling, then floated, then struck the floor on her side. Ann didn't want to think about what the plane must be doing. She clambered upright and bolted past a flight attendant, strapped in her own seat.

"Ma'am!" the woman shouted, and reached out to grab Ann's arm. Ann slipped away and ran past.

Near the front of the plane, she stopped, gripping onto a low silver handrail before entering first class. The restroom was opposite her; it was closed, and marked OCCUPIED.

"Michael!" She had to shout—the whine of the engines, the crashing luggage—the screaming—was all deafening. She tried to open the door, but of course it was locked. She looked around for something to pry it with—there was a kitchen just beyond. Maybe . . .

She felt a hand on her shoulder and turned around. It was the flight attendant. She leaned close: "You've got to sit down!"

Ann shook her head and pounded on the door. "My husband's in there!" she said.

The attendant was having none of it. "He's safer there than coming out," said the attendant. "There's oxygen in there. The cabin's depressurizing. You need to return to your seat."

Ann tried to pull away, but the attendant's grip was strong. "You have to obey my instructions ma'am. It's for everyone's safety—"

She didn't finish. There was a bright flash as she spoke, sending spears of lightning in from both rows of windows—and it illuminated a bright silver briefcase, shooting through the air up the aisle.

The case hit the attendant in the back of the head. She collapsed into Ann. She stepped back and let the attendant fall to the floor. She bent down—on the attendant's skirt, there was a plastic spring and a set of simple keys. Ann stretched it out, and found one that matched a keyhole underneath the handle of the restroom. The plane lurched then, and the floor tilted sharply. Ann held tight until the plane righted. She inserted the key and clicked the sign to VACANT. She let the keys snap back to the attendant and slid open the door.

The electricity seemed to be working fine in there; the lights inside the restroom flickered, occasionally flashing as bright as the lightning outside the plane. It played across a sight that at first Ann couldn't fathom.

It was Michael. His pants were around his ankles and his linen shirt was unbuttoned, pulled back over his shoulders so it hung tight around his elbows. His head was cricked back, tendons taut under his chin. His penis was hard—and it swayed back in forth in front of him, as his hands made claws to clutch at the air. His head swung around to look at her, but it was as though he couldn't see her; in the light, his pupils had shrunk to pinpricks. And around him—toilet paper floated, draping in the air in what seemed like a cage. Droplets of blue fluid hung in the air. Gravity had been utterly suspended in that tiny room.

He began to turn away from her, toward the little mirror over the sink—rotating in the air, unfettered to the deck. The muscles in his still-pale ass tensed as he looked in the mirror—looked at something, Ann saw, that was not precisely his own reflection.

The thing in the mirror made its face into a rictus—of anger, maybe, or something else. But Ann peered around at Michael's face, and thought it far less ambivalent.

He was smiling.

And he was hard. More than hard. He was *engorged.*

There was a popping sound then, as the light in the restroom shattered, and it was all dark again. Ann tried to reach in—to stop him—but she heard a shout, and the floor shifted beneath her again, and there was a flash of silver as the briefcase that had taken down the flight attendant leapt up from the floor and struck Ann hard in the side of the head.

She crumpled.

iv

And she was on some kind of bench.

It seemed to be made of wooden planks—not finished, not even sanded. She smelled woodsmoke. Or maybe not, not *wood*smoke. The smoke of burning dung? What made her think of that? It was pungent, not unpleasant—but dung? Why would she think of that?

She sighed and opened her eyes. She had thought of that because she'd invented it. The dung of cave bats was what the tribe who was charged with guarding the Insect burned in their cooking braziers. It was more plentiful than wood, and burned hot and long through the nights. And sure enough, that's what was providing the light in this place . . . a small windowless room, halfway up the tower where the Insect was to have dwelt.

She sat up, put her bare feet down on the thick pine floor. She was wearing a long dress of velvet, a deep blue, with sleeves that fitted her arms tightly and extended just past her wrists. It was the sort of dress that an out-of-favour royal might wear in the Tower of London at various times in history.

The light came from two braziers that hung from chains hooked into ceiling joists. There was a door, made of thick planks of maple. There was a small barred slit at eye level. The door was, of course, barred from the other side. Although she couldn't see it from here, Ann knew it was a stout bar. She had put it there herself, just as she'd invented the dung and the bench and the wood.

"A prison of my own design." She stood on toes to peer out the slit. A rusted iron cover was drawn across the other side. She tapped on it. There would be a guard there. He would be careful, draw the cover open with the haft of his spear perhaps.

The cover drew aside.

"Hello, Miss." The guard was not standing too close to the slit, so Ann could get a look at him in the dim firelight.

"You were on the plane," she said. The guard rubbed his fingers through close-cut hair. He smiled. Ann had not seen him smile when he was sitting in the row next to hers, telling her to calm down. He stepped closer to the door, until their eyes were only inches apart.

"Not anymore," he said. "Your husband still is though."

"What?"

"He ain't going anywhere, miss."

V

And she was on a mattress. There were linens. It smelled of ammonia. A machine was beeping. It was hard to focus her eyes on the dim light sources, the odd shapes in the space that she now occupied. She lifted her arm. There was a bracelet around her wrist. She touched her head; there was a bandage taped to her forehead, and it stung, deep, when her fingers brushed it.

It was oh-so-mysterious, but only for a few seconds.

Ann was no fool.

She wasn't on the plane anymore. She was in a hospital, somewhere. They had bandaged her forehead where the case had struck it. The bracelet on one wrist was a hospital bracelet.

She inferred from this that the plane had not exploded, had not fallen into the sea, had landed in some way.

Okay, she thought.

Everything's good.

It wasn't good.

Here is what had happened according to the representative from Air Canada, who met with Ann after the doctors had pronounced her fit for visitors. There was turbulence, and it wasn't expected, and it did some damage to the aircraft. The damage was serious. It had nearly brought the aircraft down in the ocean, the damage was so serious. But the pilots were able to regain control at 1,000 feet, and fly with only one engine all the way to Miami, Florida, where they made an emergency landing.

There was more, but Ann didn't absorb much of that, because the representative, whose name was Carolyn something-or-other and was just about Ann's age but seemed so much older, had already told her the most important thing.

Michael had not survived the landing.

Ann was a widow.

Were there tears?

When she came to her senses next, Ann was sure there must have been—even as she felt nothing but iron in the middle of herself. Her husband, Michael Voors, had died in the air, after . . .

After . . .

She must have cried herself to paralysis.

THE TRICASTA EXPERIMENT

i

She had fallen in with a bad crowd in junior high school. That was how Ann's mother would put it. Ann didn't agree. They weren't bad, really. Just odd.

There were five of them—three boys: Luke, Ryan and Bruce. The girls: Courtney and Leah. They were all in the gifted program, like Ann, and they were all underachievers, like Ann.

They were, as Ann's father put it one night over dinner at the Lake House, slaves to the dice. Philip thought that was a good joke, and in Ann's defence, told both their parents that the pastime was "a better form of birth control than the Pill." But that didn't get much of a laugh. Their mother quietly pointed out that spending time drawing up mazes populated with monsters and devils was walking a bit too close to the line for a girl with Ann's history.

"Whatever," said Ann, swirling her mashed potatoes into a little crater for the melting butter. "It's just a game."

"It's like a religion," said her mother. "It's got its own bible."

"Bib*les*," said Ann. "And not even. They're just rules."

They were borrowed rules, then. There was the *Player's Handbook*, which taught the novice adventurer everything she needed to know about making a character, be it thief or fighter or cleric or magic-user; the *Dungeon Master's Guide*, which got into the architecture of making up imaginary continents, and the tombs and caverns and fortresses that riddled their mantle; and the *Monster Manual*, which told you everything you needed to know about the devils and monsters that dwelt inside.

Ryan loaned them to her after she promised not to (a) write in them, (b) tear them, or (c) spill anything on them. They were stupidly expensive—the whole set came up to nearly $100—and you couldn't do without them, running a long-game, in-depth Dungeons & Dragons campaign like Ryan's.

Ryan was in Grade Nine—in just a few months, he'd graduate on to the district high school. But he'd been running his campaign, on an island called Tareth, since Grade Seven. The island was a geographical jumble that intentionally or not, resembled a face; thick jungles hugged the southern coast like a beard, cut off by the arid plateau of the Sun's Anvil, that rimmed the southern third of the island in a jack-o-lantern smile topped by a range of mountains that Leah kept calling the Mustachio of Death, for obvious reasons, but Ryan maintained were known as the Grim Spires.

A great freshwater lake might have made a nose, although it was further to the east than the west, and the towns that dotted the northern coast and followed the three rivers that drained from lake to sea did not make for eyes. But the Sun's Anvil still grinned.

Ann wanted to make her own continent, her own campaign. She had begun work on it while she was still exploring the jungle temples of Ith, looking for a fabled jewel known only as the Fisherman's Lure, along with Leah and Courtney—a sort of audition session that Ryan ran in the cafeteria back in September. Ann's continent looked more like Italy—she thought it might fit in just a few hundred kilometres to the west of Tareth, across a treacherous ocean filled with sharks and reefs and kraken. It would join to a larger land mass to the northwest that was omnipresent but effectively unreachable, fenced off by swampland and foothills and a Great Wall. The wall was her big brother's idea. Philip was nearly finished high school and had been studying Chinese history, and was of the view that every ancient Dungeons & Dragons world needed at least one Great Wall.

He helped Ann with some of the geography, too—made sure that the terrain was realistic enough nothing could be mistaken for a happy face, and helped her come up with names for her towns and lakes and rivers that didn't immediately suggest the B side of a heavy metal album.

"You can still have monsters crawling through a burial cairn that's just called the Cairn of Saint Lucius," he said. "Not every cave has to have 'Fang' in its name."

They came up with a decadent former imperial hub, based loosely on Rome, that still ruled the place even though it had gone monotheistic in the past hundred years. They named it Tricasta, because the city was divided into three districts which cast out from a central fountain, fed by a trapped water elemental spirit. Her name, Ann decided, was Casta.

Philip quietly suggested that was a pretty cheesy way to name a city, but he couldn't come up with anything better. He was finishing his senior year, and had his hands full: playing basketball at the Varsity level, maintaining better than average grades, and managing a teen romance of considerable tempest with Laurie Weston, nearly a year younger than he, the middle child in a family of five boys, two of whom were teammates of his. It was complicated.

Ann disliked Phys. Ed., was bored by basketball even from the point of view of a spectator, and while she was fond of Ryan, she did not think she would like to date her dungeon master just as a rule. And her grades? They were as unspectacular as her generally uncomplicated life.

Ann liked it that way. Philip could play at sports and excel at calculus and explore and agonize over the body and mind of the mercurial Laurie West. Ann had other priorities.

With geography and ecology established, Ann busied herself with the care and feeding of the Empire of the Eternal Fountain.

As Leah drily observed just before Christmas, the empire was fed with the blood of their player characters.

"Seriously, Ann, you are one murderous dungeon master." The root beer in Leah's glass foamed to within a millimetre of the top before she stopped pouring. The plastic bottle made a clicking sound as she set it down beside her now-redundant character sheet.

"You guys do it to yourselves," Ann replied. "If Halgreth wanted to live, he could have had a long career as a castrato in the Cathedral of Tears."

"She's right," said Ryan. "The Archbishop did make the offer before we rescued you. All you had to do was say thanks but no, I like it here."

"Don't be such a dick," said Leah.

And Ann said, "That's what the Archbishop said," and that cracked them all up.

They were at the Lake House that day, in the basement rec room where Ann had set up the game table. It was not the full crew; just the girls, Ryan, and Ann. Luke and Bruce, skeptics to the end, had other things to do than play in Ann's girly little campaign.

It was Saturday—the Christmas break was just thirty hours old—and Ann was hosting the day's game, which was scheduled to go for another five hours before their rides showed up to end it all. Leah would, in practical terms, be in for a long wait; the party was exploring a network of caverns underneath the Coliseum of Dusk, in a deep valley some fifty leagues south of Tricasta. The entrance had collapsed behind them, so there was no easy exit—and as poor dead Halgreth was the party's only cleric . . . there was no one in practical earshot who could be prevailed upon to cast a resurrection spell and bring him back.

So there would be nothing for it. Leah would have to sit on the sidelines, watching as the party lashed her eviscerated corpse to a makeshift litter, and rolling up a new character or three while the rest of them fought their way through the Corridor of Bones, swam an underground river and battled the Arch-Liche of the Games in his inverted tower that clung stalactite-like above the nearly bottomless Cavern of Souls.

No two ways about it. It sucked to be her.

"Let's take a break," said Courtney. "Out of respect, you know, for the dead." She patted Leah's hand.

Ryan shrugged. "I gotta take a wizz anyway." He pushed the chair out from the table and headed upstairs.

"Yeah, don't take all day," said Ann.

"Just enough time to figure out a strategy to survive this fuckin' death march." He grabbed his copy of the *Dungeon Master's Guide* as he passed Ann, and Ann took it back, then covered the maps behind her screen.

"Easy cowboy," she said.

"Yippee kai-yay, motherfucker," said Ryan, and Courtney cracked up.

Ann grinned and leaned over her notes, thinking about some of the things she'd have to change in the dungeon now that Halgreth had bought it. If the party lost one more member, they'd be wiped out by the Arch-Liche and its army. She considered for a moment whether to cross out the Balrog she'd set to guard the Gossamer Bridge—to give them a sporting chance. She was literally poised to do that when Courtney piped in with a suggestion.

"You know," she said, as Leah hunched adding up the Wisdom points on the dice she'd just rolled, "when Ryan was running his Tareth campaign, shit like this didn't happen."

Balrog's in, thought Ann, but what she said was, "You want me to go a little easier on you, sister?"

"Not easier, exactly. But . . . remember in Tareth when we got into the treasury?"

Leah sat up, and nodded. "Yeah, Ann—that was where you picked up that sweet Bag of Holding. And the Vorpal Blade."

"And that invisibility ring," said Courtney. "I didn't hear you complaining it wasn't tough enough then."

Ann nodded at Leah. "You got another cleric there?"

She shook her head. "Wisdom's just 11. Won't make the cut."

"Re-roll it," said Ann.

"The whole character?"

"Just the stat," she said. "If it's lower than 11, keep the first roll. Otherwise . . ."

"You want me to make another cleric?"

"You're going to need one where you're going," she said. "Don't worry—I'll find a place to introduce him, before you get there."

Leah nodded and rolled again. "Seventeen!" she crowed, and Ann nodded.

"Take better care of this one," she said.

Ann shut her binder with all the notes for the dungeon and got up.

"Where you going?" asked Courtney.

"Going to pee," she said, and headed for the stairs out of the basement. "You guys want anything from the kitchen while I'm up there?"

"Nah," said Courtney, and Leah rubbed her arms.

"Maybe crank up the heat in here," she said. "I'm starting to freeze."

Leah was right. It was freezing, outside and in. The sky was clear and blue, and the air was still, but as Ann walked past the French doors to the deck, she could see frost starting to rim the glass. It was too early for the lake to have frozen over—that didn't usually happen until mid-January—and looking out, she could see little eddies of the sharp wind crossing the middle of it. She flipped the light on in the kitchen—the brightness outside made the interior of the place greyer by definition, somehow lonelier.

Her parents had taken the car into Toronto for some last-minute Christmas shopping, and Philip was over at Laurie's place for the day. Ann and her friends had the place to themselves.

She didn't really have to pee. She figured she could squeeze one out if pressed on the matter. But yeah . . . she was hoping to run into Ryan. She had no time for Leah's dramatics, and she wanted to confer, dungeon master to dungeon master, on the best way to deal with a troublesome player. She figured she'd catch him on his way out of the little powder room in the hall between kitchen and living room.

She flipped on the hall light, and waited outside the door for a moment. Bounced back and forth on her feet once, then tapped on the door.

"Hey Ry, you okay in there? You—oh."

There was no light coming from under the door. She opened it, and sure enough—the little two-piece was empty. And cold. She could see her breath as she leaned inside. The room had been shut up all morning.

"Ryan?" Ann shut the door and headed into the living room. It was dark too, nothing but the reflection of the kitchen light in the screen of her dad's rear projection TV. Ann stopped at the base of the stairs to adjust the thermostat. She put it to 24 degrees, and flicked the side of it with her thumb, as though that might kick-start it.

Light filtered down through the slats on the bannister. That was it, then. Ryan had used the upstairs bathroom, with the Jacuzzi tub and the full-length mirrors, and all her mom's New Yorkers—or her "hometown papers" as she called them.

Ann started up the stairs. She stopped at the first landing, wondering for a moment—would Ryan think it was weird if she followed him all the way upstairs to the big bathroom, when the powder room was *right there*? Would he think she was following him? That she liked him?

But he had been up there awhile. She might be just going up to see if he was all right.

"Sure," she murmured, and climbed to the second floor. The bathroom door was wide open, but it was dark in there too. The light, such as it was, was coming from around the corner of the hall.

Her room.

Ann rubbed gooseflesh down on her forearms. She didn't call out his name this time, just padded along the hallway, stepping over the board that squeaked, and turned the corner. The door was half-open. Ryan was sitting on her bed, facing away from her. She needn't have been so stealthy. He was wearing her headphones, so oblivious that he just about jumped out of his skin when she grabbed his shoulder with one hand and yanked off the phones with the other.

"Shit!"

"What the hell?"

"I'm sorry!" Ryan sat bolt upright, his eyes wide. The headphones were in his lap, hissing with the noise from the machine beside her bed. "Shit, Ann, I'm sorry. I was—"

"You were snooping around in my room!" said Ann. "I can't believe it!"

Ryan blinked fast and slid off the bed so he was standing, facing away from her, toward the window in Ann's room.

"Look—I'm sorry. I shouldn't have been in here."

For just another second, Ann felt like she could hit Ryan, like that was going to be the only thing for it. But the mood passed. He was really sorry. His head hung low enough that his jaw touched his chest, and his eyes, normally wide and brown, were crinkled with what seemed like genuine regret, sincere apology.

"You didn't go through my drawers, did you?" Ann had heard about boys stealing girls' underwear. Evidently so had Ryan; he shook his head emphatically.

"Look, I'm really sorry. I was just walking by, and saw the cool old tape deck."

"Ah. The machine."

"Yeah. No one uses tapes anymore. I wanted to see what you had."

"Yeah, it's not that kind of tape deck," said Ann. The tape deck was an old Emerson model, with two cassette player-recorders. It was sitting on top of a broken digital tuner that wouldn't pick up the radio but amplified the tape through the headphones. It had been at Ann's bedside for years.

"You're telling me. That's some weird stuff on it."

"You were listening to my tape," she said, and immediately felt stupid. She had, after all, caught him listening to her tape. But saying it felt creepy; he might as well have been going through her drawers, stuffing underpants into his pockets.

"What is it? It sounds like hypnotherapy or something."

"How do you know what hypnotherapy is?"

"My Aunt Eva is into all that stuff," he said. "She's a little nuts for it. Your parents make you do that too?"

Ann sat down on the bed, picked up the headphones. She held it to her ear for a second: a sound like the ocean; the voice of Dr. Sunderland, counting up the alphabet. She set them down and pressed the stop button; the machinery clicked and the ocean stopped.

"It's just something I do," she said. "You won't tell anyone, will you?"

Ryan shrugged. "Why would I?"

"I dunno. You could tell everybody I was a bed-wetter and needed hypnotherapy . . ."

"You a bed-wetter?"

Ann made a show of sniffing. "Not last night," she said, and Ryan, laughing, said "Good one."

She nodded, face hung in a half-grin, and Ryan sat down on the bed beside her. The room was east-facing, so the afternoon light left the room grey and shadowy as the rest of the house. In certain lights, the bare walls were a light pink; the uncluttered floor a deep cherry. An old clock radio blinked 4:56 on the otherwise clear dresser top.

"Love what you've done with the place," said Ryan.

"I don't need a lot of stuff," said Ann. She felt like she was apologizing.

"Well it's not because your dad's poor," said Ryan. He looked at her. "What's that tape for?"

"It's, um . . ."

Ryan waited a moment. "Don't feel bad," he finally said. "Aunt Eva has a whole handbag full of cassettes. And crystals, too. Every time she comes over, she's exorcising the evil spirits and opening up the gateways to the divine. Nothing you can tell me will surprise me."

"When I was younger," said Ann finally, "we had . . . some problems. The tapes help with that. I'm supposed to listen to them every night as I go to sleep."

Ryan nodded sagely. "So it *is* bed-wetting." Ann punched him in the arm and told him to shut up.

"All right," she said finally. "You want to know?"

"I'm asking."

She leaned close to him and whispered: *"I used to be possessed by the Devil. Things would fly around the house. Knives. Nail guns."* She grabbed his arm, hard. "Axes," she said aloud, and made a *chk-kk!* sound at the back of her throat—like an axe might make, embedding itself in a skull. "That's why I can't have any axes or other sharp things in the room."

"Yeah, right."

"No foolin'," said Ann.

"Well whatever gets you through the night," he said. "I hope this guy didn't charge you too much for it, though."

"Don't know how much, don't care."

"Yeah, your dad's not poor."

"Stiiinkiiing riiich."

"Well the main thing is that you feel better," said Ryan. "That's what all this is about. The placebo effect. That's what mom says about Aunt Eva. She helps people trick themselves into getting better."

Ann took a breath—opened her mouth, to shoot something back. But she couldn't crack wise this time. She felt her face flush. It scarcely would have been worse if she was listening to tapes to stop her from bed-wetting. She met Ryan's eye. Ryan leaned back and smirked at her. Then his head tilted, and his eyes narrowed with terrible purpose, and he came in close.

He was aiming for her mouth. But Ann was too quick. His lips brushed her cheek, and before he could do anything else, she scooted to the foot of the bed and got up.

"Come on," she said. "They'll be going through my notes by now."

Ryan shrugged and followed her downstairs. They'd been gone awhile. By the time they were back at the table, Leah's back-up cleric was all finished, and the furnace had done its work. Even the basement was toasty warm.

ii

When Ann was very small, there were a couple of Christmases that they spent in Long Island, New York, where Ann's mother's family came from. But in recent years, they tended to keep closer to home. Ann was not sure why that was. Her parents just said they didn't want to travel much, but it was pretty clear to both Ann and Philip that something had changed between their mother and her parents. Their grandmother Mavis would phone on Christmas Eve, but it was always their father who would take the call.

This Christmas, she called during dinner. Their mom craned her neck, checked the call-display on the credenza phone, and looked to their dad. "Them," she said, and her dad pushed out his chair and picked up the phone

"Hello, Mavis," he said. "Merry Christmas to you too." He leaned against the door jamb. "It's pretty cold here, too. A bit worse than last year, I'd say." Their mother scooped out a spoonful of mashed potatoes and plopped it next to the capon's left thigh on her plate. "They're fine," he said, looking first at Ann, then Philip. And, "I don't think that's a good idea." Pause, as the phone squawked. "We've talked about this." He sighed. "I'm sorry. I will. Merry Christmas, Mavis."

And he hung up, and went through to the kitchen to get another bottle of wine. Their mother's glass, just filled before the phone rang, was empty.

Things were better with Nan.

It was just Nan; Granddad had passed on when Ann was five. But it had been good with Granddad too. He was a giant of a man, with a full head of grey hair and a thin white beard—like Santa Claus with a subscription to GQ. That was Nan's joke. She had a lot of jokes; she even found a way to laugh at Granddad's funeral.

Now she lived by herself in a big ranch house outside Barrie, just a couple of hours from the Lake House. There was usually a Christmas Eve call from her, too, but it was a little longer, everyone talked on the phone, even as the purpose was to figure out the timing of their visit for late lunch on Christmas Day.

Lunch being loosely defined in this case, in that they wouldn't generally get there until two o'clock, and food wouldn't be out until four.

Philip explained the drill as they pulled away from Laurie's house in town. Laurie sat in the back seat with him, her red hair tied in a ponytail, otherwise garbed in a pair of black tights and a short-cut ski jacket that wasn't really warm enough for the day. So she bundled under his arm, nodding and listening, watching the houses go by as they pulled out. This was to be her first time at a LeSage family Christmas, and Philip wanted to make sure she knew what to expect.

"Same every year," he said. "We get there at two. Nan's been cooking since, like, six in the morning. She is a demon in the kitchen, seriously. Don't get between her and her Dutch oven." Laurie laughed, and Ann, on her own in the middle seat of the minivan, grinned and thought: *Seriously. Buuuuull-Shit.* Philip was laying it on thick.

"So there's no prayers or anything, like your folks do. Nan's not really Christian."

"That's okay," said Laurie. She and her family were Baptist or something, some fundamentalist thing, and they prayed a *lot*. Philip did not, but he tried to be nice about it. Ann privately thought this would be the end of them, which was okay by her. But on the other hand, Philip had managed to steal her away from her family on this, the afternoon of the birth of her Lord and Saviour. Maybe it *was* true love.

"Nan likes singing, though. She has a guitar, an old classical guitar, and there will be singing. She likes Bob Dylan and the Beatles. After dinner, you're going to have to sing along. You up for that, West?"

"Yes sir," said Laurie.

The houses were gone now; they'd hit the traffic light at Highway 89, which was barely a highway so much as it was a two-lane blacktop weaving through the woodlots and fields of southern Ontario farm country. Ann found herself humming along with Laurie, as she dutifully joined Philip in an off-key rendition of "If I Had a Million Dollars." When their dad called over his shoulder that Barenaked Ladies was a long way from John Lennon, Philip shouted back, "I'd buy you a stress tab," and everybody cracked up.

"What's a stress tab?" asked Laurie.

"Nan always says that," Ann explained. "'Take a stress tab,' whenever anybody gets too tense."

"So what—it's like Prozac?"

"I think it's a vitamin pill. From the Seventies," said Philip. "So y'know . . . mushrooms . . . speed . . . caffeine."

"Goofballs," said Ann. "Staples."

"That's pretty close," said their dad, who was either in on the gag or hadn't heard over the road noise. "I think it's vitamin B complex."

"Got it," said Laurie, and Philip said, "Good."

"So Laurie," said their mom over her shoulder, "you're graduating this year too?"

"That's right, Mrs. LeSage."

"What comes after that?"

Philip cut in. "Foreign Legion," he said, and Laurie hit him in the arm.

"I'm deciding," she said. "I've got applications in to Queen's, and McMaster, and Western."

"She's a wizard at math," said Philip.

Their mother turned around. "Will you let the girl speak, Philip?"

"Don't make me come back there," said their dad.

"I can take care of myself," said Laurie, and punched Philip again.

"Now it'll never heal!" Philip grabbed his arm and gritted his teeth. He pressed his forehead against the windshield, making a halo of condensation on the glass. The sun had gone behind some cloud, and it seemed like a shadow fell across his face with it.

"I think I'd like to go into medicine," said Laurie. "Have to keep my grades up for that, but that's the plan. Probably Queen's is my first—" she paused. "Wow. Look at that."

"What?" said Ann's mom, but Ann could see, looking at the road past her mom. It had been a pretty dry December so far—there'd just been two snowfalls earlier in the month, and both had melted. It looked as though they were driving into the third.

It was a wall of white, maybe a half a kilometre ahead. They had crested a hill, and were heading down into it; a translucent veil of snow, blowing across the road, through the field to their right and between the trees of the woods to their left.

"A white Christmas," said Philip. Their dad switched on the headlights and the wipers, and their mom looked into it. Her shoulders clenched.

Laurie said, "Cool," and shivered.

"Could you turn up the heat please, Dad?" said Ann. She was feeling it too. A chill was creeping up her arms.

"Sure," said her dad. He turned the dial beside the radio and the fan kicked on. A blast of icy air came out of the vents.

"Aw, shit," said her dad. "That's just perfect."

"What?" said her mom.

"Radiator. When the heat goes off, that's usually what it means. The radiator's leaking."

He slowed the van down and put on his hazards. "We're going to have to stop somewhere."

"Where? There's nothing."

Her mother had a point. The snow was coming hard now—from where Ann was sitting, she couldn't even see a bit of the road.

"Why do we have to stop?" asked Laurie.

"The radiator is what provides heat in the car—it's the heat off the engine," said Philip. "If there's no heat, it means the radiator's not working. And that means the engine could overheat."

"Yeah," said their dad, "that's right. But I don't want to stop right now—bad visibility—too easy to get hit by another car coming up behind. Too—"

There was a sickening lurch then, and Ann felt the seatbelt bite into her shoulder, as the van fishtailed. Laurie gasped and Philip shouted, "Whoa."

Good.

Ann clutched the shoulder strap of her seatbelt as their dad pulled the steering wheel. Underneath them, the tires slid and screamed, and outside, a car horn dopplered in and out. And then there was sunlight, and the air blasting through the vents was suddenly hot.

Ann looked out the window.

The van was in the middle of the road, bisected by the yellow no-passing lane. On either side, farmers' fields stretched and rolled up to lines of trees at the edge of vision. The snow had stopped; the sky was clear. The radiator, given the sudden heat, was on.

"Shit!" Their dad shook his head, turned on the ignition, and pulled around and back into his lane, gunned the motor and got up to speed. Ann hadn't noticed the car coming down the gentle slope until it sped past them.

"Wow," said Laurie. "Wow."

Ann felt Philip's hand on her shoulder. "Hey," he said, "you okay?" She nodded, and he leaned forward and whispered, "We okay?"

Ann bent forward, held her arms tight around herself. She felt as though she might shake apart. Her mother was looking back at her over the seat.

"Annie," she said, "remember your words."

Ann nodded. She began to recite them. *Belaim, foredawned, sheepmorne, overwind . . .* Not speaking aloud, but listening for them, letting them bubble up. *Belaim, foredawned . . .*

Laurie was asking what was going on, and Philip was explaining that it was just a thing to help Ann with her stress, and her mom was saying "good, good," when her dad said, "shit" again, and Ann opened her eyes.

The snow had returned. It wasn't enveloping them this time; but to their left, and their right, and yes, behind, it was keeping pace—a great white pincer, that rolled across the fields, overtaking the van by degrees. The sun yellowed through it, as it rose higher and farther.

Good.

"We need to go back," said Ann. "This isn't—this isn't the radiator."

Ann's mother twisted around and touched Ann's arm. "Annie," she said, "your *words*."

And Ann thought about those words, as she listened for them again, and thought about that other snowy day—by the lake, in a room just as white as the snow outside, with Dr. Sunderland, sitting in that black office chair while she curled on a couch, repeating, "belaim"—which wasn't even a word—and "foredawned"—could be a word, but wasn't—and the rest, as a light flashed irregularly in the corner of her eye. And she thought about the time she'd become impatient—that she'd "had it!" And got up and tried to open the door, as Dr. Sunderland watched, and nodded, and in that way he had, begun to recite the alphabet, *A* and *B* and *C* and so on . . . And Ann thought about the new word, the one she'd heard in her room coming from Ryan's lips. . . .

Placebo.

She looked it up on Yahoo after he left that night. A substance with no medical ingredients, but which tricked a patient into believing that it provided a cure. Enabling the patient to provide the cure to herself.

Good.

Behind her, Laurie was using her own words, about the valley of the shadow of death, and Philip was saying "Easy, easy," and her mother twisted around and reached and held Ann's hand tight as the sky became a deathly yellow, like flypaper, and the pincer closed, and the van became black and the vents blew hard, lashing snow, and gravity shifted.

It's all right. You're safe. Shh. Hush. You're safe with me.

Ann was cold.

She couldn't breathe. Not at first. She coughed, and she drew a great wheezing breath so hard it seemed to crack her ribs. She was cold. And wet.

She sat up. Her ears were ringing, and she was dizzy. She was at the bottom of a ditch. She had cracked through ice and was sitting in swift, running water. She got up, a sloshy, muddy job, but not impossible. Her arms and legs all worked, and although she was dizzy, she wasn't blacking out. Three years ago, she'd fallen down the short flight of steps from the deck, and those were the questions her dad has asked her: *Do your arms and legs work? Are you dizzy? Does it seem like things are getting darker? How many fingers am I holding up?*

There was no one nearby to ask her that last question. But Ann thought she could get the answer right if anyone did ask her.

She was cold. Colder than it had gotten in the van—when she'd fallen against the seatbelt, and the air had filled with the moaning sound of metal tearing, and the yowling of tires slid sideways, and a cracking sound . . .

And, as the seatbelt released her—

Ann leaned forward to climb the edge of the ditch. It was sunny again, and the heat of the sun felt good on the back of her hands, her shoulders. Her thighs stung under her sodden jeans. She slipped on the icy mud, and fell. "Help," she murmured, reaching up.

Her fingers found a hand. It was warm, and she reached up with her free hand and grabbed it too. "Thank you," she said, and found purchase in the muck. Three pushes, and she was over the top—alone, on the side of the highway.

Ann hugged herself and shivered as a bright red SUV crested the hill ahead of her, sped past. She couldn't even tell which way it was going.

"Help!" she said as its taillights vanished around the bend in the other direction. "Help!" She started to run after it, stumbled, and fell into gravel.

She remembered sky, first that awful yellow, then blue—and then rotating, and looking down. The van rolled across the highway like a toy underneath her. She had thought it was a toy, hadn't had time to put it together as she turned again.

And saw someone.

A tall figure—standing at the crest of the hill, from where the car had come.

Help! Ann didn't articulate it this time, as the figure turned towards her, and raised two arms, and then two more, longer than those two, beneath that.

Ann let herself go. She felt the gravel, sharp against her face, and although it hurt, she pressed it there. And waited.

The next car that came by announced itself by its siren. The hands that helped her up were warm, and brought with them a blanket.

And when they crossed the crest of the hill moments later, the figure was gone.

iii

They hadn't gotten far enough to go to the hospital in Barrie, but that wouldn't have done any good anyway. The only one who needed serious medical attention was Philip. Their mother had died at the scene—the doctors and police wouldn't tell Ann exactly how it had happened, but Ann remembered her mother, twisted around dangerously in the front seat, holding Ann's hand. Ann imagined that she had been torn in half when the van hit the bridge abutment. Their father had lived long enough to be put into an ambulance. But there was internal bleeding, or something, and they hadn't been able to keep him alive even as long as Laurie, who had made it to the E.R. before she was pronounced dead.

Philip needed help. He had suffered head injuries, and had cracked his spine at the second vertebrae when the van had whipsawed back into the road and begun to roll out the other side of the bridge. When he arrived at the hospital, doctors took a look at him and called for an airlift to get him to Toronto.

Ann stayed at Fenlan. She had relatively few injuries, but the water and the cold had put her into a state of acute hypothermia. This was something the doctors and nurses at Fenlan knew how to deal with, given the local snowmobile club's propensity for racing across the lake in the dead of winter.

Nan came. She sat by Ann's bed, and held her arm, and told her how much she loved her, and how things would be fine, and she would see, unfortunately underlining it all with jags of tears and curses. Ann had never heard her Nan curse before, and Ann suggested, through trembling lips, that Nan should stop cursing because it was not very ladylike.

That was the sort of joke that Nan normally might appreciate but she gave no indication of doing so this time. She became quiet, her mouth drawn, her eyes narrowed.

"You're a good girl," she said.

But she didn't sound as though she meant it.

It grew warmer. Ann felt her fingers and toes. A man came from the Ontario Provincial Police—Constable Reid. He had a red face and blond hair that was a bit darker at the roots. He was the one who'd found her by the side of the road. He brought her a stuffed dog, with soft furry ears and big sad eyes. She took it, and held it close. He asked her if she remembered how she got there, in that ditch, how she'd gotten out of the van before it crashed. Her Nan sat on the other side of the bed, looking down at her hands.

"I remember being in the air," Ann said.

"Were you wearing your seatbelt?"

"Yes."

"Okay. Do you know if your daddy was doing anything?"

"He was driving."

"I see. Just driving?"

"There was a lot of snow," she said. "It came up all of a sudden." And she told him about how the heat hadn't worked, and how her dad thought it might be the radiator, and how it had started up again, right before the snow. Nan asked if this was necessary, and Constable Reid rubbed the back of his neck and seemed to make up his mind.

"Okay, Ann. I'm not going to trouble you about this any more than that." He put a hand on the edge of the bed. "I'm so sorry. I guess . . . you'll be heading home with your Grandma soon."

"No," said Ann, and Constable Reid gave her a look that suddenly had a raft more questions, and Nan gave her a look that nearly broke her heart.

"Oh, darling," she said, "don't worry. We'll make a nice room for you, and—"

"Not yet," said Ann. She thought of the man on the ridge, with an extra set of arms, and that hand that had pulled her from the ditch. . . . And as she flew through the air . . . the face.

And she said, "I can't go anywhere right now." She didn't add, *It isn't safe for you.*

The Fenlan Medical Health Centre was the name of the hospital. It wasn't big enough to have its own full-time grief counsellor; for this, it employed volunteers. But just because they were volunteers was not to say that they weren't good at their job. For Ann, they called in their best. His name was Mr. Small, and he was the sort of fellow who took pains to live the opposite of his name. He was kind of heavy, and had a bushy head of whitening hair, and a long beard that was fully white. He used to be a negotiator for the teachers' union, and was spending his retirement in Fenlan, he told Ann, "For my sins."

"I'm sorry you had to miss Christmas," she said.

"That's okay," he said. "We're here for you right now. I see Constable Reid has given you a nice present."

Ann nodded and held the dog close.

"You given him a name?" asked Mr. Small.

Ann shook her head.

"I'll think of one. I promise."

"That's okay," he said. "I wouldn't give him a name either right now."

"My parents are dead," said Ann suddenly. The words came out fast, like she'd upchucked them. She didn't know what to do after that, and Mr. Small didn't seem to either. They were sitting in the pediatric room, which was a playroom for kids much smaller than Ann. There were wooden blocks all over the table between them. Mr. Small picked one up and turned it in his hand, as though studying it for clues.

"It's okay to cry," he said finally. "But it's also okay not to cry."

Ann nodded. She thought that she wouldn't cry, not then in front of Mr. Small. She had cried a lot—when she got into the back of the OPP cruiser on the side of the highway, again when they drove past the ambulance and the other police cruisers, and she caught a glimpse of the van, or its underside, exposed obscenely to the passing road. . . . When she saw Philip, on a body board, wheeling through the emergency room. She couldn't even talk to him, or see him properly.

"I was talking to your Nan just now," said Mr. Small. "She's a really nice lady, isn't she?"

Ann nodded. Her Nan was a very nice lady, she guessed.

"She loves you and Philip a great deal."

"I love her," Ann whispered.

"That's good," said Mr. Small. "But Ann, can you tell me why you don't want to go with her?"

Ann thought about how to phrase it.

"Are you afraid?"

Ann nodded.

Mr. Small set down the block, slid it to one side, as though it were actually a barrier between them. "Now you can be honest with me," he said. "Are you afraid of your Nan?"

The legs of Ann's chair made a groan as she pushed her chair back, and she shook her head. She saw where this was going, and it wasn't what she meant. Mr. Small thought Ann was afraid that Nan was . . . maybe a pedophile, or hit her and Philip, or drank too much and said things.

"That's not it," said Ann. "I'm not afraid of her. I'm afraid . . . for her."

"Can you explain that?"

Ann sat still again. She could explain it, sure. She could explain that Nan might find herself driving back to Barrie with Ann in the back seat of the car, and how the windows might frost over and the snows might come, and how a great wind might lift the front wheels of the car off the road, and flip it around, and kill Nan too and maybe Ann and maybe Philip too. She could tell Mr. Small that Nan might go down to her basement and check on the furnace one night a week from now, and find the door to the basement locked behind her, and then see . . . see it, just an instant before it got to her.

Yeah. She couldn't tell Mr. Small any of that. He'd think she was crazy. Maybe she was—or maybe it would be best to be treated that way: taken away to a hospital where she could be filled with drugs and just shut down.

Ann sighed, and looked up. Mr. Small met her eyes, blinked twice—expecting an answer.

"I'm bad luck," she said. "Really bad luck. I'm afraid . . . it'll rub off on Nan."

Mr. Small nodded. He actually seemed to relax. He set back, and pushed the blocks even farther to the edges of the table. Like he was clearing the very last of the debris between the two of them, and they could just level with one another. He tucked his chin down.

"It's easy to think that. Take it all on yourself. Sometimes, that's how we make sense of things, when really terrible things happen. But you have to know, Ann. You really had nothing to do with what happened in the car. It wasn't your fault."

Ann looked at him and thought about that, and thought about how it might be true. It wasn't her fault—any more than it was when light bulbs burned and exploded, or a wind came up and lifted the surface of the lake into the sky. It was the Insect at work; not her. The best she could do was control it—keep it dormant. That was what she'd learned at the lodge. That was what she did every night, when she listened to her tapes and whispered the mnemonics that Dr. Sunderland had made her memorize. She was the gatekeeper, and the Insect was the wicked one—the mischief-maker.

The murderer, now.

And yet. Ann *was* the gatekeeper. She had kept that gate shut for many years, following the instructions that had been given her. She'd been diligent; a good student. A good girl, Dr. Sunderland had told her.

Had she gone bad? Had she betrayed the virtue she'd held on to so strongly? These thoughts tugged at her, as Mr. Small sat across from her, surrounded by blocks of wood that, she knew, could fly into the air at once and pummel him bloody.

Had she gone bad? Or had she simply opened her eyes—seen what Dr. Sunderland and the clinic provided, were nothing, really . . . nothing but a placebo.

"I know it wasn't my fault," said Ann finally. "But I need to have some help."

"Of course you do," said Mr. Small. "We can talk as long as you want."

"Thank you."

They sat quietly for another moment. Mr. Small asked her if she wanted to pray, if that was maybe what she meant, and Ann shook her head firmly.

"No," she said. "But I do need to talk. Can I please call a friend?"

She could, of course.

iv

Christmas made it easier.

Ryan and his folks had just finished dinner. His father answered after the first ring. He was a little tipsy, his words slurring a bit. He called for Ryan in a sing-song, "It's a gir-ul, Ry. Anything you want to share?"

And as the phone clattered, and for a moment Ann could hear the din of a Christmas at home: glass clinking—a squeal, from some baby who'd stopped in—condescending laughter from a crowd of adults. And then it all cut off, as Ryan took the phone, sheltered it from the noise of the room.

"Hello?"

"Hey, Ry," said Ann.

"Ann?"

"Yeah."

"Uh, Merry Christmas."

"Yeah."

"What's up?"

Ann didn't, quite, get the nerve to tell him everything then. She wasn't crying—she was feeling pretty strong, for the moment. But telling Ryan the story would crack all that. More important, she wouldn't be able to rely on Ryan to do what she needed to have done—right away, really, as soon as possible. Mr. Small was sitting at the low table, surrounded by all those blocks, and her Nan was out in the waiting lounge . . . waiting, to take care of her.

"I need to talk to your Aunt," she said. "Is she there?"

"Ye-e-es," said Ryan, taking a what-the-fuck tone. "She's staying the week for Christmas. How come?"

"I think," said Ann, "that I need one of those exorcisms."

"What?"

"I'm not safe," said Ann. "The placebo failed."

The Devils' Advocate

i

"I don't want to fly back."

"That's understandable. Sure. I can't say I'd want to get into the air after something like that. We can put you on a train, if you like."

Ann shook her head. Carolyn waited, a question in her eye.

"I'd like to rent a car. Drive back," she said.

"Do you think that's a good idea? You've suffered a head injury. And . . . a terrible loss. It's days back to Toronto."

If that's where I was going, Ann thought but didn't say. She looked away. Carolyn was a tall woman with dyed-blonde hair. She had a deep tan that made Ann think about Michael's lobster-red sunburn, and that made her think of the terrible fire in Tobago, and that drew her to the plane, the spinning cabin . . . Michael, spinning.

"I'll sign a waiver," said Ann. "Rent me a car. I'll sign a waiver that absolves you from any liability." She met Carolyn's eye. "That should be worth something for you. For the airline."

Something passed over Carolyn's eyes then, and later, Ann wondered if the Air Canada representative wasn't considering just that—absolving her bosses of all responsibility.

It passed quickly. Carolyn smiled gently, shook her head. "You shouldn't make offers like that," she said, "without your lawyer."

"What lawyer?" asked Ann.

"Your family isn't here yet but they've sent your lawyer along," she said.

Ann shook her head, as if to shake the words into place; as it was, they were a jumble. "Family?"

Carolyn looked at her, nodded, and as though she had only then made up her mind. "Mrs. Voors, I don't think we should be talking any details right now. Your lawyer called us and said he'd be here in an hour."

"What family?"

"We'll make sure you're not disturbed," said Carolyn. "You've been through so much. You just have a quiet talk with your lawyer. No one'll bother you."

"What lawyer?" said Ann again, but Carolyn was already out the door.

ii

His name was John Hirsch. He was a partner in a Miami firm that had three other names besides his on the business card. He was not tall—Ann guessed maybe five-five—and he was losing his hair, although not excessively; studiously untidy tufts of dark brown hair colonized the crown of his head. But he was fit and hard, and tanned like Carolyn. He wore a light grey business suit and a tie the colour of arterial blood.

Hirsch had to explain it twice. He was on retainer with a local friend of Ian Rickhardt's. Ian had called in a favour to engage Hirsch's services for Ann.

Hah, thought Ann. The "family" that Carolyn had spoken of. Family. *Right*.

He crossed his hands over his middle, lowered his head. "Before we begin, please let me offer my condolences, Mrs. Voors."

She nodded thanks. He leaned forward, for just an instant, looking into her eyes as though he was looking for something.

"Do you mind if I sit?"

Ann pointed toward a little armchair.

"I don't want to seem ungrateful," she said as he sat. "But I need to ask you . . . What do I need a lawyer for?"

"Hopefully not very much," said Hirsch. "If all goes well, not much more than an advocate. An agent. We're helping deal with the return of your husband's remains. That's pretty straightforward—but it's nothing you want to spend your time dealing with, I'm guessing."

"Thank you," she said. "But that's not all, I'm guessing."

"No," said Hirsch. "There are troubles you might encounter in the next while. I'll see you through 'em. Just follow my lead."

"I don't want to sue the airline."

"Didn't say you should, although under other circumstances I might consider it. No, the problem is a bit more fundamental. You don't know it yet, I imagine . . . but you're on the roster to be interviewed by the FAA."

"The—"

"Federal Aviation Authority. They're looking into this flight, the incident, and particularly your husband's . . ."

"Death," she said, more sharply than she'd have liked. Hirsch smiled, but his eyelids fluttered strangely. He reached for a box of tissues next to the bed and held it out to Ann. She waved it away. He shrugged.

"Right now we're doing everything we can to get you off that roster. And maybe we'll succeed. But here's the thing. You were found unconscious right outside the restroom. Along with a flight attendant. I haven't spoken to her, or seen her testimony . . . but I'm willing to bet she's reported that she found you there before she was struck unconscious. Right at the door of the restroom, with your husband inside. There will be questions arising from that. We need to work on how you'll answer them."

"How do you mean? I went to the restroom because I was worried about my husband. It seems pretty—" and Hirsch raised an eyebrow, and at once, she got it.

"Oh. They'll think I was in there with him."

"By the evidence," said Hirsch, "someone was."

"And they'll think that it was me," said Ann, nodding, "doing, what do they call it? The Mile High club?"

"That's already in play," he said. "The Miami Herald has a story online today with an unnamed source suggesting that's what might've happened."

"Wait a minute—there are news stories?"

"Mrs. Voors," said Hirsch, "this is a news story. Flight 1205 came *this* close to crashing rather than emergency landing at Miami International Airport. A Canadian lawyer with a prominent firm died returning from his honeymoon. The cause is mysterious . . . or at least, a little scandalous. There is huge exposure on this. And that's why . . . why everyone is concerned, that should it become necessary that you are interviewed, you might respond . . . intemperately."

"Why would I do that?" asked Ann.

"You tell me."

At that, for the first time since she'd regained consciousness, and learned about the death of Michael Voors, her husband of less than a month, Ann felt her throat constrict, and tears well in her eyes.

Were those tears for her husband? He had pulled her from the flames in Tobago—made good on vows to be by her side until death—and she had been unable to reciprocate. He had died and she had lived. And the life they'd had planned, such as they had planned it . . . it was just gone.

And there was the shame—the idea that the newspapers in Miami were making sniggering insinuations about Mr. and Mrs. Voors, fucking in a restroom while Flight 1205 nearly crashed—she must've been a *little slut*; he must have been *insatiable*; they both must have been *on something.*

And then there was this:

He's raping me.

"That's good, Mrs. Voors," said Hirsch. He produced a tissue from the box. "Let it all out."

You don't want that, she thought, and before she could stop herself, she said aloud, "You don't want it all out, Mr. Hirsch. Neither does Mr. Rickhardt."

More of the fast blinking. Hirsch got up, and went to the door, cracked it open. He peered down the hallway, and shut the door, firmly. It seemed that in doing so the temperature in the room dropped noticeably. Ann felt the hairs on her arms rise, and her tears freeze. A terrible thought occurred to her.

She didn't know this man. He had a business card that had his name on it, and he'd identified himself as a lawyer and he'd dropped Ian Rickhardt's name. But that in itself was no assurance. And she was alone with him in a room where he had shut the door.

He smiled, as though he'd divined her anxiety, and put both hands up in an "I surrender" gesture to reassure her.

"Mrs. Voors," he said, "I'm on your side."

Are you? she wondered. But this time, she said nothing.

He sat back down in the chair beside the bed, rocked back and forth in the seat.

"There are a range of things that can happen. This can be very serious—you could, if you play this foolishly, implicate yourself in your husband's death. I suspect that my counterparts with the airline would be very pleased, faced with evidence that you and he behaved recklessly and their crew were perfect professionals. Now look—I know that you didn't. Like I said—on your side."

"But you're working for Ian Rickhardt."

"He's paying the bill," said Hirsch. "But Mrs. Voors—may I call you Ann?—rest assured. My only interest is seeing you out of this unscathed. At least, as unscathed as possible. Because there is another thing that might emerge. And I think we both know what that is."

"Mr. Hirsch, please sit back. Just a bit."

"Of course." He had been leaning forward in his chair. He rocked back now, and regarded her.

"Now," said Ann, "what do we both know?"

Hirsch didn't answer immediately.

"What do we both know?" she said again.

Hirsch's eyes darted away from her, to a corner of the room. He rubbed his arm and looked back at her. His face was flushed, and his eyes widened, almost hopefully.

"It's here, isn't it?" he said.

Ann sat up and pushed herself against the headboard. Somewhere at her shoulder was a button to summon a nurse—although she hadn't used it since her arrival, not being that kind of patient.

"Yes," Hirsch said, "you can do that. Call in a nurse. But you remember what happened on the plane, don't you? When it came out. Do you really want to expose a nurse to that? Do you want it to get out?"

Ann found the button. It dangled from a wire that was velcroed to the headboard. Her finger brushed it.

"What do you call it now?" he said. "The Spider?"

"That's an arachnid."

"Ah hah. Right. The Insect."

"The Insect."

"And it's here."

"It is."

Ann dropped the help button. The exchange had happened fast and cold, and it had hauled her down, as down a staircase, as into a cellar. How had he drawn it out of her? Was this a trick he used on the stand?

Those were questions that circled for just a moment. Because the ugly answer they circled was obvious, and terrible in its implications.

He knew about the Insect. She hadn't told him anything. John Hirsch had come to her room, on retainer from Ian Rickhardt, after the Insect had very nearly crashed a plane and killed her husband, and he'd brought that knowledge here with him.

And now, Ann found herself agreeing with him. Whether the Insect was emerging or not right now, calling the nurse wasn't the best use of her time.

"What is Ian's, um, *friend* really paying you to do?" she asked.

"Oh, just what I've represented. Ian wants to make sure you get out of this and back to Canada safe and sound. He wants to minimize any fuss with the FAA, and would like the news stories to stay away from him. But fundamentally, he wants to make certain that you're looked after."

"But that's not your whole game," she said.

"Quite so, Mrs. Voors," he said. "I'm working for Ian; I'm paid for by his friends. And I . . . well, I sometimes take my own counsel. And Mrs. Voors—there is another option. We might be able to avoid the FAA altogether. At least for a short time. My firm has a relationship with a private clinic outside St. Augustine. It is used by several plastic surgeons in the Greater Miami area as a recovery facility sometimes. Right now, it's empty. I can, I believe, have you moved there—and arrange a later date for your interview."

"Why would I do that?"

"Recovering from the grief at the loss of your husband?"

Did Hirsch smirk for an instant? *Prick*, Ann thought, *he did.*

"That's one reason. The other reason, the real reason, of course, is only obvious to you and me."

"The Insect. Which you apparently know all about."

Hirsch nodded. "It's freezing in here," he said. "Colder than south Florida air-conditioning. Didn't you notice?"

"As you mention it."

"Yeah, you girls never notice that on your own. You're too used to it. All those spooky drafts . . ." Hirsch got up and stretched, hooking his thumbs in his belt loops. He walked around to the foot of her bed, and picked up a green plastic bedpan. "What's this doing in the middle of the floor? I bet this wasn't here when your Air Canada rep was here talking to you. And—" he craned his neck, to look at the small washroom off the hospital room "—I swear, the light wasn't on in there when I came in."

"Stop it."

Hirsch looked at her, eyebrows raised. "Mrs. Voors, I tell you honestly—right here, there's nothing I can do to stop it. Any more than you can. Isn't that right?"

Ann felt tears welling up, her throat constricting. "Fuck off."

Hirsch shook his head. "Don't think so. I think, though, that we can calm this thing down a notch, if we keep from the potty mouth. Isn't that right?" The last sentence he spoke at the ceiling, as though something hovered there. Possibly something did.

Without looking down from the ceiling, Hirsch continued.

"I gather that Ian Rickhardt visited you on your honeymoon. There are stories going around, about that visit. The terrible fire. Might I say—" he looked at her now "—Mr. Rickhardt reported enjoying himself terribly at the fire. He should have; he went down specifically for that purpose."

Ann thought again about what she'd seen: Ian Rickhardt, turning slowly in the air as the Insect rampaged through the guest house. The expression he wore on his face . . . rapturous. Orgasmic.

And the words that the Insect conveyed to her, on the plane . . .

He's raping me.

Ann felt the tightness in her throat well up, and this time, Hirsch didn't bother with the tissue. He set the bedpan in her lap.

It caught nearly all the vomit.

They called a nurse in for that. Ann smiled, and thanked her, and when she asked what had brought it on, Ann said she didn't know.

"Well you've been through a lot," said the nurse. "I'll tell the doctor."

She pulled away the sheet that had caught a few flecks of the vomit, and pulled a new sheet from a cart.

"You figure you two are about done here?" she said.

Ann had looked at Hirsch, then back at her and said, "No. We still have some more things to discuss."

The nurse closed the door. Ann thought she heard something click in its latch, roughly, as though the lock were being asked to do something it had never done before.

Hirsch reached into his jacket pocket, and removed a small stainless steel hip flask. "Scotch," he said. "I don't know if your stomach is up for it—"

Ann took the flask before he'd even properly offered it, and drew a long swallow. It burned down her throat but her belly welcomed it like an old friend.

They sat quietly for a moment. A breeze crossed the room, slow and cool, as though it were coming from a distant place to the north. The fluorescent bar over the bed flickered, ever so slightly. Hirsch started, and looked sharply at his shoulder, as though he had been touched there. Ann offered him the flask back, and he took it, drew a mouthful.

"What's it doing?" he finally asked.

"It might not be doing anything," said Ann. "It might not even be here. After a while, your imagination can do almost everything the Insect can. It might be getting ready for something big. It never does the same thing twice. But . . . I don't think it's going to be bad."

Hirsch screwed the cap back onto the flask and slipped it back into his pocket. Ann rubbed her temple; the whiskey was good, but she felt the beginning of a headache, and that was probably partly to blame. Still, she wouldn't say no to another slug. Or three.

"Ian Rickhardt raped it, I think," she said. "I think my husband—Michael did too."

"I think you're right," he said softly. "That's what it's for, as far as they're concerned. That's why they trained it, all those years: to be unable to resist them. I hope it understands that's not what I'm going to do."

Ann shivered as the sheets of her bed billowed up her thighs, an icy wind manifesting underneath them.

"I hope so too," she said, and looked at him. "What *are* you going to do, Mr. Hirsch?"

"Nothing it doesn't want me to."

"You'll understand if I'm skeptical about that." Ann looked around. The chill seemed to be leaving the room. Nothing that she could see was in motion. "You'll understand if the Insect might be."

"Is that meant as a threat?"

Ann shrugged. Inwardly, she tallied it up. They'd never met, she and this lawyer, who said he worked for Ian Rickhardt—who hadn't so much as telephoned. He knew about the Insect. He wanted to take her somewhere safe.

Where no one else could see her, or find her.

And he knew about the Insect. And the only living people who knew about the Insect besides herself were her brother, who hadn't spoken in a decade, and Eva, who was down with a stroke.

Even Michael . . .

Well, if he knew anything, he wouldn't be saying. Not where he was.

"What are you smiling at?"

She hadn't realized she had been. She blinked.

"Look," said Hirsch, "I think I've got a bit of an idea of what you're going through. You're not the first woman that's been caught in Rickhardt's mill. It's like you're cut off from a piece of yourself. Things don't connect like they should, isn't that right? You're out of joint."

"What are you talking about?"

"I'll lay it on the line," said Hirsch. "You probably have no idea—but you're well-known in certain circles. The . . . thing that you've got following you around, maybe inside of you. It's a commodity to men like Rickhardt, in those circles. Do you understand?"

Ann thought she did. "That's how you know about the Insect, isn't it? Because you're a part of those circles too."

Hirsch puffed out his cheeks and exhaled in a silent whistle.

"Lay it all on the line, I guess?" He grimaced. "Yes. I have been."

"And you're not now."

"Something like that."

"And you want to protect me from your old friends. No. Not me. You want to protect the Insect. Keep it for yourself."

"That—"

"—is exactly what you want to do."

Hirsch looked away, and his shoulders hunched a bit—like a preteen boy caught with porno. It was as good as an admission.

Ann went on. "You were never nervous about the prospect of the Insect coming out, were you? You were . . . you were excited. I've seen that before. You can't wait to see how it goes; you can barely hold yourself back—"

"Mrs. Voors," he said, "you've got—"

"Well Mr. Hirsch, let me clue you in. If you were to meet my Insect in the washroom back there, it wouldn't go well. It would smash your head into the toilet. It would bend your spine to the breaking point. It would bend it *past* that point. It would kill you. If you were lucky." Ann slid away from Hirsch as she spoke, until finally she was standing, on the opposite side of the bed. "But you might like that. You might just like that," she said.

"Mrs. Voors," he began, and she cut in:

"Stop calling me Mrs. Voors."

Hirsch opened his mouth to say something else, but the breath caught in his throat. He half-stood—or at least that was how it seemed at first. As Ann watched, the lapels of his suit-jacket rose higher, as though they were tugging him. His arms spread, like wings starting to unfurl—and as the front of the jacket spread, Ann could see the fabric of his shirt creep up his chest, as though pulled by invisible fingers.

Ann stepped away so her back was against the drapes. The room was freezing now; she could see her breath in front of her face. She reached behind the drape—the sunlight through the window was warm on her hand, nourishingly so. She wanted to pull herself behind the curtains, bask in the Florida sunlight. But she couldn't look away.

Hirsch was bending backwards, his hips thrust outward. His belt snaked through the loops of his trousers, slipping finally to the floor.

"Oh," he said, in a soft, little-boy voice. "Oh thank you."

How like Michael he was, then. Not Michael in the aircraft, spinning in the small space . . . No. Ann was struck how similar he was to that first date—lunch, on top of Toronto. Watching the salt and pepper shakers dance across the table.

Michael Voors' dream come true. How hadn't she seen it?

"Are you enjoying yourself?"

"Hmm?" Hirsch spared her a glance through slit eyes. "You can't imagine," and he gasped as his trousers shifted a small rotation, making a frosted mist in the air in front of him.

"That's why I'm asking you," said Ann. She couldn't imagine, obviously. Through the whole of her courtship—her marriage . . . she hadn't imagined. She hadn't even *seen*. "What do you get out of it?"

His eyes cracked open, just a little wider, and regarded her lecherously. "Do you . . . want to come see?"

The waist of Hirsch's trousers was stretching out, the button undoing, the fabric sliding down his hips. They were muscular, tan, and glistened with sweat. And he was hard. She did look away, and although she fought it, crept a few inches farther behind the curtain. She looked outside sidelong, squinting in the afternoon sun as it bleached out the air-conditioning units on the rooftop below her window.

"Because you can," he whispered. "Rickhardt . . . your poor late husband . . . never had any use for their wives. Their vessels. That's what they call you, you know. A vessel. Because it's all the 'geist for them. But . . ." he paused, and cried out softly, but Ann didn't look to see what had caused him to do that ". . . we're not all like that. Some of us love our women. Some of us . . . see the godly in you."

Ann's sun-warm hand clenched into a hard fist. "Thank you, Mr. Hirsch," she said.

"You should come over here, Ann. You haven't ever felt your own . . . the Insect's touch, have you?"

"What's it like?"

"It's . . . it's like death."

"How genuinely tempting."

A chuckle. "Not death. But . . . you're familiar with the term 'petit mort'? Little death?"

"I know the phrase." Ann's fist pressed against the hot glass. "So it's like an orgasm."

"Like an orgasm. Yeah. But a genuine little death. When the 'geist touches flesh—in the way it's been trained . . . it doesn't just touch flesh. Goes straight . . . straight to the soul, straight to the Infinite. When you come . . . you come—into *being*."

"Back up," said Ann. "The way it's been trained?"

"Well-trained. Yours . . . the Insect . . ." He grunted—low in his throat, almost lower than he should have been able to do. "The best we've done."

Ann shut her eyes and swallowed hard. She thought again about Michael—sweet, unremarkable Michael Voors—and how she had met and married him without question, even as sex with him hardly brought her to orgasm, never mind into *being*; even as Ian Rickhardt came into their home and bullied and belittled her, and Michael did nothing; even through fire on the shores of Tobago and onto an airplane back to Toronto, one she had no business boarding, so her husband could find his *being* a mile in the air. . . .

The Insect wasn't the only one who'd been well-trained.

"Come on out, Ann," said Hirsch. "Taste the Infinite."

Ann clutched the curtain . . . the sun was blessedly hot. She froze in its heat, immobile.

"Get out of here, Mr. Hirsch," she said.

He didn't answer this time. Outside, face pressed against the glass, Ann could hear the faint wailing of an ambulance siren. Something in the belly of the hospital's HVAC shifted, and Ann felt a rumbling vibration through her forehead.

"Get out," she said again, and when there was still nothing, she pulled herself away from the window, and looked to see what depravity the Insect had inflicted on her new lawyer.

"Oh." She barely whispered the exclamation, and stumbled over to her bed.

John Hirsch was back in his chair. His trousers were buckled around his waist; his belt through every loop. His hands, strong and lean, were on the armrests. His eyelids were slack again; his mouth pulled down on the right-hand side. Saliva dribbled down his chin.

Ann took a shivering breath, and reached for the button to signal the nurse. Her thumb hesitated over it for just an instant before she pressed. She got back into her bed and pulled up the sheets—and only then, began to scream.

Mister Sleepy

i

9:55 p.m.

Ann: Hey

Jeanie: Hey grlfrnd! How was the honeymoon?

Ann: Bad. U didnt hear?

Jeanie: Hear what?

Ann: Michael died.

Jeanie: OMG! I didnt!

Ann: *http://www.miamiherald.com/2013/11/03/307680604/1-dead-after-727-forced-down-in-freak-storm.html*

Jeanie: Oh my God. I saw that on CNN. I didn't know . . . had no idea it was you.

Ann: It was yes.

Jeanie: You home safe?

Ann: Not exactly. Check these out:

http://www.miamiherald.com/2013/11/05/3080609/feds-probe-death-of-canadian-lawyer.html

http://www.miamiherald.com/2012/11/05/3080610/mile-high-club-more-than-a-myth.html

http://www.miamiherald.com/2012/11/06/3080612/mile-high-widow's-lawyer-succumbs-to-stroke-in-meeting.html

10:05 p.m.

Jeanie: Oh God, grlfrnd. You home safe now?

Ann: On the road. Soon as I could, checked out and rented a car. I'm in

10:07 p.m.

Jeanie: Ann?

Ann: I'm in Alabama. Sorry. Thought I shouldnt say. But doesnt matter. Not like I was being charged with anything. Driving home off highways. Staying in motel.

Jeanie: Driving home? Glfrnd, thats a long haul. Why not fly? Take train?

Ann: No public transit. Just me.

Jeanie: You sure that safe?

Ann: Safer travelling alone. Nothing will happen if I travel alone.

Jeanie: Why would anything happen if you werent? U ok?

Ann: Im ok.

Ann: Im not ok. Obviously.

Jeanie: Im sorry. Michaels gone. Of course ur not ok. Didnt have time to get to know him but he seems like a great guy.

Jeanie: ***Seemed***.

10:15 p.m.

Ann: Michael was a liar.

Jeanie: Ok.

Ann: He never wanted to be with me.

Jeanie: Did he cheat on u?

Ann: Yes. Not in the way you think.

Jeanie: Was it some internet thing? Did u catch him in a chatroom? I was with a girl who was into RP, some real weird shit. With strange Dudes. Dumped her ass when I found out.

Ann: Good 4 u.

Jeanie: That what he was doing?

10:25 p.m.

Jeanie: Ann? Grlfrnd? U there?

10:29 p.m.

Ann: Sorry. Hard to describe in chat.

Jeanie: But he was cheating.

Ann: Worse. Dont want to get too specific here. Google keeps these things recorded.

Jeanie: Dont buy the Do No Evil mission statement, hmmmm?

Ann: lol

Jeanie: Me neither.

Ann: Grlfrnd, I need u to do me favour.

Jeanie: Ok.

Ann: call up lesley.

Jeanie: BIG FAVOUR!

Ann: dont want to call her myself.

Jeanie: U 2 have a fight?

Ann: i need u to get her to check on philip.

Jeanie: y dont u just have that rickard dude check? Hes helping.

Ann: no.

Jeanie: y not? lesley & I barely spoke at ur wedding. really awkward.

10:44 p.m.

Ann: i really need you to. need u to erase this chat when done. cant call lesley. U need 2. tell her to check on philip. pls.

Jeanie: U arent ok. Where in alabama are u?

Ann: just pls do this.

Jeanie: OK. Where he staying?

Ann: Hang on.

Ann opened another tab and googled the Hollingsworth centre, copied the link into their Gchat, and when Jeanie asked again, once again didn't say exactly where she was: in the "business centre" of a woodsy little motel complex outside of Mobile. The midsized car she'd rented on her credit card was parked outside her cabin. Her luggage, filled with honeymoon clothes and toiletries and such was still in the trunk. As she evaded another question from Jeanie, it was finally sinking in that although she had left the hospital in Miami with only mild protest from the airline, and the intensity of the FAA investigation suggested by Hirsch had not materialized—she ought to be taking matters more seriously.

The fact was, she was on the run.

The last call she made on her mobile phone was to Krenk and Associates. That was outside Tallahassee. After a short, teary conversation with Krenk's assistant Noah—during which she assured him she'd take as much time as she needed and he told her to see that she did—Ann popped the battery out and tossed it and the phone into a drive-through garbage bin. She was staying off interstates and taking secondary roads as it was, but her knuckles whitened as police cars drove by—and then as she thought about it more, and realized that the police might not be her problem—her breath stopped when she observed the same car behind her for more than a few minutes.

She stopped at an ATM in Gainesville to get a cash advance on her credit card, and then, although it would have made more sense for her to continue north, she cut west through Alabama—and found this motel, this sort-of motel, that was willing to take cash and no credit card as an advance on a room for the night. She was exhausted, she explained, which was true, and then lied: she told them her name was Ann Brunt, and she made up a confused story about a stolen wallet at a diner down the road—a wallet that didn't contain a bank roll of mad money she kept in her pocket. The place was family run, had the look of being off the grid—she'd been banking it was the kind of place that would let her do these things.

And after a while, Ann established that it was, and they understood, and even let her use the "business centre," which was really just an adjunct to the front office with a couple of old PCs hooked up to the old router. As Jeanie signed off, Ann cleared the cache and shut the browser. She sat a moment, rubbed her temples and shut her eyes.

"Y'okay in there?"

Ann looked up and made herself smile. "I am," she said. The owner's name was Penny. She was middle-aged, a little on the heavy side with short-cropped blonde hair and cheeks rosy like there was a chill, which there wasn't tonight, particularly. Ann liked her.

When Ann had come in, she was met at the desk by a whip-thin man who wasn't at all comfortable not seeing a credit card.

But Penny had set him straight with a few questions. "How much we charge a night? She got that much there on the counter? Okay, then what's your problem?"

The man turned out to be Roy, her husband and co-owner of the place, and as it turned out, not the final word on payment policy. Also, not the one who took the overnight desk duty.

"Been a hard time, losin' your wallet like that," said Penny as Ann packed up at the computer. "Lucky thing you got your driver's licence and all."

"Lucky," she said. The word felt funny, saying it.

"Okay. Well you need anything else?"

"Think I'm okay," she said, and Penny nodded.

"You don't mind if I help you clear the cache," she said. "You missed a couple steps."

Ann blinked. "Sure," she said, and Penny scooted a chair over, and laughed.

"Don't worry—I wasn't snooping on your chat. But I got a feeling you don't want to leave a trail of breadcrumbs right now."

"I—"

"Shush," said Penny. "Wasn't snoopin', but couldn't help noticing you sobbing as that chat went on. Brought back memories. I been where you are."

Ann thought she might not have been there exactly, but she didn't say that. "Thank you," she said.

"He do that to you?" Penny motioned to the bandage on Ann's head. Ann shook her head no.

"An accident," she said. "But thank you."

Penny nodded as she clicked through preferences windows on the browser.

"Mine hit me," she said. "Not this one—he's husband number two. But husband number one—he had a temper. And he had his views on things."

"I'm sorry," said Ann.

"Don't be. He's gone now. But it sure wasn't easy making it that way. I had to run off in the night—took his truck, so he wouldn't follow me. 'Course he called the cops, like I knew he would. So I ditched it next town over. Hopped on a bus, headin' to Mobile, which decided where I was going."

Penny closed the browser and shut off the machine like she was folding a set of towels.

"But oh, I was scared. Thought I might wind up in jail, or worse, back home. With him. And I did at least five stupid things that'd make it easy for him to track me. I was jumpin' at shadows."

"I know about that."

"I know you do," said Penny.

Ann looked at Penny, Penny looked right back. Ann wondered for a moment: did they have her picture in the Miami papers? Did they put that picture on CNN, or on the internet on some blog that innkeepers in rural Alabama looked at to while away the day? Had Penny seen her picture—worked out that she was that "mile high" widow from Florida?

"Easy, girl," said Penny. "I understand, that's all I'm sayin'. If you like, I know some numbers of folks in Mobile—they can set you up someplace safe, where you can think things through. Y'aren't alone."

Or not, Ann thought. She smiled, weakly and said thank you to Penny.

"Things aren't like that," she said. "But thanks. I've been on the road for a long time, and it's better that I just get some rest. You and Roy are a real godsend for that."

"Sure," said Penny. "I apologize for intruding. It's just that when you been through something, you start seein' it in everyone else."

"You're a good person," said Ann.

"I am," she said. "And in that spirit, here's a word of advice."

"Yes?"

"Park that rental car you got around the side of your cabin."

"I'm sorry—"

"Don't apologize," she said. "It's harder to see from the road. Just move it, or I can get Roy to if you like. Then you'll have done one less stupid thing than I did."

ii

The motel was called the Rosedale Arms, and it, like the sign that advertised it on the road, was ticky-tacky cute.

The sign was lettered in sweeping cursive script, all meticulously cut out of a wooden board with a mitre saw, and painted rose red on the whitewashed background. The cabins had the same colour scheme, brilliant red on the eaves and white on the side. They were tiny, but well enough appointed—and they were set reasonably far apart from one another.

That was another reason that Ann had picked this place. She didn't want to be too close to any other travellers as she tried to hold it together through the night.

There wouldn't be many in harm's way this evening. As she crossed the grounds from the office, she saw only one car: an old-model station wagon, parked by a cabin three away from hers. Ann hoped that might be safe enough. Of course if she did things right, it'd be safe enough next door to her.

She popped open her trunk and moved her bags to the front door to the cabin. Then, she did as Penny'd told her, started the car, backed it up, turned it to the side and tucked it around the side, nudging it up to the front of the propane tank.

As she shut the ignition and the lights off, the little girl standing there waved at her.

Ann sat frozen in the dark. There was a moon out, not full, but casting just enough light to see her.

The girl was wearing a sweatshirt and jeans cut off at the knee. She was black-haired. She was standing by the propane tank. Not smiling.

Ann opened the driver-side door.

"Hello?"

There was no answer; really, Ann hadn't expected one. The Insect had been quiet since she'd left the hospital. It had let her drive, let her do her business, given her the time she needed to deal with things.

If it manifested now—well, no apology necessary.

Ann stepped out of the car. The air was warm and rich with the sweet smell of the trees, a faint tang of vegetable rot.

Nothing moved outside; not even the cicadas sang.

Ann drew her fingers together in fists and held them at her side.

"Fine," said Ann finally. "I'm going to bed."

She shut the car door and locked it, and went around to the front of the cabin. She didn't check the back seat of the car to see if the girl had gotten in there now; she didn't look over her shoulder as she opened the door. She didn't bother to check corners in her room, or make a note to see if anything had moved, seemingly of its own devices, while she was outside.

Almost a day ago, the Insect had nearly killed a lawyer from Miami, just a day after it had killed Ann's husband.

But Ann was starting to work it out. As far as her own safety was concerned, the Insect wasn't a problem. It was the people around her who were at risk—who so often came to harm.

The cabin had two rooms; a bedroom-kitchen, and a bathroom off to the side. There was a TV, old CRT-style, and a little kitchen with a microwave and a small fridge. Three lights, two on either side of the queen-sized bed. One in the middle of the ceiling. In the middle of the fan. There was an air-conditioner built into the wall. There were a couple of chairs and a little table. But aside from those, there was little that wasn't nailed down.

Ann lay down on the bed. She shut her eyes, and descended the ladder of colours that put her in the place where she had thought things were safe, without realizing . . .

For her, everywhere was safe but there.

"I'm here to talk to you, if you want to," said Ann into the unformed dark.

That was how it was, now; since the hospital, since the airplane, she hadn't been able to properly imagine the tower, the place where the Insect might be held at bay. It was an imaginative exercise from the get-go. And now, Ann's imagination felt used up; or at least, the images she'd used to hold things together, drawn from her fantasy Dungeons & Dragons world, were just too childish to do the work.

Maybe that was it.

Perhaps the darkness was empty, perhaps not. When she tried entering it, during little rest stops on the way, she certainly imagined her share of ghosts. Her mother visited her once, clad in a fleece vest and a pair of blue jeans, her eyes difficult to discern. She asked Ann if she were happy, over and over, so much so that Ann found herself speaking the question aloud to the empty car. "Are you happy? Are you happy? Really happy?"

The ghost of Michael sometimes made his presence known. Ann saw him in the shadows, balancing a saltshaker on the tip of his finger, whistling tunelessly with his back to her, once looking at her directly, idly masturbating as he rocked back and forth. He didn't say anything, and Ann didn't prompt him.

As she lingered in a filling station restroom, Ann thought she might feel the presence of Eva, even though the darkness at that moment was absolute.

Who knew if any of it was real? Eva claimed clairvoyance for herself, but never presumed that was what she was teaching Ann.

When she'd agreed to help Ann through the loss of her parents—when Ann had confided in her, about the Insect—Eva had made it plain.

You're letting this thing rule you, that's the problem. It thinks it runs things. For a while, the exercises you learned from those other people did the trick. Now, it's found a way around them. So. We've got to find a way to tell it to be quiet, and keep it quiet when you're not talking to it. So let's play a game, she said.

And that's what the game was—another exercise for gaining control. Ann thought these manifestations were nothing but a signal that she'd lost control; pieces of her unconscious, coming up to talk to her like waking dreams.

She had to get past that. She called out into the dark again: "I'm right here. Talk to me, please."

There was a rustling, a squeaking of wheels—the sound of a sheet being drawn.

"Hey, sis."

Ann didn't answer immediately. Once again, the Insect would not speak with her, and her unconscious mind supplied her with a different companion.

This time was the cruelest yet.

"Philip," she said.

"Don't sound so excited to see me."

"I can't see you."

"No? I can see you fine. Must be a trick of the light."

"Or you're a ghost."

"Can't be a ghost. I'm alive and well. Ghosts are the dead."

"Or the Insect."

"Or the Insect, that's true. You think I'm the Insect? Because I can see how you might. Fucker's done everything else to you. To me. Why not fake my voice here in your head?"

"Except the fact that you're saying this, now disproves the assertion."

"Because the Insect would never think of *that*."

"Do you want me to just open my eyes and stop talking to you?"

"It, um, would be the sane thing to do, sis."

Ann found herself smirking.

"All right," he said. "Crazy as she ever was."

Philip's voice was the voice he had at seventeen, at Christmas, as he helped Ann make up names for imaginary cities and speculated about his romantic fortunes and occasionally stuck up for Ann at the dinner table. When his spine was whole and he didn't need help.

When she could rely on him.

"Michael's dead," she said.

"No way."

"They didn't tell you?"

"Folks don't tell me much," said Philip. "I think I must make them uncomfortable."

"Well yeah. He's dead. Pft. No more. Gone—"

"I get it. I'm sorry, sis. I don't know what to say. I remember when Laurie died . . . you remember her, right?"

"Couldn't forget her."

"Well I couldn't talk about it, but it tore me to shreds. I really loved her."

"You were only together for a few months."

"Same as you and Michael. Long enough to know."

Ann considered that. "Not really," she said.

"Wait a second—are you telling me you might not have truly loved Michael Voors?"

"I don't know. I mean, I married him, right?"

"I was there."

"We were good together, right?"

"Uh huh."

"But you know—he betrayed me."

"Did he now?" Philip asked.

"So I don't—"

"What?"

"Are you making fun of me?"

A knowing chuckle drifted out of the darkness. "You're kind of full of shit sometimes, you know that?"

"Oh am I?"

"Oh yes. You are. Look. Michael Voors was a really stand-up guy. I remember when you brought him by the first time. You introduced me, and being who I was—I was just lying there. And Michael leaned over, not too close, and looked me in the eye, and introduced himself again, and not batting a fuckin' eyelid, told me how happy he was to meet me. Those things are always weird—I'd stand, you know, if I could."

"I'm sorry."

"You're forgiven. Now stop interrupting. Michael kept his cool around me, and I admired that. Really polite."

"Just what a girl looks for in a man," said Ann.

"If you say so. I mean, you picked him, right?"

"I'm not so sure that I did, actually."

"Oh really?"

"Really. I think that I didn't have too much say in whether or not I'd marry Michael. I think I was manipulated into it."

"Wow."

"Yeah. After Michael died—well *when* Michael died. I caught him . . ."

"Caught him what?"

Ann struggled. "Doing it."

"Doing it. With who?"

"The Insect."

"Whoa."

"Yeah. Whoa."

"Okay," said Philip. "Let's say, for the sake of argument, I been watching CNN, and I know all about what's been going on in Florida."

"Okay."

"Let's say that I know about this 'mile high' club thing, but was being too polite to bring it up with you."

"Sounds plausible."

"So let me ask you this. Was Michael 'doing it' with your poltergeist during the flight?"

"Yes."

"And was all of that turbulence that nearly brought your plane down—was that all caused when things got . . . how shall we say . . . out of hand?"

"It was."

"Okay. Now are you sure—"

"I don't think it was the first time. And I don't think just him. I think Ian Rickhardt—"

"Asshole."

"Yeah. I think he did it with the polter—the Insect too, in Tobago. I saw it. I wasn't sure what I was seeing. . . ." Ann recalled Rickhardt again, turning in the air outside their villa as the world combusted. "But I think he was. . . having sex with it. And I think the Insect . . . it doesn't like it."

"Hmm. Man fucks ghost. I guess if you can describe it, there's someone who's into it."

"More than one."

"Well there's the late Michael Voors. And Ian Rickhardt. So that's two of them, I guess."

"There's more," said Ann. She told him about Hirsch, and his display in the hospital room.

"Shit."

"He's not dead, but he can't move. He's like—"

"Like me. Yeah. And Auntie Eva—she's had a stroke too. That's interesting, don't you think?"

"You don't think—"

"Well Eva, bless her, had it coming. She was eating poutine before your wedding, as I recall her saying."

Ann bridled. "And Philip—you are okay, aren't you?"

"Right as rain."

"But I mean, you can tell me that. I got Jeanie to talk to Lesley, to check up on you."

"I'm just fine."

"I mean, I'm not just talking to myself, and—"

"Hey, hush. You want this conversation to continue, don't go too far down that road."

"I'm sorry."

"You're into some important shit, here, little sister. You want to keep your eye on the prize."

Ann peered into the darkness. She thought she could discern shapes there—not of Philip, but of some kind of architecture. Were there stairs? A faint shape of a window, covered or dark, by the first landing?

"It's interesting," said Philip. "Hey, remember the innkeepah?"

"Penny?" Ann squinted into the dark; it really was taking some form. "Oh. You mean—"

"Yeah. The camp."

"I do remember the innkeepah. That was Dr. Sunderland, right?"

"He was a creepy old bastard."

"He really helped us, though."

"Yeah. Did you ever let him touch you?"

"Ew. No."

Philip was quiet for a moment, and Ann thought she heard a click—and far off, down a long hallway, a light came on.

"Well, that's good. He touched me."

"What?"

"Not like that. But I remember a needle."

"Philip! What?"

"You were there. We were in the music room—remember?"

"Not too well."

"Mom and dad were sleeping. He had us in there listening to some kind of boring music. Pan pipe or something."

A kind of music started to echo down the hallway. Ann could see that it was lined with doors—but not doors such as she might have found in the Insect's world. It had more of an institutional feel; there were little windows in them, and light filtered dully through them. Maybe they were classrooms. The music came from one of these; it was slow and almost atonal. Ann recalled listening to it as she sat on a beanbag chair in a brighter room, blinds drawn against the snowy winter. Dr. Sunderland sat there cross-legged in a pair of track pants and a sweatshirt, on his own beanbag. Ann was watching, as he fiddled with a wooden box, as Philip sat there beside him, knees up, hands leaning back like he was getting ready to crab-walk.

Dr. Sunderland nodded to Philip, and whispered, "Hold still," as he opened the box and removed a syringe, and when Philip pulled away, he slowly, firmly, took hold of Philip's arm and inserted the needle.

"Yeah," said Ann, "I remember."

"And I was out cold," said Philip. "And it was just you and Dr. Sunderland. And what did he say, Ann?"

"'Now, you're isolated,' I think."

"And then?"

Ann swallowed. "'It's just the three of us.'"

And Sunderland had reached into the box, and pulled out a scalpel, which gleamed in the light. And he let it go, and watched as it floated there in front of him. Philip lay still, but he was still aware—still awake. Dr. Sunderland climbed to his knees, and backed away, and watched as the tiny blade moved through the air, slowly, towards Philip's face.

"It's just the three of us," he said to Ann again. "And Philip."

Ann remembered that much.

"Did he . . . let it cut you?"

"I didn't get cut," said Philip. "I remember that. But the knife came really close to my face. I was terrified. Scared shitless. So were you. I remember you sitting up and yelling for it to stop, and yelling at Dr. Sunderland to make it stop. And you yelled at it. And you yelled at me. And do you remember how Sunderland's face got?"

Ann thought about that. He was biting his lower lip, his shoulders were really stiff, as he watched the knife hover there, closer and closer until the blade caressed Philip's jawline.

"And then he . . . it was like he barked," said Ann. "I remember that. It was like a dog." She frowned. "And you didn't get cut. It was like he called it off. With a bark. That's weird, isn't it?"

Philip chuckled. "Yeah—you were pretty young. So was I. And maybe he did call it off. But you know something? That's what it sounds like. Sometimes. A shout. A bark. It can sound that way . . . when a guy comes."

Ann found herself walking down the corridor now, past that flight of stairs leading up. At the far end, something was heading toward her.

"Ann," said Philip. "Is that you?"

"Coming," said Ann. "He was one of them too. Hirsch said there were a lot of them watching me. And he was the first of them."

"Ann," said Philip. "Ann—I think I'm in trouble." The figure drew closer. It moved very quickly for coming along such a long hallway.

"I need you."

It wasn't Philip, Ann realized.

Any more than the disembodied voice who'd been speaking with her was, telling her things that really—she already knew.

Philip was back in Canada, living by the good grace of the trust fund their parents had left him. He might even be safe there.

And the figure that emerged from the corridor . . .

That was someone else.

The doors flung open. Light streamed in.

The figure stuttered through the shafts of that light, one after another, transforming each time. A little girl—the one Ann had seen outside? No. An old man—perhaps the one who'd helped her from the ditch, and showed her the way to the wreck of the family's minivan? No. A policeman? A scientist?

Ian Rickhardt?

By the time it stood face to face with her, it was none of those. It was the Insect. Finally, it had granted her an audience.

When it spoke, its voice was the sound of splintering wood.

The door hung open. A man wearing a pale blue windbreaker, the top of his head covered in close-cropped hair, stepped inside with measured haste. He was sweating, and tense—but he didn't seem especially afraid.

He had something in his hand. A gun? No. Not a cell phone either. There were prongs coming off it at one end. It was a Taser.

He kept his back to the wall as he examined the bed, the luggage that sat unpacked at the foot of it, peered into the washroom. He looked under the bed too.

The bathroom door was closed. He approached it warily, almost diffidently—who knew what might be waiting inside? It could just be the occupant, having a quiet pee. It could maybe be something else.

With his free hand, he turned the doorknob and opened the door. The bathroom was dark. Inside was a toilet and a short bathtub, a shower. The light over the sink and mirror was the only light in the room. He flicked it on. There was a jangling sound as he moved the shower curtain from one side to the other.

At length, he re-emerged from the room. The two prongs at the end of the Taser flashed nervous blue as he idly flicked the switch.

He went to the bed, lifted a pillow to his face . . . sniffed it. He set it back down. There was a small window looking out the back of the cabin, into the woods. He checked it. Latched shut. He knelt down, peered under the bed.

As he was doing so, the barrel of a shotgun entered the cabin—preceding Penny, who held it at the ready. The man was preoccupied; he didn't notice anything until he heard the pump chambering a shell.

"This is not rock salt, sir," said Penny. "I aim to shoot you dead."

She was wearing a deep blue housecoat. Her hair was uncombed, and stuck out from her left ear. The man looked up and began to rise.

"Raise your hands," she said. "I will shoot you dead."

"I heard you, ma'am." The man's voice was high for one so big. He had an accent that was hard to place. Not quite the same as Penny's, but close. He stood the rest of the way, and raised both hands. The Taser went into his coat pocket, smoothly. "I'm here with my wife. Just checking in later."

"Oh are you?" Penny didn't move. "Well she ain't here now. She's gone."

"I can see that," said the man. "Please put the gun away, ma'am. She's gone, but she left her car and all her things behind. Do you know where she might've gone?"

"You got no business here," said Penny. "She wants to talk to you, she'll call."

"It's really best that I find her."

"Uh huh. She a danger to herself and others, by any chance?"

"You—you have no idea." It was hard to say, but he might have been trying a smile.

It was the wrong approach. The shotgun wavered.

"I can shoot you right here," said Penny. "You're in my place—broke in. Looks like you got a joy buzzer there, counts as a weapon." The barrel of the shotgun wavered only slightly as she braced it. "I'm within my rights. And it'd solve a lot of problems if I did that. Get you what's comin' to you."

"Now ma'am—" the man's voice got a little higher "—there's no need . . ."

"I think there is," she said.

And the shotgun flew from her hand.

Penny screamed, as it tumbled in the air for an instant—pointed at her—and the man barked, "No!" and moved fast.

He pulled the Taser from his pocket, and ran fast around the foot of the bed. Penny was frozen, staring at the shotgun, suspended in the air—twirling slow like a baton—so it was easy for him. He jammed the Taser into Penny's side, and she spasmed and fell to the floor, her housecoat obscenely askew. The man stood over her for a second, but looked out the door, and held his hand up in a calm-down gesture.

"Thank your friend for me, honey," he said. "That's enough."

"Okay," said a voice—a little girl's voice. "But let's go from here. Mister Sleepy says it's scary. He needs a cuddle."

"He's not the only one," said the man, and glanced down at Penny. "Crazy fuckin' bitch."

And with that, he flicked off the light, shut the door, and was gone.

The shotgun landed on the bed.

A moment later, Ann settled down beside it, as the Insect lowered her gently from the rafters, where it had safely hidden her from the moment the bad man with the poltergeist came to call.

iii

There was a lot of beer in the fridge at the Rosedale Arms' back office. And it was a good thing, Ann thought; there was a lot to process, for everyone involved.

The office was actually a screened-in porch, with a cone-covered lamp dangling from a chain and wire in the middle of the ceiling. It offered a view of the cabins. Penny and Roy sat with frosty cans of Budweiser in front of them; Ann picked a Corona, downed it quickly, then took another.

"First things first—that wasn't your husband, was it?"

"No," said Ann. "My husband's dead."

"By your hand?" asked Penny. When Ann didn't answer right away, she nodded.

"I feel comfortable askin' about that, because you saw me nearly shoot that fella dead on your account. So I'm guessin' you didn't kill him exactly, but it's not that simple."

"My husband wouldn't have died," said Ann, "if it wasn't for me. But it was his own fault."

Roy didn't say anything, but he gave Ann an appraising look as he took a noisy sip from his Bud.

"Fair enough," said Penny. "Any idea who it was that I almost murdered?"

"I don't know," said Ann. "Not exactly. I think he might be one of my late husband's . . ."

"Kin?" prompted Roy.

"Associates," said Ann.

"He hooked up in the mob?" asked Roy. "Jesus, tell us we ain't in the middle of some mob fight. We gotta call the cops."

"I don't think it's the mob," said Penny. "And we ain't callin' the police."

"Why don't you want to—"

"Hush. You know why, Ann. You saw what happened. Can't tell the police anything about that business without either seemin' crazy or lyin' about it. And cops don't like neither of those things."

Ann finished her beer, and reached for another, but Penny stopped her with a hand on her arm. "Slow up," she said. "You're gonna be drivin' in a few hours. Don't want to be tipsy behind the wheel."

"We should call the cops," said Roy again.

"Shut up, Roy," said Penny. "No cops. But." She frowned, as though doing arithmetic on the fly. "Here's who you are gonna call. Pete Wilshire. You're still tight with him, right? Well good. Miz '*Brunt*' here—" her own beer sloshed at the bottom of the bottle as she made air quotes "—is gonna need a car that's not so easy to trace as a rental with Florida plates. I know Pete can fix her up with somethin' driveable, for just a small bit of that roll of bills she's got in her handbag. After seein' what went on in that room, I can see why she won't take a bus or a train, or God forbid, an airplane. So you think you can do that?"

"Not right now," he said, "but in morning, sure. He won't be able to do it right straightaway, though."

"That's fine," said Penny. "Because once you call him, you're goin' to follow Miz Brunt into Mobile, where we'll find a place to return that rental car of hers. She can settle up there, and for good measure maybe go into a bus station and buy a ticket somewhere. Then you can pick her up, bring her over to Pete's lot, and see her off in her new car." Penny turned to Ann. "That sound good to you?"

"Sure," said Ann, and Penny said, "You're welcome."

"I'm sorry. Thank you. You don't have to do any of this."

"Well, here's how you can really say thank you," said Penny. "First off. Keep your cell phone turned off. And don't go sending revealing messages on chat programs in fancy business centres. Might be all right to buy one of those disposable cell phones, for emergencies. But I'd even keep the battery out of that, most of the time. If you can get any more cash on that credit card you lost, get it—then cut the thing up for real. Don't use it anywhere. Drive the speed limit, and stay off freeways. Though it may be tempting, don't buy yourself a gun. It's easier to get one here than pretty much anywhere else, true enough, but you still gotta show I.D. and register it. And unless you got the will to use it on a fella, it can be turned against you. Like you saw just now.

"That joy buzzer your dead husband's 'associate' has is a better deal all the way around. Easy to buy and use, and less costly. In fact, you might want to take the money you save on that and buy yourself a wig. If you're goin' somewhere after this—don't take the direct route. Zigzag a bit. Throws 'em off the scent, if they're on it. Now let me see. Is there anythin' else I can think of?"

As she thought, Roy got another couple of Budweisers out of the fridge, popped them both and handed one to Penny.

"Oh yeah," she said. "Get yourself an exorcist. But not the kind uses snakes and potions. Those ones are liars."

The Plains

i

Ann checked her Gmail at a public library in Atlanta. She didn't sign in to chat. There was an email from Jeanie, though.

> Hey Ann
>
> Call me, would you? Everyone's really worried about you.
>
> Lesley checked and your bro's fine. He's checked out of the Hollingsworth place. He apparently consented. Michael's friend Ian is taking him back to his place where the wedding was. He stayed there before, so it should be okay. I remember they had a room for him and everything.
>
> They finished arrangements for getting Michael's remains back. There's going to be a memorial, but they want you to be there. You should be there. Lesley got in touch with Ian and he said to tell you to please come home. Or at least answer your cell phone. He said to say you aren't in any trouble. He's sorted everything out with the airline.
>
> I know it can be really hard, and I know what you told me about Michael. I can't imagine what you must be going through. But you have to know people love you and want to help you.
>
> Love
>
> Jeanie

Ann pressed the "reply" button, and thought about what to write. She finally typed:

> Hi Jeanie,
>
> Tell Lesley to get Philip out of there! These guys are sick! They're going to hurt him. I can't call you, because they might hurt you too. In fact—you should get away from your place for a while and don't tell anyone where you are.
>
> There's a man with short hair and a blue jacket and a little girl whose friend Mister Sleepy is just as bad as the Insect. He might show up at your door. He might not tell her to stop.
>
> Run!

She didn't send it.

Jeanie didn't know about the Insect. She didn't know about Mister Sleepy. How would that email read to her? Ann didn't want to seem crazy; didn't want to set off any alarm bells that weren't already ringing. What the hell had she been thinking?

She had been following Penny's advice along the road. Roy's friend Pete ran a used-car lot out of an old filling station up the highway, and he had a surprisingly extensive stock of vehicles. After some hemming and hawing, she settled on an old Chevrolet campervan. Roy agreed, it would be easier to find camp grounds that took cash than it would motels. He and Pete had a quiet word out of earshot of Ann, and they figured $2,000 would be a fair price, given the vehicle's age and the smell in the upholstery and level of rust and so forth. Ann thought it was a steal, but kept her mouth shut on the matter.

Ann hadn't bought a gun, and she hadn't bought a Taser either. She did manage to find a wig shop in Mobile, and got a red wig and a pair of big disguisey sunglasses too, and in the outlet store up the road, a pale blue jean jacket that was unlike anything else she owned. She did buy a mobile phone with a disposable number on it, and did max out her card on a cash advance—another $5,500 was what she could arrange. She bought a bus ticket to New Orleans and put it in the pocket of that jean jacket. Then she headed northeast in her fancy new van, her credit card broken in two at the bottom of her purse.

Was all that enough? If she'd done all this straight out of Miami, would Mister Sleepy and his master have been able to find her in the Rosedale Arms? Had they really tracked her by the license plate of her rented Toyota and a Gchat in the business centre? Or had they used something else?

Were they still on her trail even now?

Ann closed the email without sending it, then changed her password—something that she should have done a long time ago. She logged back in, just to make sure when she noticed the sender of a new message in her inbox.

mailto:evafenshaw23@hotmail.com

She didn't have much time left, and it was a long note. So she opened the email, and despite the risk, summoned a library page to find out how to use the printer in this town. When it was finished, she deleted the email, signed out, and cleared the cache—just like Penny'd shown her.

She hurried back to her van with the printout, to read it through. Because that was the one piece of advice from Penny she hadn't yet been able to follow.

She had not yet sought out an exorcist.

ii

Blessings, Ann

Oh I don't know where to start. I love love love love you. I hope after everything that has happened you are okay. I know you know that I was sick for a while. I had a bit of a stroke. I don't want to bore you with details, but it was very hard for me to move or to talk for a little while. I'm better now but not all better. I can go on the computer and I can do my stuff. I had some very good helpers to keep me going. There's an in-home care division from the Hollingsworth Centre and they really helped a lot.

That's me. Now you. First I am so sorry. I heard about the accident in the airplane on the news. I am sorry. Michael was a good man. I could feel it when I checked him, my way. He really loved you and I know you loved him too. I am praying for you.

I know from reading your emails you sent me from Tobago, that you were having a hard time with the Insect. I wish I could have helped you. But they didn't tell me about all the calls and messages that came in when I was sick until later.

I still have a hard time moving. But I can type, and I can pray. If you call me, I might be a bit hard to understand. But in the meantime, I can remind you of what we learned.

Remember when we first met? It was in the hospital—after another crash. I remember you there, so small, in that playroom. It was Christmas, and my nephew had told me I had to go, and of course I did.

I had a rest just now. This is a lot of typing.

You were so frightened there. They didn't know what to do with you. You wouldn't go away with your Nan—you wouldn't even go back to your room. You were afraid that things would start to happen. That you wouldn't be able to control it. That the Insect would come out and tear the hospital to pieces. Do some harm.

You told me everything. You were such a brave girl. And you told me, "Get rid of this thing. Make it go away. Ryan says you can. So do it please."

I told you of course I would. I would spend all the time with you I needed to make sure the thing inside you went away.

I think now you understand that I couldn't really do that. That was a white lie I told you, because I couldn't tell you then what we later learned: that you can't make something go away that's part of you. You can control it. You can make it behave. You just have to learn how to talk to it.

Eventually we used your Dungeons & Dragons game.

But that day we did a simpler thing. We just did a little chant: "Shut up. I know you're there. But shut up right now."

You said it again and again, first with me, and then on your own. I left you for a little while alone in the room, chanting this over and over.

I spoke with your Nan after that alone. She was very skeptical about my methods. A lot of people are. Particularly people who believe in the traditional religions. But I explained to her about the importance of this, and the counsellors at the hospital agreed, and so you were able to go home. Your old home first, then, after a while, over to Barrie to live with your Nan.

She was a dear. I hope you remember her that way, still. You only had a few years with her before she passed on. But she loved you and Philip dearly. We became good friends. I like to think we still talk.

So here is what I want you to do. Every time you see the Insect start to assert itself, I want you to say, "Shut up! I know you are there!" And I want you to think of your Nan. Nothing happened when you were with her. The Insect kept its peace. Nothing happened for many years after you lived with her. When you moved in with me for those years, we kept it under control. But it all started with this:

Shut up.

I know you're there.

But shut up for now.

My dear Ann, I hope that helps you for now. But should you want more help, please call me. I promise, this time I'll answer myself.

Love love love

Eva

Ann folded the sheets and slid them into the glove box of the van. It was late in the afternoon outside the library in the parking lot. Minivans and SUVs were pulled up by the sidewalk, letting kids off. On the steps outside, an elderly man with a ponytail and a thick beard sat on a bench, thumbing through a thick volume. Ann pulled the disposable cell phone from her handbag. It was an old-style flip phone.

She opened it, and from memory, dialled Eva's number.

iii

"Hello?"

"Hello Eva. Don't say my name if there's someone else in the room right now."

"Mm. All . . . all right."

"So there is." Ann sighed. "All right. Eva, I got your email. I've made a copy and printed it. You do the same when we're done."

A pause. "Yes."

"Good. Now. There are some things we need to talk about very quickly. I need you to listen to me."

"Yes."

"First. Ian Rickhardt is not to be trusted. He is a—"she wanted to say prick, but knew better than to use that kind of language with Eva "—a wicked man. So was . . . so was Michael. They—" Ann paused. She tried to form the words to describe what had happened, exactly, in a way that Eva could understand.

"They're perverts," she said finally. "They both knew full well about the Insect. They . . . they exploited it sexually. Does that make sense?"

There was a silence on the other line.

"Ian has taken Philip. They've taken him from his home care. Apparently he consented to it. But I'm worried he doesn't understand. I think he's in trouble."

"All right." She sounded less certain. But then she added, "Just a moment."

The phone muffled—a longish silence as these things went—and she was back.

"All right. I've sent David away. He was here just now, helping clean up. I've asked him if he could take out the garbage, and he hopped to it."

"Who is David?"

"He's with the home," said Eva. She was still speaking slowly, hesitantly, stumbling a bit over consonants. "He's been helping me ou'. Out."

"Okay." Ann thought about that. Hadn't a David told her he was Eva's nephew? She wasn't sure, and didn't want to get into it with Eva now. "Well. Don't talk to him about any of this."

"Of course not. Now tell me, Ann. Did the Insect cause that plane crash?"

"It didn't quite crash. But Michael caused it. He raped the Insect, Eva. Ian did too."

"Goodness," said Eva. "Goodness."

"He wasn't a good man. Neither of them were."

"Ann," said Eva, somewhat more deliberately, "how precisely did he rape it?"

Ann felt her throat rise. Outside, a woman crossing the parking lot glanced at her, and looked away quickly. Ann might've done that herself, seeing a woman like Ann in the cab of a burned-out campervan, crying. "I—I don't know, precisely. But it told me. It told me it was happening."

"How did it tell you?"

Ann drew a breath. She swallowed, and steadied herself.

"I can't stay on this phone very long," she said. "You've got to trust me. There are a group of men, who do this to the Insect. To poltergeists. I've met them. They have some sick relationship with them. They . . . they call people like me a 'vessel' for their . . . for their real brides. Michael was one of them. And Ian Rickhardt's one of them. And I think he's kidnapped Philip."

"Do you want to call the police?"

Ann wiped her eyes. The tears were gone as fast as they'd come. Something else came up in its place. A hard certainty. Eva wasn't alone in the room, wherever she was. This wasn't her; there was more than a stroke at work here.

"Eva," she said, "you're not really alone, are you?"

"I'm alone," said Eva. "But I'm also listening to you. And this . . . this doesn't make sense. You've had an accident in Tobago, and another one on the airplane back. With tragic consequences. But it's only that you've slipped—you've let go. So what you need to do, is get it back under control. And you're on the phone right now, and I think we might just be able to do that."

"All right," said Ann.

"Good. Now, Ann, I want you to visualize the safe place."

Ann shut her eyes. There was nothing but darkness.

"Do you have it there?"

"Yes," said Ann. "I'm in the tower, and there's sunlight streaming in the windows, and there are unicorns dancing outside."

"Unicorns?"

Ann opened her eyes. The sun had gone behind a cloud, and the wind was whipping up.

"I'm sorry, Eva. I can't."

"You don't want to, you mean."

There is no can't, only won't, thought Ann crazily.

"It's past that," said Ann. "The Insect has escaped. I tried to get it back in. And I couldn't."

"Ann," said Eva sharply, "the Insect hasn't done anything. It can't escape, if you don't let it. Now let's take a breath—fill ourselves up with energy. Breathe deep—"

"It's *killed*, Eva. The Insect has *killed*."

On the bench by the library, the man shut his book, and peered up at the sky. The quality of light was changing; Ann could feel a prickling on her arms.

"Ann, you need to take control of this thing. You need to put it down."

The Insect had killed. That was true; it had killed Michael, while he tried to rape it. It had taken Hirsch, the lawyer, to the very edge of death and held him there.

And when Ann was facing a kidnapper all her own, it had lifted her high in the air, free from harm—and it had saved her.

It would take more than a placebo to keep the Insect anywhere it didn't want to be. More to the point, it would take more than that to keep it anywhere Ann didn't want it to be.

Outside the car, a woman with a stroller shouted to her husband, and pointed to the west. Thick drops of rain splattered on the car windshield.

"Eva," said Ann, "I want you to be careful. Don't trust David. Don't trust Ian. If you can, call up your nephew Ryan and get him to take you away from home."

"Ann?"

Ann swallowed, and smiled as the western clouds fattened into deep, greenish-black things.

"Just go," she said. "Go stay with Ryan."

Ann clicked the phone off, and cracked its back and pulled its battery out. She dropped the battery out the window, turned the ignition, and pulled out of the parking lot and onto the long and twisted road ahead of her.

She had to take it. Philip needed her.

Whatever anyone else said, she knew it to be true.

The Candy Robot

i

And then she was three.

They had a party for her. It was her third birthday party really, one that was just for her. The first birthday was marked with a brunch in their living room where other parents with little children came around and ate bagels and smoked salmon and talked over their children's heads, and Ann just jumped and grinned in her playpen while Philip caroused in the dining room with a pair of twin girls who were only a year older than he.

The girls weren't there at her second birthday. Neither was her dad. He was off talking to investors in Boston, and Ann and Philip and their mom were stuck in Long Island, with their grandparents. Mom's mom and dad. It was a nice house, and there was some cake, and Gran even lit a couple of candles and put it in the top. But it was quiet, and rainy, and nobody came, and their mom seemed distracted the whole time.

This birthday was better. It was a real party.

Ann was a nice kid. She had friends. There was a play group at the local park that her mom took her to; they met every day at eleven, moms and dads carrying silver thermos-mugs of coffee and diaper bags as the kids clambered over swings and seesaws. Ann had formed meaningful friendships with a little girl named Robyn, a trio of boys whose names she could never get straight—Nick, Stevie and something-or-other—and another little girl, with long braided dark hair and the biggest smile Ann had ever seen. Ann couldn't pronounce her name, but she always won at hide and seek. There was also a puppy, whose name was Buster, who was sometimes there with Robyn's mom. He was brown and liked to cuddle.

Ann's mom thought she should invite all of them to a big party at their house. There would be cake and games. Kids would all bring presents, and they would go away with "loot bags." Ann loved the idea of loot bags for her friends. She wanted to know what loot Buster would get, and had a bit of a tantrum when her dad said he didn't think Buster should have a seat at the table.

But Ann was a nice kid. So when she made up the invitations, she didn't make one for Buster. When she handed them out next day at play group, she just gave him a pat.

Philip was almost as excited as Ann. He, after all, had had six birthdays now—three of them big-production-number parties. The last one had been an outing to Chuck E. Cheese with all his friends from kindergarten. He explained to Ann that soon she would be big enough for a Chucky birthday. But in the meantime, a birthday party at the house would be just fine.

Their mom cleaned up the basement for the party. It wasn't super fancy—she was always complaining about the wooden panelling and the tatty carpet. But with birthday decorations and little plastic chairs and a couple of Fisher-Price tables (one borrowed from Robyn's mom), and the piñata shaped like a robot hanging from the dropped ceiling, she admitted it didn't look too bad.

The kids started to show up at lunchtime. First there was Robyn and her mom and dad. They brought a big paper bag covered up with fluffy paper on top. And a card. Ann wondered if this were a present too. One of the boys (whatsisname?) came with just his mom next, and then another boy came along with his mom, who was also looking after whatsername, who was grinning bigger than ever, and carrying her own present, wrapped in bright paper and tied at the top. Ann couldn't guess what it was.

And then the last boy came, who Ann was pretty sure was called Stevie. They were very happy, all of them, to get things underway.

There were two parties. One in the basement, with a bowl of bright red punch, and hot dogs and chicken nuggets and french fries. There was a second one upstairs, in the kitchen and dining room. There, parents and guardians gathered, drinking grown-up drinks and waiting their turn to come downstairs to watch over the party.

Later birthdays would be more structured. That morning, Ann had picked out the toys she was willing to share, and had them laid out in neat rows in the corner nearest the laundry room. There was a pin-the-tail-on-the-donkey game tacked up to the wall, but it was clear early on that this was beyond most of the guests' abilities. And there was the piñata. But that was for later.

The festivities began with an inventory of the toys. Ann solemnly told her guests which was which, as her dad videotaped.

"These are my Rainbow Brites!" she exclaimed, pointing at a little clutch of bobble-headed dolls, and their unicorns. "That's Jem!" She grabbed the more humanly proportioned blonde doll and waved her around, fast enough that her neck would have snapped if she weren't plastic. "And this!" And she picked up a different doll, whose hair was more mane than coif and who carried a big sword in one fist—and roared: "SHE-RA!"

Philip cracked up. The girl guests headed in to look more closely. The three boys looked on curiously, but kept their distance.

"Philip," said their dad, apprehending the problem before anyone else, "why don't you go get your Star Wars toys."

Philip, who was also a nice kid, ran upstairs to oblige. And Ann settled down with the Rainbow Brite dolls, to arrange a pecking order.

Robyn went for She-Ra. And the other girl—she must have gone for some punch. It was just Robyn and Ann until lunchtime.

There was trouble at the table—someone hadn't set quite enough spaces, and Nicky had to stand for a little while. He kept trying to sit on the smiling girl's lap, but Ann told him he couldn't.

"That's rude!" she said.

But Nicky was a baby, and started to cry. So the girl said it was okay and got up.

Ann was impressed; she didn't cry at all. She just nodded, and went upstairs with her hotdog and juice cup.

Probably to tell her mom.

ii

"Okay," said Ann's mom, "who wants candy?"

There was general agreement that everyone did. This, after a big piece of cake with icing that was white, and pink, and blue, and multiple sippy-cups of red, sugary punch. The party had not had its fill of sugar.

"Okay, here's the game," she said. "There's lots of candy. But can anyone guess where it is?"

"Inside the robot!" squealed Ann, and Robyn yelled "No fair!" because of course Ann was on her home turf. The boys sat quiet, rocking back and forth on their chairs, waiting to see how things would play out.

"That's right. The robot there is all full of candy. We're going to have to get it. Any idea how?"

"Bang it with a stick!" yelled Nicky.

Ann's mother said yes, this was so, and pulled from behind her back a long stick, wrapped in colourful paper. In her other hand, she held a blindfold. "But no peeking," she said.

"You have to hit it hard," said Philip, who then asked if he could go first. But Ann's mom said no, Philip was too big and strong. And it was Ann's birthday, not his.

Ann wanted to be a good hostess, though, so she said she would go later.

Robyn got the first whack. The blindfold was giant on her head—it made her look like she had bug eyes, thought Ann. Ann's mother turned her around twice, and Robyn teetered off toward the punch bowl. The kids yelled at her that she was going the wrong way, and eventually she made it back to the robot and clobbered it.

It was no good; it just swung back and forth slowly, and Ann thought: *Robyn's too little.*

The boys took their turns; each giving the robot a good wallop but not really making a lot of progress. Finally, it was up to Ann, and it was about time; she was jumping from one foot to another, and had to go pee but wasn't going to say as long as that robot still had its candy in it.

"Now let's see how the birthday girl does," said her mom, and put the blindfold over her head.

The blindfold was made of a velvety cardboard, and it didn't fit perfectly; light leaked in on the side. Ann thought she might be able to see out the sides if she turned her head just so. She couldn't see much, but she could make out the shapes of her friends.

"Okay baby," said her mom, "you ready?"

"YES!" she screamed.

From somewhere nearby, she could hear her dad laughing as her mom's hand fell on her shoulder, turning her around and around.

"Okay," said her dad, "everybody stand back. The birthday maniac has a stick!"

Ann cackled on cue and started forward. "No no no!" shouted her guests, and so she turned around, and ran forward. She felt a pair of hands on her back, pushing her away, and her mom yelled, "Hey! No touching, now, Stevie."

Someone shouted something that Ann couldn't understand. She took a few more steps forward, but someone else shouted, "No! Not that way!" right in her ear. Someone else hollered, "Yes! That way!"

Ann felt her breath get quicker. She thought about all the candy that must be in that robot. And she started to think that maybe if she didn't get that robot quickly, the candy would be gone. That would be sad. That would *suck*, like Philip would say.

She might have started to cry then. She felt the tears welling up in her. But if she let that happen, on some level she knew that would be it—she wouldn't be able to swing hard enough if she was crying too hard.

So Ann swung.

Philip finally took down the piñata. He did it without a blindfold, because at that point their parents and the other adults had concluded that blindfolding little kids and letting them swing sticks around in a relatively small basement rec room was not the safest thing.

Ann had already apologized to Nicky. The stick had hit Nicky hard across the cheek when Ann swung it. It had missed his eye—it had not, "Thank God," her mother said, broken skin. Probably it wouldn't even bruise.

Still, Nicky didn't like it, and wailed to high heaven while his mom held him close and told him it would be okay. Stevie was whimpering too—more in sympathy. Ann was flat-out bawling—because even at this moment, when she'd raised a weapon and smashed it across the face of the little boy whose name she was positive now was Nicky . . . she was a good kid. And there was no acknowledgment of that—no absolution whatsoever—here. When she said she was sorry, Nicky just buried his face deeper in his mom's breast. When she said she was really sorry, raising her voice so that Nicky would be sure to hear it, her mom just took her over to her chair and gave her a hug.

Finally, her mom patted her on the shoulder, and pointed over to the piñata, where Philip stood ready—grinning incongruously.

"Okay, Philip," said their dad, who stood behind her, "show that robot what-for."

And Philip wound up, holding the stick in both hands, pulling it nearly all the way around his back, somehow, and swung with all his might.

The air at Ann's third birthday party was filled with candy.

iii

Things wound down. Ann opened some presents, and said her thank yous.

It was a good haul: a little baby girl doll, with a bottle; a paint set with Star Wars teddy bears; a colouring book with some puzzles in it too; and a play set with toy ponies.

By four o'clock, it was over. As her dad set about cleaning up the basement and her mom took her upstairs to the bedroom, she was fidgety and cross—and couldn't quite figure out why.

"Nap time, now," said her mother as she set her down on her bed on the bottom bunk.

Ann yelled that she didn't want to sleep, and as he climbed up into his bunk on top, Philip agreed. But there was no arguing. Nap time meant nap time.

Philip climbed up to the top bunk, and the frame shook as he adjusted himself to at least shut his eyes if not actually sleep.

"Happy birthday," he said, and Ann said, "Happy birthday."

But something was bothering her. There was something missing. She turned that over in her mind as she drifted off to sleep. There was enough food, and there was a lot of play, and she'd said goodbye to her friends like she was supposed to, and the presents were great.

And then she thought about it. She had opened presents from every kid except for that girl from the play group. She still couldn't remember her name, but she definitely remembered that when she arrived, she was carrying a box with a ribbon on it.

Where was it?

Had she gotten mad and taken it home with her? Ann hoped not.

In fact, she bet that it was downstairs in the basement, or maybe by the door from when she came in. Ann thought she should go and see.

She waited until she heard Philip's breathing get slow, like it did when he fell asleep, and very quietly slipped out from under her covers. She crept across the floor of their bedroom, and cracked open the door, and came out into the upstairs hallway. That was fine. She would keep going.

She checked the bathroom, in case she had left it in there. She climbed down the stairs, backwards, which was safer, and had a look by the front door. Nothing. Her mom and dad were in the kitchen, and she didn't want to go there right now because she might get in trouble. So instead, she went straight to the basement door in the dining room and climbed down.

The lights were out in the basement and Ann was too little to reach the light. But the little windows by the driveway made it just bright enough to see. So she did the backwards-climbing thing again, and went right down to the basement floor. Her feet made a candy wrapper crinkle, and then it stuck to her sock.

She looked around. There was still wrapping paper on the floor, and she looked through that. But nothing.

She was about to give up, when she heard a tick-tick-tick sound from behind the wall. There was a little door but she knew she wasn't supposed to go back there. That was where the furnace was, and furnaces were for big people.

Of course, she had just had a birthday. She was bigger now than she ever was.

Ann went through the door.

And sure enough—there it was! A little box with a ribbon wrapped around it! Right there beside the furnace. Which was ticking, faster and faster.

Ann picked it up. She wouldn't open it here. She hauled it upstairs, and being very quiet, snuck up through the dining room and living room, back up the stairs. She tiptoed along the hallway, and back into the bedroom.

She very quietly got back into bed, and then set about unwrapping the present. The ribbons were hard to remove—they were held on with the stickiest glue ever. But Ann got them off. Then the paper, which was all bright red, had to come off. She tried to take it off quietly, but didn't do so well at that. It made a rrrrrRIP! sound that she was sure would wake Philip. But although the bunk bed went thunkity-thunk, Philip didn't come down. So she opened the rest of the paper, and underneath that, found a simple cardboard box like one for shoes.

She opened that up fast. "Ooo," she said. "Birdy!"

It was a beautiful blue bird—with a dark blue head and pale blue wings. It was curled up in a bed of plastic straw. Ann touched it. It was so soft. Its little eyes were shiny and black. Also, it smelled.

Thunkity, went the bunk bed.

Ann looked up at the ladder. There was a pair of little legs, not much bigger than hers, standing on one of the top rungs. It wasn't Philip—he was much bigger. Ann was still puzzling it out when the legs took one step, and another, and disappeared into the top bunk.

The whole bed swayed a bit. More than a bit.

Ann put her birdy down, and slid out from under the covers and got onto the floor.

She stepped back so she could get a good look on top.

"Hey," she said.

The girl looked back. She was sitting up in the bed, grinning wider than ever. Her eyes looked kind of like the bird's eyes in this light—all black and glittery. But friendly.

"Thank you for the present," said Ann.

The grinning girl bounced a bit. She didn't say anything, but Ann could hear Philip murmur something.

"It's nap time," said Ann. The girl nodded vigorously. She bounced some more, and looked down at where Philip would be. Ann couldn't see Philip.

"You should go to your mommy," said Ann.

The girl bent over and disappeared behind the edge of the top bunk.

There were no more *thunkities*.

Ann rocked from one foot and then the other. Of all her friends from the play group, Ann thought she liked this girl best. But this was very strange behaviour coming from her, all the same.

Why was she still here? Where was her mommy? Everyone else had gone off with their mommies.

Ann started to climb up the ladder. She wasn't allowed to do this, but she had done so anyway a couple of times. Because, while she was a nice kid, she was also a curious kid. And the top bunk was great; there was a window up there for one thing. It was a great view, and once she had come up with Philip to look at the sunset through it.

It was dark and grey when Ann climbed up this time. Drops of water hung on the screen outside the glass.

The light made the grinning girl look like a black-and-white picture where she lay, cuddling Philip around his chest with her skinny arms. Philip was fast asleep, and the girl was holding him at his back. Her eyes were closed too, like she was sleeping. But Ann didn't think she was sleeping; she was breathing too fast. It sounded like she had the sniffles. Philip shifted, and she shifted too, so she was holding him even tighter.

Ann stood on the rung right under the top rung.

"You need to go home," she said, and the girl opened her eyes. They flashed dark, like little marbles.

"Find your own bed," said Ann. "You go there."

The girl pulled away, her arms pulling back from around Philip's chest.

"He's my brother, not yours," said Ann. "Go home."

The girl stood up on her little legs, so her head brushed the ceiling.

Then she reached down, and ran a finger over Philip's cheek, and bent down, and stepped out the window.

Ann clambered onto the bed, and pushed her face to the glass to see where the girl had gone. Even though she squinted, she couldn't tell. It had become even darker. The girl had gone somewhere into that. There was no way Ann would be able to tell where.

Philip stirred and blinked. Ann curled up beside him, and he put his arms around her. Ann didn't think she'd get to sleep after all that commotion, but she did, all the same.

The Bridge

i

The Insect came to her, finally, in a campground outside of Bloomington, Indiana.

Ann had been following Penny's advice—zigzagging across the country rather than making a straight-up run for it. She'd been mindful that the man with the buzz-cut could still be on her, even though he'd been scared off at Rosedale. Or Mister Sleepy had. But who knew if he might try and pick up her trail elsewhere?

So she stayed offline and kept her new phone battery-free. And when she needed to sleep, she looked for off-season campgrounds, where she could get a shower, but generally avoid even small groups of others.

The Winding River campground was where she ended up her second night on her meandering, under-the-radar trip home. And it was perfect for her needs. The campground was on a road lined with cornfields, nestled in a copse of trees between farms. It was not in fact on a river, but the owners had fashioned a pond that they stocked with fish. This far into the fall, they didn't have many customers; at the lodge, they were happy to hook the van up to power and turn on the water in the bathroom for her. Ann thanked them, picked a spot far from the lodge, and cracked a bottle of some interesting-looking California zinfandel, to watch the sunset.

She hadn't actually thought to pick up anything to eat. The wine hit her hard as a result. She was asleep before the stars came out.

At midnight, Ann woke up, throat torn with reflux bile, on the little bench beside the kitchenette. She had not even put up the roof to open up the bunks to sleep properly, so her neck hurt, too.

None of that had woken her up, though.

The cab light was on.

It was on because the passenger side door was hanging open, up front.

There was someone in the passenger seat. Wasn't there?

Yes. The door shut and the light went out, which meant that the shape she saw, the head bobbing on the thin neck, the tangle of hair . . . that had to be real, because the door had shut. And someone had to shut the door.

"I've got a gun," lied Ann. She hoped the hoarseness in her voice overrode the quaver.

The only answer was a squeaking sound, of flesh rubbing against painted metal perhaps. Ann peered forward. No good. Too dark.

Ann reached across the miniature counter top, found the light switch. A little fluorescent bar over the hotplate stove flickered to life.

The passenger seat was empty now, so far as she could see. Ann swallowed hard—her mouth felt like it was full of chalk—and she crept toward it to confirm, grabbing the neck of the wine bottle.

And as she did, she sighed. It seemed as though the seat were empty. She put her hand on the headrest, and peered over to be sure, and she swallowed even harder—because she hadn't seen the thing that was there.

It was a bird—its head cricked in toward its breast. Its back was bright yellow, its wingtips black and grey, a tiny black crown on its head. It was surely dead.

The squeaking sound resumed. It seemed to be coming from all around her. It took her far too long, she thought later, to place it.

It was the sound of a finger drawing across the windshield of the van; making words in the dew.

STOP DAWDLING
TAKE US HOME TOMORROW NIGHT
I WILL HELP

ii

There were four places to cross the border that would take Ann to Ian Rickhardt's place in Niagara. The most obvious one was Niagara Falls. East, she might have crossed at Buffalo. West was the crossing between Detroit and Windsor; roundabout, but still convenient.

Ann chose the farthest; the little city of Port Huron, not far from Flint, Michigan and kissing distance from Sarnia.

It was a long drive from Bloomington. And Ann stewed as she made it. She was a Canadian citizen, driving an Alabama-plated vehicle. She might have to surrender that at the border. She had heard stories about border officials taking a car apart to see if it was running drugs or weapons. She might wind up in custody.

She had read about exit searches. It was something the U.S. border guards could do if they wanted, for any reason they chose. Once they stopped you . . . they could do anything they wanted.

She knew she could disappear under such circumstances.

She'd hoped to make it by dinnertime, but the weather wasn't with her. A lashing rainstorm hit at Fort Wayne, so bad that she had to pull off into a rest stop for almost an hour, and traffic crawled along the interstate. She stopped in Lansing four hours later for a rest and something to eat.

By the time she hit the city limits of Port Huron, it was closing on midnight, and the storm had tapered somewhat, so she could make some progress. But her windshield wipers were on high and the heater was blowing full on.

As Ann drove through on the I-69 and the wind picked up, she began to wonder just what kind of help the Insect was going to provide.

She had to slow up on the on-ramp to the I-94; a transport truck was pulling off to the side, leaving just enough room for her to get around. As she passed it, she thought she saw something sparking underneath. She kept going.

She merged onto an empty I-94 and thunder rumbled. Had that been a lightning strike somewhere, reflected from the truck? Signs indicated the upcoming Blue Water Bridge. Lightning flashed again and in the aftermath, it seemed as though the world had gone dark.

It took her an instance to realize that it had. She flashed her high beams on. Ahead was a small building at the roadside, and as she passed it, she saw in her rearview that someone had stepped outside, was waving a glowing blue cone.

Ahead, another figure stepped into view, waving her to stop.

She braked and pulled off to the side.

The figure was in rain gear; she came up to the window of the van and rapped on it with her flashlight.

"Step out of the car, Ma'am!" It was a woman, thick-featured. About Ann's age.

Ann said that she would. But when she turned back from unbuckling her seatbelt, the woman was gone.

There was a *thump!* on the roof of the van. Ann caught a movement in her side-view, as a glowing flashlight rolled off the top. An instant later, the woman fell too.

Ann looked outside. More figures were running over from the building. The woman on the ground wasn't moving.

There was a squeaking sound then, and Ann looked around.

Written in the growing condensation on the windshield:

DRIVE.

Ann put the van into gear and drove. Ahead, she could barely make out a dark bank of toll booths; as she approached, the bar rose in front of her.

She heard a muffled shouting sound that might have been screams as the rain relented, momentarily, under the awning. Then the rain hit again and she pushed on across the dark bridge.

Ann found she was barely breathing; the cabin of the van was getting cold—just as it had been at Christmas, when the Insect killed her parents and paralyzed her brother.

She had been waiting for this to happen—for thousands of miles, she'd been waiting for the Insect to manifest on the road, maybe in the midst of a traffic jam as she hit rush hour outside some Midwestern metropolis. There had been times, she had to admit, that she had wanted it to.

Now, it was just her in the van. There were no crowds of people outside; no lines of cars waiting to make it through the checkpoint. She wondered if the swerving truck on the on-ramp might have been part of the cause of that. She wondered what the Insect had done to the traffic approaching the checkpoint farther back on the I-94, to keep it back, then waited until the last American crossed into Canada, before cutting the power.

Whatever it had done, Ann felt coldly certain the Insect wasn't killing her. It had never been killing her, it had never really tried to, and it wasn't going to start tonight.

Lightning flashed, throwing the suspension cables over her head into a sharp relief. Ahead, she could see the Canadian customs checkpoint. Like the toll booth she'd passed through, these were dark—except for the tops of what looked like streetlight poles. There, something sparked.

Cameras, Ann thought, feeling the certainty in her gut. *The cameras are shorted out.*

"You heard my thoughts," she said aloud as she accelerated toward the Canadian border. "You heard how fucking scared I was—to be coming at the border with Alabama plates and the face of the Mile High Widow. So you helped."

At some point, Ann had stopped muttering and started shouting.

As her headlights illuminated the Canadian border checkpoints, she swallowed her words and sat straight. Ann knew she should just fly through here, faster even than she'd passed the toll both—that's what the Insect told her to do.

But she couldn't quite make herself. She'd been terrified of this encounter; but something in her, some base programming, made her slow down.

She rolled up to one of the dark booths. Someone was inside it—she could just make them out through the window, which sat about a foot higher than her line of sight. The booth was open, and a hand clutched the edge of it.

The hand disappeared as she rolled by slow.

Ann knew that she should have just pushed through. She had a clear run, if the cameras were all down. No one would know she crossed; her Alabama-state camper van would be hers.

She rolled her window down, and craned her neck to see.

Behind the counter, the agent—it was hard to tell much other than by the close-cropped haircut, it was probably a man—sat bolt upright in his chair. He looked to be staring straight at Ann.

"Are you—okay? Do you need help?"

The man made a high noise that sounded like it was coming from the back of his throat.

"Go through, Ma'am," he said.

Ann shivered, as an icy breeze passed between them.

"Go on." His voice was high. "Go through fast. Get help."

Ann took that as a pass. Through she went, past the dark secondary search, where she noted sickly four cars and a minivan were pulled over, to have their belongings searched. She didn't stop this time, but kept to the path—swerving only once, to avoid a garbage can that had blown into the road.

iii

The weather cleared up as she passed through Sarnia. The streetlights came on again. In the oncoming lane, police cars sped toward Port Huron, but until Ann had passed a few on-ramps, she was blessedly alone on the highway.

As she drove, she wondered just how alone she was. Had the Insect remained at the border crossing, wreaking mayhem as was its wont? Had it released her, now, to make the long drive past Sarnia, through London, and eventually southeast?

An hour out, she found a highway rest station, and pulled into it to get some gasoline—order some coffee. There were TVs on in the central dining area, tuned to CTV's news channel. None of the half-dozen or so late-night travellers clutching their travel mugs paid it any heed, and why should they? The weather scroll showed cool but clear skies ahead; the stock market seemed to be ticking along normally; and as for news?

It looked as though the main story this morning was about the Prime Minister, and a couple of senior ministers, and judging from the stock footage, the Alberta oil sands. Ann wasn't sure. She had been on the road, not paying attention to Canadian politics.

There was nothing about the Mile High Widow. Not a hint of any trouble at the border.

But there probably wouldn't be, not yet.

Tim Horton's was the purveyor of caffeine and carbs at the rest stop. Ann didn't care for their coffee but made an exception. It was rich and stimulating, and she thought she could drink a gallon of it if she had to.

And she had to, because there would be no night spent at a campground tonight.

Soon, the CTV screens would light up with news about what had happened at Port Huron. At the very least, about a dead or badly hurt U.S. border guard. Possibly about a terrible auto and truck crash on the I-94.

Maybe, about hell opening up at Canada Customs and Immigration.

Whatever the totality of that was—Rickhardt would know that she was back in Canada, and where she was coming from.

And then . . .

Then he might just start hurting Philip.

Ann finished her coffee, tossed it away and headed to the rest room. She'd showered and cleaned up at the campground the day before, and that showed. If she'd had to, she could have put on a good face at the border.

Even now—after everything, Ann congratulated herself silently. She didn't look desperate at all.

Empty Vessels

i

There had been a limo waiting for Ann and Michael when the wedding was done. Ann had thought it was vulgar, and later, when she finally mentioned it as they were waiting for their flight at Pearson Airport, Michael would agree. Rickhardt had ordered it; a long SUV-style limo, the sort of thing rap stars and upwardly mobile movie actors rode around in. It had been idling outside the winery for a couple of hours before they finally departed in it.

Ann had rolled down the window. There was a long gravel road from the concession line leading into the vineyard. On one side of it, rows of grapes blanketed the land to the south. To the north, there was a higher line of orchards. She couldn't see a thing this time of night, but she liked the scent off the vines; it was fresh, and good.

Michael put his hand on her arm and told her that he loved her, and Ann smiled to herself.

"Do you now?" she said, intending it to be flirtatious. But she wasn't good at that sort of thing, obviously.

Michael took his hand back. "Of course," he said.

That was then.

Now, Ann had trouble even finding the place. She'd bought a road atlas for North America back in Alabama, and she had to stop and refer to it three times. She might've excused that by the simple fact that she was coming at it from the west, and the numerous times she and Michael had driven here had been from the east—from Toronto. Fatigue might've had something to do with it; she'd been on the road for nearly a dozen hours.

But as she slowed down and stopped at the last turn, and just sat, staring into the dark—she thought that might not have been it.

On some level, she just didn't want to do it. Or more precisely, she did want to—but she feared it.

"What are we going to do?" she said to the dark. "I need to get Philip out of there. But I can't just do that. We need to . . . we need to plan."

Ann felt a cool breath on the back of her neck. "Ah," she said.

She shut her eyes. The spectrum of colours drew across her thoughts wordlessly, and she breathed deep. She had seldom come to this place so wordlessly. Might that be because she had, on some level, stopped fearing it?

She felt the deeper darkness; and coalescing before her came the corridor, the stairs, the doors along it, all shut.

"This is the new tower, isn't it?"

Yes.

The word came as a rattling of lockers, as though this high school corridor were the Insect's throat.

"And you're finally talking to me—not just sending messages in the morning dew.

Yes.

"Well thank you." Ann took a breath in the world; here, the air smelled of sweat, and furnace oil. "Can we make a plan?"

We already have.

The lockers stopped rattling entirely, and were quiet.

"What is it?"

And Ann felt the breath again at her neck. She turned.

There was nothing but darkness. Behind her now, the lockers started slamming, open and closed.

Ann opened her eyes.

The transmission shifted into drive, and the van began to move through the intersection. The signal indicator switched on. Ann slammed her foot on the brake, but it wouldn't move. She took hold of the steering wheel, tried to turn it straight; but it was no good. It turned to the right, and the van wobbled down the concession road.

Ann mashed her hand down on the horn; it tooted once, briefly, then became as immobile as other things. In desperation, she twisted the ignition key, and tugged on it. It stayed put.

The van accelerated, and the blue light of the dashboard indicated the headlights had switched to high beams. Far down the road, she could see the Rickhardt Estates sign on the road—a deep purple backing with a delicate curled font in white that mimicked the label. It was two kilometres off.

Ann undid her seatbelt, and twisted around to look back as the van continued on its course. It was dark there; no sense of any presence, or any movement whatsoever. She was about to try and crawl out of the seat—head back there—when she heard the squeaking sound again. She turned to look.

Words were appearing letter by letter—and disappearing, wiped away as fast. She could make out:

TOP IT STOP IT

. . . before the wipe took the entire thing and left the windshield clean, and dry.

The van lurched to the left.

Out the front window, she could now see lights, at the end of a long narrow roadway.

She swore. The van was taking her along the drive to the Rickhardt Estates.

And she was pretty sure it wasn't the Insect doing it.

The van was going more slowly now. She tried to open the door, but of course it was locked. She shuffled over to the passenger side, tried it too, expecting and receiving nothing. She twisted around in her seat and kicked at the window, but it held firm, and so she kicked again.

The van stopped, and there was a shudder as the engine shut down.

The van began to rock back and forth. The engine started again, but this time it went into reverse. There was a crunch, and Ann was thrown in her seat. The van switched gears, pushing forward and turning and lurching through the narrow ditch at the side of the drive. It bumped again, and crashed through branches. It was going into the orchard.

The window fogged, and in it, the words

RUN

wrote themselves, followed by

I WILL HELP.

The driver's side door swung open as the van snapped the trunk of a young apple tree and juddered to a halt.

Ann didn't waste time. She pushed the door open and stumbled out. Back at the road, she could see flashlight beams cutting through the dark. There had been a car shadowing her—without its lights on, obviously. But now they were on and it was three-point-turning into the orchard.

Ann stepped into the shadow of the van before the light could catch her. Without even giving her eyes the chance to adapt to the dark, she ran.

She made it a long way before stumbling; the trees were in rows, and she kept going straight through. Behind her, the headlights speared through the trees, the now-leafless branches. When she finally stumbled, it was more from exhaustion; the adrenaline had been spiking her along for the past six hours. It was a resource of very diminishing returns.

Ann fell against a narrow trunk, gasping for breath. She wanted to vomit, but held it back. She needed to hunker down, find a place to hide. She thought about climbing the tree she was leaning on. It was an apple tree, small and not very high, but the branches were low. She gave it a try. Something in her shoulder started to tear. She let go, and fell back to the loamy earth.

"Fuck." She sat there, huddled against the trunk of the tree—feeling like nothing so much as a field mouse knowing there were owls about.

But the light was gone. The low clouds glowed slightly to the east, and the south, where lights from towns reflected back. But even that seemed muted. And the orchard had become very quiet. It was almost as though she had stepped over a ridge when she slipped from the tree—fallen into a cleft or a valley where she was entirely alone.

After a moment, Ann stood. She was feeling better. At least she had caught her wind.

She started to piece together what had happened. Of course, they had been waiting for her here. These men may have had enough connections to hire a hit man and a Miami lawyer, but they didn't have the means, clearly, to watch every border crossing twenty-four hours a day. On the other hand, they'd known that one of the few places she'd be going was right here, if she were coming back at all.

So here was where they'd waited. Ann hadn't considered that but it made sense—it was a logical way to grab her, if that's what they were going to do—and if they didn't want to involve U.S. law enforcement to do it for them.

They hadn't wanted that. Which was why they'd sent Hirsch to the hospital, and offered up a respite home in St. Augustine, against the bogeyman of Ann's humiliation in front of the Federal Aviation Authority.

She began to shake. Part of that was the cold—it was three in the morning in November, and she wasn't dressed for it. But that was a small part. More chilling than the cold was that realization: they'd seen her coming.

She pulled her legs close to her and tucked her head into her knees. Like a tongue to a broken tooth, her mind settled back on the colours of the spectrum. But there were no colours; just the words: Red. And orange.

Yellow.

Yellow.

Light.

"There."

Ann opened her eyes. The speaker turned the mag-light away from her. He was taller than she remembered, had a bit of a paunch that had been hidden by his broad shoulders. His brush-cut hair stood out in spikes, by the light cast by the other flashlights that wove through the tree branches like searchlights, moving toward her.

"Are you hurt?" asked the man. His voice sounded different now than it had in her cabin in the Rosedale Arms.

"No," said Ann. She pushed herself back against the tree trunk; the bark bit into the thin denim jacket she'd bought on the road.

"Good. You hit my truck pretty hard; back of your van took most of it. Should have been wearing your seatbelt."

Ann looked up at him. The other flashlights were shining on both of them now, and she could see his face. His hair was greying, but he didn't look much older than forty.

He looked kinder than he had tossing her cabin, Taser ready in one hand. . . .

She murmured to the Insect: *Kill him.* Shame came and went, like a wave over beach pebbles. *Kill all of them if you have to.*

He smiled a bit and bent down as one of the flashlights came up beside him. It was held by a child, or someone very small; it just came up to his waist. It wore a hood. As it moved into the light, Ann saw that it was a little girl. Dark-haired—ten years old, maybe twelve. And yes. The same girl she'd seen for an instant outside the cabin. Of course.

"She's trying," said the girl. "But Mister Sleepy has it all sewn up. Don't worry."

"I'm not," said the man, and patted the girl on the back of her head. "Thank you, Mister Sleepy," he said, looking not at her but into the night sky. "Thank you, all of you."

The branches rustled as though there were a breeze, and the man extended his hand down to Ann.

Because she could think of nothing else, she took it. He hauled her to her feet, but it was hard to stand.

"I'll try and be a gentleman," he said as he slipped his arm underneath hers.

"See that you do," said another voice from behind her. It was one that Ann thought she might recognize. Just then, she couldn't say from where. But he didn't speak again until much later.

"Now come on, Mrs. Voors," the first man said.

He led Ann for a few steps, then dragged her, and finally—apologizing again—bent down, drew his other arm behind her thighs, and lifted her.

"You're shaking like a leaf."

"She's afraid," said the little girl, "of Mister Sleepy."

Ann shivered, and shut her eyes. She didn't fight; it was as though all the energy had fled from her. She felt as though she were deflating.

"Who are you?" she asked.

He said something, but she couldn't make out what, exactly.

ii

The music was not especially loud, but it was too loud to ignore. It was choral. It reminded her of Orff, a bit. One of the middle bits of *Carmina Burana*. But more primitive. *Carmina Burana* as arranged for piano movers and orchestra.

Ann opened her eyes. Her mouth was very dry. Her head was propped up on sofa pillows. The rest of her was prone, on a sofa. It felt velvety and lumpy. But it was warm. She looked around; she was in a large room. There may have been windows, but it was hard to tell; thick green curtains hung along two of the walls. The other two walls were painted burgundy. There was a stained pine dining room table, and some chairs near Ann's couch, and an overstuffed dark leather recliner.

The room was not brightly lit, and what light there was came from the far end.

That was also where the music came from: the speakers next to a big, flat screen TV. Ann propped herself up and looked. There was a game playing on it—a first-person shooter type of game, but with a bow and arrow rather than a big gun, and the fellow wielding it was running around some mountainous terrain on a beautiful autumn afternoon. The view was only partly occluded by a high-backed leather chair, faced away from Ann.

Ann swallowed. It hurt a little to do so. She put her feet on the floor. The game shifted to a menu screen, showing a compass rose of choices.

"Mrs. Voors?"

Ann stood, carefully.

"It's Ann," she said. "Yes. Hello Susan."

The chair turned around. Ian Rickhardt's wife, Susan Rickhardt, was clad in a dark fleece sweater and pale blue track pants, thick-toed feet proudly bare. The music from the game had devolved into a series of grunts: the piano movers were hefting the Heintzman up the stairs, Ann thought, and suppressed what she was pretty sure would be a crazy laugh.

"You're awake," Susan said simply.

"Barely," said Ann. And it was true; she felt doughy, as though something were holding her down. Something might have been holding her down, she realized. It was somehow easy to forget that she had just been abducted; it was in fact impossible to remember the point at which she had apparently passed out. Which she must have, because here she was, on a couch in this very simply appointed room, looking at Ian Rickhardt's wife playing a video game. She wasn't a guest here. She was a prisoner. Was Susan Rickhardt the one they'd left to guard her?

"I take it this room is somewhere in the winery?"

Susan shrugged. "I call it home," she said.

Ian's wife Susan—the simple fact of her—had always been a puzzle for Ann. She was heavyset and dull-eyed. The only time she'd seen her out of sweats was at the wedding, when she'd also had her dark, too-thin hair done as nicely as you could ever expect. When they'd first been introduced her hair was as it was just now—flat on her scalp, unwashed. Susan had shaken her hand perfunctorily, almost sullenly. She didn't seem like the sort of woman a man like Rickhardt would marry. It would have to be love—though Ian didn't seem to be the type for that.

When she remarked on this to Michael, he'd just winked, and said, "She must have hidden talents."

Ann had slugged him in the arm and called him nasty, but she hadn't really been angry. It was one of the few times he'd shown anything approaching lechery, and she thought then she wouldn't mind if he showed it more often.

If only she'd known.

Ann shook her head. Something was dulling her now; the same weird fatigue that had knocked her out in the orchard.

Focus, she thought, and asked: "Do you know where Philip is?"

Susan Rickhardt picked up the game controller from where it nestled in her lap and tapped a button. The compass rose vanished and she was back at it.

"There's a dragon on top of that hill," she said. "I'll take it down, soon as I can find the path up."

Ann stood, wobbling a bit, crossed the room. There was no other chair in front of the TV so she knelt beside Susan.

"Skyrim?" said Ann, and Susan nodded.

"Best Elder Scroll yet," she said.

"So I've heard," said Ann. "You've been at this awhile, I see."

The bar at the bottom of the screen showed she was running a character at Level 48. Susan didn't answer; she was absorbed in the game.

After a moment, Ann got up. She was steadier on her feet—far steadier, certainly, than she'd been in the orchard. She walked over to the curtain, peeked out the tall window behind it. There was nothing to see but dark; so she'd either slept a long time, or not long at all.

There was a door, behind the sofa where Ann had been sleeping, next to a long mahogany credenza. It was a double door, stained dark, with brass handles. Ann went to it, and turned a handle.

It wasn't locked. Ann pulled it open a crack. There was a hallway beyond, lit by halogen pot lights. She shut the door quietly and leaned her back on it.

Back at the TV, the battle for Skyrim continued. Susan appeared to be sneaking up a cliff, approaching a camp of barbarians with arrow notched.

"Save the game," said Ann. Susan responded by letting an arrow fly and killing a lean woman wearing a headdress. Her two companions got up and began looking around for the source.

"Save it," said Ann again, as she crossed the room back to the TV. Susan put two more arrows into the men. One of them fell dead; the other was strong enough to take it. He drew a sword and moved to attack.

Ann stepped up to the TV stand, and pressed the eject button on the game console. The screen went dark. Ann turned around and faced Susan.

"I'm sorry," she said. "It's time for talking. Play later."

"You are a little bitch," said Susan. She tried to look around Ann, to the screen. "Put it back in."

"Okay," said Ann, "I will in a minute. But first. Where is Philip?"

"Put it in."

"Where?"

"Put it—"

There was a knock at the door.

"Tell me where my brother is, Susan. Please."

Susan didn't answer. She pushed back in the chair, like she was pulling away from something. Her eyes became wide. She shook her head quickly, like she was trying to dislodge something.

The knocking resumed—louder this time.

"Should I get that?" asked Ann, and Susan shook her head no.

"Why not? Is it someone you don't want to talk to?"

"Put it back in, now," she said.

"Is it Ian?"

"No."

"If I put this back in," said Ann, wagging the disk back in front of her, "will that stop?"

Things happened very quickly after that. Susan drew back, like she was experiencing g-forces in an airplane, and then launched. The chair skidded backwards on the floor, and suddenly, she had hold of Ann's wrist.

Ann stumbled back as Susan kept pushing, and Ann fell against the TV. It toppled backwards and with a wrenching crash, fell to the hardwood floor behind it.

The pounding abruptly stopped.

Susan let go of Ann's wrist, and Ann righted herself.

Behind her, the two door handles turned down.

"What've you done," said Susan. Her voice was flat. Dead. She couldn't even make it sound like a question.

The doors swung inward, until there was maybe a foot of space between them.

"It's your poltergeist, isn't it?" Ann said

And from the look on Susan's face, she could see that she'd guessed it.

Susan had been Ann many years ago, when Ian Rickhardt married her: a young woman who'd had a poltergeist in her from her childhood. And she had sat here, cared for, playing console role-playing games, while Rickhardt carried on. She was a vessel.

She was shut down.

"Does the game ordinarily keep it at bay?" asked Ann. But Susan wasn't answering; she'd turned around and was staring at the door. Her breath puffed visibly, giving her a smoker's wreath of mist. She was trembling, now.

Terror circled Ann too, looking for an opening, but Ann wouldn't give it one. She drew a breath of the newly cold air and stepped close behind the older woman.

"What do you call yours?"

"Little," Susan said, her voice shaking. "I call it Little, though it's not. You're a bitch. Always were."

Around them, the curtains started to billow—as if perhaps a figure moved behind them. Ann shivered, and Susan's breath condensed in little clouds.

"I used to play Dungeons & Dragons," said Ann. "I used that to keep mine quiet. A magical D & D kingdom where I made all the rules. It worked for a long time. Never thought about trying a video game."

Susan looked around the room, her eyes narrowed into a squint.

"It's not like that," she said.

"Then what is it like?"

"You don't control it," said Susan. "You don't keep it *quiet*. That's not your job. The only thing you have to do, is stay out of its way."

The curtains fell back, and were still.

"All you have to do," said Susan, "you stupid little bitch, is stay out of its way."

Susan moved behind the table, to survey the damage that was done to the TV. Its glass screen was cracked, and dark. She knelt down and ran her finger along the line in the glass.

"I don't know where your brother is," she said, not looking up. "I saw him when he showed up a day ago, but Ian said it might not be for long."

"Did he say where he was going next?"

"Home," said Susan. "He said he might go home."

"So he's left here, definitely," said Ann.

"He's left here definitely."

"And you think he's gone back to the rest home."

"Ian said he was going home."

"So Ian knows where he's gone?"

"I guess," said Susan.

"Thank you," said Ann, and Susan looked up at that.

"Sorry I called you that word," she said. "That's not how it was supposed to go when you woke up."

Ann tried to smile. "I'm sorry about the TV."

"My fault," said Susan. She stood up, and frowned and nodded to herself. "I'm the fuckup. I was supposed to offer you some wine. Maybe something stronger. I got caught up. Stupid game."

Ann felt a chill up her arms again, but this time, the drapes were still. This chill was familiar in its own way. She'd felt it on the road, at the end of a long day driving, as she pulled into a campground, and thought about opening up the cooler in back.

"Is there wine here?"

"Over there," said Susan, motioning to the credenza. "Some nice stuff. You should have a glass."

"Not sure I feel like wine right now. Philip—"

At that, Susan finally cracked a grin. "Oh, come on now," she said. "I already told you. Philip's gone."

Ann looked at the credenza, and at Susan. She shook her head.

"I shouldn't. Not until—"

"Until what?" Susan motioned to the credenza again. "You're not going anywhere for at least a few hours. And really—when haven't you felt like a nice glass of Ian's wine? Just check it out."

The credenza was more than it appeared.

When Ann opened the doors, she found inside a small bar refrigerator, installed next to racks of tall stemless wine glasses and a rack of six bottles of red wine. The refrigerator contained another six bottles of white. Ann selected a Gewürztraminer. Rickhardt Estates did a good job with the Gewürzt.

There was a giant corkscrew contraption on the shelf below the glasses. To the uninitiated, it was a puzzle box, but Ian had this model in his kitchen and early in their acquaintance he'd showed Ann the trick. Ann unfolded and twisted and pumped, and the pink rubber cork disappeared in the thing's belly. She pulled out two glasses, holding them between three fingers by the rims as she set them down, and poured.

It was only after she'd joined Susan back at the wreckage of the TV that Ann noticed. The doors leading to the hallway, right beside her, were shut.

"Sure," said Susan, taking the glass, "just one."

"I don't remember this part of the house," said Ann. They were sitting on the sofa, each tucked against separate armrests. Susan Rickhardt was back in her Buddha pose, legs crossed up under her, her wine glass cradled in her lap. She was looking at her lap.

"You're not in the house," she said.

"We're at the vineyard, though. I don't remember this from the winery either."

Susan nodded. "You never came out to this part. It's the conference centre."

"Didn't know there was a conference centre."

"It was no secret. But I can see how Ian wouldn't give you the tour."

"We had our wedding here. You'd think we'd have at least talked about using this—"

"You'd think you two would've talked about a couple things."

"You know what I mean."

"Sure. They don't do weddings here," said Susan. "That's what the new building's for. Wasn't that one nice enough for you?"

Ann emptied her glass and reached down for the bottle. It was mostly empty.

"Damn," said Susan. "I'll get you another one."

"It's not that," said Ann. "But . . ." she struggled to put the thought to words. Wine didn't usually hit her this hard. ". . . but let's put it on the table. This isn't a conference centre, is it now?"

Susan bent down and rummaged under the credenza. "You want to move to red, or another Gewürzt?"

"What goes on here?"

"I think more Gewürzt. You like that special, don't you?"

"It's nice, yes. What goes on here, Susan?"

"For you and me," she said, pulling a fresh bottle from the fridge, "nothing much."

"That's not an answer," said Ann. "There was a—manifestation, a poltergeist a minute ago. Was that, um . . ."

"Little? I dunno."

"How can you not know?"

Susan smiled. "One of many, dear."

Ann stared at Susan Rickhardt. She'd called her dear. A few minutes ago, Ann was "a little bitch," who'd interrupted her video game. It was as though this were a different woman, now, talking sweet and pouring her drinks. That chilled Ann almost as much as the thing she'd just let slip.

"What do you mean, many?" Ann said. "How many?"

Susan went on. "The boys are in town," she said, "and with them, their wives. This conference centre, it's a little like a running party. There are, oh, a dozen couples here. The boys do their thing. And the wives . . . we wait. Keep ourselves occupied."

"Occupied with what?"

"Oh," said Mrs. Rickhardt, "with whatever we like. Used to be a big World of Warcraft junkie. Skyrim's my poison, these days."

"I can see."

"And yours—" Mrs. Rickhardt came back with the bottle, and topped up Ann's glass. "Well."

Ann put her glass down. "What's going on here?"

"Oh," said Susan, "the same thing that's been going on all your life."

"What do you mean by that?"

Susan nodded sagely, as though she were revealing a great truth.

"You're vanishing. Just like the rest of us did when they shrove us off. Now drink up. It'll be better if you drink up."

Ann did not remember when she had her first drink. It was probably wine. It was definitely wine. But it wasn't at home; her parents were not among those who believed that children should be weaned on wine, or that brandy was the best medicine for a sore throat.

She didn't remember when, either—other than it was in an innocent time. She must have been very young. She didn't know how young, but she remembered the moment. It was like stepping into a winter wind, hard enough to steal your breath; a kiss, welcome but still a surprise. The sharp, happy flavour of a good idea. It tasted like luck.

It still tasted like luck. It had always tasted like luck. That first sip of wine had always tasted as sweet, and as fine, as that first time.

Ann thought: *I could disappear into it.*

"I'm not disappearing," said Ann. She stood up. "I don't know what 'shrove' means. But I don't think I'll stay to find out. I'll be leaving now."

Susan Rickhardt looked at her, and set the bottle down.

"You might want to think about that," she said.

Ann shrugged. "I don't see anyone here who can stop me."

Susan smiled at that and she laughed, in a way, as Ann opened the door on the empty hallway.

"You noticed that, did you?"

Ann turned. Mrs. Rickhardt looked back at her steadily.

"They don't need to stop you," she said. "There's nothing you can do anyway."

Ann shut the door on her.

iii

It *was* a conference centre.

Ann couldn't believe that she'd mistaken it for Rickhardt's home. She couldn't believe that she hadn't been here or noticed it before; it was clearly a major facility.

The hallway should have been her first clue. It was a little wider than you'd expect in someone's home, and there were semi-circular seats between the doors. Little brass sign-holders were beside each door, where you might put your itinerary for that particular room. The rooms had names, too—named for grapes: Merlot, and Chardonnay, and Pinot Grigio—inscribed in script over the lintels. Lighting came from silvered sconces on the wall, casting their beams to the ceiling, and to the burgundy carpets.

Ann stood there a moment. The air here was warm, conditioned—she flexed her hands, waiting for the chill, or the flare of heat, that indicated a presence here. There were women here—possibly in each room—and they might all be like her, carrying their own Insects, and Littles and Mister Sleepys.

Away from Susan Rickhardt, Ann allowed herself to consider the fact: for the first time since the Lake House, she truly was in a haunted house.

A haunted conference centre, excuse me.

Ann started forward, hands fluttering slowly at her side, feeling the warm air for the iciness of invisible spectres.

The hallway continued a long way, turned at a stairwell, then opened up into a space not unlike the tasting room in Rickhardt's winery.

It was better appointed, though; something the Krenk team at Ann's architectural firm might've done. For the first time in weeks, Ann found herself appraising space like an architect.

The ceiling opened up into an arching dome, like the inside of an overturned boat. Iron-hooped chandeliers hung from crossbeams on black chains. Behind the bar, wooden wine racks sat empty. Thick oak pillars touched the beams on each side, like piers in the nave of a cathedral.

Tall windows lined one wall—but it was still deep in the night and the only illumination came from a banker's lamp overhanging the space on the bar where one might find a computer and till.

In its place sat a polished brass container, with a gleaming steel lid.

Ann's running shoes squeaked on the wooden floor. It was the only sound in here. She approached the bar.

"Would you like to be left alone for a moment?"

Ann froze in the middle of the room. Ian Rickhardt stepped out from behind the tasting bar. He was wearing a white, open-necked shirt and a pair of green khakis. His feet were bare. His hair was damp, as though he'd just showered and dressed. He gestured to the light, the container.

"I'm sorry for your loss, Ann," he said.

Ann blinked. She pointed to the container—"Is that . . ."

Ian nodded. "Michael's remains."

Right. It was not a container. It was an urn.

"You cremated him."

"I'm so sorry," said Ian. He stepped closer to Ann. "You disappeared," he said. "In Miami. You went right off the grid. Can't blame you, really—after that shit show that Hirsch put on for you. But you were gone, we couldn't find you anywhere, and decisions had to be made."

"You found me in Mobile," said Ann, and Ian raised an eyebrow.

"Did we now?"

Did Ian know? Ann kept her face impassive, but she wondered now: did Ian know that when his agent had come into the cabin in the Rosedale Arms, Ann was tucked away . . . by the Insect, who knew enough to hide, then?

Did he not know, and did she just tell him?

Ann cleared her throat. "How is Mr. Hirsch?"

"Oh, you don't know. Of course you don't. Full recovery. Back on the squash court like nothing happened."

Ann looked at Rickhardt. He looked back, shook his head, pursed his lips.

"He's alive," said Rickhardt. "Doesn't have much to report. On account of, well, the *stroke*. But I expect inside that shell of his, he's happy as a clam."

Ann stepped close to the cylinder. On one side, there was a little engraved plaque.

MICHAEL VOORS
1979-2013

"I don't think so," said Ann, running her finger around the steel lid. "You weren't there."

Rickhardt shook his head. "You don't know Johnny like I know Johnny."

Ann took a breath. Once again, the reality of her situation caught up to her. Here she was, in an empty hall with Ian Rickhardt, who'd come to Tobago to . . . what? To rape the Insect? While she was on her honeymoon, with the man who couldn't get through one short flight before he did the same thing to it?

Hirsch had warned her about Rickhardt . . . had promised something better, something she'd find in a spa in St. Augustine. Ann hadn't believed him about that.

But she did believe him about this: Ian Rickhardt was dangerous.

He'd demonstrated this many times over. He'd sent people after her. He'd sent something else after her. He'd had those people overpower her, and take her virtual prisoner.

"Do you want to cry?"

"What?"

"I'm sorry. Maybe not cry, but have that time alone. Over Michael's ashes. I can leave you for a moment. Given that you're here now, I should have waited before authorizing the cremation. I'm sorry. That was bad of me."

"I'm fine."

"Should I leave? Give you a moment?"

Ann sighed, and took her hand from the urn.

"How do I do this?" she said quietly. Ian didn't answer, just raised his eyebrows in a question. "How does it go? Michael was a rapist. You're a rapist. I've had to put up with and internalize this shit. So how do I talk about it, to you, in a reasonable and rational way?"

"We're rapists," said Ian. "I see."

"Ian," said Ann, "can we just drop the pretense? I saw what you did in Tobago. I saw what Michael did on the plane. And I know about you and your friends. What you do."

"And what is it we do?"

"You rape poltergeists." She said it very quickly, so that it came out as almost a single word: *yourapepoltergeists*.

"No, Ann, we don't."

Ann shut her eyes. She felt like she was going to vomit. She nearly did, as sour acid filled her mouth.

She summoned the spectrum, a slow ladder to the depths. She murmured: "Red, yellow . . ."

"Hey," said Ian, "You're doing Eva Fenshaw's trick now, aren't you? With the colours, and your little prison, aren't you?"

Ann opened her eyes, expecting to see Ian's smirk—like when he showed up in Tobago with his wedding video, but really to elbow his protégé out of the way and have first-night privileges. He wasn't smirking, though. He leaned against the bar, comfortable.

"How do you know about that?"

He shrugged. "Eva told me about some of the stuff she does at the wedding. She's a great gal, but she likes to talk. We did some healing exercises together, and she told me about the prison."

"She just told you everything."

"Well, not just me. But she does like to talk. When she got sick—when that stroke hit . . . she was very talkative indeed. Told us a lot of things that we missed, after that incident with the minivan. Your parents. Philip. That girl—Laurie?

"That girl."

"Eva's like a mother to you, isn't she?"

"Oh, fuck you," said Ann, and at that, Rickhardt did smirk.

"I have to confess, Ann. I'm actually a little nervous, talking like this, upsetting you," he said. "Do you have any idea what's going on right now outside this place? The state of Michigan is on an orange terror alert. The Port Huron crossing's a mess right now; the Blue Water Bridge is completely shut down. CNN's saying there are three dead on the U.S. side. Homeland Security personnel. Doesn't get more serious than that. The Canadian side isn't reporting any dead. But it's a mess too. They're talking about cyber-terrorism, too. Given that you made it here, I'm assuming that means that somehow, you shut down and wiped all the video surveillance. Because otherwise . . . they'd have caught you on the drive here. They might've shot you, if they'd seen it all." Ian shook his head. "Surely there was an easier way to get back into your country of birth. Even if you didn't want to be detected. But oh—it gets very serious, when the Insect goes a-walking, doesn't it?"

"It did that to Hirsch," said Ann, "and it can do that to you."

Ian nodded. "It did that to him. It also killed my dear friend Michael Voors. And your parents, didn't it?"

"Don't," said Ann. Her voice was low. She surprised herself by the fury in it.

"So don't *you*," said Ian. "Don't call me a rapist. Because, I'll tell you. Coming from a woman who's committed . . . let's see. Patricide . . . matricide . . . and what's the word when a young bride murders her loving husband? It'll come to me. Point is this: you really aren't in a position to call rape."

"I didn't do any of that," said Ann.

"Right," said Ian, "it was the Insect. A being that has nothing to do with you."

"Why are you doing this?"

"You just threatened me, Ann. That your Insect would also harm me, in the way that it did John Hirsch."

"Hirsch told me about you," said Ann. "And the others. And the things you did."

Ian nodded. "And that's why we're having this conversation. Part of the reason. Normally, I wouldn't worry about you. I'd just leave you with Susan. You two could catch up, play a little Skyrim, get good and toasted on the fine wines of Rickhardt Estates. But the fact is, you're not going to do that. I figured that out for certain when you, ah, wrecked that rather nice television set in the Cab Franc room."

Ann looked at him. "Did Little tell you about that?"

Ian laughed at that. "Little? Susan's 'Little'? No. With one or two notable exceptions, the 'geists don't run our errands. We also have webcams. A couple of us were keeping an eye on you. We wanted to see how you'd interact . . . if you could be, uh, integrated."

"Integrated."

"Yeah. See, when Michael brought you home, that should have taken care of it. But things took a turn for the worse. . . ." He looked down, then up again. It was like he was checking notes, Ann thought. "Here's the thing, Ann. We want you back here. And on some level, you want to be back here too."

"Bullshit."

"No," said Ian, "you do. If you didn't—you would never have come."

Ann shivered. Was the room chilling? Was the Insect manifesting around her? She rather hoped that it was; she wanted it to reach through Ian's flesh, and pinch together some blood cells into a clot, as it had with Hirsch.

She rather hoped that it would just kill everyone right now.

"I don't want to be back here. I want my brother back. Where is he?"

"All right," said Ian, ignoring the question pointedly, "you don't want to be back here. But I'll tell you, kid—the Insect sure as shit does. That's why it led you home."

"You're playing games," said Ann.

"I'm not," said Ian, "at least not with you. The reason we're having this conversation is simple. Because the Insect, as you call it, is back exactly where it wants to be. But it's tied to you, Ann. There are some of us who think that in fact, it *is* you. It can't stay, if you don't."

"Such shit," said Ann, but Ian shook his head, and pointed at the urn.

"Look," he said, and Ann did.

The urn no longer gleamed metallic in the light. It was covered in hoarfrost—as though it held liquid nitrogen, or some other frozen matter, rather than the cooling ashes of Michael Voors. It looked like nothing so much as an eggshell.

"It's telling you it's okay," said Ian. "It's calling you to go see it."

The egg started to throw off tendrils of mist, and Ann opened her mouth to call bullshit once more. But she couldn't. Not really.

She didn't need to see words written in the frost to understand that.

The Tower of Light

i

"I'd apologize for not telling you about this place," said Ian as they climbed down a sweeping set of stairs past a long, empty registration desk and a little lobby, "but really, I don't feel I owe you that. If your boss Krenk had won the bid to make my winery—if he'd shown the vision . . . then you probably would have had an idea all on your own what was happening here. But in the end . . . couldn't trust him."

"Because it's a secret conference centre," said Ann.

They moved past the registration desk and into a glassed-in corridor. Outside, Ann thought she could see the dawn coming—a hint of pink over treetops.

"Because I couldn't trust him," said Ian. "When you're involved in something like I am—we are—trust is paramount."

"Like a bottom trusts a top," said Ann. "You've got to keep your safe words straight."

Ian gave her a look.

"It's not like that," he said, and she said, "Of course it's not."

The corridor went down a gentle slope, and turned. Double doors at the far end led to the Octagon Ballroom, according to the signage. They stopped there. Ian thrust his hands into his pockets and looked down at his bare feet, as though he were waiting, for something.

"This would have been a good place to hold the wedding," observed Ann, and Ian chuckled at that.

"Who was it who a moment ago said we should drop pretense?"

In spite of herself, Ann smiled. Ian folded his arms and leaned against the glass.

"It's not rape," he said. "But I can see how you'd think it is. Because it's certainly sexual. And consent . . . well, it's complicated."

Ann leaned against the glass opposite him, folded her arms to mirror Rickhardt. "I have to hear this," she said.

"You ever read any of Stephen King's stuff?"

"I started the Dark Tower series in high school. I read the book with the story about the boys going to find a body in the woods. Otherwise, you can imagine his stuff might not be my thing."

"Yeah. He also wrote a non-fiction book, early on, called *Danse Macabre*. He came up with a hierarchy in it, of the sort of thing that a writer of horror fiction aims for. It's a hierarchy of fear. At the bottom is the simple gross-out—torture, or maiming; up from that is horror: the face of the monster, giant fucking bugs, zombies on the march. And finally . . . there's terror. King calls that the finest emotion of all. And in that—we are in agreement."

"All right. So what does this have to—"

Ian kept going. "Yeah, so here's how he describes terror. It's the cold hand that touches you in the dark. It's coming home and realizing all the furniture in your house has been replaced by furniture that's exactly the same. It's the knowledge that reality is tearing away underneath you. That there's a dark place underneath it that has nothing to do with you, except that it maybe wants to eat you.

"That, Ann, is the nub of it. It's more complicated than that. But that is what we all share—and what you and I share too."

"I don't think we share anything."

"Well it may be true that we don't share the sexual component. If that's what you're guessing."

"Hirsch seemed to think that there was more to poltergeists than sex, though."

"Yes," said Rickhardt, "he does. I think it's fair to say that the American guys like to think about it that way. I think it's in their national character; they can only enjoy something if they pin it to manifest destiny, divine will. So of course, the 'geists are a gateway to the divine. What else did he tell you?"

"He told me about you," said Ann. "He said he'd protect me from you."

Ian smirked. "Those guys can be pretty judgmental down there in the sunshine state. But you knew enough to not fall into his arms, didn't you?"

"The Insect decided that for me."

"It made the right choice. They have a place outside of St. Augustine. Visited there once. They were inducing comas at the time. They thought it enhanced things; unleashed the Id or some shit. But it was a bad idea. I don't think they're doing that anymore. But still. Nowhere you'd want to go."

"So terror," said Ann. "You're telling me that this is a kink for terror."

"It sounds so tawdry when you reduce it to that. The Americans take it too far in the other direction, maybe. But there's a big difference between what we do in these walls . . . and what goes on at a German fetish bar, say. Those people are playing a game, with their leather costumes and safe words.

"We're doing the real thing, Ann. When we stare into the abyss—it really is staring back."

"And yet, in the end it simply arouses you sexually."

"There you go again, being all reductive."

"Is there a more nuanced way that I should be thinking about this?"

Ian opened his mouth to speak, then shook his head and smiled, a little sheepishly.

"So it's like *really* raping children rather than just looking at child pornography," said Ann, "if you were a pedophile, I mean."

"A 'geister," said Ian, not smiling now, "is what I am."

"That's a cute name," said Ann. "But I'm willing to bet that when I came to you 'geisters' attention, I wasn't much more than eight years old. Hirsch told me that much . . . that they'd been watching me for some time. And there's that little girl I met. With what—Mister Sleepy? Tell me—is Dr. Sunderland a 'geister too? I remember that Philip warned me about him. Did he touch Philip?"

"Wow," said Ian, "cards on the table."

Behind him, the sky was lightening. Ann could see it resolving behind the bare branches of the denuded woods around here. The tree branches descended down beneath the floor so it became clear that this wasn't just a covered walkway between buildings. They were on an enclosed bridge, crossing a ravine.

"He at least worked for you, didn't he? We thought he was helping us—but he wasn't, was he?"

"He was helping you," said Ian. "You either would have burned down your house or been in the nuthatch within a year if you hadn't gone there. Sunderland put your 'geist, the Insect, someplace safe. Someplace where it couldn't hurt anybody, and nobody could hurt it."

"And it worked great."

"It worked for a long time. We should've been following closer. The accident . . . that should've tipped us off. But it didn't fit the profile. So you got away from us for a while."

"And then—Michael."

"He was a good kid," said Ian.

"He was a rapist. A fucking liar," said Ann.

Ian nodded in agreement. "He was a liar. He had an agenda in your marriage that he didn't tell you about. But I'll tell you—he would've treated you well, if he'd had the chance."

"How would that have worked? He'd keep me in white wine and video games upstairs, while he and his friends, what—terrified each other to orgasm in the rumpus room?" Ann shook her head. "Where the hell did you find him, anyway? And did you promise me to him? It really did seem as though we just met, the way . . . you know, *normal* people meet."

"Michael I found on the internet," said Ian. "You think of us as this terrible secret society, and while it's true that we communicate—really, it's not a big secret. We're a community. We have websites and chat rooms just like anybody."

"How perfectly innocent of you."

"Well I wouldn't go that far. But we pay attention to those chatrooms—because that, really, is just the modern variation of how all of us got involved with each other. Me, I was bit old for that. I came to this through EC horror comics, those Warren magazines . . . *Famous Monsters of Film Land*. I met people. . . . Well, Michael just signed himself up on "Spectral Women," and we started up a friendship. Good thing for him, too—he was still in Capetown, and would've got himself killed if he stayed there longer."

"He didn't speak a lot about South Africa," said Ann.

"He was taking a lot of risks. His family had a bit of money. His dad was a lawyer, like him. He'd had a post with the government, during Apartheid, gone into practice afterward. They had a nice big house. A compound, really. You could spend your whole life there, not step out at all. Got the sense it was designed for that; Mr. Voors had some enemies. Or at least, he thought he did."

Ann's fists clenched, but she kept them at her side. *You have some enemies too, Rickhardt.* "What risks did he take?" she asked.

"There was something going on around his house—maybe those enemies at work. Michael told me about some experiences he'd had as a little kid. Faces at his windows; cold drafts. It might have been the real thing. It probably was. And it was terrifying. But of course—"

"—he got to like it."

"He did," said Ian. "He saw it all as a mystery at first, like he was in one of those boy detective books, where the haunting would turn out to have a perfectly rational explanation for the thing that he saw."

"What did he see?"

"Would it help you understand if I said Michael saw a beautiful, naked girl?" Ian chuckled. "I don't know exactly what he saw. I'm sure he didn't know exactly what he saw. He was only twelve, when he started into it."

"That's young," said Ann, and Ian gave her a look that she couldn't quite apprehend.

"Ten years later, he could have learned everything he needed to know with a Google search. As it was, he did his work the old-fashioned way. He left the compound. He went to the library. Started asking around. He visited shops. Found out about séances, and covens, and 'secret ceremonies.' Got him robbed a couple of times. Could have got him killed, given the times. Finally, years later, he got himself mixed up with a *sangoma*—a witch doctor, sort of a healer woman. *She* was a beautiful girl, now. Not much older than him."

"Did she seduce him?"

"Oh, in a way. But by that time, he'd found the websites—the chatrooms. She was showing him things—and he, the little idiot, was taking pictures and telling stories and bringing them to us, uploading them to a room we had running on GEnie."

"What?"

"Before your time," said Rickhardt. "But the point is, they were up there. Where anybody could see. That was when I noticed him. They were real treasures. There was one in particular—of a human femur, dug out of a grave it looked like, floating in the air above a woman, who was floating herself, just a foot off the ground. It was taken in a Capetown slum, in what looked like early morning. The sun made it all golden. I got in touch with him directly, because I wanted to know if it had been manipulated. He offered to show me the negative."

"Negative?"

"He shot it on film," said Ian. "No camera phones in those days."

"That sounds risky," said Ann, and Ian allowed as it was.

"I tried to steer him away from that—if nothing else, it wasn't making it any easier with his family, who didn't like him consorting with the *sangoma* and her friends, and there was trouble there too. Michael very nearly didn't make it out of there. Do you know what necklacing is?"

Ann nodded. "Michael told me about it on our first date," she said. "He didn't use the term. He just called it a tire thing. But I looked it up."

Back when that was the worst thing that I thought Michael brought to this relationship.

"Yeah, it's never far from his mind. You fill up a tire with gasoline, put it around your victim's neck and light it on fire. Watch him die. It takes a long time.

"They got as far as pouring the gasoline in the tire and putting it over his head, before they let him go. It was a warning. He'd followed his *sangoma* girl to an exorcism for a little girl. The family had been ANC, during Apartheid, and they were, shall we say, private people. They caught him taking pictures. They wanted to make sure that didn't happen again, but didn't quite want to kill him. Still—the display made an impression."

"He didn't tell me about that part."

"Of course he didn't; he was ashamed of what he did. He was a liar, and he was compelled toward these things . . . the 'geists. That compulsion—we all accept it, but nobody's proud of it. But he wasn't some monster. None of us are." Ian rubbed the back of his neck and looked outside, over Ann's shoulder. What was he looking for? "Most of what he was, you knew: an immigrant from South Africa who took his law degree at Osgoode and didn't speak with his father anymore. I sponsored him, and I helped him with his tuition, and he stayed with me in Toronto while he was studying, and he became—yes, like a son to me."

"And from pretty early on, you had him zeroed in on me."

"It was all he ever wanted," said Ian. "He would have treated you well."

Dawn broke over the woods. It was a winter sky, although winter had not yet come. Ann wondered if it would storm. She thought that it should. Storm had followed her from Alabama, through the midwest and across the border, in hail and rain and funnel clouds. It should be here now.

But there was no storm outside; thin branches reached up from the depths in a deathly stillness. The clouds overhead hung quiet and thin. It all lay beyond clean, dry glass. There were no messages for Ann, or anyone, in this landscape.

Ian was watching the landscape too. In the morning gloom, he seemed hunched, small, and very old. His face was sallow, and dark rings cradled his eyes, which cast over treetops—looking for any sign of life out there. It seemed, for that instant, as though the breath caught in both their throats, each of them trapped in droplets of psychic amber: a kind of limbo. Neither of them wanted to take a step further. They'd been killing time at the threshold, telling ghost stories about Michael Voors here at the end of the night.

Now the light had come.

Ann imagined them on another bridge—the one that she needed to cross every time she needed to obtain entry to the Insect's prison. The pallid morning light grew over the ravine, and it seemed as though the treetops themselves sank as the earth distended below them. The plate glass on either side might as well have been open gallery windows, extended from the flagstone floor to the thatch and timber roof, separated by Grecian columns, wrapped in dark ivy. The door at the end was thick oak, bound in iron, held tight by a bar, and twelve sturdy locks. And the light, awful and sickly as it was, filled the hallway here and gave it its name.

The Hallway of Light.

"Ian," said Ann finally, when her breath found her again, "what's behind that door?"

"You don't have to go," he said, "if you'd rather not."

"It's the Insect, right?"

Ian said nothing. He shut his eyes tightly, bit on his lower lip. In the Hallway of Light in her mind, he was a shrivelled gnome, shrinking and crumbling in the sun. Ann studied him.

"Oh my," she said. "Ian. You're terrified."

Ian didn't answer.

She nodded. "Whatever's behind that door. It's as good as it gets for you, isn't it?"

Ian whispered to himself.

"Well I'm not afraid," she said, and knocked on the door three times, sharply.

ii

When the door opened, Ann wondered briefly whether the hand that opened it would be human. This time, it was. She recognized its owner immediately.

"I didn't catch your name back in the orchard," she said.

Mister Sleepy's babysitter had changed clothes.

Now he was wearing a crisp white tunic and matching trousers, both made from loose-woven cotton. Ann had seen ensembles like this in Little India on Gerrard Street.

"It's Peter," he said. "Hello, Mrs. Voors. Hope you're feeling refreshed."

"As you'd expect."

"Quite," he said, and looked over to Ian, and nodded. Ian nodded back.

"Well why don't you come in, Mrs. Voors."

Peter stepped aside, and beckoned Ann into a small sitting room, with couches like the one Ann had woken up on to either side of the door. Opposite walls had small dark wooden tables underneath mirrors, with table lamps on each.

There were no windows. On the far side of the room, there was another set of doors much like this one. They were propped open, to darkness.

"How's your little girl?" Ann asked.

"She's just fine, ma'am. Though as you've probably guessed, she's not my child."

Ian jumped in: "Peter's up from Tennessee. With his niece. Isn't that right?"

"That's where you're from," said Ann. "You probably don't remember, but you and I met. In Mobile."

"I reckon we did meet, Mrs. Voors, at least nearly," said Peter. "Glad you made it here safe."

Was he glad? Ann had to wonder. He was a southerner: probably one of Rickhardt's judgemental Americans; maybe from the same little coven that'd spawned John Hirsch. If he'd taken her at the Rosedale Arms, she doubted he'd have brought her here, to Southern Ontario. Assuming he could have wrangled her and the Insect, likely she would have wound up in whatever facility they'd built at St. Augustine.

If the opportunity arose, would he do that now?

He didn't give her the chance to ask. "I'll tell the Doctor you're in," he said. "Excuse me a moment, please."

"The Doctor?" Ann asked as he stepped through the doors and into darkness. Ian said nothing.

"What is this place?" said Ann finally.

"It's the Octagon: which is to say, an octagon. We pitched it as an homage, to the old octagon houses that used to be safe houses for the Underground Railroad here in Upper Canada."

"Back in the day. When slavery was more, um, institutionalized? Nice juxtaposition."

Rickhardt barked a laugh. "Good one," he said. "Of course, the octagon has other symbolism too. *Older* symbolism."

Ann wouldn't bite. "And it's a ballroom?" she said instead.

"It's not. 'Ballroom' is what's written on the plans we filed with the township."

"So no weddings here," said Ann.

"No," he said. "Maybe next time."

Ian sat down on one of the couches. Ann made a point of sitting on the other. "Must have cost you a fortune," she said, and Ian nodded.

"As you can tell by now," he said, "I'm not what you'd call stingy. And," he added, as the door beyond them swung open, into the darkness, "I'm not alone."

Ann blinked, as the man who was surely the Doctor stepped from it, into the light.

"Look at *you*," said Charlie Sunderland.

He had lost some hair, and gained a little weight, but not so much of either, given that Ann had last seen him more than fifteen years ago.

He wore a pair of dark slacks, a white shirt and unlike Rickhardt and Peter, dark leather shoes. He stepped forward, gingerly shut the door behind him. He looked as though he'd gotten some sun.

"You're all grown," he continued, as he moved to sit on Ann's couch. Ian withdrew perceptibly. It was as though Dracula had stepped into the room. Or more aptly, Josef Mengele.

If Ann looked at him in just the right way, she thought she might scream.

She had guessed about Sunderland being here, being involved; Ian had as much as confirmed it.

But the fact of him, here—it was a blunt, visceral thing; the dangling string off the end of a long continuum that had begun in a little room years ago, and continued in another little room in the woods, and finished here. She crossed her legs and folded her hands on her knee, and knitted her fingers together tightly.

Sunderland smiled gently.

"I can imagine," he said, "that you're angry with me."

Ann shut her eyes. She imagined that she was angry, too. She didn't say anything though.

"Well, you might have cause to be," he said. "If nothing else, I didn't do a very good job then, in fulfilling my promise to your parents."

"That's true," said Ann, opening her eyes again. "You didn't do any kind of job.

"They died, because you weren't trying to help me at all. You were trying to turn me into what—a courtesan?"

His smile faded a little, and he looked at her. "Oh dear," he said. "I may have left you with the impression just now that I am here to apologize to you." Dr. Sunderland ran a forefinger along the back of the couch; if they were sitting any nearer one another, it might have seemed as though he were trying to seduce her.

"You've been drinking," he continued, "a lot. And you're exhausted. You haven't really slept in nearly twenty-four hours—possibly longer. Most of that time, you've been driving, and for most of that drive, you've been terrified. You have no capacity left, do you? You don't even know why you're here right now."

Dr. Sunderland spoke in slow, measured tones that had a lulling effect. Ann drew a deep breath, and blinked.

"So why," he said, "don't you simply repeat the words again: 'Belaim, foredawned, sheepmorne . . .'"

"Fuck off," said Ann, and at that, Dr. Sunderland was quiet. He blinked, as though he'd been slapped. Ian, on the other couch, started to get up, but Sunderland motioned for him to sit.

"We are very close to a thing right now, Ann," said Sunderland. "A very big thing. And you're angry, very understandably angry. Would I be too far off the mark if I said that you thought you might be able to disrupt this thing of ours? Perhaps hurt myself, and Mr. Rickhardt here, and the rest of us?"

Ann didn't answer.

He sighed. "We do need you here right now. If you want to use your time here, attempting to call down the heavens on all of us . . . well, that's up to you. I'd understand."

"You don't think I can."

"You know you can't," said Sunderland. "If you could, you would have by now."

"Ask Mr. Hirsch what I can do," she said.

Sunderland ignored the comment. "We are on the edge of something very big, Ann. I think on some level you know that. I think that is why you came back here."

"I came back here," she said, "to get my brother."

Sunderland nodded. "And you're still here, even though you've been told that he's gone 'home.' Why do you suppose that is?"

"Because . . ." Ann took a breath, stifled a yawn ". . . because I don't believe that."

And he smiled, broadly. "That's an excellent instinct you have," he said.

Ann sat up. "Is he here?" she asked, and Sunderland motioned with one long arm to the doors, now shut.

"Through there," he said.

iii

Rickhardt tried to hold Ann's hand as Sunderland held the door open for them. Ann pulled away. Sunderland was right in some of his observations; she was exhausted, and the wine from the other wing of this place had left a sour taste in her mouth. The world had a shimmer to it that she recognized, from the morning after all-night study sessions. But he was wrong: that she came here, on any level giving a shit about the *thing* that Sunderland and his 'geisters were on the verge of discovering, or extracting, or whatever it was he had planned; and oh, he was wrong about the fact that she had no power.

She was sure he was wrong about that.

He had to be.

Darkness enveloped her as the doors shut behind them, and Ann fought an instant of panic. Should she have taken Ian Rickhardt's hand? The air was suddenly icy cold, as though she'd stepped into a big refrigerated room. The only sound was her own heartbeat, which accelerated in a rush of adrenaline. Screaming might have helped; but as it had moments before, her breath caught still in her throat. She couldn't so much as whisper.

She could walk, though, and she did so, stumbling forward, hands held in front of her. It seemed as though she were running down a ramp of some sort.

The darkness split in front of her in a vertical line of dim light. As it spread further, Ann could see that what was opening was a curtain being drawn—they had stepped into a small circle defined by a thick curtain. It rattled aside on its bar on top, and as it did, Ann found her breath. She stepped forward, and as she did, she was struck by the truth of it:

This wasn't a ballroom at all. It was a tower.

It was a pit.

They were standing on a wide balcony, that circled an octagonal atrium measuring perhaps thirty feet across. A single pillar, with a spiral staircase, ran up the middle; a narrow walkway extended to the staircase from a spot opposite where they stood.

There were more walkways: the balcony was one of at least three; there was one maybe ten feet over Ann's head, and another as far below. The floor, as she peered over, was a dozen feet below that. It may have gone down further; Ann's angle of view didn't afford her much opportunity to see, and the only light came from an octagonal skylight directly above, and this morning it didn't offer up much.

But she could tell that in each of the eight walls of this place, there was a curtain, like the one she'd just passed through—one on each level, one on each wall. Each of those curtains, Ann guessed, would lead to another door: and that door would lead to . . . what? A space that would be a slice of the octagon pie. At least as big as the little lounge they'd found themselves in. She found herself mapping it in her head—grasping for some measure of orientation.

Ann approached the railing. Like the finish on the balcony, it was made of dark wood, and the rail was padded with what felt like real leather. She leaned on it, and tried to look down, then up. The lattice of the skylight reminded her of a spider's web—an effect that she expected was the intent of whichever architect Rickhardt had finally hired to build this thing. It looked like some 18th-century idea of a prison, or an insane asylum, where the cells ringed the atrium, and the guards watched from the middle. A panopticon.

"See, Ann," said Ian Rickhardt from behind her, "just keep holding on."

On the other side of the chamber, one of the curtains wavered. Something moved out—Ann was sure she could see it, a small figure—but it was gone as fast as it had come.

"Ann," said Ian, so close that she could feel his breath on her neck. Ann shifted aside, and turned.

Ian wasn't there. He was standing an eighth of the way around the balcony, gazing dreamily into the centre. His left arm was hanging out from his body, at about twenty degrees, his fingers curled and spread—

—as though he were holding someone's hand.

Dr. Sunderland leaned against the wall, beside the curtain they'd just come through. He had his arms folded tight, but despite the body language he didn't seem perturbed; just cold, like Ann. He motioned her to come closer, and she came.

"It is a poltergeist that is holding Ian's hand," he said quietly, nearly whispering it in Ann's ear, "in case you hadn't guessed."

Ann swallowed hard.

"And he thinks it's me," she said. "Holding his hand."

"Oh, I think it's dawning on him that it's not," said Dr. Sunderland. "Look."

Ian was looking at Ann, and looking down at his hand, his eyes widened in marvel and, Ann supposed, that terror he so craved. Dr. Sunderland smiled.

"It's one of the games they play," he said, "before it gets more serious. The spectral hand, holding your own, in the dark. You think that it was your friend's hand. But when the light comes on, and you say, 'Thank God you were there holding my hand,' your friend says: 'I wasn't holding your hand.' It's an old Shirley Jackson trick."

"Shirley Jackson?"

"*The Haunting of Hill House*?" said Dr. Sunderland, and regarded Ann. "No? Well I can hardly blame you for staying clear of haunted house novels, given your upbringing. But it's fair to say that Shirley Jackson's the Marquis de Sade for the 'geisters."

The curtain behind Ian billowed, and for only an instant a shadow fell across Ian Rickhardt, and then his shirt billowed too. He bent down, as though he could see something more than just moving shadows, shifting curtains. Sunderland shook his head bemusedly, and pushed himself away from the wall.

"Mr. Rickhardt!" he called. "We do still have business, yes?"

Rickhardt seemed to consider that, but Ann suspected it was for show. "You take care of it," he said. "I'll catch up."

As they watched, he fell to his hands and knees and crawled through the curtains, and was gone.

iv

"The heart wants," said Charlie Sunderland wryly, "what the heart wants."

The air seemed to warm as he spoke—or rather, the chill began to flee. Ann felt her shoulders relaxing, and only from that realized how tightly hunched she'd been. Sunderland also flexed his fingers. He looked at Ann.

"Now I will apologize," said Sunderland. "We're not all like Rickhardt. Some of us—"

"—are like Hirsch?"

Sunderland nodded. "Some are like him."

"And you aren't like either of them."

"I'm not," said Sunderland, and he flexed the fingers of both hands, as though re-introducing blood flow into them. "Would you please follow me?" he said, and headed around the balcony to the little bridge to the staircase.

They climbed down the narrow spiral, past two other floors. On each of them, Ann saw eight more sets of curtains. She asked what was behind them.

"Rooms," said Sunderland, "some of them containing poltergeists. Several of them also containing men."

"Is Philip in one of those rooms?" she asked sharply, and was surprised when Dr. Sunderland merely nodded.

Ann halted between floors, clutching the twisting metal bannister.

"Is he safe?"

"Oh no," said Sunderland.

"Don't joke," she said.

Sunderland shrugged and said, "All right."

He circled the spiral once, then stopped as he realized that Ann wasn't following.

"You don't remember much from our time together, do you?"

Ann peered down at him through the empty risers. "I remember more and more," she said. "I remember the three of us—and the knife. But you drugged us, didn't you? Up at that lodge of yours."

"Only as needed. But you remember the knife. I'm not quite sure what that refers to."

"There was a scalpel," said Ann. "You set it in front of Philip, as he slept, after you'd injected him, and it floated—"

"Floated?"

"Yes. It was 'just the three of us,' you'd said. After you injected Philip with something to knock him out. You said you needed to isolate me. You explained, 'now it is just the three of us.'"

"And you remember this?" he said. "Did Philip tell you about it?"

Ann thought about that. It had come to her as she imagined talking to Philip, as she shut her eyes in the Rosedale Arms. Philip had reminded her. But she was there.

"I remembered it."

"Fascinating," said Sunderland softly. He climbed back up around the spiral, so he stood nearly face to face with Ann.

"What's so fascinating?"

"All that did happen," he said. "I injected Philip with scopolamine that day. There was an . . . event involving a scalpel. But I don't see how you could have known about it, Ann."

"Why is that?"

"You weren't there."

Ann took a step backward. "What—"

"It was just Philip, and myself . . . and as it turned out, the Insect."

"I was there," said Ann, and before she could say more, Sunderland raised his hand.

"I don't doubt that you were," he said, "on some level. In some form. But physically . . . physically, you weren't present."

Ann considered that. He was drugging them. Of course he was drugging them. *Jesus wept.*

"Tell me, Ann, does the Insect speak with you? Tell you things, from places you can't possibly be?"

Ann clutched onto the railing, with both hands.

"Are you going to tell me where Philip is?" she asked.

"Not just at the moment," said Sunderland. "I'd like you to answer my question, though."

The railing on the staircase was iron, and although the air was warmer here it was cold as ice as Ann gripped it. *Don't let him touch you*, Philip had said, that time they had first gone to Sunderland's clinic in Etobicoke. She shut her eyes, tight enough that colour flashed across her retinas in a sheet of red.

"What were you doing with Philip," she said, "when I wasn't there?"

"Treating him," said Sunderland sharply. "Now answer my question. Does the Insect speak with you?"

"All the time," said Ann, returning his tone in kind. "Now what did you do to Philip? Did you touch him?"

"No. I did not. Had the Insect told you that I had?"

The red fractured and lightened to an orange, and a yellow. The metal was freezing cold.

"Where is Philip?"

It wasn't just the metal, now—the air chilled around her, and that chill deepened into her bones. Ann's teeth began to chatter.

Sunderland put his hand on Ann's arm. It was hot by contrast, and although she tried to throw him off, he held tight.

"I never touched Philip," he said. "I was treating him."

"You were treating me," said Ann. "I remember that much."

"Ann—Ann, open your eyes and look at me."

This Ann did, as green images blossomed from within the yellow in her retinas.

"If I were only treating you," he said, "I would have only brought you to the lodge."

"I was the one with the Insect," said Ann. She could barely speak through the cold.

"Ann," said Sunderland, "please come down the rest of the way. I want to talk to you, and run some—"

Sunderland didn't finish. There was a fierce gust of air that whirled about and robbed Ann of her breath. She shut her eyes, on a bloom of violet on her lids. She half-expected when she opened them again to find Sunderland gone, plucked from the stairs and smashed to the ground—or perhaps against the skylight.

Sunderland hadn't moved.

"I want," he said levelly, "to talk to you and run some tests. Tell that to your Insect. Tell it—tell yourself, that when we do this, it'll be time to meet up with Philip."

"I want to see him now."

"Ann. No. Not quite yet. We have to take this process step by step. You're in a fragile state right now."

Ann thought to herself: *I could just push you right now, over the edge of this goddamn staircase. I bet I could do that, fragile as you say I am. I bet I could.*

But she knew that she wouldn't. In spite of all that had happened, Ann was a little dismayed and a little relieved to realize that she didn't quite have a murder in her.

The staircase bottomed out on a concrete floor. Ann was surprised to find that she could see—from above, it had seemed pitch black. But this far down, her eyes adjusted to the gloom and the skylight did its work. The central park was illuminated with a dull light. Like the floor of a barn. Its walls were lost in shadows between sturdy steel girders and wooden crossbeams. Ann squinted up the column of light. This whole structure, basement to roof, couldn't have been any less than a hundred feet.

That would be a long way to fall, Ann thought. Sunderland might have been thinking the same thing; as soon as he stepped off the staircase, he had discreetly moved himself underneath the lip of the lowest balcony, and leaned against the girder there, almost in the manner of an embrace.

"Come on," he said. "Let's sit and talk."

Past the pillar, Ann could see that a small living space had been arranged: another couch like the ones upstairs, and a little table, and two wing-backed armchairs. There was an antique-looking floor lamp between them, with three orchid-shaped shades, unlit.

Ann waited for Sunderland to settle on the couch, and selected the farthest armchair.

"Let's get this done," she said.

Sunderland steepled his fingers in front of his face. In the dark, he might have been smiling.

"Mr. Hirsch," he said. "I wanted to ask you about him."

"I'm . . . sorry about that."

"Really? Why should you be sorry? You didn't do anything. The poor man had a stroke!" Sunderland shifted so he leaned forward. "Thank God he was in a hospital when it happened."

"What did you want to ask me?"

"What was he up to? What exactly?"

"There was trouble with the FAA, of course. He was there to represent me. Didn't you read the papers?"

Sunderland reached up to the light and pulled a chain. Two of the three lamps glowed. They didn't cast much light beyond the circle in which they sat—the rest of the space seemed darker in contrast. But Ann got a good look at Sunderland's face. He'd moved his hands, and she could tell for certain: he wasn't smiling at all.

"What was he up to, in the hospital room?" Sunderland's eyes were lost in the shadow of his brow. He shifted to the very front of the sofa, his hands wringing in front of him.

"What do you think?" Ann snapped. "What was Ian up to? What are any of you up to? Do you want a detailed description?"

Sunderland sat back a hair, opened his hands in a gesture of appeasement. "All right, no. I'll be more direct. Was he . . . praying?"

In spite of herself, Ann laughed. "Praying? No." She thought about Hirsch, letting his trousers slide off him, letting himself be taken—like a noon-hour philanderer at a suburban rub-and-tug. "Not praying." Sunderland sat quietly, eyebrows raised slightly, waiting for more. "He was making an offer."

"Yes," said Sunderland. "An offer to take you away. To St. Augustine, yes?"

"That's where he said. Ian tells me they're religious whack-jobs there. And that I'm better off here."

"Well yes, he would," said Sunderland. "Did you think it was a good idea to go with him? With Hirsch, I mean?"

Ann thought about that. She'd been pretty hostile to the idea at the time—but in retrospect, it might've made sense. It might have been for the best. She'd left Miami on her own, and left a trail of victims as she went. Penny and her husband at the motel probably wouldn't get a good night's sleep for a month after what they'd seen; and the border . . .

There were corpses at the border.

All that might never have happened, if Ann had gone along quietly—let herself be locked up, or put into a coma, or whatever it was they did there. Or, she supposed, if she had kept the Insect under control in the first place.

"I didn't think it was a good idea," said Ann. "No."

"Were you afraid that he might abduct you?"

"I think those fears were founded, given everything."

"Fair point. But did you have them?"

"Sure," said Ann. "He laid out my situation for me pretty . . . pretty starkly, I think."

"And he didn't pray."

"You keep coming back to that," said Ann. "Closest he came was offering me communion, from his hip flask." Sunderland seemed not to understand, so Ann elaborated. "Scotch. He offered me a slug of scotch."

"Ah."

"Not what you had in mind," said Ann, and Sunderland shook his head.

"Should he have prayed?" she asked. "Because he's part of that religious sect. Who would he be praying to?"

Sunderland opened his mouth to answer, but something changed in his expression and stopped and looked over Ann's shoulder.

"He shoulda been prayin' to your Insect," said a child's voice. "That was his grave mistake, an' he paid for it dear. Ain't that right, Doctor Sunderland?"

It was the girl—Peter's niece. Ann recognized her from the vineyard.

She was wearing a fresh white bathrobe that was too big for her. She grinned a little sheepishly as she saw Ann looking at her.

"Hi," she said, and Ann said "Hi."

She turned to Sunderland. "It's okay now. Mister Sleepy's taken care of everything. Everyone's back in their rooms." She crossed the sitting area to Sunderland's side, and whispered something in his ear, pointing at Ann with her thumb as she did so.

"Thank you, Lisa," he said.

"Where's your Uncle Pete?" asked Ann.

"He's resting," said Lisa. "Late night."

"Ann LeSage, please meet Lisa Dumont." Dr. Sunderland got up.

"How do you do?" said Lisa. She didn't come over to shake Ann's hand, but she waved again. She smiled, but looked at Ann sidelong—like she was trying to put her finger on something. Ann knew the feeling.

"I'm doing pretty crappy, thanks."

Lisa took a step back, and Dr. Sunderland stepped up and put a hand on her shoulder.

"It's all right," he said to her, and Ann heard, in her ear: *It's all right*, like an echo. She only felt the hand on her shoulder by its sudden absence; when she looked, she saw nothing behind her but empty air.

"All right, Lisa," said Dr. Sunderland. "We need to talk, Ann and I. Go and see to Mister Sleepy."

Lisa stuck her tongue out at him.

"Mister Sleepy can take care of himself," she said.

Dr. Sunderland looked at her, and seemed about to say something to object. But finally, he shook his head.

Lisa sat down in one of the chairs, curled her legs up under her and looked at Ann levelly.

"You look bad," she said.

Ann rubbed her eyes. They stung. "I'm not sure how to take that," she said.

"Yeah, don't take it wrong. Like you said, you're feelin' crappy. I get it."

Lisa gave a quick, nervous-sounding laugh, then went quiet, and started to twirl a lock of hair in her fingers. Ann couldn't really see her face in this light. But she felt her eyes on her.

"The Insect is pretty scary," Lisa finally said.

Ann agreed. "Mister Sleepy is pretty scary too," she said.

Lisa shrugged.

"Mister Sleepy gets it done. He always did. But yours. It's *hard*. It'll do anything."

"I don't know about that," said Ann.

Lisa leaned forward. "Mister Sleepy knows," she said. "The Insect is big. That's why old Mr. Hirsch ought've been prayin'."

Ann didn't disagree.

"Mister Sleepy says it's going to eat you up."

"Lisa!" said Dr. Sunderland. He had moved across the room, just at the edge of the light. "You know that's not so. Don't listen to that, Ann."

"Quiet, Doctor," said Lisa, in a voice so bossy it nearly made Ann smile. "You don't know."

"What do you mean, eat me up?"

Ann's eyes slowly adjusted to the dark. She could see that Lisa looked very serious.

"Well it's nothing new," she said. "The Insect's been eatin' you for years. That's what Mister Sleepy says."

"Ann—" said Sunderland. But although Lisa didn't so much as look at him, he cut off.

"Mister Sleepy says the Insect will eat everybody before too long."

Ann squinted. Charlie Sunderland was gone now.

"That's why I wanted to talk to you," said Lisa.

"I'm sorry?" said Ann.

"Mister Sleepy says if I ask you nicely, maybe the Insect won't eat me." Lisa was talking more quickly now. "Mister Sleepy can be real helpful. That's what he's made for. He's not like the girls; he's not for *that*. Mister Sleepy's for helpin'." She held her hands together in front of her. "I hope the Insect ain't too mad about Mister Sleepy helpin' catch you. You know I let you go, back at that motel, right?"

As Lisa spoke, she began to sob. And it dawned on Ann: this little girl was begging. Ann reached over to touch Lisa's arm.

"It's all right," she said, and it must have been the wrong thing to say. Lisa recoiled, drew her arm back to her shoulder, and scrunched away in the chair.

Then she cried even harder. "I'm sorry! I don't mind if you touch me, not really!"

Ann's hand fluttered back. *Oh God*, she thought. And then she thought about Lisa's Uncle Peter Dumont, and Ian Rickhardt's flaccid defence of their shared predilection, and she wondered. Mister Sleepy wasn't for *that*.

What about Lisa?

"It's all right," Ann said. "I'm not going to touch you if you don't want me to."

Lisa calmed down, but only marginally. She was still terrified. She swallowed, and folded her hands into her lap, and looked at them.

"I can help you, y'know," said Lisa. "I can help you talk to the Insect. That's good, right? I can help you and the Insect do whatever you want."

Ann wasn't sure that the Insect needed anybody's help. But the offer was interesting. It certainly brought up some questions. Lisa Dumont wasn't more than eight years old—just a little younger than

Ann was when she visited Dr. Sunderland's offices in Etobicoke, and they were all trying to figure out what exactly was happening when the lights went out at the Lake House. Ann didn't even have a name for the Insect then. Lisa Dumont had somehow developed a genuine rapport. So much so, that she and . . . and Mister Sleepy could actively work as a team—and offer their services.

How had it been when Lisa rolled in with the 'geisters here? Did she offer them services? Did her uncle?

What did Lisa and Mister Sleepy get in return?

The temperature was dropping again—more rapidly this time. It was as though a door had opened onto an icy winter night, and the frozen breeze was being drawn inside. Lisa was looking around rapidly now, head turning this way and that, as though she'd lost her way suddenly.

"P-please," she said, "Mister Sleepy says he'll be good."

In the centre of the room, a shadow moved. Ann looked, and at first there seemed to be nothing.

"Take me with you," she said. "I c-can teach you how to talk with yours. We're not like the other ones. We can work together."

That wasn't quite right, though; as Ann looked the shadow returned again, a blurred smudge across the concrete floor. It was circling the chamber, whatever thing it was that was casting it.

"Don't," said Lisa, and the shadow sharpened. "Please!" she said. "Please!"

Peter Dumont appeared on the staircase, coming down. He bent, peered under the lip of the bottom-most balcony.

"Easy, hon," he said. "Just calm down—everything's fine."

The words of Lisa's uncle didn't seem to have too much effect on her nerves. But they sure shut her up—she drew a deep breath.

"Doctor Sunderland says you've been telling stories, now," he said.

Ann reached over to touch Lisa's arm. This time, the girl didn't pull away.

"We're in danger here," Lisa said.

"No," said Peter. "Not at all. Ol' Mister Sleepy's got it all under control." He finished coming down the stairs. At the bottom, he folded his hands in front of him.

"It's past Mister Sleepy," said Lisa. "Insect's goin' to get us."

"It's not going to get us." Peter looked to Ann. "Mrs. Voors—if you'd excuse us, we have to have a talk."

"I think I'll stay," said Ann. "For the moment."

He sighed. "The Insect can't do anything for right now. It's here under control. Its husband lost control of it. But now it's back."

"Its husband hasn't," said Lisa. Tears were running down her cheek now. "He hasn't lost control."

"He's—excuse me, Mrs. Voors—he's dead, sweetie."

Lisa shook her head slowly. "He never died," she said.

"Mrs. Voors, I really got to apologize," said Peter as he crossed the floor. His breath clouded in front of him. "She's a good girl. She doesn't mean—"

Ann felt her ears popping an instant before it happened. Peter Dumont's left shoulder jerked back, as though he'd been struck—and then his right joined it, and he started to fall backwards.

He never hit the ground. Lisa screamed as the air rushed past them, and Peter's feet left the floor. He hovered there for an instant—eyes comically wide—and then a gust of wind nearly knocked them all down, and Peter was gone.

Lisa's scream gurgled quiet as the air rushed from the space, and Ann felt her own breath hitch, and she feared she might suffocate.

The instant hung between them. Ann looked at Lisa, and she thought: *The husband wasn't dead?*

Michael was still alive? He was ashes; it didn't make sense, no sense at all.

Before she could puzzle it out, the body of Peter Dumont fell to the floor. From the way he landed, on his stomach, head turned hard to the right . . .

Ann had no doubt he was dead.

Then came a tap-tapping sound—as from a sudden summer hailstorm, here in this gigantic octagonal silo. The stones bounced on the concrete, and it was only as some of them careered into the sitting room that Ann realized it wasn't hail.

It was glass, from the skylight, utterly pulverized.

It had not made a sound when it shattered.

The "hailstorm" stopped as fast as it had begun.

The only sound in the space was the quiet sobbing from Lisa, and a wind that howled over the now-open rooftop. Ann stood carefully, but it was still too quickly. She felt the world grey a bit, but she steadied herself on the back of the chair for the moment.

Lisa got up. She tiptoed gingerly through the broken glass and knelt at her uncle's side. Under the light from above, she looked almost angelic, as she leaned over Peter's body and studied it—as though looking for an "on" switch to make him move again. A breeze came up, hard enough to lift the ends of her hair. She was no longer sobbing.

Ann walked slowly to the middle of the chamber. The wind picked at her jacket, tugged at her hair. It was icy, but it didn't chill her.

Lisa looked up at her, and up into the light. Her face was streaked with tears.

"He's gone," she said.

"I'm sorry," said Ann, uselessly. "Your uncle . . ."

"Not him," she said sharply. "And he's not my uncle. Not really. *Mister Sleepy.*"

Ann frowned.

"Mister Sleepy's dead. Mister Sleepy's dead too."

Ann reached out to touch her, remembering only at the last instant how it had upset Lisa, and withdrew.

"My God."

Ann turned. Dr. Sunderland emerged from behind her. His hair was dishevelled. A bruise was darkening on his face, and as he stumbled closer, she saw another one around his throat.

He hurried past Ann to Lisa, and knelt down beside her. The glass crunched under his knees, but if it cut, he didn't let on.

"Oh, Lisa," he said, "I'm sorry."

She looked at him. "Mister Sleepy's dead," she said again.

Sunderland said, "I know," and he put his arms around Lisa and held her—over the body of her kin, Peter Dumont, shattered with the glass as he fell from the top of the Insect's tower. Then Sunderland did a thing that she had never seen him do before.

He let Lisa go, and put his hands together—and began to pray.

Ann stepped back. She had no business in this place, this tiny circle between little Lisa Dumont and her "therapist" Charlie Sunderland, and the corpse. Ann's place was elsewhere.

The wind told her so.

She stepped around them, quiet as a ghost, and started back up the staircase.

V

Ann stopped climbing when the stairs ran out. The open air was just beyond her reach at the top of the tower. A part of herself understood that really, she had climbed out of a shaft—the Octagon was not that high off the ground—on a more fundamental level, she had begun to understand this place for what it was: a tower, where the Insect might sit, a prisoner.

It was not just the Insect being held here, of course; the 'geists tied to an unguessable number of women were kept here, kept in thrall to the appetites of their men.

And then there was Philip.

Of course he was here. In one of these very rooms.

She crossed the narrow bridge from the stairs to the balcony. It only made sense, to start at the top.

She found a curtain, and slipped behind it to the door, and opened it.

A rail-thin man with jet black hair cut long stood in front of a bathroom mirror, in a suite of rooms that resembled a decadent hotel room from a century ago. He was naked. He regarded himself steadily, as the deep red wallpaper surrounding the mirror undulated with faces and hands. The man's lips trembled, half-open, and a pink tip of a tongue showed itself as he looked deep into the glass. Something in there was transfixing; he didn't appear to notice Ann when she looked in, and he barely flinched when the straight razor lifted itself from the water glass on the vanity, opened and caressed the soft, lean skin at the base of his jaw.

She withdrew, and chose another curtain from those circling the balcony.

Behind that one, a door led into a hideous kitchen—floor, ceiling and countertop all panelled with the same yellow Formica. The refrigerator was a Frigidaire; the stove, an old harvest gold electric range. The room was spotless, except for what looked like pink cake icing, stuck in prints the shape of a child's hands, on the ceiling. Watching them long enough, you could see them creep from one end of the room to another. A small, muscular man was curled on the floor beside the sink, where a garbage disposal hummed and crunched.

The next curtain in the Octagon had more money behind it: a wide, tastefully spare living room with deep chestnut floors that gleamed, furnished with several pieces Ann took to be Louis XIV. The only sound was the ticking of a grandfather clock. She looked around the room, and determining it empty, shut the door. Something heavy fell as she did so, but when she opened the door again to see, all was as it had been.

Ann continued. She looked in on a room furnished as a little girl's bedroom; another, made up as a 1970s living room, complete with RCA television set and teak stereo cabinet as long as a coffin; a suburban two-car garage, with a '70s-vintage Gremlin parked to one side, a wall of power tools along the other. The Gremlin was bright red. A man sat inside it, staring into the rearview mirror at the empty back seat—terrified, like the others.

That was the purpose of these rooms ringing the Octagon; small, familiar spaces where scenarios were tailored to the needs, which is to say fears, of the membership. Little curated rooms at Ian Rickhardt's otherworldly fetish bar. *The Haunted Hotel. The Accursed Kitchen. The Demon in the Gremlin.*

Like the *I-thought-you-were-holding-my-hand* Shirley Jackson game, they were each crafted to help cultivate that sense of terror that Ian Rickhardt said all these men craved.

And they were each haunted—by the poltergeists that Rickhardt and his friends had raped into submission.

As Ann quietly shut the door on the garage and stepped back through the curtain, she thought: *The only thing terrifying about these rooms is their existence.*

She stepped through the next curtain and door—there were only three more on this top level—and turned the handle. This one smelled of antiseptic. The walls were covered in green tile, and there were IV stands and great hot lights, and carts full of instruments, surrounding an operating table, upon which was splayed the tiny corpse of a vivisected bluebird. There was the sound of a tap running, which she thought might be coming from behind a set of swinging double doors.

She would have closed the door then and there, but it occurred to her that this might be a place they'd have put Philip; it certainly had the life support equipment he might need.

Ann stepped into the room and went through the double doors.

It was a surgical scrub: there were hangers and drawers at the back of the room, where smocks and masks hung, and folded up rubber gloves were stacked neatly on shelves. Bisecting the room were sinks, six of them in an island, three backing on three. The water was running in the middle sink opposite Ann. Looking over the low tile divider, she could see a pair of child's hands, reaching up over the sink's edge, scrubbing themselves with a foamy dark soap. She couldn't see more of the child from where she was standing.

Ann stepped around the bank of sinks, but as she did so, in just a blink, the hands shifted to the other side.

"Now you can't get out," said a little girl's voice, "without going past me."

Ann considered: this should have really thrown her, the trick of shifting sides on the surgery-prep sinks, the little-girl sing-song voice, happily informing her she was trapped; the likelihood, given that this place really was filled with ghosts, not just little tricks, that in fact she most likely was trapped.

But Ann didn't feel a thing. And she realized, looking at those hands in the sink, a little blue around the nails, that she had never, truly, felt anything. This font of terror that Ian and Michael kept coming back to, and Sunderland couldn't stop *studying*, and the fellows down in Florida worshipped, was dry for Ann.

It made sense. After all, for most of her life—she was the one washing her hands in the sinks, trapping her victims in the wash-up. Ann was the font.

Ann stepped around the sinks to head back to the operating room. Something flickered in the corner of her eye. She didn't pay it any heed. She felt a tiny hand gripping her ankle. She kicked it away and kept moving. A child's face, lips blue, long red hair streaking down her face to half-cover eyes that shone like dimes in a puddle, appeared in front of Ann's face. She walked through it and pushed open the doors.

These poltergeists couldn't make the terror. Not like the Insect could, for a simple reason. They didn't kill.

The bluebird on the operating table writhed and sang as Ann opened the door, and let it shut behind her.

As far as Ann knew, it kept right on singing, even as Ann pulled open the curtain into the Octagon, and felt her breath freeze to rime on her throat, at the sight of the one who stood there waiting for her.

vi

Philip LeSage towered over her.

He was tall—a head taller than her, easily.

He was not strong.

His shoulders hunched around his hollow chest. His arms, thin as broomsticks, were held aloft, as though waiting her embrace. The freezing air goosefleshed his pallid, naked skin. His eyes stared out at her from sunken hollows, and his mouth twisted from grin to grimace as his head bent slowly, side to side—the only acknowledgment he seemed to give of his own impossibility, there on the catwalk beyond the curtain.

"Oh God." Ann whispered it as the ice spread from her throat and along her nerves. Philip was a quadriplegic. Normally he couldn't do much more than lift his little finger; he could barely control the movement of his own head.

But of course, it wasn't Philip.

His hips swayed, his naked member swinging semi-erect between tree-branch legs. His hands settled gently on her shoulders and his face drew closer to hers.

"I couldn't have you searching the whole tower."

The voice was a low buzz, from rattling glass and humming wires—the wind.

The Insect.

Ann pulled back. "No," she said. "No, stop it."

Philip pulled back too, his mouth twisted around another word that translated, easily: *"Have it your way. I'm going home."*

He turned as if on point. His bare feet touched the balcony floor, and moved in a simulacrum of walking, around to the ramp that led to the staircase. Ann sat frozen for a time, watching him. When he got to the stairs, he turned back—the Insect turned him back—and he beckoned.

Ann felt like she was encased in ice; it physically hurt to walk, nearly. But she followed. Philip looked like a giant's skeleton from this distance, with just bits of flesh and tufted hair. His eyes were black pits in the grey light coming from above. Ann joined him on the staircase, and together, they moved down.

Was that why he had decided to stay here? Ann had thought Ian might be lying about Philip's choosing, but this made sense: the 'geisters offered him mobility of a kind, hauled along by the unseen hands of the poltergeists. Was that what made it home for him?

God. He was so tall.

It had been a decade since Philip had stood; it had been a decade since Ann had seen him upright. He was a giant when she was a little girl, but that had changed with the bed and the chair, laying him flat or folding him up. Now, his arms folded around her, holding tight with muscles that were barely sinew, nerves that were dead wiring.

This must be agony for him.

Philip stepped off the stairs and onto one of the narrow bridges. They had only gone down one floor and were back on the level onto which she and Rickhardt and Sunderland had originally arrived. They crossed the bridge quickly; Philip's stride was improving—or more realistically, the 'geist's ability to manipulate Philip's numb limbs was growing stronger.

They passed through a curtain halfway round the Octagon. It would have been directly above the kitchen set-piece, unless Ann missed her guess.

"Let me get the door," said Ann, first to Philip, then, absurdly she thought, again to the air around them. But she had to: she didn't want the Insect twisting him more than necessary. This wasn't good for him. What was all this motion doing to his spine?

Philip "stood" to the side as Ann turned the handle, and as she looked through, into this room, she realized something. No one had lied. Not Ian Rickhardt, not Susan Rickhardt, not anyone.

Philip *had* gone home.

But for the empty scooter set by the thick burgundy curtains, this space was a note-perfect recreation of the kitchen, living and dining rooms of the Lake House.

Ann stepped inside, and beckoned Philip—or the thing that bore Philip—to follow. It even smelled familiar . . . that still fresh scent of spruce sap, latex paint, and bacon, the last of which their dad liked to cook way too much of.

It was incredible, in the attention to detail—and the totality of the effect.

Philip came into the room. Any pretense of walking was gone. His feet slid across the tile floor, the tips of his toes squeaking like pencil erasers. His arms dangled listlessly. His head lolled, so much so that Ann thought that he might have fainted from the indignity, or possibly worse . . . that in its puppet game, the Insect had killed him.

But he blinked, his head righted, and for a moment he looked steadily at her, as he had countless times. In this very room.

No. In a room that this room strongly resembled. But not here. Not this room.

All appearances to the contrary, they were not home.

Philip hovered and then settled into the seat of his scooter. His arms lifted and folded over his lap. The Insect adjusted his head so that it fit comfortably into the rest.

Ann took a dining room chair and brought it next to Philip. She sat beside him, and put her hands on his. The flesh was clammy. She heard him exhale raggedly. She might have done the same.

"I made a mistake," said Ann, looking her brother in the eye. "I shouldn't have married Michael."

Philip made a quiet noise. *I know.*

"I thought I loved him—but I didn't. And he didn't love me either."

Philip looked away.

Ann leaned in. "Have we had this conversation?"

Did he nod then? Or did the Insect?

"Did you talk to me," she said, "in that dark school corridor?"

He turned back to her and met her eyes again. There was no nod this time, no shake of the head.

But there was an answer.

The room turned icy—and there came a familiar squeaking sound. Ann turned and looked toward the mirror above the telephone. It had frosted over. And written on it were the words:

YES.

"All right," said Ann, "am I talking to you now, Philip? Are you talking to me?"

WE ARE

Ann stared at the glass as the words faded, and considered that "we."

Did the Insect belong to both of them? Did the Insect talk to Philip, just as it had to Ann?

Perhaps so. Perhaps, that was why Rickhardt had brought Philip here, to this facsimile of the Lake House, as it looked in the 1990s, when Charlie Sunderland had collected such detailed information about the LeSage family's domestic arrangements. Ann walked over to the curtains. They were thicker than the ones that had hung in the living room of the Lake House at any time Ann recalled. But they covered a more damning anomaly; there was no window here that could look out onto the lake, or the woodlot that surrounded the real Lake House.

Was that the nature of all these rooms she wondered? Each slice of the Octagon, a slice of memory from . . . a 'geist and its vessel?

The 'geisters had gone to great lengths to quarantine the 'geist from the vessel early in life—so they would grow apart, like two branches from a split tree-stem. Were these rooms, then, a means to draw the 'geist out, from the point of that separation?

And was this room—their presence in it—an attempt to do something more, with the Insect, and Ann . . . and Philip?

Ann turned and leaned against the curtain, the hard wall behind it. The refrigerator door hung open in the kitchen at the other side.

She crossed the room to close it, and as she did so, the upper cupboard doors opened.

Pale blue plates and bowls were stacked neatly—they were of a pattern that caused a sharp lancet of nostalgia in her. They matched the coffee cups that were stacked next to them. The bins that held pasta and rice and cereal against moths were in their place. The refrigerator was stocked with jugs of milk and a big carton of orange juice and a good dozen bottles of beer, and the freezer overtop was filled with tupperwared leftovers and frozen vegetables.

Ann's hand hovered over the beer.

You could just disappear into this room, couldn't you?

Ann pulled her hand away and shut the refrigerator door, and turned to lean on it to keep it shut. The mirror in the dining room was frosty again, but for the words:

YOU COULD JUST DISAPPEAR INTO THIS ROOM,
COULDN'T YOU?

She could disappear, just like Susan Rickhardt disappeared. Like the other vessels disappeared; not into some boozy distraction . . .

well not only into some boozy distraction . . . but into her actual childhood—into the mire of *bona fide*, pure nostalgia; life as memory. It was a tempting pact. The frost faded and dribbled down the glass, obscuring the words. Ann looked at her melting reflection. She looked ghastly. Her eyes were hollow and dark, her hair hung in rattails over her face. The jean jacket she'd worn here was filthy, and her shoulders hung low.

She was exhausted, and thirsty, and hungry. . . .

And she had found Philip, which had been all she'd been thinking about for more than twenty-four hours . . . and the Insect too—she'd found her way back to the Insect. She'd found her way home.

And she was done.

Ann turned away from herself, and stumbled to the sofa, where she let herself collapse, into the Insect's tender care and her brother's protective supervision.

As she dozed off, she had the definite sense of the two of them—the Insect and her brother—sharing a knowing glance.

HOMECOMING

i

Ann slept deeply.

She lay on the narrow ledge of the sofa cushions. She'd thought to jam a corner pillow between her neck and the sharp edge of the sofa's arm. She stretched as she slept though, and the pillow slid out, so that her neck cricked against the arm as though it were broken.

Ann worried about that, as she observed herself. She was outside her body; as far as she could tell, she was observing from a vantage point near the living room's ceiling. The dying might see themselves this way: extended from their bodies, their own 'geist, while their heart slowed and stopped and their brain began to starve, and vanish.

Had the Insect done this, as she lay down—reached down and turned her head, just so—and cracked her neck? She could not believe that were so.

And sure enough, it was not. Ann soon observed herself turn, draw her knees up tighter to herself, and twist her head into a more comfortable position.

So Ann was not dead.

But she thought about what Lisa Dumont had told her, and Susan too: that the Insect would devour her. Was this a place she sat now, on the precipice of the Insect's throat?

Ann worried about Philip, too. He sat alone in his wheelchair by the curtain, head bent to one side. Was he asleep? Ann didn't think so, but of course you couldn't tell with Philip. She didn't like that he was alone. Since the accident, Philip always had an attendant near; the Hollingsworth Centre made sure of that. If he were to aspirate, there would be no one to help him. He could choke to death. They really did need to get out of here. But of course in order for that to happen, Ann needed to wake up. And that didn't appear to be happening any time soon.

After a time, the door opened. Charlie Sunderland stepped in. He had changed clothes—he was wearing what looked like a long, purple bathrobe, the same shade as the bruises on his face.

He looked out the door and held up a finger to someone. Ann found herself curious about who that might be, and her curiosity brought her lower, so she could see.

It was Ian Rickhardt, also wearing a bathrobe. He lingered between doorway and curtain, hands jammed deep in the pockets.

Sunderland crossed the floor to the kitchen, eyeing both lolling Philip and sleeping Ann. He opened the refrigerator, and bent down to look in. He was counting the beer bottles. He wanted to see how many of them Ann had drunk. She could not read his reaction to the evidence that she had had none of them.

Ian stepped into the room now. He was followed by others, one or two of whom Ann recognized: the thin man from the hotel bathroom; the smaller one, who'd been in the kitchen scenario; the man from the Gremlin, maybe—she hadn't seen much of him, but a thick salt-and-pepper moustache made it likely. There were—Ann counted—five others, all wearing those bathrobes. They were made of something like silk, and quilted with a diamond-shaped pattern.

Sunderland was kneeling beside Ann.

Ian stepped around and looked down at her. "Is she done?"

Sunderland looked up at him and smiled tightly.

"*Whatever walks in Hill House, walks alone*," he said, and Ian chuckled nervously. "Yeah. I'd feel better if we could have talked a bit before this. Reaffirm it. But it looks as though everything's all right. Like a bee to honey, here she is."

"Pat yourself on the back," said Ian drily.

The other men spread across the room, hands spread delicately at their sides, as though they were trying to keep their balance on a world with strange gravity. They looked around, as though seeking something out in the corners and the shadows. None of them looked to Ann where she watched from the ceiling.

Ian turned to Philip. "How you holding up?"

Philip swung his head up and made a noise at Ian. Ann understood it to mean "Ready."

Sunderland went to Philip's side. He put a hand on his forehead, as though feeling for fever. "You've been very brave."

Philip made another noise. This one Ann couldn't translate. Sunderland seemed to understand it, though. He turned to Ian.

"Philip is ready to join the circle," he said. "Could you get his robes?"

Ian snapped his fingers, and one of the men—a taller one, with feathered blond hair, brought a folded bathrobe. Sunderland took the robe and in series of quick, professional moves, wrapped it around Philip and threaded his arms through the sleeves.

Ann drifted lower, as her curiosity about Philip grew, so that she was able to look directly into his eyes over Sunderland's shoulder. They were damp—from exhaustion, from tears . . . who knew?

Ann wanted to think there were tears there. She looked for some sense that Philip wanted—needed—to be rescued from this perversion.

Don't let him make you take your clothes off, Philip had told her, the first time they went into Charlie Sunderland's office.

He had been afraid of Sunderland, then. He had not wanted to talk to Sunderland at all, about the things that he had seen, in his room. Now . . . now, he was throwing in with them—letting Sunderland put clothes on him.

"*They're rapists.*"

Ann didn't precisely speak the words—whatever force it was that had drawn her from her slumbering body, also robbed her of lips, a tongue. But she still had voice, and she could hear it.

So, it seemed, could Philip. He twisted his lips back from his teeth, and swallowed hard, and said, "Nyuh."

"*No.*"

Ann spun in the air, searching vainly for the source of the voice.

"*They're not rapists. They are worshippers.*"

The Insect. It was the Insect.

"*They know better, after what we've shown them. They remember Michael Voors. They remember John Hirsch. Peter. They know what we are. They know we're not their plaything anymore. See how they come before us?"*

Ann turned and looked down. The men were forming a circle—a circle that encompassed Ann's sleeping body, and included Philip.

Why was he including himself in this thing? The Insect had destroyed him . . . taken his limbs, his voice . . . his parents and his girlfriend. Why would he worship?

Why would you worship that thing? Ann called to Philip, but he couldn't, wouldn't answer.

"*He abandoned me. He knows better now too.*"

Ann felt the voice at her shoulder. She turned to it, with great effort. And for the first time, she saw the Insect, hanging above her, long hair dangling over mandibles and great, multifaceted eyes gleaming like giant blackberries.

Ann looked into that eye—and instinctively, the way another person might throw up their hands to ward off an attack or crouch down to protect their vitals, Ann tried to visualize the descending rainbow: *Red, and Yellow . . .*

"*No. You should know better than that too.*" And over her, the Insect's mandibles extended—and took hold of Ann's limbs—and drew her in.

She vanished utterly, but only for an instant.

She felt herself returning to her body, breath returning to her lungs, and her eyelids flickering open—and watching the men in their circle sway, in some fetish-court perversion of religious ceremony. Her mouth was filled with stale bile, the peach-fuzz sour of unbrushed teeth. She started to get up—as though she could physically flee what was happening to her; as though it were all but done.

She fell back, pushed as if by an invisible hand. Her eyes fluttered shut again, and she was in darkness—a freezing, numbing pool.

Little Lisa Dumont was right. The Insect was devouring her. It had been, for all her life, in slow, measured bites. It might have stopped, as she grew into herself. But the work of Charlie Sunderland had made sure that didn't happen. It had kept the Insect cocooned, let it grow on its own, even as it sucked the life—the soul—out of Ann.

But then she thought—that wasn't quite right.

The Insect wasn't some alien species, come in a shipping crate from far-off lands to denude Ann's being like the bark off a tree. It was a part of her—at its most removed, a vestigial twin. Or perhaps, a purer part of herself—a part unsullied by the daily exposure to the world that ground at Ann, the rest of her, as she made her way through it. And had she rejoined the Insect now, newly innocent herself, having passed through her flesh as though it were a filter?

Was the act of that moment—a matter of purification?

"None of us are pure."

"What do you mean?"

"Oh Ann. Remember."

ii

The Lake House living room. Again. But empty. The curtains were half-drawn, and the remains of afternoon sunlight streamed in.

She could see the lake—and the boat, the *Bounty II*, hauled up onto the shore, mast cracked, gouged hull covered in a shrink-wrap tarpaulin. A TV was on in the basement. Something with a laugh track.

She was not drawn to it.

There were other sounds. The Lake House was young, and its bones were still hardening, setting into themselves. Softly, in the corners, it moaned.

Upstairs a faucet turned, and the pipes hummed behind the walls.

She thought about taking hold of those pipes—of bending the copper, snapping it, stopping the water. She could do it if she wanted to.

She didn't want to.

She moved from the living room, past the kitchen, and into the stairwell of the Lake House.

Ann's father sat on the stairs. He was wearing a pair of dark wool dress pants and a white shirt, top button undone. Tufts of hair poked out. His elbows were propped on his knees, his hands hung limp in front of him, and he stared ahead, into the empty front vestibule. He seemed very young. His hair was dark, and too shaggy; he had put off his haircut for a few weeks too long. His eyes were blinking rapidly. His mouth hung.

She was curious about that. But they didn't linger to satisfy it.

Ann had no say. She may have once. But this was nothing but memory. A conversation, with herself, reminding her of where she had already been.

Up they went. Ann's father shook his head as they passed, and pushed himself up, his knees cracking as he hung onto the bannister and climbed down off the staircase.

The second floor hall now. Five doors: one, to the home office; another, to a spare bedroom; Ann's room; Philip's room. The bathroom. One floor up, and the master bedroom. Another bath. Big windows and its own deck, overlooking the lake.

No need to go there.

There was a long red and green rug on the floor of the hallway. They slid it along—so that it accordioned against the home office door. Perfunctory terror for the next person who saw it.

The bathroom door was closed. Behind it, the shower ran hard enough that steam crept out from underneath the door.

There.

Followed the steam.

Into a room of it.

The bath in here had a sliding door of frosted glass. Behind it: Philip LeSage. Lathering up his hair.

They slid over top of the door. There was Philip. Tall and strong. Eyes shut against the water. They circled him. Ran fingers like rope over his throat.

His hands dropped from his head. Eyes opened.

"It's you," he said.

They turned off the water.

"It is," he said.

They reached, and flickered the lights—on and off, on and off. Then off.

"You were in my room last night."

They moved through his hair, drew it back from his face. He held his head back so the soapy water flowed down his back.

"You've been there before. I know that."

They withdrew. Philip did too. He sat down on the edge of the bathtub.

"I don't mind," he said. "I'm not afraid."

He was lying about that. He was trembling, soaking wet and naked, against the tile. His voice was high.

"You have everyone else scared. Not me."

His backside squealed against the tile as he slid around. He turned the water on again, set the temperature, then started up the shower. He got under the stream of hot water, and the trembling stopped.

"You turned the lamp shade around. You opened the closet door. You left me a sparrow. You kept touching me."

They thought about stopping the water, or making it cold, or too hot.

They didn't want to do any of those things.

"It's okay. You can touch me if you want."

He finished rinsing off, and shut off the water. In the dark, he found the handle on the shower door and slid it open. He stepped out into the dark, groped around on the wall until he found the light switch.

"If you're there, I'm going to turn on the light."

He flipped the switch and the bathroom lit up. Philip looked around, almost disappointed to find himself alone. Even the fog on the bathroom mirror was smooth, unblemished by even punctuation marks.

"I think you've been doing this a long time," he said. "I think you've been around this family since when I was a baby."

He took a towel, wrapped it around his middle.

"Maybe you've been around before me." He cracked the door open, peered out into the hall. Satisfied they were still alone, he shut the door. "Maybe from Nan's family. Mom says she rhymes with 'witch.' Maybe that's where you came from. Maybe you came in with Ann on her birthday. I don't care. I wanted you to know . . ."

He leaned on the door, as though holding it shut against something.

"I like it when you come to my room. You can always come see me there."

Could they? They moved in on Philip—wrapping him in tendrils of steam, holding him close in adoration. He began to tremble again, and he did not pull away, and after a moment of that, the trembling turned to a shudder, and he was still.

"You can always come see me," he said again. "Always, always."

They believed him.

The bathroom door, open.

Philip, crossing the hallway, heading to his room, noticed the rug, all bunched up. Clutching his towel tighter around his waist, he walked down the hall and took hold of the end of the runner rug, pulling it back straight. As he finished, the door to Ann's bedroom opened.

Ann. Seven years old. Unrecognizable to herself, with a pageboy haircut and green corduroy overalls.

"What are you doing?"

Philip shrugged. "The rug was all bunched out. You might have tripped."

"You should put clothes on. I can see your wee."

"Fuck off."

"You fuck off."

"You can't see anything. And cut out the swearing."

"Fine." She leaned against the door. "I didn't make the rug bunch up."

"I didn't say you did."

"I think the ghost did."

Philip, shrugging. "Maybe. Whatever. Shouldn't be left like that."

"Someone might trip."

"You know it."

"I hate the ghost."

Philip stood up straight. "Don't," he said, and tightened the towel again. "I'm going to put on pants."

"I didn't do it," said Ann as Philip stepped into his bedroom. "Stupid ghost did it."

Philip closed the door and Ann was alone in the hall. She looked straight at them.

"I hate you!" she shouted. When she went back into her room, she slammed the door.

See? None of us are pure.

iii

The circle of men had fallen to their knees, in an approximation of prostration. With the exception of Philip, who sat lolling in his chair, looking at Ann, still asleep on the couch. She was turned away now, so her face pressed into the backrest cushions.

"Belaim," said Charlie Sunderland, his head downcast to the floor. "Redawn," he continued, working his way through the words he'd taught Ann to chant, as a way to rope the Insect in when the chairs started shifting, the windowpanes vibrating. *Sheepmorne . . . Overwind . . .*

It had been a game when they'd sat up late at Sunderland's lodge, practising the words—the whole family, chanting them together, in their own little circle, learning Sunderland's nonsense words to banish the demons into the night.

Philip had sat in that circle—straight-facedly reciting the words with everyone else. When they were alone, he would make up other words—"fuckitutilly," "scroticalific," "snotufical"—and Ann would crack up.

Now, he couldn't even articulate the words with the other men—but he looked deadly serious.

And why shouldn't he?

He had learned what happened when he didn't take the Insect seriously. When he'd brought Laurie into the Lake House . . . brought her to his bedroom, held her close as she squirmed out of her sweater and jeans . . . kissed him, and took hold of him, and with touch and caress and kiss, brought him from shivering arousal to shuddering climax.

He had learned, the price of betrayal, of abandonment.

Now, see how he comes crawling back. See how they all *come crawling back.*

The words from the 'geisters continued: a sweet, insensible cadence that lulled, like an old song, like a strong, sugared liqueur. Philip swayed, and sang them too—each time around, his pronunciation getting stronger, as though he, too, were training himself to absorb the words.

On the sofa, Ann stirred.

She stretched a leg out, and then another, and rolled over onto her side. She brought a hand to her forehead, brushing hair out of the way, and blinked. She swung her feet to the floor, and sat straight, and shakily, stood, looking around at the circle with measured disinterest.

The men didn't stop chanting as Ann rocked back and forth to build a bit of momentum, finally got to her feet, and made her way through the circle to the kitchen, and the refrigerator.

She opened the first bottle of beer and finished it in two long swallows.

The men stopped chanting as she opened a second bottle. Ian Rickhardt looked to Charlie Sunderland, who nodded at him.

From the ceiling, she and the Insect watched, as though they were pinned there, as Charlie got up, crossed the room and whispered into her ear.

The corporeal body of Ann Voors nodded, and swallowed half of another beer. And leaning on Dr. Sunderland for support, she let herself be led from the room.

At the ceiling, Ann tried to reach for herself as the door opened—to follow. It was no good. Ann watched herself take a final swig of the beer, dangle it between two fingers, and disappear as the door swung shut.

Fuck. If she'd had arms, she would have wrapped them around herself, curled up, as the reality dawned on her. She would have shut her eyes tight. *Fuck fuck fuck fuck.*

"Don't fuckin' swear, Sis. Not very ladylike."

iv

Ann opened her eyes.

She stood in the middle of the dark gymnasium, casting her gaze among the shadows, the beams of sickly light that came in through the high windows. It was cold in here. Snow blew outside. Climbing ropes dangled from the darkness of the ceiling like trailing man-o-war tentacles. At either end, basketball hoops were bent up.

"Where are you?" she called. Her voice sounded very small and weak to her, more frightened than she thought.

"I'm here," said Philip. His voice had an odd echoing quality that took Ann a moment to place. There was a loud thumping sound then, a great drumbeat, and it hit her: he was talking over a PA system—tapping the microphone in the office for the school PA system.

"Is this the high school?"

"Fenlan & District Secondary School, that's right. If . . . if you hadn't gone to live with Nan, you'd have gone here too."

"It's awfully dark," said Ann.

"There's a light switch over by the door."

"Can't you turn it on?"

"What do you want, me to hold your fuckin' hand?"

It wasn't entirely dark. As Ann became accustomed to it, dim light entered from high windows. Barely enough to see by.

Ann crossed the floor of the gym to what looked like a big set of double doors at the very edge of the brightest pool of light. It wasn't exactly clean; things crunched under her feet, like peanut shells. Ann looked down as she stepped into the light. They weren't shells; they were bugs . . . beetles and flies, curled up dead. Ann brushed out a path for herself with the toe of a running shoe she hadn't worn in fifteen years. She crossed back into shadow, and felt on the wall until she found a row of switches, and flipped them on.

"That's better," she said. Fluorescent lights flickered in rows on high over the court. At the opposite end, wooden bleachers had been pushed against the wall emerged from shadow, as did a deep green banner crossing the wall, announcing that this gymnasium was home to the Fenlan Panthers. Philip had been a Panther.

It didn't look like any Panthers had been through in a few years, though.

The walls were also streaked with rusty water-marks, where pipes seemed to have burst. Wind whistled through a broken pane up high. It was cold in here—cold as January, cold as a visit from the Insect.

"What've you done, Philip?"

"Oh, chill."

"Literally." Ann tried the double doors behind her. They opened a little ways, then stopped. "Seriously. What've you done? I watched myself walk away—my body walk away. Where am I?"

"You're at the high school," he said. "You've been here before."

"So we did speak—when I was on the road."

"Yeah. It's a place I've put together. It's where . . . where she and I talk."

"She?" Ann leaned on the doors, hard. They gave a little bit, then stopped again. It was as though something were wedged against it.

"Yeah. After the accident . . . the crash. Sometimes, I'd wake up here. Back at school. She'd be here."

"Laurie," said Ann, although she knew that wasn't so, and a yowl of feedback over the PA system confirmed it.

"Not Laurie. No. She doesn't have a name," said Philip, "but I can tell you—she fucking hates being called the Insect."

"Ah. So *her.*" Ann stepped away from the doors. There was no getting out that way, she thought, as they pushed back shut.

"You're going to have to stay here," he said. "Good that you figured that out."

Ann moved along the wall of the gym. There were doors farther along, the two change-room doors: HOME first, then VISITOR.

"I don't really want to stay here, Philip," said Ann. "I want to wake up."

More feedback. "Wake up? Who said you're asleep?"

Ann pushed open the HOME door. It opened easily, into a big square room with a bench all around, and coat hangers. There was another door through it, which Ann guessed probably led to showers.

"I want to go back to myself," Ann said. Her voice was shaking. She wondered, was this how the Insect felt, when she locked it in a tower overlooking the loamy fields of Tricasta? "I want out of this place, Philip. You got to know, this isn't right."

"You know Sis, you might be right." His voice was louder here because it came out of another speaker, set in the wall in this smaller space. "This might be wrong. But it's all I've got. It's all I had for years. Her."

"So you're just like them," said Ann. "You've used the Insect . . . you've used *her* for your own sexual pleasure. You . . . you raped her too."

"No," he said. "I never raped her. But we've been together for so long. Since I can remember, she was there for me. And I let her down. That's why . . ."

"That's why the accident."

"I should have known better. Laurie was great. But I should have left her to her life."

Ann found the light switch, and the change-room filled with a dim yellow glow. She didn't have to listen to the rest of the story. She knew it, in a way that made her think she'd always known it on some level: how Philip, mesmerized by the red-haired beauty from History of Europe, had one night turned away from the quiet touch of her—of the Smiling Girl . . .

He had rejected her. Like Peter Pan casting off Tinker Bell for the womanly temptations of Wendy . . . he'd cast her off.

And yeah—the Insect, the Smiling Girl, had shown Philip just exactly what that meant.

Which is to say: everything.

Ann sat down on the bench. She stretched her legs out, and thought about it.

"You there, sis?"

"Yeah," said Ann. "Right here in the change-room."

"Okay."

"Did she . . . did the Smiling Girl visit you in here?" Ann thought that she did.

"Yeah," said Philip. "Sometimes. She was always with me."

"She was never just mine," said Ann, "was she?"

"No."

More quiet, as Ann thought about that. She wondered how much of it Dr. Sunderland really knew. He'd treated both Ann and Philip. Did he understand that the Insect, the Smiling Girl, was really a part of both of them? That both of them—Ann and Philip—were vessels to this poltergeist he and his friends coveted?

"She sure as shit wasn't yours to give away in matrimony," said Philip. "To those fucking rapists."

"Those fucking rapists," said Ann, "are the fuckers that you threw in with."

"Don't curse."

"I was duped," said Ann. "You weren't duped at all. You threw right in."

"Oh did I?"

"You wore their bathrobes—while they were doing their *Eyes Wide Shut* shit."

"What?"

"*Eyes Wide Shut*? The Kubrick movie? Tom and Nicole?"

"Must've missed it on movie night at the Hollingsworth."

"Sorry." Ann thought about that. "Fuck you, Philip. I'm not sorry. You threw in with Ian fucking Rickhardt and Charlie Sunderland and everybody else who took . . . whatever it is we share, and made it into their sex toy." She stood up from the bench, and went through the door to the showers. It smelled of chlorine in here—like a pool. She couldn't find the light switch immediately, but she didn't care. She just stepped farther into the darkness.

"And for what? So the Insect could carry you around like you're walking under your own power, and . . . I don't know, get you off? You sold me *out*. I trusted you. I always trusted you. And you sold me *out*."

The darkness deepened as she rounded a corner and the dim light from the change-room vanished. She could hear Philip mouthing something, but the place she was entering didn't seem to be hooked up to the PA system.

He made a garbled noise that might have been a protest: *You don't understand, it was all for the best* . . . blah fucking blah blah blah.

As Ann kept on, the wall she was following fell away, and she had no guide for her progress. The floor transformed as well, to what felt like hard, dry clay. She felt a breeze of cold, sweet-smelling air that cut through the chlorine smell and eventually drove it away. The breeze intensified, as the darkness became absolute and the clay hardened to stone. The sound of her running shoes shuffling along it took on an echoing quality, and Ann came to imagine that she was in an immense cavern.

She stopped walking.

"I didn't throw in with them."

There was no PA system this time. Philip's voice came from close—very close, because he was whispering. There was no light, so Ann reached out, trying to touch him. Her hand closed on empty air.

Philip went on. "They think I did. They think I'll do what Michael . . . what he couldn't do . . . and tame her for them. But I'll tell you something, Sis." Ann felt his breath, cold as winter on her neck.

"She was already tame," he said, "when you flew off to Tobago—what with their tricks, and yours . . ."

"What do you mean?"

"I'll put it to you simple," he said. "Our friend never would have killed Michael Voors, without my help."

"What the hell, Philip?"

"I couldn't stop you from marrying him. Couldn't stop you from flying off to Tobago. But when *she* told me what Rickhardt had made her do, in that beach house . . . how she couldn't do anything to stop it."

"She burned down the beach house."

"She didn't like it," said Philip, "and she demonstrated that, yeah. But she couldn't stop it. The . . . rape. They'd conditioned her. That far at least."

"But you undid that. How?"

"How do you do things, when it comes to her? I dreamed it. As you can imagine, I do a lot of dreaming."

"Like that school."

"Like that."

"How did you learn to do that?"

"She taught me. She learned how to do it from you and passed it on to me. You know. The stuff you learned from that old lady. Eva."

"I know," said Ann. "But it doesn't seem to be working right now."

"Isn't it?"

"There's no school here," said Ann. She held out her arms and turned around. "It's all a big, dark cave."

"Fuck."

"There's a breeze coming from one direction," she said. "I bet it's the way out."

"Fuck," said Philip again. "I'm sorry. It's hard to concentrate."

Ann started in the direction of the breeze. "How's that?"

"You fucking try concentrating," said Philip, "when you're *flying*."

"Flying?" said Ann, and Philip said, "Oh." And the cavern became very quiet.

"Oh," said Ann after a moment.

"*Oh*."

At that, Ann became very quiet too.

The Insect was near. It might have been right behind her, long-fingered hands hovering at her throat. It might no longer have fingers, but great mandibles, and a vampiric sucker in place of a mouth. It might have just been a girl, smiling.

It might have been anything.

Ann tried to put the idea out of her mind. There was, after all, also a breeze. By the rules of this place, that should take her out. Ann started walking. Was the Insect following her footsteps? She tested the hypothesis twice—stopping short and turning, arms outstretched. Each time, her fingers closed around air—and Ann was lost, until she found a trace of the wind.

They marched into it. It led her along the bare rock, and she stumbled for a moment as her feet found a stone step, and then another. She began to climb. There were many steps; Ann was disinclined to count, after hurrying up the first dozen or so. The stairs turned back on themselves three times, and when they finally levelled out, Ann thought she could make out a faint light ahead, casting on a gleaming fall of minerals down a sharp cut of rock.

Ann hurried toward it—quickly, but not so hastily that she missed the fact that the floor here dropped away a good distance before the wall, leaving a deep chasm. The floor now became a ledge, crawling along the near chasm wall. The light was off toward her left—a bluish glow at the edge of her vision—so left she went.

As she clambered along the uneven ledge, it began to dawn on Ann that this light, the breeze, did not necessarily point the way toward escape. It might—in one of her old friend Ryan's dungeon crawls, it probably would. *You feel a breeze—and there seems to be some light coming down the southern passage.* And the party would hurry along, hauling their sacks of loot and golf bags of magic swords. But that was Ryan's game for you.

Fucking little people pleaser, Ann thought unkindly, and kept going.

The chasm widened as she went, until the opposite side was all but invisible. Partly it was the distance—partly it was the phosphorescent mist that filled this great space. The mist had a sharp smell to it, like vegetable rot—and Ann worried that it might be toxic. She supposed it didn't matter if it were; this place wasn't real, after all, not in the physical, biochemical sense.

As she went on, the ledge levelled out, and the bare rock was replaced by broad cobblestones. The cliff wall behind her, conversely, became craggier. In the distance, she could hear the sound of fast water—rapids, or maybe a waterfall, and she also thought she might have heard the sound of wings beating—*leathery wings, as those of gigantic bats*—and perhaps deep, mournful moaning—*from the souls of the risen gladiators, waiting for their final judgement in the Corridor of Bones. . . .*

"Ah," said Ann aloud, and listened as her voice echoed back across the great chamber.

She thought she might know where she was. And as she took three more steps, and the ledge separated from the cavern wall and became a kind of bridge, she became sure of it.

These were the caverns beneath the Coliseum of Dusk—in the middle of which hung the Arch-Liche of the Games' inverted tower, a thick basalt uvula that dangled from the greatest cavern's throat.

She wanted to applaud, as the tower emerged from the mists—carved with runes that she and Philip had devised on the remains of a tablet of scientific graph paper, dotted with arrow slits and balconies, illuminated in parts with firelight, and the screams of the giant glow-bugs that the Arch-Liche had enslaved the last time he'd walked in the world's moonlight.

Ann smiled. For the first time since she was a child, she truly felt as though she were coming home. By the time she was halfway across the bridge, she couldn't help herself: she was running.

In the first room—a wide entry hall—a fine meal was set out on a long oaken table. Ann avoided it, remembering it as a trap: the succulent venison that topped the centrepiece was really the carcass of a gigantic spider, basted in its own venom. The bunches of grapes were flesh-burrowing grubs, that would render an adventurer paralyzed, if she failed to make her saving throw. The entire banquet—the suckling pig, the mounds of honeyed yam, the links of sausage, all of it—was poisonous, its true nature hidden by the cunning illusions of the Arch-Liche. The only thing safe to consume on the table was the wine, thick and dark and infused with a healing potion that would undo the effects of all but the most fatal of the poisons.

If Leah and Ryan and the rest of them had ever gotten that far in her campaign, they would have been so impressed. And, Ann was sure, so dead.

Ann bypassed the banquet, and moved farther into the tower. She visited its dungeons, near the top, where the Arch-Liche, in an unholy pact with the ruling families of Tricasta, kept hostage some of their more troublesome political enemies. She spent some hours in the Hanging Gardens, where pale vampiric flowers drank the blood of cave-blind rodents and blossomed into glorious crimson for hours afterward. She slept the first night in the Arch-Liche's laboratory, where he had invented his glass automaton guards to watch over his treasury and mind the doomed gladiators. The laboratory was deserted, but the forge was easy to light, and it kept the place warm.

The next morning, she found her way to the kitchens and made herself a proper breakfast, absent both illusion and poison, and took the bowl to the Liche's private chambers at the very bottom tip of the tower. She was delighted to find the Golden Telescope of Scrying there, mounted as she hoped, and settled in to observe all the goings-on in Tricasta and the lands surrounding it.

The next day mingled with the one after, and the one past that, and so on. The Arch-Liche, if he even still occupied this tower, never made himself known. Ann had the entire space to herself.

There were no mirrors in the Arch-Liche's chambers, nor anything even polished enough to cast a reflection. But while Ann could not look upon her own face, she could look at her hands and feet, and notice how quickly the scant colour from the Caribbean sun faded. She was becoming like alabaster, like bone, here in these new sunless chambers. When she looked down on the afternoon siestas at the fountain in Tricasta, Ann found herself squinting at the brilliance. Her joints made clicking noises when she bent to pick up a cup. Her teeth seemed to be looser in her mouth.

In these tiny measures, she came to understand that she was dying. She was wasting away—vanishing. In the belly of the Insect.

And she understood also: she did not wish to die here.

She wished she could speak with Eva, and she thought about trying to contact her now, using the telescope or one of the great spell tomes in the library. But she knew that she couldn't. Eva understood herself to be a master of the psychic realm—able to send stores of energy to needy souls like Ann, speak to spirits and communicate via the power of the Universal Mind.

But Ann had to remind herself that the prison Eva had helped devise for the Insect had failed. Her intuitions about Michael—her assurances that he was a nice man, a good match, probably good in the sack—were as wildly tone-deaf as was her misplaced trust in Ian Rickhardt, who'd been able to draw out the deepest of Ann's secrets with nothing more convincing than smarmy patter and mediocre flattery. And Eva had utterly failed to ferret out Philip, Ann's own brother, and his lifelong betrayal.

Eva had shared a house with Ann. She had helped her through terrible trauma—the loss of her parents, and later, of her Nan.

But when it came to this business, Eva was nothing more than a fraud—most charitably, an unwitting fraud. She had no way into this place—this prison, literally of Ann's own making.

Philip might listen to her call, now. He might help her. Ann wandered to the upper galleries of the tower—nearer its own, inverted base—and considered how she might do so. But she could conceive of no incantation by which to call him, that wasn't comprised of her tears. He was her brother and she had loved him and it had been . . . what? A lie?

She stepped onto the south balcony, high enough that the ceiling of rock was visible barely a dozen yards overhead. It was freezing out here, cold enough that she felt it in her bones, her thickening joints. Her breath rattled in her throat.

She didn't want to vanish. She let her hands fall to her side.

Warm fingers entwined with hers.

Ann squeezed as breath tickled her throat. *Thank God you were here to hold my hand.*

She let herself be turned around, to face the girl.

She had dark hair tied into snaky braids, and darker eyes. She wore a long pale tunic, and black boots with toes that curled on themselves.

You, mouthed Ann.

She was tall, and she filled out her tunic as a grown woman does—not like the child that Ann remembered distantly; not like the creature, the Insect, that Ann had come to understand her to be. She had grown and shifted in so many ways, but for one:

Her smile was still wide as the world.

Don't vanish, the girl mouthed.

Ann leaned in, and kissed her. She closed her eyes, and as she did so, many things did vanish, into darkness, and into silence. But not Ann, and not the girl either.

The two of them stayed put.

They were it now.

A Sip of Sémillon

Susan Rickhardt poured them each another glass, killing the bottle.

It was not a Rickhardt Estates label. Susan had just finished explaining how she liked this stuff, from Rosewood Estates, a little bit better than a constant diet of the house wine.

They were sitting on the long tasting bar, maybe a dozen feet from the urn that held Michael's ashes. Ann vaguely recalled that Charlie Sunderland had left her here, in Susan's care. *Just sit here,* he'd said. *Your friend Susan will keep you entertained.* And Ann had said . . . what? Nothing, probably.

The clock over the bar showed that it was coming up on the lunch hour. Susan had changed clothes. She had put on a woolen skirt and a loose-knit grey sweater that Ann thought actually flattered her somewhat. She had fixed her hair—maybe gone for broke, actually taken a shower.

Hard to say, though. The only light here came from the tall windows that lined one wall, and it was inconstant; the clouds were moving fast, and they rippled across the sun to make a shadow-puppet show under the great wooden dome of the tasting room in Rickhardt's backwoods conference centre. Ann had no doubt that the windows were new as everything else in this space, and strong as money could buy. But the wind still rattled them in their frames.

The electricity had gone out some time ago.

"Ian was thinking about planting Sémillon about a year ago.

Never did, and that's fine by me," said Susan. "Ian's got no touch for decent wine. These Rosewood people do it better than he ever would."

Before Ann had escaped the tower and returned to herself, her lips had been about to say, *Tastes fine to me.*

"Tastes fine to me," she said, and she let her eyelids flutter closed for a moment—to savour the wine, and turn attention to . . .

Well, to that other business.

The lights in the ceiling of the Lake House rooms sparked bright and died.

Ian Rickhardt and his friends didn't quite know how to take it—sudden darkness being, under the right circumstances, delicious for men such as they.

But the sharp and growing smell of ozone—the flickering light of flame from the electrical outlets in the kitchen, beside the sofa . . . that was a different matter. Four of them pointed it out, and made for the door, stumbling over chairs and a coffee table.

Another grabbed a cushion from the sofa, and tried to use it to suffocate the flames at the outlet in the living room. He screamed and jerked as electricity coursed through him.

The door handle was stiff, and the four of them struggled with it before it finally gave way. It opened, onto a bright, greenish light, and a howling wind. Two of them simply vanished through the opening, while the other two were able to swing the door back, and shut it.

Ian Rickhardt had come prepared. He had a small LED flashlight in his pocket, and flicked it on.

It proved unnecessary, however, as the electrical fire in the wall touched onto the drapes. Philip LeSage, floating above them, was illuminated in flame, grinning insensibly.

Rickhardt had stopped smiling as the room began to fill with smoke. The sprinkler system cut in, and he flinched, shading his face against the spray of icy water.

Others crawled on the floor, trying to stay below the smoke, heading for the door, beyond which a titanic wind roared, and beams snapped. He shouted for each of them to find something to hold onto, and as they did so, Ian hauled open the door and pressed himself against the wall behind it.

Ears popped as the wind drew the air and the smoke out—and for a moment, the fires slowed. the doors to the cupboards swung open again as one, and dishes flew and smashed in the wind. The sofa overturned, pillows spewing behind it like entrails. But the men held tight. The only one drawn out the door was the one already airborne. Philip LeSage, held tight in the Insect's embrace, flew head-first out the door, and was snatched in the bright twister that tore at the belly of the Octagon.

Ian Rickhardt didn't look to see where he went. As the balcony outside the Lake House room disintegrated, he gasped wonderingly, and reached down, and took hold of himself.

"You ever play any D & D?"

"D & D?" Susan Rickhardt looked perplexed a moment, then made the connection and nodded. "Oh, Dungeons & Dragons. No."

"I'm surprised," said Ann. She swirled the bottom half of her glass of wine. "Seems like it'd be a natural for you."

Susan shrugged. "I came to my habit late in life," she said. "When I was a teenager, I was more of a Ms. Pac Man kind of kid."

Ann nodded. "I played a *lot* of D & D," she said. "A lot. From junior high school, all through university. It was a real lifeline for me. Also, wicked fun."

"Wicked, now?"

Ann took a delicate sip of the wine and shut her eyes. She thought about the grand plaza in Tricasta, and how that world's sun would paint the stones a rich gold as it set, the streams of water from the great fountain there sparkling like gemstones. There were pinkish marble benches surrounding the fountain, and on these adherents to the doctrine of the great water elemental Casta would sit, burn a cinnamon-tinged incense in special brass philtres, and contemplate Her greatness. When Ann described it the first time, Ryan had rolled his eyes and Leah had giggled, and for that moment, Ann had been embarrassed and thought she might be on the wrong track.

Ah, but when the sun went down—and the adherents began to chant a deeper rhythm—and Casta Herself emerged, a terrible cascade like a waterfall, falling up to the heavens . . . she could tell by the widening of Ryan's eyes and Leah's sharp intake of breath . . . she'd done it right.

Beauty was a prerequisite to terror. And yes—when it finally came, the terror was exquisite.

At least it was from Ann's perspective.

"I always wanted to learn how to play it," said Susan. "I mean, it's pretty much like Skyrim, but in your head, right?"

"Yeah," agreed Ann, turning her attention even as she said the words, "in your head. But it's not for the faint of heart."

And her eyes flickered, and she thought about that.

The faint of heart.

Charlie Sunderland wasn't an MD—by any reasonable academic standards, he wasn't even a doctor—but he'd gleaned enough over the years to know how to administer a hypodermic and manage some basic first aid. He thought he might be able to set a bone, if it weren't a complicated fracture. He was pretty good with CPR.

He was heading back from the conference centre, where he'd dropped off Ann—right on the covered bridge—when the tornado descended into the middle of the Octagon. He couldn't see the twister itself—the roof of the glassed-in bridge blocked it perfectly as it descended. But he stared, frozen, at the greenish cloud that surrounded the vortex. The roaring wind left a ringing in his ears when it passed and drove him to the ground, in abject terror.

Sunderland was not an MD, but he was no fool either—he had after all compiled the file on the Lake House, and the Bounty II. He knew what the Insect was capable of.

He may not have understood why it had come to pass, but he understood what had happened. The Insect had broken free. The plan that they had all made—to do with Philip what they had not been able to do with Ann, and bind it tight—had broken down. Somehow.

And now—this.

The walls of the Octagon remained standing. Sunderland was amazed, although he knew he shouldn't be: tornadoes in nature could be alarmingly selective. One house might be reduced to matchsticks; a neighbour's might survive untouched.

And this . . . this was not nature.

Dr. Sunderland opened the door to the Octagon. It was dark inside, which he took to be a good thing; it might mean that the chambers surrounding the centre had survived. There might be survivors.

There was a first aid kit somewhere in this room, and a good one. Rickhardt had boasted about it when they'd arrived. It was above one of the sofas, attached to the wall. If there were light,

Sunderland could have found it easily. In the dark, he had to feel around for it.

As he searched, he called out: "It's Sunderland! I'm going to try to bring help! Shout if you can!"

No one shouted as he searched over the first sofa. He moved around to the other side, through the grey, changing light of the day. He was about to call out again as he reached out to the wall behind the second sofa.

He found he had no words. There was nothing to say, as the cool, dry hand wrapped around his own.

And her eyelids flickered.

"I used to dungeon master," said Ann. From Susan's blank expression, Ann could guess that the woman had no idea what she was talking about, so Ann explained: "I would be the one who made up the place where the adventures happened. In the game, I'd describe what was happening there, and the players would react." Susan nodded, slowly, in that nervous-but-encouraging way that people who'd never rolled up a first-level halfling thief did, when Ann tried to explain how a game of Dungeons & Dragons went.

"Basically, it comes down to this," said Ann. "I'm the one telling the story. If the characters run into . . . I don't know, a band of trolls . . . I'm the trolls. If they meet a dragon—it's me. If the bridge they've just crossed crumbles into dust . . ."

"You," said Susan.

"Me."

Susan got up from her stool, and went around to the other side of the bar. She opened up the refrigerator and got out another bottle of the Sémillon.

"Sounds wicked," said Susan.

Ann chuckled. "Yeah. I used to play *rough*. Not everybody's cup of tea."

"Not for the faint of heart."

"Right."

Susan refilled Ann's glass nearly to the brim. Ann widened her eyes and laughed. "Sure that's enough?" she said, and Susan laughed too.

"We got big merlot glasses in here somewhere, if you'd like some more."

Ann let her smile fade a bit.

"No," she said. "Thank you."

Susan came back around the bar and sat down by Ann again. "It's okay," she said.

Ann blinked. "What's okay?"

"You're all gone now," she said. "It's done. You can just relax."

All gone now.

Ann thought about that. Earlier that morning, in the dark, Susan had predicted just exactly this: that she'd be eaten up soon. So had Lisa. The Insect would devour everything. And now, according to Susan anyway, that had happened. The Insect had devoured everything. Ann was here by herself now, or rather her flesh was . . . And Susan—or the flesh Susan left behind—was here helping her to adjust. To her new life—as a vessel that largely stood empty.

Of course, that wasn't precisely what had happened—not to Ann at least.

Ann was, for the first time in decades, entirely whole.

Ann climbed off her stool. She swayed a little bit, what with the wine in her, but steadied herself with the stool. She walked down the bar to the urn that contained Michael's ashes. She ran a finger up the cool metal.

"Tell me," she said. "Does Ian have an up-to-date will?"

Susan shrugged. "I don't know."

"Michael and I made out wills," said Ann. "Part of the elaborate plans we laid for our wedding. It made sense; we both came into the marriage with considerable assets, after all. Michael owned property, had investments. I . . . I had my part of my parents' trust fund. You probably should have done the same thing."

Susan shifted on her stool. "I'm sure I'm looked after."

"Hope so," said Ann. She left her wine glass on the bar and crossed the big room to the bank of windows. It had begun to rain, but the wind was blowing the right way, and not a drop of it touched the glass. The view was perfect.

Susan came over with both glasses—Ann's dribbling a bit over the rim. "What you looking at, Annie?" she said, and then added, "Oh," as she came closer, and saw.

Ann took the glasses from Susan, and set them down on a nearby table. "There was a storm," said Ann. "It was terrible—a tornado. It touched down on the Octagon, and tore it out from the middle. You can see the pieces of it—there—and there—and that thing." Ann pointed to a twisted helix of metal, sprouting from the edge of the ravine like a broken bedspring. "That's the staircase, I think." The trees that must have covered the grounds outside the tasting room were just as mangled. There was a wide swathe where the branches had simply been sucked away, leaving cracked stumps in their place.

"That's one of your husband's friends," said Ann, pointing at a slender figure, clutching a blood-red bathrobe around himself as he staggered away from the ravine. The rain was coming hard and it lashed at him, but he didn't stop. "We weren't introduced when I came across him in the Octagon. Do you recognize him?" Susan must have taken the question to be rhetorical, because she didn't answer. "All right. Well watch carefully. I am going to cause him to trip, and fall forward into mud." The man did so, arms wheeling comically as he fell to his knees, and then his face. "He may wish to get up," said Ann, and indeed, the man tried to do so, his narrow elbows emerging over his back, as though he were to begin a push-up. Ann smiled slightly and shook her head. "But I don't wish it," said Ann. It was difficult to see precisely, but it seemed as though something—a tree branch, perhaps?—reared up, and fell onto his back. His arms were splayed in the mud, and as he tried to manoeuvre them back under him, more branches seemed to come up from under him. "He won't be getting up," said Ann, and sure enough, he showed no more signs of it.

In the course of this work, Susan had dropped her wine glass. The floor here was carpeted, and it prevented the glass from breaking, and also absorbed the wine around Susan's feet. From the way she wrung her hands together, eyes wide and mouth half-open in terrified dismay, it could have been the result of another kind of accident.

"So here's the thing about dungeon mastering," said Ann. "You can play rough—take-no-prisoners, re-roll no stats. But it doesn't work at all if you're not giving the players what they want. And it doesn't work if you're not giving them what you want them to have."

"Why did you ask me about a will, now?"

Susan's formidable brainpower made Ann smile. "Ian's going to die in a minute," she said. "I just hope he didn't go leave all his money to some 'geister spa in Florida. You don't want those ones looking after your future."

Susan drew a breath, and held it a moment, behind pursed lips. Ann looked outside. The man in the mud was asphyxiating. Just to look at him, you'd think that he'd already died, but he hadn't—he was trapped in himself, his mouth and nostrils filled with slick muck, memories flashing like lights behind his blocked-shut eyelids, terror fading to despair, and finally—dull, drowned acceptance.

"Don't kill him," said Susan, and Ann said, "I think it's too late for him," then thought about it again and said, "Oh. Ian. You mean Ian?"

"I mean Ian." Susan's voice took a low turn—like she was putting on the tough, letting Ann know that she also meant business.

Ann let her eyes flutter shut. "I'm not sure there's much to do for him, either," she said. "The good news is that the burns from the fire are superficial. He got out before that could take him. His legs are broken, though. And there's a fracture in his spine, too. Might be paralyzed. Hard to tell at the moment. He's conscious, but he's at the bottom of a very deep hole right now. There is a dead man on the ground not far from him, and a little girl—Lisa. Yes, Lisa Dumont. She has quite lost her mind. Or she thinks she has. She hasn't yet realized the truth. So now she's singing. Can't quite make out what the song is. Some lullaby. *Sleepy-time, sleepy-time* . . . She's giving him a look. She knows what he did. And he knows it."

"How do *you* know all that?"

Ann turned around. "I'm there too." She met Susan's eyes, and the act of it seemed to drive Susan back. There was that terror, right there, in her eyes.

"Oh Annie," she said, whimpering, "you . . . you're not you. You . . . you faded. And now—it's the Insect in you, isn't it? It got back in. And now that's all there is."

Ann considered that.

"I don't think I've faded," she said. "No. And as to the Insect being back in me?" She shook her head. "There's no such thing as the Insect. There's only me. There was only ever me."

Susan kept backing away. Ann followed, keeping the same distance between the two of them.

"Do you want to save Ian's life?"

"I don't want you to kill him," said Susan.

"I never intended to kill him. Or save him." Ann stopped in the middle of the room, under the great bowl of its roof. "I thought I'd leave that to you."

Susan's eyebrows rose and she looked down, as though she'd worked something out.

"He's in what's left of the Octagon," said Ann, helpfully. "You are too."

To Ann's disappointment, the last part was lost on Susan. "Thank you," she said, and turned and half-ran across the room, and down the hall that led to the bridge. Ann sighed, and let her eyes flutter again—and watched as Susan ran a short distance farther, then come up short, on the empty space between the conference centre and the Octagon ballroom. The bridge had been torn down, and now there was nothing but twisted metal and fractured timber, tumbling down into the ravine. The Octagon loomed on the other side—literally, a smoking ruin. Susan fell to her knees and wept.

Ann shook her head. She shouldn't have been surprised. Susan played Skyrim, and World of Warcraft. She was used to being led along a path. She was not a dungeon master.

There might have been a time that she had the capacity. But that time was past. Susan and her 'geist Little were two things now. Two things they would remain, until they found the courage to embrace one another.

And Ann had been wasting her time talking to Susan.

Ann left her wine glass on the table in the conference centre. She returned to the tasting bar, and hefted the urn containing Michael's ashes. It was heavy but not burdensome, all things considered; after checking to see that the lid was screwed on tightly enough, she tucked it under her arm, and headed away from the Octagon, and poor despairing Susan Rickhardt, back to the meeting rooms at the far end of the conference centre.

With the electricity down, the hallway was a veil of shadows. Ann held the urn tighter, and stepped through. She could make out the shape of a bannister and the first few steps of a stairway to her left, but ahead, it was all darkness. It brought to mind the high school where Philip had dwelt. Except instead of classrooms and lockers lining the walls, there were big doors to meeting rooms and uncomfortable little benches along the way. Would the doors swing open suddenly, lighting some terrible spectre that ran towards Ann down the corridor, from the gymnasium?

No.

Ann took a step and two wall sconces to either side flickered to life—the hidden bulbs casting an irregular glow like gaslight. She smiled, and continued, and as the next set of sconces lit up, the last pair went dark, with the popping sound of cracking bulbs. If they'd been in a linen closet in the Lake House, they might've started a fire. They still might here, Ann thought as the second set of bulbs cracked. She stepped up her pace, and that seemed to do the trick; the light followed her down the hall, leaving the darkness behind her and cutting the darkness ahead.

She passed doors: the Pinot Grigio room, the Chardonnay Room, the Merlot. All of them were shut fast. She thought about opening them, and in response, the Amarone Room's door handle cricked down. But Ann didn't really want to look inside, see another poor wretch like Susan passing the time. So the handle returned to its place, and Ann left it in darkness with the rest of them.

Finally, the hallway ended and she reached another set of double doors—these ones glass-panelled. Beyond, she could see a dimly lit reception area, with a long desk as you'd find in a hotel, more comfortable chairs. There were windows here, and another set of glass doors, leading outside. Ann pushed on the first set of doors twice. The first time they were locked. The second, they opened easily.

The last few drops of rain pattered softly as Ann stepped out of the conference centre, onto the gravel of the parking lot. The woods rose up around the lot untouched, limbs bare but undisturbed by anything other than a moderate breeze. There were a dozen cars in the parking lot; some of them looked expensive. The camper van sat between two more modest vehicles—a cherry red Toyota hybrid and a deep blue Town Car. The van needed a good wash, even after all that rain.

There wouldn't be any more rain for a while. As she stepped into the middle of the lot, and set the urn containing Michael's ashes down in front of her, the clouds began to thin. They drifted apart in gossamer strands, to reveal a wintery blue bowl of a sky.

She looked up, and waved.

Philip did not wave back. He was too far up for it to be visible in any event—drifting against the winds like a kite on a string.

But Ann knew he hadn't waved; she hadn't allowed it.

ACKNOWLEDGEMENTS

Each novel is a different game for me, but there is a reassuring consistency to the people who help and support and love, and thereby earn my gratitude each time. So it is with *The 'Geisters*. The members of the Cecil Street writers' group and the Gibraltar Point summer writers' group all gave excellent advice: to whit, Madeline Ashby, Michael Carr, Laurie Channer, Rebecca Maines, John McDaid, Elizabeth Mitchell, Janis O'Connor, Helen Rykens, Karl Schroeder, Sara Simmons, Michael Skeet, Jill Snider Lum, Dale Sproule, Rob Stauffer, Caitlin Sweet, Peter Watts and Allan Weiss all share much of the credit and none of the blame for the contents of this book. That goes double for Sandra Kasturi, who's edited all my books to within an inch of their lives so far, and has at various points brought this one back from the dead. ChiZine Publications has, as usual, delivered along with Sandra, a crew of phenomenal artists, editors, publicists and publishers in the persons of Erik Mohr, Kelsi Morris, Brett Savory, Helen Marshall, Laura Marshall, Sam Beiko, Danny Evarts, Michael Matheson, and Beverly Bambury, who contributed to both the genesis of this project and the launch of the last one in 2012, in a continuum of support, encouragement and aid. The phenomenal singer/songwriter Kari Maaren composed and performed a theme song for *The 'Geisters*—I had it on a nearly continuous loop during the final edits in early 2013. And of course my agent Monica Pacheco and the Anne McDermid Literary Agency provided consistently excellent support, advice and representation.

ABOUT THE AUTHOR

David Nickle is the author of numerous short stories and several novels. He lives in an east-end Toronto hayloft with science fiction author Madeline Ashby and a very bad cat, and spends his days covering Toronto city politics for the Toronto Community News chain of community papers. He has at least one more novel in him. Possibly more.

MORE FROM DAVID NICKLE

RASPUTIN'S BASTARDS
978-1-926851-59-4

Monstrous
Affections
David
Nickle

MONSTROUS AFFECTIONS
978-0-9812978-3-5

EUTOPIA
978-1-926851-11-2

EMB
RACE
THE
ODD

THE INNER CITY

KAREN HEULER

Anything is possible: people breed dogs with humans to create a servant class; beneath one great city lies another city, running it surreptitiously; an employee finds that her hair has been stolen by someone intent on getting her job; strange fish fall from trees and birds talk too much; a boy tries to figure out what he can get when the Rapture leaves good stuff behind. Everything is familiar; everything is different. Behind it all, is there some strange kind of design or merely just the chance to adapt? In Karen Heuler's stories, characters cope with the strange without thinking it's strange, sometimes invested in what's going on, sometimes trapped by it, but always finding their own way in.

AVAILABLE NOW

978-1-927469-33-0

THE WARRIOR WHO CARRIED LIFE

GEOFF RYMAN

Only men are allowed into the wells of vision. But Cara's mother defies this edict and is killed, but not before returning with a vision of terrible and wonderful things that are to come . . . and all because of five-year-old Cara. Years later, evil destroys the rest of Cara's family. In a rage, Cara uses magic to transform herself into a male warrior. But she finds that to defeat her enemies, she must break the cycle of violence, not continue it. As Cara's mother's vision of destiny is fulfilled, the wonderful follows the terrible, and a quest for revenge becomes a quest for eternal life.

AVAILABLE NOW

978-1-927469-38-5

THE MONA LISA SACRIFICE
BOOK ONE OF THE BOOK OF CROSS
PETER ROMAN

For thousands of years, Cross has wandered the earth, a mortal soul trapped in the undying body left behind by Christ. But now he must play the part of reluctant hero, as an angel comes to him for help finding the Mona Lisa—the real Mona Lisa that inspired the painting. Cross's quest takes him into a secret world within our own, populated by characters just as strange and wondrous as he is. He's haunted by memories of Penelope, the only woman he truly loved, and he wants to avenge her death at the hands of his ancient enemy, Judas. The angel promises to deliver Judas to Cross, but nothing is ever what it seems, and when a group of renegade angels looking for a new holy war show up, things truly go to hell.

AVAILABLE NOW

978-1-77148-145-8

MORE FROM CHIZINE

HORROR STORY AND OTHER HORROR STORIES ROBERT BOYCZUK [978-0-9809410-3-6]

NEXUS: ASCENSION ROBERT BOYCZUK [978-0-9813746-8-0]

THE BOOK OF THOMAS: HEAVEN ROBERT BOYCZUK [978-1-927469-27-9]

PEOPLE LIVE STILL IN CASHTOWN CORNERS TONY BURGESS [978-1-926851-04-4]

THE STEEL SERAGLIO MIKE CAREY, LINDA CAREY & LOUISE CAREY [978-1-926851-53-2]

SARAH COURT CRAIG DAVIDSON [978-1-926851-00-6]

A BOOK OF TONGUES GEMMA FILES [978-0-9812978-6-6]

A ROPE OF THORNS GEMMA FILES [978-1-926851-14-3]

A TREE OF BONES GEMMA FILES [978-1-926851-57-0]

ISLES OF THE FORSAKEN CAROLYN IVES GILMAN [978-1-926851-43-3]

ISON OF THE ISLES CAROLYN IVES GILMAN [978-1-926851-56-3]

FILARIA BRENT HAYWARD [978-0-9809410-1-2]

THE FECUND'S MELANCHOLY DAUGHTER BRENT HAYWARD [978-1-926851-13-6]

IMAGINARIUM 2012: THE BEST CANADIAN SPECULATIVE WRITING
EDITED BY SANDRA KASTURI & HALLI VILLEGAS [978-0-926851-67-9]

CHASING THE DRAGON NICHOLAS KAUFMANN [978-0-9812978-4-2]

OBJECTS OF WORSHIP CLAUDE LALUMIÈRE [978-0-9812978-2-8]

THE DOOR TO LOST PAGES CLAUDE LALUMIÈRE [978-1-926851-13-6]

THE THIEF OF BROKEN TOYS TIM LEBBON [978-0-9812978-9-7]

KATJA FROM THE PUNK BAND SIMON LOGAN [978-0-9812978-7-3]

BULLETTIME NICK MAMATAS [978-1-926851-71-6]

SHOEBOX TRAIN WRECK JOHN MANTOOTH [978-1-926851-54-9]

HAIR SIDE, FLESH SIDE HELEN MARSHALL [978-1-927469-24-8]

NINJA VERSUS PIRATE FEATURING ZOMBIES JAMES MARSHALL [978-1-926851-58-7]

PICKING UP THE GHOST TONE MILAZZO [978-1-926851-35-8]

BEARDED WOMEN TERESA MILBRODT [978-1-926851-46-4]

NAPIER'S BONES DERRYL MURPHY [978-1-926851-09-9]

CITIES OF NIGHT PHILIP NUTMAN [978-0-9812978-8-0]

JANUS JOHN PARK [978-1-927469-10-1]

EVERY SHALLOW CUT TOM PICCIRILLI [978-1-926851-10-5]

BRIARPATCH TIM PRATT [978-1-926851-44-0]

THE CHOIR BOATS DANIEL A. RABUZZI [978-1-926851-06-8]

THE INDIGO PHEASANT DANIEL A. RABUZZI [978-1-927469-09-5]

EVERY HOUSE IS HAUNTED IAN ROGERS [978-1-927469-16-3]

ENTER, NIGHT MICHAEL ROWE [978-1-926851-02-0]

REMEMBER WHY YOU FEAR ME ROBERT SHEARMAN [978-1-927469-7]

CHIMERASCOPE DOUGLAS SMITH [978-0-9812978-5-9]

THE PATTERN SCARS CAITLIN SWEET [978-1-926851-43-3]

THE TEL AVIV DOSSIER LAVIE TIDHAR AND NIR YANIV [978-0-9809410-5-0]

IN THE MEAN TIME PAUL TREMBLAY [978-1-926851-06-8]

SWALLOWING A DONKEY'S EYE PAUL TREMBLAY [978-1-926851-69-3]

THE HAIR WREATH AND OTHER STORIES HALLI VILLEGAS [978-1-926851-02-0]

THE WORLD MORE FULL OF WEEPING ROBERT J. WIERSEMA [978-0-9809410-9-8]

WESTLAKE SOUL RIO YOUERS [978-1-926851-55-6]

MAJOR KARNAGE GORD ZAJAC [978-0-9813746-6-6]

"IF YOUR TASTE IN FICTION RUNS TO THE DISTURBING, DARK, AND AT LEAST PARTIALLY WEIRD, CHANCES ARE YOU'VE HEARD OF CHIZINE PUBLICATIONS—CZP—A YOUNG IMPRINT THAT IS NONETHELESS PRODUCING STARTLINGLY BEAUTIFUL BOOKS OF STARKLY, DARKLY LITERARY QUALITY."

—DAVID MIDDLETON, *JANUARY MAGAZINE*

ALSO AVAILABLE FROM CHIZINE PUBLICATIONS